I0785562

WEAPON OF RULERS

BLADE OF TRAESHA BOOK II

KELLY COLE

ALSO BY KELLY COLE

Daughter of War

Copyright © 2022 by Kelly Cole

All rights reserved.

No part of this book may be reproduced in any form or by any electronic or mechanical means, including information storage and retrieval systems, without written permission from the author, except for the use of brief quotations in a book review.

Kelly Cole Books ISBN 979-8-9853212-3-4

kellycolebooks.com

Cover Design by Ellen Kenneda

Instagram @comicoffii

For Hannah and Sarah. I love our friendship and how much you two were there for me during the writing of this book

CHAPTER 1

Icouldn't relax fully. Not with Levi driving, the lack of safety straps, and Silken likely on our trail. However, as we sped away from the lot where we had just stolen our transport truck, I finally pulled in a full breath. The transport's wipers squealed as they rid the front window of melting snow. It was dark enough that if I unfocused my eyes, the white flakes blowing past were all I saw in the headlights. Levi leaned forward as he navigated the dirt roads leading out of Vichi. This far from City Center, the apartments were dark, crumbling, and ready to collapse. I focused on the snow. I focused on Natasha's hand in mine, fingers stiff with cold from our dash through Vichi's streets.

My body finally still, my mind struggled to catch up with the night's events.

With Audrey, Hue, Gale, and Levi's help, I had broken into the Command Hall. That alone was mystifying. I could only hope Hue and Gale had gotten away after planting the explosion that had distracted the guards so we could enter.

It still seemed too good to be true that everything had worked out so well on our end.

I had faced Silken yet again. His words continued to echo in my head. *I'll return your team. I'll let you fight. And when we win, you'll share in our glory. I know my people. I know you. Power is the only thing worth fighting for. Power means freedom. It means security. It means never going hungry...*

I had burned everything tying me to my old position as a Bellovian commander. That shouldn't bother me with my parents dead and my brother using an alias successfully. My duty was to Natasha now. But Silken had threatened my old team and was traveling with Yike currently. My stomach turned painfully each time I remembered his words. I took a deep breath and tried to refocus my thoughts. I had to think about all this one step at a time.

I had just rescued the queen of Traesha. *That* was the most difficult to wrap my head around, even as I held her hand. Weeks ago, I hadn't even known Natasha was alive. Now we sat together in the backseat of the stolen transport, all our emotions bare between us. I could feel every pop and spark of feeling twisting through her chest. Anxiety, fear, relief, giddiness, regret. Hope, hope, *hope.*

I had accepted my duty as *resa magsai* to protect her and help her reach whatever goals she had for my mother's country. Actually, as *resa* and full-blooded Trish, I should probably start thinking about Traesha as *my* country even though we were fleeing the city I called home all my life.

From this point forward, my desires weren't my own. My decisions had to be made as a duo. My previous life goal to infiltrate the commanders and take them down from the inside while risking only myself was suddenly laughable. Now Natasha needed me to free a country. To raise a country back from the ruin the Bellovians had left it in. My future was to protect the Trish for the rest of my life while struggling to balance their ideals of peace, love, and strength.

A lifetime of commitment to the girl beside me.

I couldn't afford to let her down. I had to get her to Floria and our people there. I needed to stand by her side as we bargained with the Florian king, a man I only knew from Bellovian propaganda: power-hungry, weak, tyrant, lazy, unfit. I had to believe he was better in person. Hinze had only mentioned his father in passing, but if he was the sort of man to raise Hinze, I wanted to believe he was good and would treat us fairly.

Hinze. The thought of him made my chest squeeze. Everything depended on him and my Bellovian friends at the Front. All people I had let down and abandoned. All people who had to come second to the girl beside me from now on. I glanced at Natasha. If my plan didn't work, if I failed her in this, an entire country could crumble. Traesha needed her and the power her presence could give the land. The gods created the triangle and Natasha was the missing peak. For her and my mother, I had to get us across the Front. I couldn't fail.

Another pang in my chest. But it wasn't the time to think of bloodstains and an empty childhood home and a missing *magsai* sword. It wasn't time.

My duty as *resa* had to be the single focus of my future. It spread before me in a tunnel of time and energy condensed to one purpose.

I shivered.

The boulders surrounding Vichi came into view, catching the light of the transport's beams. I braced myself, looking at Levi. His concentration never faltered. I didn't know this section of the city, but I should have known better than to doubt Levi's sense of direction by now. Spinning the wheel hard enough to send the bed of the transport fishtailing, Levi slipped into a gap between rocks with only a brief scrape of metal. I hoped this hidden entrance would be enough to throw off anyone pursuing us. Silken's little transport might have easily crossed the plains and mountain switchbacks between Vichi and Traesha, but it wouldn't be able to handle the terrain on this side of the city. Even my father's cycle would have had trouble. I'd never been in this section of the boulders, but being here flooded my mind with memories of training and shooting and my father looking at me with approval over his scarf.

I forced the thoughts from my head yet again. It wasn't time. I had to focus on what was happening here and now. I had to focus on Natasha. *Always focus.* Until Traesha was free, she was all that mattered. Maybe even beyond that. Being *resa* meant Natasha was my priority.

She squeezed my hand. I met her pale green eyes and saw understanding there. A flare of grief from her own emotions. She had known loss recently too. The bond was so strong it was almost harder to shake off the weight of her pain than my own.

It was nearly invasive. I felt the elation Natasha was still experiencing from her sudden freedom. She could feel my relief that she was by my side, just as I felt her wariness toward Levi and Audrey with their black hair and Vichi accents. She knew the pang of longing I felt toward Vichi. I tried to stifle how much I still connected to the city, still encouraged by the thought of rebellion. I could sense her glee to be free of the commanders and in a position to work toward their downfall. She longed for revenge. I tried to let that sensation fuel me too, but all I could think about was the starving we left behind and Nico, sure to return home soon to find his apartment ransacked.

People were not meant to feel the emotion of two. I hoped we would learn more control. Some form of balance. We would need to be strong for the next steps.

The next steps. My team. Silken's threat. Would we even be able to find them at the Front? Or had we used all our luck freeing Natasha? Even if we found them, there was still a good chance they would refuse to help. I pulled out the small knife Oken had given me. I kept it tucked in my boot, its presence unforgettable. He'd freed me. He'd given me a way out of Shalta. But he also may have been the first to tell Silken my heritage. To tip the commander off about my potential plans to search for Natasha.

I spun the knife between my fingers. Despite all this, my stomach fluttered with the possibility that I might see Oken again soon.

"Finley!"

I jumped in my seat and caught my knife awkwardly, slicing my middle finger. As quickly as the blood welled, the skin under it healed. Natasha frowned at the finger, flexing her own hand. She'd saved me the pain before adrenaline subsided. How strong was she to heal it so quickly? Had she just been watching, or had she felt the wound before I did?

"Finley!"

I started again. How long had Audrey been calling my name? Thus far, we'd been sitting in what I could only call a stunned silence, none of us quite believing we'd pulled the rescue mission off. I knew I wasn't the only one struggling with spiraling thoughts.

Of course, Audrey was the first to recover. Nothing seemed to phase her.

"Yes?" I bit out the question, wiping my finger off on my black leggings.

"Focus for a second, would you?"

My stomach clenched. *Always focus.* My mother's words. Bloodstains and the smell of lavender and *magsai* swords. "I *am* focused."

"I just want to know if you feel like being more forthcoming yet. Rennie might help us cross the Bellovian side of the Front, but you never said how we're getting into Floria."

I frowned and spun my knife again, ignoring the twinge of annoyance from Natasha's side of the bond. I could practically make out the words *"you better not cut yourself again"* from her emotions alone.

To get into Floria, I needed to contact Hinze. Could I depend on him to answer my call after leaving him behind to bleed in that dungeon?

I suddenly missed the days when friends were unimaginable and out of reach. Depending on people who weren't family was not a challenge my childhood taught me to face.

"I have an idea. But even if it fails, the Florians aren't as aggressive. We shouldn't have that much trouble getting past them."

Levi and Audrey shared a well-timed snort.

"So... we don't have a plan?" Levi asked.

"I'm working on it."

I tried pulling up an image of Londe in my mind's eye. I needed to talk to him. But a stirring of fear from Natasha snapped me back to the present situation. Levi had taken a sharp turn only to reveal a fallen pine tree. He barely slowed in time, coming to a halt right as the longest branches scraped against the front of our transport.

"Now what?" he asked. Audrey and I gave him a look. He let out a shaky laugh. "Oh, right."

Audrey and I got out of the truck and quickly removed the pine from our path. The second time we stopped for an obstacle, I paused before placing my hands under the boulder that was cracked down the middle.

"What was that? In the basement of Command Hall?" The more I replayed the events of the last few hours, the more details caught up with me. The Bellovian man I killed shouldn't have been that strong. And Audrey had known what we would see down that hall.

She shouldn't be so strong. There was still dust from the brick wall she'd smashed through in her hair.

"I told you. Experiments."

"Gifted Bellovians?"

Audrey gave up on waiting for me and heaved the boulder out of our way on her own. I watched it roll. She returned to the truck without another word.

Yes. Gifted Bellovians.

When I wasn't helping Audrey clear our path, Natasha and I spoke Trish quietly in the back of the transport. We explored our bond, discovering I was slightly more sensitive to her physical discomforts than she was to mine. She felt sharp pains but not the less pressing concerns. She blushed when I confessed I could feel even that she needed to relieve herself. She got out with Audrey and me the next time we had to stop. Natasha went off between two boulders for privacy. The entire time she was out of sight, my hair stood on end. I focused on the bond. I knew exactly how close she was and that she wasn't alarmed or hurting. Until she was back in sight, I relied on that to assure myself she was okay.

This protective instinct was a persistent, distracting tug in my mind. I hoped I'd learn to navigate it.

Natasha asked me more about my background. I told her briefly how my father taught me to fight and shoot in these boulders. Then about the Bellovian school system and its focus on battle strategy. She nodded and listened carefully, noting how she could use me in the fight ahead. Plotting how best to exploit my knowledge and physical abilities.

And it didn't matter how I felt about that. I remembered how I looked to her in the Command Hall when I held a man's life in my hands. She nodded and I killed him. The feel of a neck cracking with death. I was *resa magsai*. Born for her to use.

I asked my own questions. How she wanted to rule. What her grandfather taught her about leadership and Traesha. I was trying to determine her capabilities as much as she was mine. I breathed fully when she spoke about fairness, peace, and love. Her eyes lit when she talked about the Trish and all her hopes for our people.

I wanted to ask her how she imagined the Trish interacting with the war, but her focus was clearly on saving our country. We could worry about the next steps once that was accomplished.

Finally, we cleared the boulders. Natasha and I relaxed into the seat as we left Vichi behind. Snowdrifts became an issue. The truck handled most of them well enough, but we had to get out and push it a few times until we hit the plains and the blowing wind made it hard for the snow to stick. From there, we drove on into the night, heading east toward the Front.

By unspoken agreement, we ignored the fuel gauge's steady descent. It was late enough that Natasha's head was bobbing with sleep when the engine finally sputtered to a stop. We were stranded in the middle of the Bellovian plains. Anxiety crawled up my spine unhelpfully.

"We should sleep in here while we still have shelter. It'll stay warm for a while." Levi spoke softly as if the truck had actually died.

"A truck in the middle of the plains stands out," I said. I hated the thought of staying still, not when Silken was pursuing us. "We should leave and put distance between us and it. In fact, we should double back a bit and cut north rather than heading straight to the Front. Try to throw the commanders off. We can't just be sitting here if they're following us." It would take them time to find our trail, but Silken had access to a transport truck like the one we sat in now and who knew what else. Unease had me reaching for my door handle. "And moving in the dark is safer. We can sleep during the day."

When I finished talking, the wind whistled past the truck, cold and unwelcoming. Natasha pulled my mother's coat tighter around her body. They didn't like the idea, but Levi was already nodding reluctantly.

"It gets warmer the closer we get to the Front," I continued, trying to sound upbeat. It fell flat, so I dropped the attempt.

We covered our faces with scarves and hoods the best we could and jumped out of the truck. As we began our trek, I realized although the wind felt brutal where it stung my eyes and found every small gap in my clothing, at least it was blowing away our footprints in the thin layer of snow. It wasn't long before the grooves the truck had left vanished. Eventually, I turned us north, following the stars as my mother had taught me. Mags's was the brightest to the north. *"That one leads to Traesha,"* she'd told me, *"And Traesha gives us strength."*

I scanned the dark plains for village lights or some other hint of shelter.

"I haven't seen stars like this in years," Levi yelled through his scarf. Natasha's eyes immediately turned skyward and softened with appreciation. I didn't think Audrey heard him over the wind, but when Levi pointed up, she looked too. Her expression didn't change, but I saw her glance up again after a few steps. The clouds had cleared to occasional, fast-moving wisps, giving us a view of millions of twinkling specks. It was beautiful enough that I forgot about my frozen toes for a second. I reached and squeezed Levi's hand, grateful for the distraction.

With the wind in our eyes and stars watching over us, we pressed on.

"What are you thinking about?" Natasha asked sometime later. She was so curious about me. The stars began to disappear as the first hints of sunlight touched the sky.

"Trying to find a place to stop for the day." I was getting worried and she could probably feel it. We'd walked for hours with nothing but the snow-dusted plains in sight. Walking had lent us some warmth, but we needed to stop eventually. Sleeping without shelter was too dangerous to risk in this cold. Maybe Levi was right and we should have stayed in the transport.

Natasha nodded. It was just so strange being together. On one hand, it felt like I'd known her for years through our shared dreams and the bond that had pestered me for weeks. On the other, we were two girls who'd grown up in near opposite situations with completely different roles expected of us in Traesha's customs. It was disorienting. It would take a long time to get used to someone reading my emotions so well. People's eyes usually just slid past my face when they saw it wouldn't give anything away.

Natasha felt it all over the bond. Knowing I couldn't lie to her gave me a brief spurt of panic. Remembering I didn't have anything to hide from her calmed it.

She was the one to spot the village when it appeared. The relief was short-lived.

"What is that?" The wind calmed enough for Levi and Audrey to hear my shout. They turned with me to stare at the sky behind us. A strange shape had appeared.

"A bird?" Levi guessed.

"I may have grown up in a city, but I've never seen a bird like that," Audrey said.

Natasha, who hadn't grown up in a city, nodded her agreement.

"It's technology. It must have come from Vichi. We need to move," I said, voice tight with a new panic at the threat.

We started to run. I could easily keep pace with the Bellovians and looked over my shoulder constantly at the circling, flying object. It had a small, rounded body and some spinning propellers on top, keeping it in the air. It dipped and swerved around the area where we'd left the transport. It was looking for us.

The wind beneath it was picking up the dusted snow, creating a flurry as intimidating as the strange flying craft.

"I'm going to look closer," I declared. Natasha narrowed her eyes. Even with the scarf, I knew she was opening her mouth to protest. Levi and Audrey focused on running. "I'll hide in the flurry. I just want to see what it is."

Natasha sighed. "Fine. Stay safe."

"Should I take it down if I can? Or lead it away?"

Natasha glared and turned to help Levi as he stumbled.

Her quiet contradicted the vengeful *yes* that sang in the bond. She wanted the threat gone.

"Find shelter as soon as you can. I'll be back soon."

I turned and skipped to the flurry. It was alarming to realize how much further Natasha and I could have traveled without the Bellovians. I was nearly blinded by the swirling snow, but at least I was mostly hidden. The flying machine was circling back toward the transport. I skipped to duck on the abandoned vehicle's opposite side, peeking over the transport truck's bed.

Now I could see the strange contraption. It was sleek and black like most Bellovian military equipment. Flighter 001 was painted in red on both sides. It looked brand new, the window clean and glossy. This made it easy to see who was inside the cab.

Silken leaned forward, staring at the transport. His companion gestured forward, likely arguing which way we'd gone. Silken was frowning. My stomach dropped when he shook his head, pointing north in the direction of the village.

I had to stop him. I should have stopped him in Vichi. My people were tired, on foot, and no match for this flighter or the commanders within. From how quickly the flighter appeared and moved, they'd likely had hours to rest and plan while we were navigating the boulders to get out of Vichi. They'd just flown over them. I didn't have time to think about the implications behind this ease of travel. The flighter above seemed to have room for only two passengers, but imagining such a craft weaponized was terrifying.

I moved to the cab of the transport truck and looked inside. Maybe with my new strength, I would be able to throw something hard enough to take out the flighter. But the transport truck had been empty when we took it and remained empty now that we left. I frowned, moving around the truck to keep out of sight as the flighter circled it once more.

With the flighter directly in front of the transport and flying low, an idea came to me. I paused. Was I strong enough? Audrey had left her door open. It wobbled from the wind of the flighter, but the damage the truck had endured in our escape meant Audrey had to use her gift just to open and close the warped metal. I skipped back about twenty feet and stopped, exposed. I lined up my shot. I saw Silken's eyes widen opposite the truck. He opened his mouth to shout to his companion, but I was only visible for a blink. I skipped forward. I lowered my shoulder and slammed it up into the door, sending it off its hinges and into the sky.

I heard the impact of the door and the following crash but didn't look back. I'd slowed Silken down for now. Of that, I was sure. But somehow, I knew he was still coming. The flighter hadn't been that high. The door was not deadly enough a weapon. Natasha pulled at me. I needed to get my people to safety. Hopefully, our head start would be enough.

CHAPTER 2

The air was tinged with green; it was the only clue I needed to orient myself. Traesha. A tension clung to the dream. The frustration of the land flooded my mind. I knew where I was. It was such a relief not to be lost in the Command Hall that I forgot to worry about what it meant that I was traveling in my dreams even after finding Natasha.

The trees pulled at me and whispered, their reddish-brown bark and vibrant leaves shifting erratically. I couldn't pick apart their incoherent words. I hummed, hoping to calm them. It worked briefly.

The queen. The queen, *they hissed.*

I have her. We'll be back soon.

Royal blood, royal blood.

Before I could react, the scene shifted. I was thrown into the familiar fields. A boy my age was pulling up vegetables from the ground. I recognized him as Savha's friend, the one who hadn't wanted our help when we came to Traesha for Natasha.

He looked so tired. So defeated. A bruise was healing along his jaw and his hands shook. Two fingers were missing on one. He looked as angry as the trees felt. He'd been right. Things were *worse for them now that we'd interfered and failed. But I hadn't failed. I had found Natasha.*

I opened my mouth to tell him we were coming and we wouldn't leave the Trish behind to suffer this time.

I woke instead. Natasha wanted out of our shelter. She was awake and anxious, her nerves likely what had driven me out of my dream. Maybe her anxiety had given me that dream and I hadn't actually been in Traesha. It had felt so real, though. I moved to leave our hiding place, crawling over Levi and smacking his hand away when he sleepily reached for me.

I stuck my head out of the opening of the overturned wagon. The area around us was still, the old mining equipment abandoned and silent. I pulled myself the rest of the way out with Natasha behind me. Once she was clear, I covered the opening with our bags again, blocking the wind for Levi and Audrey.

We'd reached the village outskirts without further incident after the flighter crashed. We'd debated whether we should stop to rest when we came across all this mining equipment, but our exhaustion ultimately determined our decision. The land spiraled into a pit below us, the earth stripped of coal or iron. I didn't know enough about mining to be able to tell.

I had kept watch for about an hour, waiting for the villagers to go explore the source of the crash, but no one came. Eventually, I joined them in the wagon, but judging from the sun's position, I hadn't slept very long. It was still early in the afternoon, the sun bright enough to feel almost warm when we kept out of the wind.

I stared down at the quarry while Natasha relieved

herself. The only reason people settled in Bellovi and its baren cold was the coal and iron discovered beneath the plains. The cheaper coal was a blessing to those struggling to stay warm throughout the country, but when war broke out and the railroad tracks were cut off at the Front, the lack of demand put many Bellovians out of the job. The land was dotted with deep, spiraling mines, neglected equipment, and yet more hungry families. I wondered where Floria got their energy now. Many still relied on older methods and gifts, but I remembered seeing some technology in Honna.

Nothing compared to the flighter. The memory of it chilled me. I needed to talk to Hinze and learn his thoughts on how it could impact the war.

Natasha was in no hurry to return to our shelter. She sat next to me, leaning back against the wagon with her hood over her knit hat and hugging her knees to her chest for warmth. I pressed close to her side for more heat. We watched the activity in the village. A young boy just within our view left his house and ducked into the family's barn. The wind carried the sound of a horse neighing to greet him.

"One of the Florian towns where we hid bred horses and had a racetrack. My grandfather taught me to ride. He loved horses. I could tell they always made him think of home." Natasha smiled a bit at the memory.

"My mom always wanted my dad to take us riding but stopped asking when the money got tighter. I've always found it strange how the stables are a luxury in Vichi and a necessity in smaller villages like this one."

"Traesha only used horses. Horses and swords and torches and boats with sails. My grandfather hated transports and guns and motorboats. He would have hated that thing we saw yesterday."

"A flighter. Or that's what it said on the side."

Natasha dropped her chin onto her hand. "From the way Grandfather talked, he dreamed of my returning to Traesha and bringing it back to its former glory. None of this technology and only Trish." I hid my wince. "He associated it all with the Bellovians even though the Florians have caught up to them in almost every way."

Natasha's face scrunched. "But I can only imagine us moving forward at this point. If I'm going to be a responsible ruler, I can't be naïve enough to think we'll ever be left alone again. I'll have to make the first Trish army now that the *magsai* are all dead. I'll have to commission guns. I'll have to invite people in from other countries because they killed so many of us that we won't have enough people to defend ourselves or tend our farms." She sighed. "I'll have to do things that shame our gods and disappoint my ancestors."

I leaned closer. "But if you don't do those things, you won't have a country to lead. And without Traesha, the gods don't exist."

"How am I supposed to make those decisions? I haven't even been to Traesha since I was a baby."

"I don't know, but I'll help you in any way I can."

She gave me one of her small smiles, only a hint of a dimple in her wind-chapped cheeks. "I know you will. I trust you. Mostly because I could feel if you lied." We both laughed and she settled her head on my shoulder. "I think you'll make the difference in all of this for me, Finley."

The weight of her words settled heavy, but the responsibility was not entirely unpleasant. It felt like I had been born to carry it. I suppose that's precisely what it meant to be *resa*.

"You've only known me for a couple of days," I teased, trying to lighten her mood.

"I've known you my whole life. Even if we didn't realize it. My grandfather used to get sad for me having to move from place to place so often. He thought I must be lonely, but I think I knew somehow that you were with me. The dreams helped."

I thought about our mutual dreams over the years and nodded. We had never spoken during those shared moments, but I knew her presence. "I had my brother, but I spent a lot of time alone and never made friends in my classes. It didn't bother me, being alone. Maybe you're right." I nudged her and she laughed. The sound high and pure. It amazed me she could still laugh so effortlessly and often.

We fell into a comfortable silence, letting the bond communicate where words couldn't. I scanned the plains at our back and village to our front, looking for a sign that Silken survived or the villagers were coming. All was quiet. Even the sky was clear of more flighters. I glanced back in the direction of Vichi and winced as the wind filled my loose hood and blew it off my head. Movement caught my eye. Natasha sat up just in time for me to jump to my feet. I pounded on the wagon to wake Levi and Audrey.

"The train! The train is coming!"

Audrey stuck her head out first. She squinted up at me and then in the direction I pointed. "I don't see anything."

"It's coming," I insisted, watching the steam. I reached around her to grab my pack and pulled it on.

"So?" Audrey asked. Despite her questions, she and Levi were readying to leave alongside me.

"We can ride it!" Levi caught on first and grinned. "Brilliant."

"It stops at the edge of town and stays long enough just for the new volunteers to get on. I remember there were ladders built along the side; if we climb up, we can ride on the roof without anyone seeing us."

"Yeah, except another flighter. Wouldn't they figure out the timing?"

"The train is fast. We can probably get away. It's our best and quickest option to get to the Front."

Audrey looked doubtful, frowning at the crowd gathering at the platform. I was about to continue pushing for it when I realized it wasn't me she was questioning. "But... it's too early," she said.

The mood darkened and we shared a look. Only Natasha was still confused. The train was coming months before the next draft of volunteers was supposed to take place. I couldn't imagine enough people had turned seventeen since my enlistment for a good number of fresh soldiers. The commanders had decided they needed more people. Only a significant shift in the war would bring this on. Something like the Florians staging an attack on Traesha. Natasha picked up on my guilt through the bond and her eyes dimmed.

We hurried toward the village as the train drew near, doing our best to stay behind cover and avoid the eyes of the villagers. When the whistle sounded, it became easier. Everyone turned to stare down the tracks, paying no attention to the barren mines in front of them. They shifted uneasily. No one smiled or cheered and not a single whoop sounded.

That wasn't right.

When the train glided into the village platform, we

were close enough to reach its side right as it lurched to a complete stop. We grabbed the first ladders we could. Natasha and I went to one and stayed low enough on the rungs that the villagers wouldn't see us from the other side. Levi and Audrey did the same a car down. We couldn't risk climbing to the roof just yet but would have to get up there before those inside the train stopped watching the platform and saw us outside their windows. My heart pounded wildly in my ears. This was a huge gamble. Natasha's nerves combined with mine and slicked my hands with sweat.

"But she's fifteen! She's just a child!" A mother's shrill voice carried over the sound of the train's engine, followed by a loud crack. I peered through the window and watched the scene unfurl. Twin thuds as the mother's knees hit the wooden platform, falling under the force of the commander's blow. Her daughter seemed confused. She reached for her kneeling mother as the commander yanked her toward the train.

"Volunteer age has been lowered. She's choosing to serve her country. You should all be proud. Now stand back!" The murmuring crowd shuffled.

"But she didn't. She didn't volunteer," the mother's protest was nearly whispered. Half-hearted. The commanders were never argued with. The war was too crucial. The punishments too harsh.

Another crack.

I stiffened and saw my shock mirrored in Levi and Audrey's faces down the train. I ignored Natasha's whispered warning and leaned again to look through the window. Over half of those inside the train looked like they'd been dragged from the Squalor. The commanders didn't usually recruit so many from Vichi's outskirts. I caught the eye of one boy. I froze. He froze. He blinked a few times before closing his eyes, letting his head fall back on the seat. My heart squeezed painfully. He had already given up the fight. He would likely be sent to the Front within hours.

The rest of the car occupants were round-cheeked, by Bellovi's standards at least, and smaller than even Mayze when we volunteered. The two years of age between us felt like everything. Children. The commanders were sending children to war. I tightened my grip on the rung.

There were few protests once the mother had been left unconscious. In short order, the train was pulling out of the station. We climbed out of the view of the windows to find our places on the roof. We had to lie on our stomachs, hold the rails, and keep our heads down against the stinging wind. Levi lost his hat and Audrey helped him get his hood up, both working one-handed as the train picked up speed. I risked the wind every few minutes to check the sky, but it was always clear of flighters.

Long after my shock burned to an angry simmer, I could feel horror continue to roll off Natasha. She was in complete disbelief. I shouldn't have been surprised by the commanders' cruel decision. I should have predicted they would find a way to reinforce their lines. The kids in the train below me were only a couple of years younger than me. Why wouldn't the commanders call on them to fight?

We stopped at the last village, and I caught Levi's eye as they took more children from their protesting parents. His gaze held a cold fury. Audrey gripped her rail so tightly the metal was giving way under her fingers. The train pulled forward again in little time. This town had so few people there were only about a dozen children they could take.

I began to sweat under my winter layers as we drew

closer to the training base. The sun was setting now, and my arms ached where they clutched the railing. I got everyone's attention and pointed to the end of the train. The cars ran smoothly over the tracks and the wind had eased with the warmer climate. I successfully got to my feet and ran in a crouched position. Everyone else followed suit. We jumped the cars and reached the caboose, lowering ourselves to the platform. I gestured for Natasha to jump down first. She straddled and then sat on the rail, paused to take a breath, and threw herself off to the side. She missed the tracks and rolled unharmed. Levi, Audrey, and I followed. I pushed to my knees in the stiff brown grass and watched the train continue, taking Bellovi's children to war.

How long would it be before I faced them on the opposite side of the battle?

"I can't believe that worked," Levi said. All we could see of the train was the trailing cloud of steam as the track dipped up and down a slight hill.

"Me neither." Natasha sighed and pulled off her gloves and coat. "It feels so nice here."

"Just in comparison to Vichi. Keep your coat for nightfall," I said.

Natasha nodded distractedly. She was looking fondly toward the sparse trees just barely in sight. We left behind some of the bulkier layers. We didn't need the weight slowing us down no matter how cold it might get at night. I was saddened to see my mother's belongings left in a heap in the grass. I kept looking back as we distanced ourselves from the tracks. Another piece of my childhood left behind.

We hiked a long while until we reached the cover of the

trees. My neck was sore from how often I was still checking the skies while everyone else grew more relaxed the further we got from Vichi.

I tried to mimic their calm. To let Natasha's excitement infect me. Yet I couldn't shake the sense we were being pursued, the nerves I felt at the thought of facing Oken again or the guilt of trying to contact Hinze and ask for more help.

We stopped eventually to catch our breath. I had my coat tied around my waist and desperately needed the stream we found. This close to the Front, we didn't necessarily trust the water and had to wait to slake our thirst as the purifying bottle we brought slowly filtered.

Levi dug around in his pack and pulled out his hand-held light and the map of Bellovi. The sun was setting, but it wasn't so dark that Natasha and I needed his light. Levi sat cross-legged and examined the map for a beat. Situated, he pointed to the training base. He trailed his fingers along the dotted line marking the train track. They were still just within view. An hour ago, we'd caught sight of the train making its return trek to Vichi.

"I'm guessing we're getting closer to base, putting us about here on the tracks," Levi said.

I nodded. The steep hill on our left was the one on which I had passed my training course. I thought of Dani, racing to sabotage me and dying days later at my feet. Levi drew his finger upward, stopping where the Front intersected with a wide river. "Last time Hue checked, Rennie was stationed around this area. She and her unit were guarding the river. Hue said the Florians had been trying to use it to float across our borders."

"So, we go north until we find this river and follow it to her?" Audrey asked.

Even with Natasha here, they looked to me to confirm plans. Her royal title meant little to Bellovians, rebels or otherwise.

"Works for me," I said. I checked the bond for signs Natasha resented my command but found none. "Let's walk that way until we find some better cover and turn in for the night. We shouldn't be at risk of coming within view of the base, but look out for anyone training in the trees."

No one argued and two hours of mostly uphill hiking later, we were gratefully bedding down in a small alcove we found in the rocks.

The next day we woke in a solemn mood. The night had been as cold as I remembered and no one had slept well with the sounds of the forest surrounding us. Levi and I fell into step together and started talking about Nico, discovering memories of him that we shared. Like how the boy he spoke of for a year non-stop had been another member of the rebellion. Levi and I could copy Nico's excited chatter and kept making each other laugh at the memories of his love-struck attitude.

"You should have seen Henry's snaggletooth, though. He looks better now that it's been knocked out. Nico claimed he was over him, but I swear he breathed a sigh of relief when it happened."

I laughed, never having seen the boy my brother had been obsessed with and enjoying the insight.

Behind me, I could hear Natasha timidly asking Audrey questions about her childhood and the rebellion. Audrey's answers were still characteristically short, but she knew the importance of swaying the Trish queen to the rebellion cause. If we did manage to free Traesha, cutting off Bellovi completely would lead to thousands starving. Audrey was a bit more open about the hardships of her past and hopes for the future. Natasha listened carefully and by the time we stopped again for the night, there was a newfound easiness between the two of them.

We stopped for camp when we finally reached the river. I dreamed of Traesha's trees and frustration and whispers that wouldn't calm. It wasn't the tug toward Natasha like I had experienced for weeks, but thoughts of Traesha were insistent in the back of my mind.

I woke slowly to find we had slept in later than I wanted. Our bodies likely needed the rest, but I cursed under my breath. The sun was already high in the sky. While we weren't on a strict schedule, the persistence of my dreams made me want to wake everyone and hurry them along. I took a breath instead. We still had to cross the Front and, after that, deal with the politics of Floria. Our time there wouldn't be something I had ever prepared for, and Natasha and I needed to be at our best. Levi and Audrey would be surrounded by people who saw them as enemies. They'd have to be wary and alert among the Florians. If we could take a moment to rest now, it would only help us in the long run.

I sat up and pressed a hand into my rumbling stomach. A quick search of both my and Levi's packs revealed we were down to two bags of dried fruit. I ate what I thought would be a fair portion and left the rest to everyone else. I picked my way out of our little alcove and refilled our purifying bottle. I drank it until my stomach stretched, trying to convince myself I was full. I sat by the water's edge and pulled off my hat to scratch my head. With my feet cooling in the water, I kept watch over our cave entrance. I took out my braid and ran my fingers through the strands. What would my hair look like entirely silver? Light like Natasha's? Steely like Fisher's? What had my mother's looked like?

I nipped that thought quickly. My mother was dead. It only hurt to speculate.

Natasha woke, sending a quick flurry of information down the bond. She followed it to my side, and I offered her the freshly refilled bottle when she sat.

"You really think these Bellovian soldiers will help us through their lines?"

"I think Rennie will, especially with Levi here," I said. We watched the river and I thought about the shift in Levi's tone when Rennie was mentioned. Did she know he had feelings for her? I remembered how comfortable she was with Oken, my mind briefly flashing to a memory of her leaning her head against his shoulder. I hoped Rennie did know and I hoped the feelings were mutual.

"What was that?" Natasha asked. I looked around sharply, thinking she'd heard something. "No, in our bond. That... hurt?"

I hesitated, fixing my gaze back on the river. "Jealousy," I admitted, my cheeks heating.

"I've been jealous before. It doesn't feel like that."

"It does when a boy is involved and you know you're being stupid," I muttered.

Natasha smiled fully, my embarrassment throbbing in the bond. She nudged me with her shoulder. "You have a crush."

"Had a crush," I tried. It was a weak attempt. Just thinking about Oken being somewhere along this same river made my stomach flutter. I fought the urge to reach for his knife in my boot.

Natasha put a hand on her chest, spreading her fingers wide. "Our hearts are connected, my *resa*. You can't hide from me." Natasha laughed and I didn't have the heart to quiet her despite our position deep in enemy territory. I splashed river water on her instead. She closed her eyes and leaned forward to let the spray hit her face. The unexpected reaction made me huff my own laugh.

Natasha took off my mother's boots and joined me in cooling her feet in the water. I cringed at the blisters on her heels and felt her relief as the water soaked them.

"Can't you heal those?"

She tilted her head in concentration, laughing breathlessly when the skin evened out on her feet. "I guess I can."

We shared a wondering look.

"I took down that flighter with a transport door. I threw guards and even after everything, I feel like I could skip for days. Do you think we're going to keep..."

"Getting stronger?" Natasha finished my thought. She shrugged. "If we want to stand a chance in this war, I hope so."

"True."

"So, your Bellovian friends are helping us here, but you never said how we're getting into Floria."

"I might be able to contact my friends over there. The prince who helped me get to Traesha to free you." If they were still my friends after I abandoned them. The guilt surfaced again.

"How?"

I tapped my temple. "One of them has an ability that makes it possible. I've been trying to contact him, but I can't yet."

I had no idea where Hinze and his friends would be at this point, but I prayed they were close enough by the time we reached the Front that I'd be able to send word and get help with crossing. We would also need to convince Hinze to take us to the Florian king and the Trish in Helsa.

"Do you think they'll follow me?" Natasha's mind had gone to the Trish as well.

"I can think of at least three of them who will. I don't know how many made it to Floria. But Savha and Fisher are my friends and I know Sam wants to find you."

Natasha stuck her fingers in the water and watched them interrupt the flow of the current. I couldn't quite read her side of the bond when I mentioned Sam's name, but the feelings weren't happy.

"He didn't trust me," I said.

Natasha wiped her hand off on her pants and sighed. "Sam was *resa* to my mother. When the Bellovians attacked, they went straight to the throne room. My mother asked Sam to stay with me. He always said she could barely stand to leave my side. She and Grandmother got hit first that day. The queen and queen regent killed in one blast along with their *magsai*. When she died, Sam and my grandfather ran with me. Sam said her death hurt like nothing he had ever felt. Knowing she would have wanted me safe was the only thing that kept him from letting them kill him then and there."

Natasha paused, frowning. She let her head tip back. The sunlight caught her face in dancing rays through the trees. "I still don't know who told or how we were found out in Floria, but one day Sam left to shop in the village and the Bellovians came. I didn't have my speed yet and my grandfather tried to protect me, but the Bellovians were strong like Audrey and he was old. The woman leading them crashed through the wall of our home. When my grandfather tried to fight, a man threw him into the other wall."

It was strange, listening to her talk and already knowing the story. My dream had been real. I only wished she had known I was with her. That she hadn't been alone.

"Sam blames himself," I said. I cringed at the memory of the cruel words I had said to him. His complete devastation in his cell in the face of our failed mission. I had barely spared him a glance before I left to save Natasha.

Her gaze hardened in response to my remorse. "We're lucky the Bellovians wanted to use me as a threat. They did more to protect me than he did."

I quickly promised myself I wouldn't fail her as he had. Her smiles were too precious; I didn't want to lose them to the anger on her face. The frustration in the bond was hauntingly familiar. My hair rose. It was similar to how the trees felt in my dreams.

A short time later, Levi and Audrey woke. They finished off the fruit and we packed the rest of our meager supplies. Then, we decided to move forward in the daylight while Audrey and Levi could still see and move carefully. Quiet steps and sight would do more for us than shadows at night, especially if the Bellovians had access to night vision glasses like the ones I had worn on my one and only mission.

We kept the river in sight but moved deeper into the trees where we could hear better if someone was coming. We made a quiet group, and I was proud of myself for having mastered moving on silent feet. Even Natasha glided through the trees as though they were making room to let her pass. Whenever I heard Bellovian soldiers patrolling, I motioned for everyone to take cover until they cleared us.

"We have to be getting close," Levi whispered the second time this happened.

We hadn't heard soldiers for a while when we moved

back to the river to refill our water. I crouched in the bank with the bottle. Audrey and Natasha went to the bushes to relieve themselves. Levi wondered upstream a bit, probably to do the same.

The water was loud. I didn't hear the Bellovian man until he burst through the bush directly behind me, his gun drawn.

"Tell me why I shouldn't shoot you," he barked, hesitating at the sight of my black braid. I warned Natasha through the bond, hoping she would stay hidden.

I was opening my mouth to reply when the man crumpled. My heart froze in my throat.

Oken stood behind the soldier, the butt of his gun still lifted where he had hit his comrade on the back of the head. He examined me where I crouched for a long moment before lowering his weapon, keeping it where he could easily aim. I froze in the force of his unreadable stare. His eyes, an amber that always looked so close to its melting point, were hard as stone.

Natasha and Audrey came out of the bushes, hands in the air, followed by Jenna Teal, her gun trained on their backs. My blood pounded with rage to see a gun pointed at my queen.

I slipped my fingers into my boot and took out the knife hidden there. His knife. Skipping around Oken too fast for their eyes to follow, I stopped and held it to his throat. I narrowed my eyes at Jenna. "Drop the gun, Teal."

"Really, princess?" Oken asked. Even standing as we were, I melted at the sound of his voice.

CHAPTER 3

" I suppose it's too much to hope you brought my cycle back to me," Oken continued, not even a hint of tension in his shoulders. I frowned and stepped away. My thoughts were scrambled. My lungs weren't drawing in enough air. Oken turned to look at me and I offered him his knife back.

"I had to leave it in Trent," I said. I stared at my hand. Why was I giving it back when he had his gun ready? My hand wouldn't move from its awkward position of offering.

Oken pushed my hand away, not bothering to look at the knife. Jenna lowered her gun, recognizing me. "Commander Larson?"

"Don't shoot them!" Rennie suddenly broke through the trees, Levi at her side, red gun in hand.

"We weren't about to." Oken's voice was flat. I swallowed.

"I have to get them into Floria," I said.

Oken's eyes flicked to take in the rest of my group before landing on me once again. "The queen?"

I nodded, grateful he didn't elaborate and knew to drop

his voice. He still sported a yellow bruise on his cheek. I had punched him harder than I thought in Traesha.

"Please, just let them go," Rennie's voice was tight with panic. She grabbed at Jenna, pulling her aim away from Audrey and Natasha.

Of course, it was then that I finally felt Londe's consciousness brushing my own after hours of trying to contact him. Forgetting his instructions, I opened my mind to him rather than picturing us talking. I felt his shock as he took in the forest scene before me. Natasha and her royal white hair in plain sight.

"We need your help crossing the Front," I told him and the Bellovians. Oken's eyebrows lowered.

"You deserted, Finley," Oken said. I wasn't expecting the bitterness in his voice. He kept it quiet so only I could hear. "I helped you before, but this is... I can't cross the Front. Some of us worry about our families back home."

My eyes filled with tears at a genuinely shocking speed. I looked down and angled myself away, wiping them away as they formed. I swore under my breath.

Hinze is on his way. Londe's words in my mind were exactly what I needed to compose myself.

I cleared my throat and straightened, though I couldn't meet Oken's eyes. The truth of his words still hollowed my core. "Just help us. You don't have to cross."

"How?"

I considered, frowning at the panic that began to bloom in my chest. How indeed? We needed an escort. Oken could tell me the patrols as well as he knew them until he was blue in the face, but that didn't mean I could navigate the forest well enough to avoid them. We only had Levi's undetailed map. Speed and timing were what we needed to cross. We couldn't stop to check a piece of paper.

"Fine. You don't have to help." I glanced at Rennie and saw she was already nodding, soothing some of the anxiety. I stepped closer to her. "Please let us pass, Oken."

He looked to Jenna and her grip tightened on her gun. I swallowed hard.

"What happens when you get to Floria?"

"We form an alliance with the king and free Traesha."

"And then?"

I hoped Natasha couldn't hear. Her focus seemed centered on Jenna's gun. "I want to end the war."

When he looked back at me, I saw the expression on his face mirrored his look when he'd gotten off the cycle for me. Indecision. Temptation.

Hope fluttered in my chest. Gods. I wanted him to come with me.

"They shot Dani," he whispered.

"I know." My throat felt thick from the tears I had suppressed. My memory flashed to Dani dead on the ground, smile frozen on her face. Natasha's face paled from my pain.

"Silken had you beaten."

"Yes."

"They're sending Mayze and a bunch of kids to Traesha to fight off the Florians."

"And that only scratches the surface. Oken, what they're doing, what they've done, it isn't right. Please, help me stop them." I fought the urge to reach for him.

Oken glanced Natasha's way. She stood as tall as she could under his gaze. He frowned and looked back at me. I did my best to keep the hope from my face, but his lips quirked, and my heart stumbled. Was he trying not to smile?

"Sars..." Jenna's voice was low with warning.

Oken sighed, opening his mouth when a commotion in the woods behind him made us all turn. Relief flooded me when he raised his gun in that direction rather than at Natasha or me. Jenna looked from Oken to Rennie, confusion plain on her face. I pulled out the short gun Levi had given me back in Vichi and kept Oken's knife ready in my left hand.

"I'm going back to Floria whether you help me or not," I said in a low voice, stepping up to Oken's shoulder where he stood watching the forest. His jaw clenched briefly, but he turned his head to look at me. It was my turn to fight a smile. His eyes had softened, returning to their familiar look of liquid gold.

The footsteps and voices in the trees passed. Oken's stance eased. He turned to face me fully, gun lowered once more. This close, I could feel his warmth. I let out a breath. Out of the corner of my eye, I saw Rennie begin to grin and nudge Levi.

"What's going on?" Jenna broke in. "Why would we help them? Who even are you?"

Natasha turned on her. "I'm the queen of Traesha and I'm going to get my country back."

The forest went quiet until Jenna let out a sputtering laugh. "You're joking!" Jenna turned to me. "Tell me you all are joking."

Natasha avoided meeting my eyes, but she felt the force of my angered disbelief. She couldn't just go around declaring her title on the Bellovian Front.

"*Shit*," Rennie drew out the word, but her eyes were lit with excitement. She raised her eyebrows at Levi.

"I know," he said, nodding.

"We can't help you," Jenna said, but her voice wavered, looking at Oken.

"I think I just might," he said it like a great admission. "You're going to Traesha?"

"Yes. Soon, hopefully." I reached for his hand and squeezed. "Come with us."

"Princess..." He pulled his hand free and scratched at his neck, debating. "Mayze is in Traesha. They, they won't tell us what's going on up there. I need to make sure she's okay. When we go, will you attack them? The kids and Mayze?"

I gave Oken a look. He went to war for his cousin. I had no doubt it had been eating at him that he didn't know how she was. "I won't hurt Mayze. You know that. We'll find her and make sure she's okay."

He stared at me for a long time. I didn't *want* to hurt anyone. I strove to only fight when necessary. Maybe Oken saw it in my eyes. He settled his long gun across his back with the strap and bent to pick up the man he had knocked out under his arms. With a grunt, Oken maneuvered him into the rushing water. As the cold water shocked the soldier back to consciousness and he came up for air, I cleared my expression and brought my gun up to point at Oken's back. His hands were already raised in surrender. The other soldier went back under. The current carried him away. I hoped we were convincing enough that if he were found alive, he would tell the commanders what he had seen and they would think Oken, Jenna, and Rennie had followed a similar or worse fate. Presumed captured or killed was much better than desertion.

I had little hope Silken would fall for it. At the Conquering Ceremony, he had known Oken meant something to me. The thought made me cold, but this attempt was better than nothing.

The smile Oken wore when he turned back around warmed my stomach. "I'm in."

"Me too!" Rennie bounced with excitement.

We looked at Jenna.

She watched the river carry away the Bellovian soldier. I hated that she looked at me with fear and guilt, worrying her bottom lip. She hadn't made much of an impression on me through training or even our mission, but I remembered the art she made in the dust of our dirty cell and suddenly hoped she would join us. I stepped toward her.

"I love to sing, but not the shouting war songs Bellovians know. The Trish songs are art and they're celebrated. *Art* is celebrated. There are still paintings hanging up in the castle in Shalta. This is our chance to fight for the world we sing about and paint. You're an artist. We must make the world match our vision."

Jenna gave me a searching look. "My family will never speak to me again. They could die. There's no way that little show was enough." Yet... her words sounded half-hearted. I knew then she would come with us.

"It's your choice to make," I said. Jenna looked at her careful hands, so incongruent with her Bellovian uniform and stature. When she looked up again, her eyes found Natasha.

"If I go, will you put up one of my paintings?" she asked. I saw the dream in her eyes, overshadowing the guilt, and I understood. I used to fantasize about audiences listening to me. About the applauses and freely given smiles.

"In the throne room," Natasha promised. Jenna nodded and our followers doubled.

THE TREES WERE ALL TOO familiar in this reach of the forest. The hair on my arms rose. I walked closer to Natasha, though she felt little fear. During my first mission, I had a sense of being haunted while here. The feeling lingered. This forest carried death and it was so much worse the closer we got to Floria. I longed for the whispers of the Trish forest, even tense as they were in my dreams. The messages whispered at least carried hope.

The last words the trees spoke to me in person repeated in my head. *Singer singer, tell them* nisashan. I let the mystery of the message distract me as we stepped over hastily dug graves, ducked under the jagged spikes of a branch shot from its trunk, and slid on bullet casings scattered on the forest floor. Some trees were cut down to create flimsy barricades and we ducked from one to another to take shelter. Where was the technology here? Where were the commanders? Oken, Jenna, and Rennie's efforts helped us avoid the majority of unranked Bellovians stationed, but it was only a matter of time before we were spotted. Hardly anyone breathed as we carefully picked our way toward Floria.

Our luck only held for so long. We were spotted passing a larger tree when we discovered a figure huddled on the other side. They were weaponless and so still with fear that I thought we had stumbled upon a body. The unranked Bellovian soldier blinked and was silent, letting us pass. They had the Squalor written in their features and survival. But we all knew if the Florians or Bellovians found them hiding, they were dead. Levi was even tenser after that.

Oken motioned to us a short time later, pressing down with his hands. We took cover behind the nearest barricade. He came close and whispered in my ear.

"Commander Chav is the last of ours," he said, nodding to the woods ahead and to our left, where the commander must be positioned. The river rushed close on our right. There must be too many stationed here to avoid everyone.

"This portion of the Front has been quieter since Traesha, most of the fighting shifted further north, but I don't know who's stationed past our team. Are we clear on the other side?"

"I hope so," I said. Londe had been silent despite my attempts to contact him again.

"I'll go take him out—" Oken started. I was already shaking my head.

"I'm not taking any chances. I'll do it. He won't see me coming."

Natasha nodded with a wry smile. Oken shifted out of my way, mirroring her grin and winking.

I even missed his wink.

I skipped to the commander, noted the single stripe on his uniform, and choked him out in the next second. Oken stood and gestured to our group to follow him. As they passed me, I settled the unconscious Bellovian on the ground and swapped my rusted short gun for his mid gun. Much better.

I skipped to the front of the group and walked next to Oken. His back was stiff and straight as we approached enemy lines. He slowed and I opened my mouth to urge him forward when the hair on my arms rose.

The shots seemed to come out of nowhere. I heard Jenna grunt and Natasha went to her side. I turned and skipped, finding the group of four Bellovians who'd been patrolling. I took out one with a jab to the throat and barely ducked in time to avoid the bullet Oken shot to take care of the other. I stood again, but Audrey's hammer came flying next, thrown with her gifted strength, and I swore as I hit the ground. Bodies fell around me.

"Finley!" Oken's panicked shout felt louder than the pop of gunfire. I jumped to my feet, looking for the new threat. While the forest was now alive with shouting and flying bullets a short distance away, no threats were imminent. I looked back at him in confusion.

He staggered forward, relief washing his features. "You know better, Finley! I thought I shot you!"

I tried for a reassuring smile, but neither of us had the time to focus on the moment.

I grabbed Audrey's hammer and threw it back to her. Almost as soon as it hit her palm, she hurled it back into the trees, but not before her target had time to get off a shot. The crunch of the hammer hitting the Bellovian woman's skull was followed by a cry of pain.

Behind Oken, Rennie collapsed. I watched her fall, horror flooding me as more shooting rang through the trees. Levi's warning shout spurred me to turn in time to avoid the bullet hitting my chest. Instead, it grazed my shoulder. Natasha glanced in my direction and the pain disappeared. She smiled as she turned her attention back to Rennie right as Oken made to lift her out of the way.

"I'm good!" Rennie said, popping up and startling Oken so much he stumbled back and gracelessly fell with a strangled shout.

This was getting ridiculous.

"Move!" I shouted as I skipped and appeared next to them, startling Oken again. He clutched his chest. I rolled my eyes and helped him to his feet. Even now, in this panicked moment, his hand warm in mine made my chest flutter. Jenna was standing in place, mouth hanging open, looking between her healed stomach and our scrambled efforts to take cover and retaliate.

We badly needed to work on incorporating our gifts into battle.

I took charge, trying to move us past the confusion of

the moment. "Rennie and Levi take left. Jenna and Audrey cover our right. Oken take point," I rattled the orders off, emphasizing my words with the appropriate Bellovian gestures. I hoped having Oken, Rennie, and Jenna lead would give anyone else we encountered a moment of confusion with their uniforms on.

They nodded and I turned to cover our backs as we continued toward the border in a slight V formation, Natasha as safe as she could be in the middle and me just behind her. I took a second to skip and grab Audrey's hammer, trying not to look at the crushed skull it had left behind. I spotted one sniper and took her out with a well-placed bullet. We passed a body taken out with friendly fire, a bullet in the back that none of us could have managed. I wasn't prepared for the rage I experienced looking down at his body, memories of Dani hitting me once again.

Senseless murder.

I stayed close to Natasha's back. It was a struggle to ignore the instinct urging me to skip with her out of danger, leaving the team behind to ensure her safety. The forest had gone momentarily quiet behind us, but we heard plenty of shouted arguments in the distance. The Bellovians didn't know how to manage an attack from behind, and surprise worked beautifully in our favor.

I nearly smiled when I finally spotted Hinze sitting casually beside the river. There were dark bags under his eyes and his long hair looked disheveled. The braid on his right side frayed like he hadn't redone it in days. Our failure in Traesha had hit him hard. His left shirt sleeve bulged with bandages underneath. Any desire to smile died remembering Garris's death and how I'd abandoned Hinze bleeding in his cell. The guilt that twisted in my stomach was too familiar.

I skipped to the front of our line, moving Oken aside with a hand on his arm. He had readied his gun but lowered it at my touch.

The prince got to his feet when he saw us and signaled to someone close by that we were to come through.

"Welcome back to this side of the war," he said with a tight smile. "You've been busy."

He eyed the rest of our group warily, recognition lighting his face when he took in Oken, Rennie, and Jenna. When he looked at Natasha, his eyes widened just enough for me to know he hadn't fully believed the message I sent through Londe.

Hinze held out a hand and I immediately reached for it, welcoming the safety of the lightness that came over me. I held out a hand to Natasha. She looked baffled but took it. I nodded for Oken to take her free hand.

"For safety's sake," Hinze said.

"This a Florian thing or...?" Oken stage whispered behind me. Rennie laughed. Hinze's grip on my hand tightened.

"Just do it, Sars," I said over my shoulder. Oken winked and took Natasha's hand. The rest of the Bellovians quickly linked up. Even with everything that had just happened, the sight of five perplexed Bellovians holding hands had me stifling a laugh. Maybe the relief of being out of danger was making me giddy. Especially when their mouths opened in little O's when they felt Hinze's ability wash over them. Oken caught my eye, his face mirroring my amusement. He swung Natasha and Rennie's hands at his side.

There was no denying how happy his presence made me. I prayed his family would be safe. That he wouldn't regret following me.

We started moving. Hinze gently pulled me forward to

walk beside him. I ignored the bushes I would typically avoid and walked through them, showing the group Hinze's ability. Natasha cautiously walked through a tree and let out a breathless laugh when she emerged on the other side.

We passed a line of Florian soldiers who gave Hinze stiff bows. I cringed, hearing another volley of gunfire. I pressed down more guilt as the soldiers readied to hold their lines. This was war. Sacrifices had to be worth making to get Natasha out of Bellovi. It could have been much worse.

Hinze felt me stiffen. "Don't worry. The elites in the area are on their way. They'll settle down the line with minimal damage."

After a time, Hinze signaled we were in the clear to let go of each other. We had reached a small, quiet clearing. He squeezed my hand before dropping it and I let my shoulders relax. He wasn't mad at me for abandoning them. He'd come as soon as he could. I hadn't lost my Florian allies. My friend.

"Is this really the queen?" Hinze asked me in a low voice. His eyes, mostly green against the backdrop of trees, were full of hope when I looked up to answer.

Confusion muddled his face when a twig snapped in front of us. Lilah stepped out of the trees, followed closely by Sam. At the *magsai's* nod, she brought her hands together. Hinze made a sound of protest. I didn't think fast enough to close my eyes before Lilah's clap rang through the forest.

And nothing happened.

Hinze gasped and stumbled back a step. I saw the shock on his and Lilah's faces and followed their gazes to Levi. His hands were raised, forehead furrowed with concentration.

I suddenly remembered Levi mentioning an ability

briefly. I realized I had never gotten around to asking him what it was. It would seem I had my answer.

"How about we just have a normal conversation here? No need for your theatrics," Levi said pointedly to Lilah.

I reached for Hinze's arm and my hand made contact with his solid bicep. He jumped at my touch.

Levi's ability took away the abilities of others.

My heart fluttered at the possibilities. The thrill of power. My Bellovian upbringing reared its head as I thought about the advantages, especially when I tested my speed with a flick of my fingers and found my Trish gifts remained unaffected. Wherever my power came from, it was different from the Florians and Bellovians. I could swear at that moment, I heard the trees of Traesha whisper in my ears.

Sam recovered from his surprise first. In the next breath, he skipped to Natasha. Sam pushed her out of our reach and knelt in front of her. I skipped back to her side, flaring with protective anger. I heard the Bellovians around me shifting. They adjusted their weapons, ready to defend us without fully understanding what was happening between Levi and the Florians. Lilah stared at her hands. Hinze looked from Sam to the guns around our circle, his expression tight with worry. Without their abilities, they could do nothing to help Sam against the threat of the Bellovian weapons.

"My queen, please." Sam paid no attention to any of this. "We need to leave. I will protect you. I swear. Nothing like what happened to your grandfather will ever happen again."

Natasha silenced him with a cold look. Her voice shook. "You failed me, Sam. I can no longer trust you with my—"

"But you trust a group of Bellovian children? Natasha, please— "

Natasha held up a hand. It trembled with the force of her anger. "Do *not* interrupt me. I may not know the Bellovians well, but I trust my *resa* to keep me safe and to make this call. We cannot move forward without risk."

Sam's eyebrows pulled together. He looked past me, searching for the other *magsai* in our midst. I folded my arms and stepped closer to Natasha. Understanding cleared his features. He let out an incredulous laugh.

"My apologies, but you are mistaken, my queen. This girl is half Bellovian. There is no way she could be your *resa magsai*. She has already betrayed the trust of the Florians by deserting them during an important battle. A battle we are now losing in our own country."

"Do not speak to me as the child you once knew, Sam." I silently made it my life's mission never to make Natasha speak to me in that chilling tone. This wasn't the girl who sat beside me by the river and giggled. This was an angry, wronged queen with the weight of a country on her back. "If I say Finley is my *resa*, it is because I know it to be fact. Finley, close your eyes." I did and felt a slight twinge of pain above my right hip. "Where did I pinch myself?" Natasha asked.

I opened my eyes and pointed to the spot. Sam's mouth dropped open.

"She left Traesha because her brother told her who she truly was. She left Traesha to save me. It only took her days. I think it is telling of your treatment of fellow Trish that she couldn't trust you to help her."

"But she is not even a full-blooded Trish...."

"She is, not that this is any of your concern. But, even if

she was half Trish, you should have listened, as you should listen to anyone with Trish blood. Now move aside."

Sam stared up at Natasha, a battle waging in his features. He wanted to say more but worried about falling even more out of her favor. His gaze flicked to me, pale yellow eyes betraying his confusion. I raised an eyebrow and shook my head just once. Natasha was not in the mood to be lenient. I could feel his silence would go further with her at that moment. Another beat and he bowed his head. Slowly, he rose to his feet and stepped aside. The submission in his posture would have been more convincing if his jaw weren't so visibly clenched.

Natasha turned to Hinze. She took him in. She saw how he curled inward without his gift, how he looked betrayed when he glanced my way, how he frowned at Sam's bowed head. I felt her confidence bloom and it made my skin feel tight. "Prince Hinze, we need to talk."

CHAPTER 4

"I need to speak to the king as soon as possible about the situation in Traesha." Natasha paced behind the desk in the grand office room Hinze had led us to in the Honna house. It had been a two-hour drive from the river to here. I'd slept through most of it, drooling onto Oken's shoulder— much to his amusement. The shared laugh felt like the first I'd had in years.

I'd noticed right away that Hinze led us to an impersonal office on the ground floor rather than the loft in his room with the map of our lands and information on Florian lines. I hadn't been able to read his expression since Levi took his power, but his shoulders never lost their tension.

When I asked how he reached us so quickly, Hinze had explained with some embarrassment that he had ridden on Sam's back, making them both weightless so they could run through the forest at Trish speed to meet us without obstacle. Sam had only agreed to skip to us on the chance Natasha was with me but had gone to find Lilah after dropping off Hinze, hoping to capture the Bellovians and me. I chose to keep imagining the hilarious visual of Hinze and Sam running together rather than dwell on the anger fueled by Sam's actions afterward.

"I've already asked Sam to make arrangements for us to get to Helsa. It is late to travel today, but we should be able to leave first thing tomorrow. It's a two-day drive by transport to get to the palace."

Natasha nodded reluctantly. She didn't want to wait, but she looked exhausted. A full meal and a night of rest would only help us to prepare to face Floria's king. We couldn't risk underestimating him. A two-day drive put us just in the *center* of the land he called his own. It seemed too much space for one person to rule.

Floria was split into eight sections, with a ruling family in charge of each area. Bellovi was the size of only the smallest family's estate. Traesha half that. Meeting King Mavrick would be nothing like encountering a commander with a few victories under their belt. As much as I didn't want to acknowledge it, it would be nothing like interacting with Natasha either. She may be queen, but she had never truly ruled. Our land was tiny compared to his own and the only reason it had drawn attention was its resources. Yet even those were dwindling. Traesha could barely feed Bellovi. Floria had an eighth of its country dedicated to farming and abilities to aid growth. For the first time, I wondered if it was more than just our fertile ground that brought on Bellovi and Floria's attention. Why *was* everyone so interested in Traesha? Why couldn't we just be left alone?

It had to be our gifts, yet at every turn the commanders and Florians had done their best to show me not even the *magsai* stood a chance against them.

What else was there? If they didn't believe in our gods,

our powers, or our lands, what did they think Traesha could do for them?

"For now, what can you tell me about the situation in Traesha?" Natasha asked.

Hinze sighed and pulled at his small braid. "We lost all the ground we initially made with the enslaved Trish when we attacked. They had given up the fight again and we were not enough to keep the commanders at bay. The country is firmly back in Bellovian hands, with the added complication of the children they sent to hold it and prevent another attempt at rebellion. They have been making hard pushes on the northern end of the Front, just beneath the Trish forest. My father has focused his efforts there, keeping the Bellovians in check and protecting the Bennick estate. A good portion of our crops come from that region. At this point, we must accept Traesha as lost. The rest of my team was already on their way back to Honna from the northern lines. They should be here tonight, and we can all make the journey to Helsa in the morning. My father called me back as soon as we contacted him and told him of our failure. We have only held off this long while we waited for a healer. I believe the losses we suffered and my capture left him more shaken than he will admit." Hinze's eyes dropped to his folded hands. I knew he was thinking about the member of his team who would never return home.

We fell quiet. I was surprised by Natasha's reaction. The queen was fuming and struggling to get a hold of the emotion. I couldn't tell if her anger was directed at the Florians, the Bellovians, or maybe even the Trish who hadn't rallied.

"There's something else," I said. Natasha looked startled when I spoke. "While leaving Vichi, one of the commanders followed us in some new, flying transport. It was called a flighter and held two people."

Hinze's eyebrows pulled together. "I've never heard of such a thing. Where do they get the resources?"

"My question exactly. The people are too busy trying to survive to spend this much time and energy developing advanced technology. Where is it coming from? And how will it put them at an advantage in battle? I don't want to imagine the implications of flight."

Hinze shrugged. "It has proven a great advantage among the Florians with such a gift, but we also have abilities to combat such technology. It will not be a threat."

I remembered the buffeting wind and sleek build of the aircraft. "Are you sure?"

"We can talk to my father about it, but I don't think these flying transports will prove a large concern."

I heard the front door open. The tones of Mesa and Londe's voices announced their arrival.

Natasha sat down on the edge of the desk, eyes far away. The anger finally shifted to guilt and worry. I could think clearer once her rage eased. She traced a triangle on the desk. My mother had often done the same for me when talking about the powers of Traesha. The people, the land, and the queen. Mags, Tash, and Finma. Strength, love, and peace.

"I need to talk to the king," she repeated. "I need a sense of the support I can expect from him. We need to save my country. It *must* be the priority."

"He will meet with you..." Hinze shifted uncomfortably in his seat. "Your Bellovian followers won't be welcomed in Helsa, though."

Natasha narrowed her eyes at the Florian prince, anger flickering again. "You can inform your father I will speak with him and will be bringing anyone who honors me by joining my cause or he will step aside as I reclaim my country without his help."

Hinze lifted an eyebrow. "If I can ask, Your Majesty, where will you get the forces to do so?"

"I was imprisoned just a couple of days ago. Since, I have found my *resa*, broken out of the Bellovian capital, and crossed into Floria with five strong and very gifted *Bellovian* soldiers, thanks to Finley. Imagine what she and I can accomplish by making our cause known in our own country." Natasha stuck a finger in Hinze's face, fire dancing in her eyes. "You don't know our secrets, our strength, or who our allies are, but I promise you and your father want to be among them."

Hinze put his hands up in surrender with an easy smile despite Natasha's cold tone. We were instantly annoyed by the patronizing gesture. The emotion crackled between us along the bond.

"I hope I never find myself in your way," he said, easing our annoyance only slightly. His eyes unfocused briefly as Londe contacted him. "I think you'll find two more potential allies have just arrived. They're very anxious to meet you, Queen Natasha."

I was happy to lead Natasha from the office. The Honna house had changed little in our absence. The polished flagstone floors were cold against our padded socks. The stacked logs of the wall drew in the warm light. I felt surprisingly comfortable in these halls. I would be sad to leave the place again so soon.

We passed Londe on the stairs. He stopped, so we did. He looked at me intently and cleared his throat.

"You all right, Finley?"

"Yes. I'm fine." I shifted under his intent gaze. We

hadn't spoken much before, and his concern caught me off guard. "Have you heard from my brother?"

His eyes shadowed and unfocused as he shook his head. Alarm rang through me, but at that moment, the door at the base of the stairs burst open. Natasha pulled me forward at the sight of Savha and Fisher's silver hair.

The couple was talking animatedly in Trish as they quickly removed their shoes, Lanis nodding his approval. They dropped to their knees at the sight of Natasha.

"This is Fisher Dossen and Savha Molvish. Savha, Fisher, this is the Queen of Traesha, Natasha Hollis," I made the introductions with a smile, but my thoughts remained fixated on the worried look in Londe's eyes. Where was Nico?

Contentment rolled off Natasha as she gestured for Savha and Fisher to rise. "Dossen... my grandfather mentioned your family name. Your parents were *magsai* ambassadors. He said they were in Floria during the attack and told me to find them if I ever needed help."

"They'll be delighted to hear that. You can, of course, count on our support."

"And mine," Savha said. "Although my family has always just been farmers."

"They were not *just* farmers. And anyone brave enough to fight for Traesha in these times has the constitution of a *magsai*."

Savha's face flushed with pleasure. Fisher gave me a big smile before opening his arms. I happily stepped into his embrace. As he always did, Fisher pulled Savha in too. Natasha laughed when I reached for her.

"This is what grandfather talked about," she whispered in my ear.

It felt silly standing there with all four of us hugging,

but powerful too. Like being in Traesha with only one piece of the triangle missing. A large part of me was in Bellovi, thinking about my brother, but the part that was here and ready for these next steps was basking in Natasha's excitement.

Anticipation raised the hair on my arms. We were so much closer.

WE GATHERED for dinner soon after Fisher and Savha's arrival. A tense silence crowded the dining room. The Bellovians sat on one end of the table and Florian's on the other. Natasha and I were in the middle, Sam on her other side, and Savha and Fisher across from us. Constant glances were traded up and down the enormous wooden table between the uncommonly quiet Bellovians and suspicious Florians. Occasionally a clink of silverware came off a bit too aggressive, adding a new wave of glances.

I attempted to break the silence. The sound of me clearing my throat startled Jenna enough that she dropped her spoon. I winced in apology and turned to the Florian side of the table. "I'm sorry I left you all in Traesha. Once I learned I was *resa,* I had to get to Natasha, but I should have helped you more."

There was silence. Natasha patted my thigh. She wasn't bothered in the slightest that I had left the Florians. In her eyes, it was simple. I had been performing my duty as *resa.* She would have been indifferent about the entire situation if she didn't feel they had failed her country. The king should have supplied more people and helped them years earlier. Natasha didn't think I should have ever been in that situation to begin with.

I forced myself to keep eye contact with the Florians. They looked tired. And Lilah's eyes were puffy. She usually kept up a constant chatter with Brea, but now she kept falling silent. She was only picking at her food, spurring Londe to say something to her when both their eyes unfocused. I remembered her screaming loud enough to trap a ballroom of commanders in her gift.

The realities of war were hitting them hard.

From her seat next to Fisher, Mesa raised an eyebrow. She hadn't looked at all happy to see me, but she hadn't followed through on the threat she made to kill me, so there was that. "It was bullshit and an apology doesn't do much, does it? Hinze still got shot. We were still locked up down there for hours until he could get me out of my cell. Garris still died." Lilah flinched. "There are tough calls to make in war. You made your choice. If you feel guilty, live with it. Just like we'll be living with the knowledge of where you stand and how little we can trust you."

The table was even more divided than I thought. No one was looking at each other now. Rennie's knee was bouncing on Levi's other side. He sat completely still next to me.

The Trish. The Bellovians. The Florians. Silence roared between us. I would argue this table represented the most progressive of our lands. If we couldn't come together, how would our countries? How would the war ever end?

Fisher looked distinctly uncomfortable. He'd grown up in the palace with most of the Florians to his right. Hinze was his best friend. Natasha the queen he just met.

I didn't know how to fix it. "We're still on the same side. We want Traesha free. We want the war ended."

Natasha shifted. One of those things was much more important to her. Did she even care about the war? I couldn't tell her thoughts through the bond.

"Our methods appear to be quite different," Mesa said, voice cool. Even with her glare and tone, I was so relieved she was talking. Silence didn't get us anywhere. She was helping me, whether or not she wanted to.

"I'm sorry I took your knife," I said, a final apology to ease my own guilt whether or not she wanted it.

"It *was* one of my favorites. I take it you lost it?"

"I gave it away. To some Squalor kids in Vichi."

Brea set down her glass too hard. "You gave some kids a *knife*?" The temperature in the dining room dropped.

I blinked. Levi stiffened at my side. I'd already told him about Leigh and Jon and how they helped me find the rebels. "She probably saved their lives. If some kids owning a knife surprises you, you have no idea what it's like trying to live in Bellovi. Especially the Squalor."

Brea backed down when he spoke. The Florians were terrified of Levi.

Personally, I felt they could only benefit from his humbling of them.

"First time I went to buy bread by myself, I got attacked in the street. And that was in the apartments." Jenna pulled at the neck of her shirt and showed us a jagged scar along her collarbone. "I was six."

"Got my first gun when I was eleven. Levi here was nice enough to sell it to me for my only coat," Rennie said, shooting him a look.

Levi shrugged and smirked. "Got to stay warm somehow. I returned the favor, though, didn't I? Gave you the best room at Gale's."

Rennie snorted and kept eating. The tension eased just slightly. I was glad to note Rennie was finally putting on weight. Audrey ate like she thought this was her last meal. Oken couldn't stop himself from moaning softly whenever he bit into his steak. Lilah and Brea exchanged a glance every time he called attention to himself. Appreciating him was a welcome distraction. When Lilah mouthed *mine* and they shared shaky smiles, I had to stop looking at them.

"We heard there was poverty, but I didn't know…" Hinze trailed off, looking closer at my companions and noting the scars, thin bodies, and hardened eyes. He had no idea.

"You wouldn't if you've only been dealing with commanders and princess over here," Oken said, pointing at me with his fork. A speck of meat hit my cheek. My face heated as I wiped it off. The Bellovians laughed at the nickname and the flying food while the Florians watched in bewilderment. My shoulders finally relaxed. I wasn't sure how to interact with quiet, watchful Bellovians.

"Most people join the war to get a decent meal," Levi said once he stopped laughing. "The rebellion is made up of people who think that's unfair, but there we are, struggling to feed ourselves anyway. Especially since Finley's dad died."

I stiffened, splashing the water in the cup I'd been drinking. Natasha shot Levi a glare and put a comforting hand on my arm. Levi jumped as Rennie kicked him under the table. Oken paused with his next bite halfway to his mouth. Hinze drew in a sharp breath, realizing his messages to Nico hadn't worked. That my family had died when I left my team and joined his mission to help Natasha.

At least Mesa's glare finally vanished. They weren't the only people I had put in harm's way to save the queen. She seemed to understand me better as I struggled to swallow the pain.

"Sorry," Levi muttered.

I was grateful when Rennie spoke up, moving us past

the moment. "I was sent to war because I got caught stealing a few rolls of bread. Easiest way to execute someone is to send them out to the Front to try and rush the lines. Not like we have the resources to lock up and feed small criminals."

The Florian side of the table was lined with shocked expressions. Mesa's face had paled. Brea set down her fork, eyeing the bounty in the center of the table. Difficult as they were, I hoped conversations like this would be what it took to make the Florians see that being born in Bellovi didn't make up a personality. That the people needed to be saved, not just beaten in battle.

I glanced at Natasha. I wanted her to feel the same way. The war had to end. What happened in Traesha was a symptom of this greater destruction happening. We couldn't escape the fight even when we freed our people. She had to see the Trish weren't the only ones who deserved our help if we could give it.

What would I do if Natasha didn't come to feel the same? What *could* I do with the bond keeping me firmly rooted at her side, the thought of separation impossible? I had to follow her. That was it.

Oken was still watching me carefully. Questions in his eyes. Comfort offered in the silent support. I looked away.

That was it.

CHAPTER 5

Natasha was given Chelsa's room for the night. The wooden walls were stained a dark shade of brown. The bedding, rugs, and curtains were all a deep red. Natasha sniffed, fingers trailing on the soft upholstery of the seat by the fire. I remembered the first time I had seen the Honna house. Well, house when Hinze spoke. It was a mansion. I had thought my room in the servants' quarter was so grand and spacious. Neither of us was accustomed to this level of luxury, but Natasha's reaction was different. She was comfortable here. It felt right to her. She grew up hoping and praying to live in a palace one day. It made me happy to see her in her element. I felt a surge of motivation to get her to Traesha's castle. To show her the beauty and comfort only our people were capable of, even though the luxury didn't sit right with me.

I'd grown up in better conditions than Natasha and every Bellovian here. But I had grown up associating every coin my family possessed as a coin the people in the Squalor would never see. My father came home every night exhausted and conflicted. He tried to improve our city's poverty yet still accepted his paychecks because he loved us and wanted us to live comfortably. He was always striving to make our country more equal. The Trish castle had been a dream to enter, but even then, my memories of it were marred with darkness. There were too many Trish enslaved. What had it been like before the invasion? Who had labored to build the grand castle while others walked its halls in comfort? Were both parties happy like my mother always made it sound?

I couldn't even imagine how I'd feel once I finally saw the palace in Helsa or the nobles who took the halls and comfort for granted so far from the Front.

I ignored Natasha's protests and told her I would sleep on the chair in Chelsa's room rather than the room offered to me on the landing below. Everything in me rebelled against the idea of letting Natasha out of my sight for an entire night, even now that we were safe in Floria and surrounded by allies. I doubted the need to stay near was an instinct that would ever go away.

"At least sleep in the bed. It's more than big enough for the two of us," Natasha said from where she looked tiny under the sheets.

I could feel in the bond she was scared. While she may feel she belonged in the comforts of the mansion, she didn't know anyone else here except Sam. The tasks ahead of us were daunting enough to chase away sleep. She wanted me closer. I nodded and crawled in next to her. It was the softest mattress I had ever felt. We tried to talk, to plan for the next day, and debate how helpful the king was likely to be, but exhaustion slowed our words and led to long pauses between thoughts. We were soon asleep.

～

I SHOULD SCREAM. I should fight. But I couldn't. Their grips were so strong and my loss so crushing. The Bellovians had been quiet and tense the whole time we traveled, but now they were ghosts moving silently around me. There was some shooting when we crossed the Front, but Bellovian soldiers quickly gave us cover on the other side of the clearing. All hope died as I was ushered into the land of my enemies.

We made camp with the Bellovians already stationed there and waited for word. Someone said they wanted to take me to Traesha. Another said they should kill me and be done with it. I was in the woods with a woman soldier for a moment of semi-privacy when the shouts erupted behind us. The fight wasn't nearly long enough. The Bellovian held her gun to my back and covered my mouth as we watched the Florians load her partners into the transport truck. It was amazing to see the Bellovians looking dazed, not putting up a fight. A boy paced, pulling at a braid in his hair. A girl with blond hair pulled back tight in a bun stood watching them closely, her hands clasped together.

The soldier with the gun on my back pushed me through the forest when backup arrived for the Bellovians and stalled the Florian's progress. She found a cycle, told me to get on, and we drove. We quickly reached a base camp, where a commander came out of a large black tent. There were transports and cycles parked hastily around it.

"The queen?" he asked. The soldier nodded. He re-entered the tent and came back with a syringe. Terror filled me. My grandfather explained the bond of the resa. I tried to reach for it. I searched my mind for any sign of a presence that could help.

"And your team?" He put the needle to my arm.

"I saw them get taken by the Florians," she said.

He slid the needle in. My head swam watching it.

"They know too much then. They'll be taken care of." The woman nodded and the world went dark. I searched and

searched for some kind of bond. A flicker. A warmth. I yanked on it, bringing the heat forward. I funneled my desperation for help into it. Darkness crowded in and I prayed they felt my call.

I woke with a start when I felt Natasha tugging at the bond in her dream. She moved restlessly across from me, still asleep. I put a hand on her forehead and tried to send reassurance back. Her breathing steadied and her body stilled.

I sighed. How often had those events plagued Natasha's dreams? Should I tell her that I had unknowingly killed her captors? Could anything truly bring someone peace after going through that?

It was suddenly clearer than ever what being *resa* meant. Everything I had done led to Natasha. The gods or some fate intertwined us. This determined friendship went so deep I could see her dreams. I swallowed and tried to relax back into the pillows, wondering if I was ready for this responsibility. If I was the right person for her to trust so completely. To lead the fighting for her. Being born at a specific moment didn't equate to competence. How could I help reclaim a country? I was glad Natasha slept on and couldn't feel my doubt. Laying there in the dark, it pressed down on me, making breathing difficult.

Sleep was far away. I needed to move. To relieve some of the tension tightening my shoulders. Carefully, I climbed out of bed and slipped out of the room. As I grew into my Trish abilities, I gained the same quiet grace I had always admired in my mother. Natasha didn't stir.

I went down the hall, glancing back at Hinze's closed doors. It was too late to try knocking. At the top of the stairs to the royal chambers, I could see firelight flickering from the direction of the shared space on the landing below. I went that way. Even though Hinze had his own office loft, I thought he would be in the sitting area. He always seemed to have trouble sleeping. I hurried my pace, looking forward to a talk with him. Hinze had a perspective so different from my own. Maybe he could help still my doubts. Turn them into something manageable.

To my surprise, it was Oken seated in front of the fire pit in the center of the room. The flames made the gold in his eyes melt and dance as he stared into their warmth. He pulled absently on a curl of his hair and let it bounce back into place. My breath caught and I cleared my throat to push past it.

Oken's pensive expression eased into his usual smile when he saw me.

"Can't sleep?" he asked. It was too late to retreat. I took the chair next to him. The blue, plush cushion was worn and accepted my body readily. I pulled my feet up and curled into a comfortable ball. The heat from the fire felt wonderful.

"Bad dream."

Oken nodded knowingly. I wondered what he had seen of the war since I had left them all. Jenna was jumpier and Rennie was nearly desperate to find something to joke about in every situation.

I remembered the hard look in Oken's eyes at the Conquering Ceremony and again back by the river. The memories pained me. Even with the hardships most Bellovians faced, he'd remained unfazed and smiling when we left for war. He'd always been a light. Throughout school and training, I had gotten in the habit of looking to him when I wanted to feel happier. But this war was getting to him. I hated it more than ever at that moment. There were so many I wished I could spare, but Oken especially deserved the same happiness he spread to those around him. I wanted to lock him away and keep him safe forever. At least I'd gotten him away from the Front.

Though the palace in Helsa may be even more dangerous for a Bellovian.

We were only just entering this war. I prayed the horrors we were sure to experience wouldn't leave Oken too altered. Wouldn't steal his smiles and contagious laughter forever.

"The silver is growing in," he noted. I lifted a hand to my bare head. I had gotten used to hiding my roots under my hat. "It suits you."

I felt my face heat and blamed the fire. Oken continued looking at me intently. I pointed at him. "You're staring."

Oken laughed, not embarrassed in the slightest to be called out. "You just seem so different now. I don't know if it's the hair, the scar, or this new purpose you have being a... what was it? A *resa*?"

I nodded but paused. "What scar?"

He leaned forward. I went still as his fingers brushed my cheek so lightly that I could have imagined their presence. When he took his hand back, I lifted my own fingers to the place he touched and felt the raised line on my cheek. His wide eyes told me he even surprised himself with the touch.

"Oh, yeah. A man shot at me through a window in Trent. A shard got me."

Oken's eyebrows lifted. "A *shard* got you?" We laughed at how that sounded. "And why was this man shooting at you?"

I explained my need for a coat and how I'd left behind his cycle. A few more questions from Oken and the whole story spilled out of me. Everything that happened since I'd looked down at Dani's dead body and the decision I made in that moment. How I couldn't fight in an army that valued its people so little. How I had to find the queen of Traesha. Oken listened intently, leaning forward, laughing in places I hadn't considered funny until just then, like Chelsa's guards thinking I couldn't fight. Telling Oken about the strangeness of the people I'd met and situations I'd come across, they suddenly seemed ridiculous. Not only that, but it was easy to talk about. The words fell out so effortlessly that it was almost like speaking Trish with my family.

I told him about talking to Nico. Finding out about the rebellion. My family's lies. How I went home and found the bloodstain on the floor. Bellovians weren't affectionate. They didn't reach out or make gestures of support. But the kindness and shared sadness on Oken's face told me enough. I ached for the home I lost, but telling Oken about it brought me more comfort than I would ever have imagined.

Maybe I wished he'd ignore his upbringing and reach for me, to touch me again, but those thoughts weren't helpful.

I pushed on and told him about rescuing Natasha, stealing the transport, and being pursued by the flighter. His eyebrows drew together. "I knew they were making something new in another section of the lot. They kept it mostly secret, but I knew someone working on the project. She said they were struggling with the mechanics on something big. Looks like they figured it out."

He asked me more about the build and sat back, staring into the fire. "I don't like it."

"Me neither." It was a relief to find someone who shared my concern. "I don't understand how they're funding all this technology."

"No?" Oken tilted his head. "I always thought it came from Detono."

My mouth dropped open. I thought I had been unique among my classmates for knowing of Detono's existence through my parent's knowledge of the outside world. Even then, I knew little about the Detonians save that they were a small, ungifted island and their relationship with the Florians was tenuous.

"How do you know that?"

Oken shrugged. "All our manuals had to be translated from Detonian. They told us not to talk about it. I even learned a little of the language. Most of our technology comes from their engineers; it didn't seem like a big leap to think the more delicate instruments and funding came from them too. Our mines provide most of the metals."

I stared into the flames with a frown. My father had to have known this. Why hide so much from me?

"I never figured out how our countries knew about each other. I don't even know where Detono is," Oken continued.

"It must be an old relationship. Back before the rebellion."

"What do the rebels have to do with it?"

"Not our current rebels. The rebellion that created Bellovi and started the war."

At Oken's blank look, I explained how a gifted family once ruled Bellovi and how they had fought Florian control. Their strength had given them the edge they needed to break away and create the Front but got them no further. Bellovian propaganda erased this aspect of Bellovi's history. Most people now thought the Florians were trying to invade and they fought along the Front to save their families from the king's tyranny.

"That makes a lot of sense," Oken whispered. We went

quiet for a long moment, both of us processing our new information.

Oken sighed. "I have to say; I'm not sure where my place is in all this. I'm more than a little worried about the Florians' reactions to us. Especially as we get closer to Helsa and the palace. The king hates us." The way he said "the king" made it clear the feeling was still mutual.

I rubbed my arm where the hand-shaped scar was hidden under my sweater. Oken was right to fear the Florians. If everything with the flighters and a Bellovian alliance with Detono came to a head, Oken was in a difficult and dangerous position here on this side of the Front. I wouldn't want to be in Floria with black Bellovian hair when the impoverished country finally became a genuine threat to the Florian king. But at least we had Levi with us. Would his ability be enough to protect my friends?

"I'm worried too." My voice came out hushed. The fire crackled. "I think it's important that they get to know us. If there will ever be peace between our people, there has to be understanding. But it's a risk. I didn't understand how worried I was until Levi showed his power. I was so relieved to have an edge against them."

Oken tilted his head. "Are you still an 'us'?"

I hadn't even realized I had used the term. That I still counted myself among the Bellovians. I squeezed my eyes shut, pinched the bridge of my nose, and blew out a breath.

"I don't even know where I stand anymore. For now, I need to help Natasha. She comes first, but I'll do what I can to keep you safe too."

Oken gave me a crooked smile. It was too sad for my liking.

"Oken?"

"Yeah?"

"Why did you give me your knife? And the cycle? And follow me across the Front? If you were that worried, you could have gone to find Mayze without this trip to Floria."

Oken looked at me for a long time, his hands curling into fists on his lap. His smile was still in place, but he almost looked nervous. My stomach fluttered.

Finally, he let his hands relax and settled back into the cushions. "I'll let you puzzle that one out, princess."

I blinked, but he turned his attention back to the fire. That was all the answer I would get. For some reason, it made me smile. I turned to the fire, too, pressing my lips to my shoulder to hide my grin.

We sat looking into the flames in the easy silence we'd always been capable of. When I glanced back at him, Oken had fallen asleep, his curls spilling into his face, his head slumped forward and to the side. I stared at him greedily with no one around to catch me. Even the view of his long legs stretched out in front of him and how he'd rolled his sleeves up to his forearms made my insides melt. He began to snore lightly. The sound nearly lulled me to sleep myself.

Nearly. I was too worried about the feelings for Oken stirring deeper in my chest. Deeper than they ever had before. He'd come here for me. I'd have to be an idiot not to understand that. He'd helped me even though it risked everything. I knew better than anyone the cost of that risk. I was so grateful. So happy. It was an unfamiliar drum in my chest.

But I needed to focus on the queen. I needed to focus on the war. *Always focus.* I couldn't let this friendship go any deeper, even if I could sit here and stare at him for hours. *Especially* since I could sit here and stare at him for hours. I forced myself to leave the comfort of the couch, the fire, and the sound of Oken. I returned to Chelsa's room and my cold half of the bed.

For the first time, I had cause to pray to Tash, god of love. I begged them to leave me alone.

WHEN THE SUN spilled through the crack in our window curtains, I got up. I'd barely slept after returning to our room. I had to fight the urge to return to the fire and Oken's calming snores for hours. Brushing all thoughts of him aside, I wandered into Chelsa's large closet and ran my fingers over the dresses and outfits she had left there. I found myself before her mirror, examining the scar Oken had touched so gently. It did give my face a different look. Before, I was always mistaken for being younger than I was. The scar made me look older and the silver roots in my hair contrasted sharply with the black, lending a fierceness to my complexion. I liked the changes. I was finally coming to look like the girl I saw myself as: a Trish who understood the Bellovians and how war worked. Not the scared Trish girl pretending to be Bellovian that I used to see.

New clothing closer to Natasha and my sizes was brought up. I saw Hinze's attention to detail in the leggings and shirts delivered for me. Exactly what I preferred to wear. When Natasha woke, she claimed a short blue dress and a pair of tights to wear under it. She pulled her hair back into a large bun that still looked elegant.

We went to breakfast, reaching the bottom of the stairs as Hinze rounded the corner.

He looked better. Rested with his hair neatly braided once more. He greeted us with a bright smile. "Good morn—"

"Hush!" I put a finger to my lips and cut him off.

Natasha's eyes narrowed; her head cocked to listen. Sam, Savha, and Fisher entered the hall, their eyes wide. Only we could hear the distant noises approaching the quiet town of Honna.

Screams. Gunshots. Whoops.

"What is it?" Hinze asked.

"Stay with Natasha." I pushed her into him. He took her hand immediately and I ran, pounding on the doors to wake everyone.

"We need to get to town *now!*" I turned and skipped back to the room Natasha and I were sharing and pulled on my boots, my movements lightning fast. Grabbing my gun, I returned to the entrance hall. The Bellovians ran down the stairs with their guns drawn and faces grim. Jenna chewed her lip. Oken watched me close for the next order.

The Florians were quick to follow, the hall warming with Brea's entrance. They fell into place behind Fisher, Savha, and Sam.

"Hinze?" I turned to him before leaving.

I could feel how badly Natasha didn't want me to go but had to ignore it. Her halfhearted tugs on the bond were nothing compared to my need to eliminate the threat before she fell to harm.

"I'll keep her safe," Hinze promised, lifting their interlocked fingers. "Go!"

We ran for town. The gates to the manor were barely open when I reached them, Savha and Fisher at my side, but I lost them quickly as I hit the open road and picked up speed. Skipping, I got to Honna first, Sam just behind me. I experienced a brief flutter of satisfaction when I outran even him.

Bellovian soldiers running on foot and riding sleek

cycles were streaming out of the tree line toward the small town of Honna. Smoke trailing from the trees revealed what had happened to the homes in the forest between the Front and the small town.

The black-clad soldiers whooped and fired their guns into the sky. Their riot of noise sent Honna's citizens running into the nearest buildings in terror. A few prepared to fight, but as Hinze said, many had abilities that barely compared to the strength of the elites. I skipped down the main street, weaving around Florians and pausing to help them up when they were nearly trampled by fellow towns-people trying to run. I scooped up a screaming child and pinpointed her frantic father's shouting in seconds. I thrust her into his arms, ignored his thanks, and kept going. The town was crumbling before the Bellovians had even reached it.

For the first time, I truly understood what it meant to grow up in a militarized country like Bellovi. This chaos wouldn't happen there. The people would all know to iden-tify the threat and how to react. They would run toward the fight, armed with whatever they could find, or they would know how to get out of the way. I remember my fifth year of school when they told us we were now old enough to be part of the former group and the classes that followed. I cursed the king for not bothering to prepare his people. This close to the Front, they should understand at least the basics.

I finally worked my way through the crowds and cleared the small buildings of the town square. The Bello-vians were halfway between the town and the tree line. I skipped to the nearest soldier. Grabbing the handlebars of his cycle, I turned it roughly and sent the man riding into the dirt. I skipped from cycle to cycle, knocking or throwing the Bellovian soldiers off one by one, hoping to slow them and give the town time to take cover or arm themselves.

The town guards joined the fight. My old buddy nearly scarred me again when his flames shot out and hit the Bellovian soldier I was running for. I dropped and slid under the fire, my momentum making a full stop impossible. I avoided any burns and rose with a glare. The guard's eyes widened in recognition before I turned away again, the scar on my bicep twinging.

There were too many Bellovians. At least three hundred had gathered to make this push against the Florians. I'd never seen an organized attack so large. Despite my efforts, they reached the edge of town. Even those I'd thrown off the cycles had gotten up, some wincing, but none hurt enough to stop. I couldn't keep holding back. I braced myself and willed my hands to be steady. I ran back and joined the line of guards attempting to help keep the Bellovians at bay. Gun in hand, I took aim.

I had slipped through the Front the day before and thought that meant I knew what it was. I was wrong. I remembered the relief of training. Watching those less skilled than I sent to fight this battle before learning how to. I thought I had avoided this fight for the near future. I had been wrong.

I had been sent to the Front after all.

CHAPTER 6

I kept expecting to see Silken's face among the attackers, but so far, he was absent. I saw no commander stripes at all. Only haggard faces of those stationed in the center of battle for far too long. Their empty gazes and nearly mechanical movements were chilling. These soldiers were past feeling. All they wanted was for this next battle to end, one way or another.

I fired a round. Reloading, I looked up to see Fisher and Savha joining the line, my Bellovians not far behind. Oken methodically knelt with his long gun to use the scope, always jumping back to his feet after only using a second to fire his bullet. Levi's red-barreled gun flashed in the morning sun. Rennie was at his side with her army-grade short gun, filling in his gaps and pauses. They worked well together. They shot with rapid precision and the Bellovians dropped from the approaching line. I saw Dani's dead eyes on some of their faces and had to harden myself, smothering something vital. Moving forward, I readied as the first of the Bellovians reached our line of defense, only to scream when he encountered a gifted Florian. I reloaded. Continued adding to the number of the dead. Each trigger pull another body dropped in the field before me and barely slowing the tide.

I caught sight of Sam. He was skipping between the Bellovians, taking the ammo they had strapped to their waist belts, easily dodging friendly fire as he went. Likely I was the only one with eyes that could follow his quick movements. I had to admit it was a good idea, but even when they ran out of bullets, the Bellovians were a force to be reckoned with.

A familiar beating of wind took my attention away from Sam. My stomach dropped. Coming over the tree line was another flighter. I couldn't summon any shock at the sight, but the Florians around me froze, losing critical moments from the battle.

It was larger than the flighter I had taken out in the Bellovi plains. Sunlight glinted against the windshield, blocking my view of whoever might be piloting. Yet something in me said it wouldn't be Silken.

A hatch opened at the bottom as the Florians recovered from their surprise and began shooting at the flighter. I swore as the line of Bellovians redoubled their advance unhindered. The Florian line broke, half only concerned with the technology they'd never seen before and the other half rushing to meet the Bellovians on foot.

A long rope dropped out of the flighter and three Bellovians began their descent, sliding down with gloves to take the burn. Their blood-red uniforms unfurled a curl of dread within me, breaking through even the rushing adrenaline. I had a wild idea and took a step to execute it, only to see Sam beat me to it. He skipped to the base of the ropes right as the gifted Bellovians joined the mob of black uniforms. With only a moment's hesitation, he grabbed the rope and began climbing. Seconds later, Sam dropped the pilot through the hatch and the flighter turned to the trees. I saw a silver streak as Sam bailed, landing on a tree branch, his lighter bones making it so the tree barely swayed. The flighter went crashing into the forest.

I shook myself from my distraction and lifted my gun to fire, only to find I had run out of ammo. I threw the weapon to the side to go hand to hand. A swift kick put one soldier down, but the other dodged my first throw. Too late, I realized I had held back. Throwing punches how my father had trained me to so I wouldn't draw attention to my speed. It cost me. The Bellovian landed a solid punch to my gut. His blow sent me flying backward. I went through a wooden market booth and hit the wall behind it, air whooshing from my lungs.

The man advanced as I gasped and struggled out of the wreckage. He stepped into the sunlight between buildings and I saw how the shadows had muted the red of his uniform.

"Audrey!" I croaked her name with as much force as I could summon. I stumbled to my feet. My ribs felt cracked. It took effort to ignore the pain and straighten fully.

Somehow, Audrey heard my summons. She burst from the chaos, already dusted as if she had been going through brick walls again. I nodded at the man stalking my way. She took in the red uniform. The challenge brought a smirk to her face and she was on him quickly. The sound of his grunts and thud of landed blows followed me as I swallowed my pain and ran to the town square. The worst of the fighting could be heard there.

My heart sank to see Oken dodging blows from a Florian man. He was trying to explain they were on the same side and carefully working only to defend. I came up from behind and knocked the Florian out by bringing my fist down on top of his head. Oken helped me drag him to safety, but when we turned around, a Florian guard raised her arms in our direction. She was lifting a huge fruit cart with her gift. She only saw our black hair. My braid and Oken's tall, muscular build. Not our lack of black uniforms or the hesitance in our eyes. The panic of battle didn't allow such observations. She pushed forward and the cart flew at us. I moved with Trish speed and pulled Oken out of the way. The cart smashed where we had just been standing. I couldn't catch my breath through the pain of moving so quickly. Gritting my teeth, I turned with Oken. We readied to defend ourselves, but Levi was there now. He took away her abilities with a wrinkled brow. Londe ran between us, his eyes unfocused as he explained our alliance to the guard without having to shout. He looked back with a concerned frown as Oken and I ran back into the fray, Oken's long gun abandoned in the dirt behind us. The fight had grown too close for a scope to be of any use.

The sharp gunpowder scent of discharged bullets stung my nose. Smoke from a fire to my right had me fighting a cough that would be too painful for the relief it would bring to my throat. The crack and thud of bodies colliding underlined the earsplitting explosions of shots fired. Someone was thrown into the fountain at the center of the square, the spray hitting us. Hinze was there, Natasha clinging to his arm while he shot off rounds into the fight. Bullets peppered the building behind them, but they remained safely cloaked with Hinze's gift.

Natasha met my gaze. I felt her reading the bond and the pinch in my features. She frowned with concentration. A sharp, quick pain as my ribs realigned and suddenly, I could breathe again. I mouthed my thanks, concerned how the healing at this distance made her sway.

I tried to get closer to her, but another Florian moved to attack Rennie just paces away. Behind me, Oken exchanged rapid blows with a Bellovian woman. His lip was split and bleeding. In a fluid motion, he got his arms around her neck and dropped to his knees, pulling her down and ending up securely on top of her with a move that looked very familiar to one I had shown him at the training base. I quickly brought down Rennie's attacker and took on a few more Bellovians. I found a short gun in a dead Bellovian's hand, jumped onto the ledge of the fountain in the middle of the square, and began picking off those who stepped into my sight with a clear shot.

Savha, Mesa, and Londe moved in closer to Hinze. The prince didn't need defending but was clearing an area for them to fight and push back the line. Sam appeared in front of Natasha. I felt only flickers of her emotions through the bond. They were drowned by the adrenaline pounding while I brought down our enemies, either with hand to hand, my gun, or the occasional knife I found in a body I was sure Mesa had thrown.

I looked up and saw Brea across from me, hands raised, glaring at the man shivering at her feet with blue lips. As his fingertips blackened and stilled, I ripped my gaze away with a shiver of my own at the unpleasant memory the sight evoked. How had I survived hours of her using her gift to get answers from me?

Someone cried out a warning on the other side of the

square. I glanced that way as Jenna turned from taking out a Bellovian soldier with a kick to the woman's temple. She spun just in time to see the Florian across from her take aim. I started forward, already seeing the hesitation on Jenna's face and the blind hatred on the Florian's. He pulled the trigger. Her eyes widened.

Fisher was suddenly between Jenna and the gun, using his Trish speed for the first time.

The madness in the square calmed for the briefest of moments. Savha let out a scream unlike anything I had ever heard. Horror clenched my throat as Natasha broke away from Hinze and skipped to Fisher's side, easing his fall when he stumbled, face bewildered. I tried to run to them, but a Bellovian woman stepped into my path, her red uniform blocking the sun. She swiped at me with her knife and in my shock, I barely registered her swing enough to jump back in time. I heard my shirt tear. I lunged and swung my body up, forcing her down quickly with a knee hooked behind her head. She hit the pavement headfirst, my bodyweight and Trish speed behind the blow. I knew she wasn't going to get back up. Bellovian gifted strength didn't protect skulls.

Panic blurred my vision. I untangled myself from the dead Bellovian and jumped to my feet, running toward Natasha, using just our bond to guide me. I growled in frustration when another Bellovian threw himself at me. From over the man's shoulder, I saw Oken standing protectively before Savha and Natasha. They bent over Fisher's still form, unaware of Oken covering them as he shot any Bellovians who drew too near. Natasha was praying. Her hands pressed to the bloody wound in Fisher's chest. I felt hope rise, thinking maybe she could heal him like Levi. But it fizzled out quickly. I could see the color had already drained from Fisher's face. His eyes stared sightlessly in my direction. I went cold.

Why did the dead always watch me?

Sam and Hinze made it to Natasha's side. Hinze put a hand on her shoulder, ignoring her screams for him to let her go so she could touch Fisher. Tears already streaked the prince's cheek.

I threw punches, barely processing who they landed on. Natasha now safely in Hinze's grasp, I let my panic fade into the anger flashing white in my vision. The rage brought a strange, cool calm with it. My punches and kicks landed with instinctual accuracy. All hesitation gone, my father's training to hold back forgotten, I slipped through the crowd, taking down attacker after attacker with brutal punches and kicks at Trish speed. I ran by Londe and Rennie, binding the soldiers Lilah held paralyzed with her arms shaking where she kept them aloft.

There were Bellovian soldiers on the rooftops shooting down into the square. I saw Audrey stagger back, blood exploding from her upper arm. I wouldn't let any more friends die today. I skipped to the nearest awning, pulled myself up, and jumped to grab a window ledge. I climbed onto the roof. I ran swift and light over the tiles. Soldier to soldier, lifting the Bellovians and throwing them from their posts. All I could hear over the pounding in my ears were Savha's sobs, Natasha crying *no no no* in Trish, and the thud of the bodies I flung into the square.

By the time there were no more Bellovians to fight and we had won, I still wasn't ready to let go of my rage. I knew what sorrow waited on the other side. I looked to the forest, hoping for more of a challenge, but any Bellovians left were retreating. The sky was clear, a growing fire the only evidence of the flighter's brief role in the battle. I clenched my jaw and watched the Bellovians disappear. It would do no good to give chase.

The fight was over. We had won and paid the price.

By the time I made myself approach Fisher's body, Natasha was pulling me there, yanking me closer with the bond. Needing me. When I was steps away, she ran at me. I held her as she sobbed and fought my own tears when her staggering grief, too overpowering to let in anger of her own, melted my rage.

I hugged her until I could stand it no more. I backed out of her arms, took her hand, and walked to Fisher's body. I knelt by his head and with my free hand, I closed his beautiful Trish eyes. Gray like a silver lining. My stomach twisted painfully.

"Until I see you next," I whispered. Savha leaned into me and I put an arm around her shaking body while gripping Natasha's hand.

As I sat and the adrenaline faded, I realized my shirt was wet. I rose to my feet and looked down. Confusion clouded my thoughts. My black shirt was ripped across my stomach, just below my ribs. I remembered the Bellovian woman with a knife. Her head cracking under my weight.

"Finley, you're hurt!" Oken's voice sounded far away.

The world tilted and went dark.

I woke slowly, the muffled voices around me gradually becoming distinct. I felt Natasha close by in a troubled sleep. She was unharmed. I relaxed just slightly.

"She's going to be okay, though?" a voice asked.

"I believe so. The queen healed a lot of it, but she was tired after trying to help..." Hinze trailed off. His voice was rough, thick with fallen tears. My throat tightened as the memories hit.

Bullets. Blood. Blows that cracked through bones. Uniforms red and black. The fight and confusion on both sides. The pain of injuries, of killing, of Fisher's sacrifice. My first battle as *resa* and a Trish boy was dead. I'd already failed our people and Natasha.

I sat up and gasped at the pain in my stomach. The blanket I was under slipped, showing my black band of a bra and bare stomach. An ugly, raised scar went almost my entire width above my belly button. The skin had been closed hastily; the damage underneath was still present. I wrapped an arm around it and told myself I was fine. It wasn't the physical pain that made my breath hitch anyway.

Hinze moved to sit next to me on the couch. He was trembling. Although nothing was out of place on his being to show we had just gone through a battle, his eyes had the hollowed look from witnessing too much death.

"Fisher..."

Hinze dropped his eyes and drew a shuddering breath. The last of my hope turned to ash. Londe lowered his tall form to kneel in front of us.

"He didn't make it." His voice cracked, but his gaze held steady. He squeezed my hand and the warmth from the gesture steadied me. Londe reached for Hinze's hand too, but his fingers went right through him. Hinze didn't seem to notice the attempted contact. Londe pulled his hand back.

"Damn," I whispered the word. It wasn't nearly enough to convey the loss I felt. "And Savha?"

"She hasn't left their... her room," Londe said. "The queen and Sam are with her."

Hinze reached over and pulled a soft sweater off the side table. I put it on. It was huge on me and smelled like the prince, but the extra fabric made it more comforting. I hugged it around myself, the pressure across my middle helping slightly with the pain. Londe eyed my arms with concern and looked ready to stop me when I made to stand. But he sat back without a word. They both watched me in silence as I left the room to join the Trish.

Jenna sat against the wall in the hallway outside Savha's room, her eyes red and swollen.

"He died saving me," she whispered, her gaze fixed on the opposite wall. She clenched and unclenched her fists. She was still in her Bellovian uniform, torn and bloody. I crouched in front of her and winced from the soreness in my stomach. I grabbed Jenna's hands. It took her a minute to grab hold of my fingers, but I stayed crouched and waited. I waited until she drew in a full breath.

"Fisher knew what he was doing," I told her. "Respect his choice and honor it. He wouldn't want you to drown in guilt when he gave you another chance at a happy life."

Jenna's eyes slid shut. I waited a bit longer before I sat back on my heels and released her hands. "Go get some rest," I said, glad she didn't notice how tight the pain made my voice. She nodded but made no move to leave.

I heard footsteps and knew they were Oken's before I even turned to look at him.

"I'll sit with her," he said. He'd changed clothes and bathed. It had been a long time since I'd seen him in something other than black. The blue shirt made him look pale. Or maybe he was just pale from the fight. My eyes lingered on the bruise I'd left on his cheek. There were more injuries marking his face now. The urge to lock him safely away hit me again.

His eyes took me in, searching for traces of the wound that had brought me down. Before he could see how much pain I was still in and worry, I nodded and turned to Savha's door. I put my hand on the doorknob but couldn't bring myself to turn it.

Oken came to a stop next to me. I grabbed his hand, needing to know he was still here and warm and solid. After a brief hesitation, he squeezed my fingers gently. He waited for me like I did Jenna. I breathed him in, so unbearably grateful he was alive and mostly unharmed.

How could I face Savha after this small brush with the happiness Oken brought? I didn't deserve this while she was hurting. When I had failed to protect our people. I should let him go.

Oken tightened his grip on my hand and centered me. The comfort wasn't fair, but I needed it. I let myself cling to him for another three breaths. I felt better when I let go. I felt stronger. The doorknob turned easily under my palm, and I stepped into the dark room. I glanced back to see Oken settle on the floor next to Jenna.

Natasha was curled at the end of the bed, her body shifting restlessly from whatever nightmare plagued her. She looked exhausted, even in sleep. I walked up and put my hand on her forehead. It took effort to send her reassurance through the bond, but I managed. She stilled, a sigh escaping her lips.

Savha sat against the pillows. Her cheeks were wet with tears. There was accusation in her gaze, the green vivid from crying. Sam leaned against the dresser to the right, his arms crossed over his chest. I walked around the bed and sat next to Savha. I couldn't tell if she wanted me near, but I grabbed her hand and pulled it into my lap. The heat from Oken's grip lingered and slowly warmed Savha's icy fingers.

I couldn't find words. Another failure.

Savha spoke first. "He really liked you, Finley. He would have done anything for you. Natasha was right there, so he probably should have felt that way for her, but the fact that you found her only made you more amazing in his eyes. He believed you'd get Traesha back for us. And now he's dead."

I swallowed. "I'm so, so sorry. I didn't know... I don't know what I'm doing. I don't know how to..." Her words settled in my stomach like a stone. I would always carry Fisher's death.

How many more would die because I brought them into this war?

Sam snorted, but it was easy to ignore his scoffing. All that mattered was that Savha gave me a wobbling smile. "You always seem like you have it under control."

"Savha, I'm sorry. I'm not—"

Her hand tightened, cutting me off. "You brought the queen back from Bellovi. Maybe that's why they attacked, or it could have been something they'd already been planning. I can't forgive what happened, but I don't think that means I blame you. Just this gods damned war. He was too young. Too sweet and beautiful. No one should have taken him from me." She turned and began to sob into my shoulder. I did my best to hold her together.

I made eye contact with Sam over her head but couldn't read his expression. In time Savha wore herself out and joined Natasha in sleep, sagging against my aching stomach. I held my breath against the pain as I gently shifted her so I could get out of the bed.

"Where are you going?" Sam asked, voice low.

"To talk to Hinze. I need to know if we questioned the

imprisoned Bellovians and how this changes our plans. We still need to get to Helsa. Take Fisher to his parents and get Natasha an audience with the king so she stops feeling useless. We need to move forward."

Sam pushed himself off the dresser. "His best friend just died."

"I know," I whispered. "I can't just stay in here." The guilt of this room would eat me. I couldn't sit still, surrounded by evidence of Fisher. Savha wore one of his sweaters. His clothes hung lifeless in the closet. His smell clung to the pillows. Flowers he'd picked for Savha gave color to the dim room. It wouldn't take long for them to wilt.

I looked away from them, blinking hard.

"I can talk to him," Sam said. "You stay here. Natasha needs you close."

I shook my head. "She has Savha and she's so tired she'll just sleep."

Sam frowned and followed me out of the room. Rennie had joined Jenna and Oken in the hall. She was holding a cloth to her scraped knee. Oken's upper lip had split again and he kept dabbing at it with his sleeve. He winced when he shifted to look at me.

"You all look like shit," I said, the words coming out rough and Bellovian and oddly comforting.

Rennie snorted. "We're fine. You and Audrey took the worst of it." She eyed my stomach and I tried to stand straight. It was getting harder. I remembered Audrey getting shot and glanced anxiously down the hall.

"She's fine," Oken was quick to assure me. "Mesa was stitching her up. The bullet didn't hit anything important."

"How's... the girl?" Jenna asked, nodding to the closed door. She hadn't even learned Savha's name yet.

"Savha is... she's sleeping." They nodded, knowing fully what I meant. Grief was nothing new to a Bellovian. "So should all you. You look exhausted." Even as I said the words, I knew they wouldn't be moving any time soon. I had less guilt walking away from Natasha because of it. No one would be getting past a Bellovian guard like that.

CHAPTER 7

I decided to check Hinze's room first, Sam on my heels. I wasn't sure what to make of his following me and chose to ignore him as I went down the hall of bedrooms. I paused at the stairs leading to the landing of royal bedrooms. It was a short flight, and for that, I was grateful.

I looked down the hall toward the room I had used during my first visit. The servant's room. It had been simple and neat and, at the time, the nicest accommodations I'd ever stayed in. I was kept separate from the Trish and Florians, still so fresh from my life in Bellovi.

I longed for the simplicity of my life then. All the secrets revealed in Traesha still made my head spin. I missed the days when my biggest problem was not knowing who I was. What country I claimed and what I'd be willing to do to end the war. The days when there was still hope for my family's safety and my humanity.

Moving forward, away from that girl, was getting harder. The future loomed with its impossibility. I was still half Bellovian, still so confused, still hurting to distraction from every loss. How would I find the strength to be *resa*? To get Natasha her throne?

Sam cleared his throat behind me and I was startled from my thoughts. I turned back to the stairs. It hurt to walk. It hurt a lot. The pain was getting worse the more I moved and I hated to show this weakness. I started up the steps, breaths turning shallow. The blood drained from my face.

I'd never realized stairs took so much more effort than a flat floor. I looked up and nearly groaned to see I was only halfway. The pain in my stomach burned hot. I took another dragging step.

"Finley?"

The concern in Sam's voice did it. I sucked in a sharp breath and tried to skip to the top of the stairs. Get it over with.

Well, I tried. My feet didn't cooperate and I tripped upward. I attempted to twist and catch myself, but Sam was there first. He grabbed my arm and righted me with surprising gentleness.

"I could have told you not to do that. I thought you were healed."

I couldn't catch my breath to answer. The world was spinning. It took everything in me to stay upright, even with Sam's support. All I wanted was to sag against the wall. But I had to press on.

"I. Am. Fine," I forced the words out from behind my gritted teeth. But I didn't shake Sam's hand off as I went for the next step and the next. It took ages, but we made it to the top.

The sweat gathered on my forehead was worrisome, but I had bigger problems. My thoughts were consumed by the memory of Hinze's lofted office and the narrow stairs leading up to it.

"You should go back and rest. Just being near Natasha will aid the healing pro—"

Whatever look was on my face, I was proud. It took a lot to quiet the older *magsai*. He pressed his lips together and I straightened and continued to Hinze's room.

Inside, the lights in his loft were on and I could hear the Florian soft accents drifting down. I called on years of hiding my expressions as I climbed his steps as quickly as I could manage. Sam followed close, hand at my elbow.

Through a fog of pain, I reached the top. My moment of victory was considerably dulled by the red-rimmed eyes around the table. The slumped postures and sniffing. My skin crawled. They'd known Fisher so much longer. I was invading their grief with my need to plan and keep pressing onward. But Londe gave me a small smile and pulled out the chair next to him for me. Brea and Lilah sat across from us at the table. Mesa was in one of the cushioned chairs toward the back of the loft. She sharpened a knife studiously. The rhythmic slice of the stone and blade was the loudest sound in the room. Once I was seated, Londe's eyes unfocused again. Hinze stood over the map, similarly absent. Were they contacting the king? Fisher's parents?

Lilah and Brea had never been so quiet. Lilah sported a dark bruise along her jaw and her high bun sagged to the side of her head. Brea poured Sam and me generous glasses of wine and pushed them across the table.

"Only thing that helps," she said with a shrug. Her act of kindness left me speechless. The liquid was still cool from her grasp.

"What do we know?" I asked softly. I didn't want to

interrupt Londe and Hinze's conversation, even if they weren't speaking out loud.

"The king is sending elites to Honna to protect them for now," Mesa said. She pulled the knife over the stone a little more aggressively.

"We think they were retaliating for the queen's rescue. They would have known if she went straight to Traesha," Lilah put in.

"They're taking the captured Bellovians to the same compound where we kept you," Brea said. "It's secure again. If those soldiers know anything, the elites there will get answers."

I repressed a shiver. "How would the commanders even know we weren't still trying to get out of Bellovi? We made such good time. And why would they think we'd go straight here? We passed at least one other town on the way," I said. The speed at which I had gotten in and out of the Bellovi still surprised me. There was a chance they made the connection between the train, Oken's team going missing, and the brief confused skirmish on the Front, but it seemed a long shot for them to guess that was all us *and* that we had gone to Honna after.

Yet, the more I thought about it, the less convinced I was that it was a stretch. That sensation of being followed crept up my spine. If anyone made all these connections, it would be Silken.

He would never give up until he had Natasha and had removed me as a threat.

"Are you sure you can trust the Bellovians you brought with you?" Sam asked. I gave him such a cool look that he raised his hands quickly in surrender. "I'm just saying it could be possible that one of them is reporting back. Can't be too careful."

Lilah leaned forward in her seat. "The Bellovians Finley brought were fighting harder than anyone during the attack, even when it was coming at them from both sides."

My mouth nearly dropped open. Sam looked equally shocked. Lilah shrugged. "I might not have been very fair to you, Finley. You were taking all this so seriously. I thought it was because you were Bellovian and loved war. But you knew what happened today could happen. You were worried about that kind of a battle. Even after Traesha, I never took them seriously. Knowing how much damage *we* could do made me too confident. I never imagined... I've never seen..." she trailed off and shivered.

Brea raised the room's temperature and put a hand on Lilah's arm. "There were so many bodies," she whispered.

"And using my abilities so much, it was exhausting. No one looked at me long enough. It was like I could barely help." Lilah looked down and Brea nodded in agreement.

"We should be training. Like your Bellovians. Like we should have when we were here last. Would you teach us?" Brea asked.

I blinked. "Of course. Anytime you want," I said, amazed at the turn in the conversation. "The Bellovians you tied up, did we learn anything from them before they were taken to the compound?"

Brea shrugged. "I was tired, but I think I was persuasive enough that they weren't lying when they said they were just following orders."

I frowned. I wanted more information. I should have known better after the vague directions of my first mission. The elites at the compound probably wouldn't learn anything further, even if they questioned the Bellovians as harshly as Brea once interrogated me.

Hinze's eyes refocused on our table. Londe still looked

far away. "My father is expecting us in Helsa," he said in answer to our expectant looks.

"*All* of us?" I checked.

"Yes. He agreed to let the Bellovians into the palace."

"What did he say about the flighter?"

Hinze's brow furrowed. "We didn't mention it."

"Why not? This is huge. If they can cross the trees so easily—"

"We will just take them down like we did today," Hinze interrupted. Sam stiffened next to me. The Florians hadn't taken down any flighters. "They probably don't have many of these flighters or we would have seen more of them today or in the north. It's just a fancier transport."

"But—"

"I am sorry, Finley, but we have much bigger concerns at the moment."

I pursed my lips and nodded. It was hard to push him when his eyes were so empty. I wanted to hug him more than anything.

"When do we leave?" Sam asked.

"I want to check on the people here, ensure they are doing okay, and wait until they have protection. Maybe give Savha a couple of days to rest. But we'll go as soon as we can." Hinze didn't wait for our response. His mind was already elsewhere as he turned for the stairs. I fought the urge to tell him to stop. To take a moment with us for comfort.

But I didn't want Sam calling me a hypocrite. I understood too well why Hinze wanted to do anything but sit still.

We sat for a moment after he left, listening to the sound of Mesa's blade. Londe was eerily far away. I cleared my throat and touched his forearm. He held up a finger. Three swipes of the blade passed before his eyes focused on me.

"My brother?" I asked. After today, I found myself missing him more than usual.

Londe's eyes softened. "Nico's fine. He's on his way back to Vichi and no one suspects he helped you escape in Traesha."

"Thanks, Londe."

I stood to leave, using the table too much to push myself up. I braced myself, lifting my chin as I thought about going down the stairs. Could it be worse than up? Sam followed me again.

"Hey, Fin," I turned to Mesa. She neatly threw the knife she'd been sharpening at me. I caught it quickly by the handle, the movement making me gasp. No one noticed. "Don't lose this one. I saw you throw in town today. Is there anything you can't do?"

It felt strange on my face when I tried to smile at her. "I'm terrible at the piano."

I painstakingly took the stairs. I was trembling when I returned to our shared hall.

"Can you check on the arrangements for Fisher's body?" I asked Sam. "I... I don't know all the Trish customs, but I want to make sure they're doing everything right."

Sam watched me close before nodding. "I will. Go rest. We need you strong."

"I am strong."

He shook his head and turned to go down the stairs. With his back turned, I put a hand on the wall to steady myself and walked toward Savha and Fisher's room.

By now, all my Bellovians were sitting in the hall. Audrey was examining the neatly stitched skin on her upper arm, Jenna staring ahead at nothing, Rennie sleeping with her head in Oken's lap and feet in Levi's. I sat next to Audrey on the opposite side of the hallway, across from Oken. His eyebrow rose watching me move gingerly. I was too busy trying to even out my breathing to assure him I was fine.

Once I caught my breath, I said, "We're leaving soon. Once things calm a bit. To go to the capital. Are you all sure you still want to come?" I wouldn't blame any of them if they said no after today. Facing the Florians and their own people in battle couldn't have been easy. It was too good an indicator of what they could expect in the days to come.

Yet there were nods all around. I looked down at my hands, overcome. I was asking so much. There was so much more risk for them here. The panic of fighting the Florians and Bellovians simultaneously would linger for me even as my silver hair grew out. I was shaken from this battle. From all the fighting I had done. From all the losses. I couldn't help but think it would only get worse.

That Garris and Fisher and my parents were only the beginning.

I cleared my throat. There were glimmers of hope. I clung to them. "You gained the trust of a lot of the Florians here today. I've never heard Lilah say anything good about Bellovians, but she nearly bit Sam's head off for suggesting you led them here."

"Finley, we're just here for you and Natasha. It doesn't matter what they think," Levi said. With his ability, he *would* say that.

"I'll do my best to deserve it," I said.

We went quiet again, guarding the room of the Trish queen. Audrey eventually gave in to exhaustion, lying on the floor right where she was. Levi's head nodded sideways, and he began to snore in the uncomfortable position. Oken laughed at him and even Jenna smiled a bit at the bright sound. I relaxed in their presence, some pain leaving as we sat on the uncomfortable floor.

Sitting upright despite the pain in my core, after the stairs and battle and stress, I couldn't say if it was sleep or pain that blacked my vision. I slipped into unconsciousness.

Traesha's trees welcomed me, angrier than ever, but offering me an escape regardless. The pain eased under their whispers.

~

THE NEXT DAY, Natasha coaxed Savha upstairs. The bed in Chelsa's room was big enough for all three of us and Natasha was disconcerted watching Savha stare at the wilting flowers from Fisher. She had to get her away. Sam watched Natasha try to make us comfortable with dim amusement. As our queen gained energy, she noticed how much pain my stomach gave me. I caught her wrist when she reached for me.

"I'm fine. Way better than yesterday after sleeping. You need your strength. I can feel how tired you are, and we can't face the king of Florian with you dead on your feet."

"You could still be bleeding inside."

"I'll go see a Florian healer."

I didn't bother. Occasionally, I felt a slight easing in the pain and knew Natasha was trying to subtly heal me throughout the day. The smaller bursts of her gifts seemed easier on her or it might just be her presence healing me like Sam said it would. Either way, I was feeling well enough to ignore the sore stiffness in my stomach.

I bounced between the groups within the mansion. The

Florians spent most of the day in the gardens where Fisher felt nearby. The Bellovians sat in the sitting area by their rooms. Their poorly contained energy was palatable and at one point, Lanis knocked on my door to tell me to make them stop sparring next to the late queen's favorite vase. Their knees bounced with nerves, and I did my best to keep them calm as they dreaded going to the palace.

At Natasha's insistence, I spent most of the time with her and Savha. Halfway through the second day after the attack, Hinze knocked on Chelsa's door.

"I like what you've done to the place," he said, only a hint of his former teasing lighting his eyes.

Natasha looked surprised, not catching that he was kidding. Savha's hollow eyes roamed the room, taking in the piles of clothes and the stacked trays I had promised to bring down to the kitchen when we finished. After my brief encounter with Chelsa, I had a good enough sense of her personality to wager this was the messiest her room had ever been.

"How are you, Hinze?" I asked.

Hinze just shrugged. He turned to Savha. "Want to walk the garden with me, Savvy?"

She blinked, eyes already filling, but Hinze just waited. He looked on the verge of tears himself. Savha went to him, willingly getting out of bed for the first time since we moved up here. Hinze took her arm and they went down the hall. I heard his soft tones and Savha responding. They were the closest with Fisher and it made sense for Hinze to seek Savha out. I only hoped they found comfort in each other's grief.

Our room went quiet with their exit. Natasha sagged against the headboard. She'd been keeping up a near-constant stream of conversation to distract Savha, even asking about complex topics like life in Traesha just to bring up something besides Fisher. Now, she let herself relax. Sam shifted where he stood at watch by the door. He turned to me and my stomach twisted, knowing the questions he had and remembering my mother's warnings. She wouldn't mind me talking about our family now, would she? If my being *resa* had been the huge secret she wanted to stay hidden? But... what if it was something else? Something even bigger she didn't want me sharing and I would give it away without knowing? With death so heavy in the air, I was hyperaware of her memory. I wanted to preserve it.

"Who is your father, Finley?" Sam asked.

"Teo Larson."

Hearing the Bellovian name, Sam's expression flattened. "Not if Natasha is correct in saying you're full Trish."

Natasha bristled but kept her mouth shut. I saw and felt her curiosity. She wanted to know my background too.

I sighed. "Well, until the Conquering Ceremony, I didn't know I had a Trish dad. Excuse me if I don't claim him."

"Your mother never hinted? What about friends she might have mentioned? Old lovers or just day-to-day life in Traesha?"

"She didn't talk about that stuff. She only talked about her happier memories and the culture. She never mentioned anyone specific. She said it hurt too much to talk about."

"Who is she?" Sam asked, stepping closer as he pressed me.

My voice cracked. "Was. The commanders killed them." It was enough to make Sam back down. Natasha glared at him and I felt her gathering herself to start comforting me like she had been Savha. "I'm okay. I just don't want to talk about her right now."

Sam nodded reluctantly.

"What about your dad?" Natasha asked. "You should tell Sam about your training so he knows what he's working with. That is if you still want him to train you to be a *magsai*."

I nodded. For some reason, my father was easier to talk about. Maybe I was just scared of Sam knowing something I didn't about my mother and uncovering more secrets, or I was just so scared to break her rules. Whatever the reason, once I started talking about my father, I couldn't stop. At times it felt like I was defending him, trying to convince Sam the Bellovians were capable of loving our people. I talked about how he'd learned Trish and held my mother close. I told him about going out to the boulders, how he'd trained me, and the school system I grew up in.

By the time Hinze and Savha returned, Natasha had fallen asleep and Sam had a good idea of my background. Savha and Hinze were giving each other broken smiles. It was apparent they'd both been crying, but they seemed a bit better. Savha had a new set of flowers in her hands. My heart broke knowing Fisher would have loved that Hinze gave them to her. He'd worked so hard to make Savha feel beautiful, to make her smile and put color in her world.

I ducked my head so she wouldn't see my tears.

CHAPTER 8

The drive to Helsa took two long days. I found myself missing the speed of skipping and even the train through Bellovi as we traveled Floria's well-maintained dirt roads in long transports with rows of cushioned seats. There was a train here in Floria, but it didn't run for passengers, just freights between the eight estate lands and Helsa.

For two days, the Florians sat quiet and subdued. Two days of nervous chatter and restless fidgeting among the Bellovians. Two days of Natasha expelling what energy she could to heal us before I caught her exhausting herself. Two days of Savha crying and shaking her head at words of comfort, curling into herself and only letting Hinze or Natasha close. The grief hit her in waves, and at times, there was no talking to her. She constantly looked out the transport's back window at the hearse following us.

Two days of Hinze's eyes unfocused, tension and sorrow lining his mouth as he communicated through Londe with the king and the estates along the Front. Two days of the Florians offering quiet apologies to the Bellovians with small kindnesses and hesitant smiles. Lilah sat next to Oken whenever she could, the two sharing quiet conversations comparing Bellovi and the palace that I forced myself not to notice.

Natasha needed me near her. Annoyance flared within her every time I left her side. "Finley, how are you supposed to heal if you won't let me do it and you keep walking away? Everyone is doing fine; you don't need to take care of them all." But her voice was brittle, betraying her real fear. It had shaken her to see me collapse right after Fisher's heart ceased beating beneath her hands. While in Honna, she felt safe in Chelsa's room, but out in the open, she couldn't relax.

We were all shaken. Fragile and too young for this war. I hated it. I couldn't sleep when we made camp. Too often, someone woke up with a horrified gasp from a dream. There was the sniffing of tears under the privacy of darkness every night. None of us could find proper rest. Still, we pressed on. There was too much to do.

Natasha and my exhaustion mingled and expanded over the bond. We spent much of the trip to Helsa sleeping in the transports with sore necks. We often sat next to Savha in the back, but on the last leg, after a stop to eat and take a break in a small town outside Helsa, we came up short seeing Brea and Lilah back with her. Savha sat between them, listening to their easy prattle. She didn't seem at all upset by their seating arrangement. Natasha and I sat in the middle row instead.

The familiar steadiness that came with Oken's presence surrounded me. He sat in the seat beside me, rolling his eyes as he used the safety strap. The drivers wouldn't start the transports until the Bellovians buckled themselves. We started off again, following the vehicle that held the other half of our people. Sam, Levi, and Rennie sat in the row in front of us. Audrey had gone in the other transport, sliding inside next to Mesa. Levi and I had exchanged a look to see her leave us.

I had barely gotten a moment with Oken since the battle. Once Natasha fell asleep against the window, I turned to him and asked in a low voice, "What do you think about the flighters now that you've seen one?"

Oken considered. His attention lingered on my face, and I thought he would touch me again for a brief, thrilling moment. But instead, he blew out a breath and rubbed his hands through his hair. "I think they'll play a big factor in the war. The Bellovians have been held back by slow travel and the Florians at the Front. The flighters remove both those obstacles."

I nodded. "Hinze isn't worried about them, though. He thinks the Florian gifts will take the flighters out easily."

"If the flighter is in range of the gift, I suppose. But that depends on the Florian, doesn't it? And imagine a flighter fitted with guns. They've made us attach them to transport trucks before. To do it with a flighter..."

"Exactly." I frowned. We considered the advantage it would give the Bellovians for a beat in silence.

I couldn't stop a yawn. Natasha had fallen into a deeper sleep than usual and her relaxation was calling me.

"What will you do?" Oken asked.

"I'll talk to the king about it. I have to warn them it's worse than they're imagining. Have to make them see the flighters are a real threat."

"And if he agrees with the prince?"

I shrugged and winced, pressing my arm into my stomach. I couldn't show the pain when Natasha was awake, or she would try to heal me. She'd spent too much energy during the fight on my ribs and Fisher and even others before him that I was slowly learning about as the days passed. I hadn't known Mesa was knocked unconscious during the battle and Natasha revived her until yesterday. It had led to Londe admitting he'd been stabbed. I remembered Rennie popping to her feet after being shot while we crossed the Front and knew that although Natasha was strong and we were getting stronger, there were limits to our power.

"Get some sleep, Finley." Oken's brow furrowed, looking at my arm wrapped around my middle.

"But..." I let my argument trail off. I nearly said I was fighting sleep because we hadn't spoken. Because I missed him. Even though I caught myself, my cheeks warmed.

Oken reached and gently pulled my head toward his chest, angling his body so I fit comfortably. My heart thrilled at his initiated contact. I melted into him. "Go to sleep," he murmured in my hair.

"Wake me when we reach the city?"

"Of course."

Oken kept his word, calling my name with a gentle shake hours later. I tried to look around him out the window and had to brace myself on his thigh when my stomach protested. The capital city of Floria was hot and bustling. Heat waves shimmered off the sand-colored buildings and streets. Most people walked or rode horses. Lilah and Brea explained from behind us that many Florians chose to avoid using electricity. They saw it as a Detonian invention that couldn't be trusted. Without Bellovi's coal, it was too expensive for many people. They relied on the old ways and their abilities.

As we drove through the crowded streets, the buildings grew taller and more modern, though the tan stone of the structures remained a unifying factor. The Florian flag, blue fabric with a white circle in the center and eight lines shooting out like a star, flew next to many of the doorways. Yet a couple had the golden triangle of the Trish flag.

Oken's arm worked as he cranked down his window, making a contented noise when we were hit with hot, dry air carrying the sweet cinnamon scent from a bakery we passed and a swirl of dust. Smell didn't carry like that in the cold of Vichi. People shouted in Common Tongue, their accents softer than those in Bellovi. They laughed more than I ever heard growing up. No one fought. I spotted artists drawing caricatures on the street corners and performers plucking various string instruments. People of all different appearances sold fruit, blankets, clothing, and everything else imaginable. They looked well-fed and happy. It was striking. No matter how much time I spent in Floria, the difference between this place and my home country still caught me off guard.

The closer we got to the palace in the center of Helsa, hiding behind a wall, the more finery the people wore. Some even had furry animals on leashes that they proudly led down the streets. It took me a minute to realize these were dogs. They looked so different from the boney animals that haunted the streets of Vichi.

The shows on street corners changed in this wealthier area. Gifted Florians demonstrated their advanced abilities. Lilah explained that many came here hoping to impress the king and join the elites. A man juggled balls of fire, a woman whistled to brightly colored birds and they circled her, and one girl was blinking in and out of visibility. Someone hovered above the crowds, their guard uniform navy and pressed. I saw a boy playing in a fountain, making the water surround him in a whirlpool as he giggled and his mother stood off to the side chatting with a friend. When the conversation ended, she waved her hand and brought down her son's water. He pouted as he stepped out of the fountain. Right before we turned the corner, I noticed he was completely dry.

Oken's eyes were wide as he stared at the Florians outside, his expression mirroring how I felt. I could feel Natasha's nerves as we approached the palace walls. She gave a wobbling smile seeing how many people bowed when we passed, recognizing the royal transports. She clutched my hand. Every time we caught sight of a silver-haired Trish in the streets, she squeezed even tighter.

Hope rekindled in our chests.

HINZE'S TRANSPORT ahead of us paused briefly at the palace gates before the heavy metal bars opened and our procession was allowed through. The long drive to the palace entrance was lined with trimmed, spherical bushes. The palace was an imposing building made of a strange, light-yellow stone. It looked impenetrable. Lower to the ground and far more rectangular than the castle in Traesha, it was still likely three times the size. Two towers rose from either end of the blocky structure and the Florian flag snapped in the wind from their points. The many windows were framed in dark gray or black. Several balconies jutted out of upper-floor doorways. I caught sight of a Trish girl high to our left. She squinted at our procession, eyes widening when Natasha exited the transport. The girl jumped in excitement and ran back through the glass doors.

I fought a smile. The palace was massive and imposing, but that was all the welcome I needed.

Two guards in Florian uniforms stood on either side of

the dark gray doors that were double their height. They bowed to Hinze before pulling them open with stiff movements. The guards did little to disguise their disgust as the Bellovians walked by, myself included.

I nearly stopped short upon entering the drafty hall. The floor was carpeted red like frozen blood on snow. Muffled footsteps came from every direction, echoing and mingling with the commanding voices of the nobles milling about. The strange stone walls were carved with arches and points and symbols I didn't recognize. Looking down the stretching hallway, I had a sense of vertigo.

"It smells like my aunt's house," Oken murmured. He stood close at my back.

The air hung with the smoke from incense, the same scent many Bellovians burned when asking for strength. Oken and I exchanged a look. Homesickness dragged at his features. I reached to squeeze his hand. He was getting better about accepting my touches, fingers instantly tightening around mine.

It was as cool inside compared to the hot, dusty city air. Hinze stepped to the side to wait for us to enter. He was entirely at ease in the imposing palace. He stood tall and nodded to the nobles walking past, greeting them by name. Their expression spoke of respect. Hinze was one of the few within these walls who had spent time at the Front.

Chelsa came gliding through a doorway to the right. She gave Hinze a fierce embrace before backing away, eyes roaming his face with concern. I softened toward her just a bit at the sight. She turned to Natasha next and dipped a quick curtsy. Natasha nodded, leaving no question of her higher rank as reigning queen. Chelsa controlled her face relatively well, but her lips twitched and betrayed her irritation.

She didn't bother to hide her annoyance when she spotted me at Natasha's side. After giving me a sneer and ruining whatever warm feelings I had over her concern for her brother, she turned to Hinze.

"Father is in a war meeting; he wants you to join him immediately and has promised Queen Natasha he will meet with her once it is over. I can take them to the Trish quarters while they wait."

Hinze looked at Natasha.

"We would appreciate that," she said with a thin smile.

"Yes, thank you, *Princess*," I added, unable to keep the Bellovian in me at bay. Rennie snickered. Oken turned his laugh into a cough. Chelsa looked confused, but she was unable to decipher the insult disguised in my Bellovian accent.

We followed Chelsa down the arched hallway, Sam and Savha leading and the Bellovians taking up the rear. Lilah, Brea, and Londe split off to find their families, Lilah making a show of telling Oken goodbye and inviting him to her family's quarters whenever he wished.

Each time we passed a glowering Florian, I glanced back at my Bellovians. They didn't seem to notice the looks they drew, too busy staring as the grand hallway opened up into a room sporting vaulted ceilings covered with hanging lights that appeared to be simple balls of blue flame. Curving stairs and hall entrances branched out in every direction. Even with so many Florians walking around, I couldn't imagine how they made use of so much space. Large buildings in Vichi were still compact and efficient. Everything had been built knowing there was finite room for a city to spread, given the boulders surrounding it. Apartments reached upward and ceilings had only been tall enough for the largest Bellovians not to have to duck.

The Florian palace was just open, lavish space.

Chelsa led us up a set of stairs and down a hall with less jarring cream carpets. After a few turns, she stopped before a massive doorway. At her nod, the Florian guards opened the double doors and returned to their positions. I could hear the soft-spoken Trish inside. The tinkling of teacups and the smell of steam off lavender tea. My heart began to race. I felt lightheaded from all the emotions thrumming between Natasha and me in the bond.

Natasha straightened her back. I met her eyes and nodded. With a brilliant smile, she entered the room full of Trish. I allowed myself a small smile when I saw her immediate effect on them. Eyes widened. Speech halted. Tears welled. Startled laughter sounded. I felt so full of emotion and power. It danced through the bond.

The smile died on my lips when I stepped fully through the doorway and saw a face I knew better than my own standing in a small circle of Trish. She broke away, features a mask of shock.

"Elise!" Sam stepped forward to greet her, arms open wide.

My mother brushed Sam aside and took my face in her hands, tears spilling from her blue eyes. The silver roots of her hair were showing at the top of the black, just like mine.

She was here.

She was alive.

I stared at her and couldn't feel anything for a moment. Even the bond was silenced in my shock.

"Finley. Oh, Finley!" My mother's thumb brushed over the scar on my cheek. She looked me up and down. Finding all my body parts intact, she pulled me into a hug. I stiffened in her embrace, emotion finally stirring. Shock shifted into something bottomless and foreign. Not any emotion I would have expected, but I couldn't fight it.

"Where is he?" I surprised even myself by the anger in my voice.

My mother jerked back. "I..."

I searched the room for his kind eyes, tall build, and black hair. "He's not here..." The realization was so chilling that I began to shake. I stepped away from my mother's warmth. "You got away? Without him? You left him? Did you even try to help him?"

"Finley—"

"Mom, where's my dad?"

CHAPTER 9

In vain, I searched the room for my father's strong Bellovian features. I couldn't stop. Even when my mother's face fell, I looked for him. I pictured the wrinkles in the corners of his eyes from years of stressful work and smiling at us. How he always took my mother into his arms after a long day, taking and giving comfort in equal measure. The love between them had been a light in my childhood. It had been the love of home and safety from the world outside. The world had gone cold when I saw the bloodstain on the carpet. It had been his.

But this... The cold was swallowing me whole.

"I couldn't, Finley. There were so many of them."

"How many?" My hands were tight, trembling fists at my sides.

"Fin..." My mother's hands fluttered like they did when she was upset, but she stopped crying.

"Did you love him, or did you just use him to get away from the invasion?" Everything was shattering. Nico's words echoed. *He's still your dad. Just like Mom is my mom.*

Lies. She would have saved him if we were the family I

thought we were. My childhood was crumbling, every memory cast in darkness.

My mother gasped. "Of course I loved him!" She lowered her voice, although everyone around us could still hear. "Finley, this is war. We can't save everyone no matter how much we love them."

They'd all lied. We all rebelled. And my father alone paid the price. I knew the strength of the *magsai* now. I had escorted Natasha out of Command Hall almost on my own. If my mother had loved him, we would be together.

I forced my jaw to unclench and cleared my face of emotions. I stepped back again, the Bellovians behind me making room for me in their ranks. Oken's knuckles brushed my own.

"May I present Queen Natasha," I said, voice flat as I tried to bury all feeling. Overwhelming relief and joy and complete devastation. I hadn't let myself think about my parents dying. Now I had to. My mother stood here without my father, the truth of my loss directly before me.

Natasha hastily stepped forward, drawing the attention away from me.

My mother and the room of Trish knelt. My mother kept her eyes on me. I hated that I was causing such a scene but couldn't find control. Natasha was keenly aware of my panicked state and sent me what calm she could through the bond. It was a gentle breeze against crashing waves.

My mother stood and turned to Natasha. "My queen. It is a great pleasure to meet you. I'm Elise Cassiwess."

Even Savha's lifeless face shifted, eyebrows lifting when my true last name was revealed. Revealed so easily. Like it was nothing. Like a simple fact I could have given Sam when I first met him to avoid all his distrust.

Like I was only a Cassiwess. The Larson half of me brushed aside with my mother's proud introduction.

The Cassiwess family was the first to become *magsai* when the royal family was the Finleys and not the Hollises. My name held the great history of the *magsai* within it and marked me as a member of the strongest, most trusted family. There had rarely been a Cassiwess who wasn't invited to the ranks of the *magsai*. My mother told me all this when I was young. I never thought it had anything to do with me. Not with my Bellovian blood and the Bellovian custom of adopting the father's name.

I was so stupid. So naive and trusting. Even since talking to Nico, I had never considered that she could be a *magsai* and not tell me, but Sam clearly knew her well.

Sam's face was full of amazement; he turned to look at me with new eyes.

"You never said you were a Cassiwess," Natasha's voice was high, drenched in startled amazement. I wanted to cringe from the pride flowing through the bond. She was honored to have been given a Cassiwess as *resa*.

The name meant little to me at this moment. I couldn't tear my eyes away from my mother. I had never seen her so clearly.

"In Bellovi I went by my father's last name." My voice was cool.

Natasha placed a hand on my arm and searched for a way to shift the focus off me again. She turned to Savha and asked where Fisher's parents stood in a low voice. The question broke my spiraling emotions. This moment wasn't about me and my mother and my dead Bellovian father left behind.

I followed as Savha walked deeper into the room, trembling as badly as I was. The Bellovians moved cautiously after me. They had no idea what had been said in Trish this entire time, but Oken's expression was dark and I felt him close at my back.

"Finley—" My mother tried again, reaching for my arm. I shrugged her off.

"What if Nico had been there?" I asked. "Would you have saved him?"

"I would have done all I could, as I did!" She was growing frustrated.

I shook my head and kept walking.

"My mother," I explained briefly to the Bellovians in Common Tongue. I looked at Jenna. "We're going to talk to Fisher's parents. The Dossens."

Her face paled, but she kept pace with us. The older couple wasn't far. Fisher's mother had his same gray eyes, his father the same dark, steel hair. Fisher's features had been a perfect combination of the two of them.

The air was growing too thin.

When Fisher's mother caught sight of Savha, her face broke into a brilliant smile. It fell away upon seeing the devastation on Savha's face. A darting glance confirmed her son wasn't among us.

"No... no, no, no!" She crumbled. Her husband tried to support her, his face draining of color. They ended up in a broken heap. Savha began to cry and knelt beside them. She lifted her hands but hesitated, debating whether or not to reach for them.

Natasha cleared her throat and spoke gently. "The town of Honna was attacked while we were there. I had just met your son the night before, but... he was incredibly brave. There were many Bellovians and h-he got shot. I couldn't save him. I am so sorry for your loss."

Fisher's mother smothered a harsh moan with her

hands. His father reached for Savha, pulling her into the hug. He bundled her and Fisher's mother close. I thought of the hugs Fisher gave freely, always reaching to include those he loved. My vision blurred with tears.

Jenna stepped forward and the Dossens froze. They eyed her warily as she knelt in front of them next to Natasha.

"The bullet that killed your son was aimed for me." Jenna's voice caught and she took a deep breath before pushing on. "I'd known him less than a day and, even then, hadn't spoken with him directly. He saved my life. The world lost a great soul, and I don't know how to repay him or you for his life. I hope to one day be as strong." Jenna ducked her head, her black braid sliding forward off her shoulder.

The room stilled. Fisher's mom studied Jenna. She shocked us all by pulling her into the hug. Jenna began to cry softly. We stood silent as the Trish family accepted the Bellovian girl. There was a shift in the air.

The loss of Fisher wasn't worth the change, but I tried to be glad for it.

I was still shaking when my mother came up behind me. I would recognize the sound of her light footsteps anywhere. Oken stiffened at my side as she approached. My stomach knotted itself and I knew I wasn't ready to face her again. It was all so much. Too much grief. I couldn't breathe.

"Finley, why don't you go get some fresh air," Natasha suggested without looking up from Fisher's parents. She was holding his father's hand. I checked the bond and found her steady. Much steadier than me, but she couldn't support me now. She had to be with her people.

"I'll be right back," I promised, voice reedy without any air to back it.

There was a balcony to the right. My mother called my name as I slipped out the glass doors. I walked until I was out of view from those in the room and then slid down the wall, crouching on my toes, wrapping my arms around my knees, and bringing my forehead down to rest on them. I thought I had mourned my parents and accepted their loss after speaking to Nico. After seeing the bloodstain.

It never occurred to me they could exist one without the other.

I held myself tightly together and struggled for air. I couldn't cry. Everything was building to a roar and I was terrified of releasing it. A stabbing, blinding, senseless pain accompanied memories of my father's expressive face. I tightened my grip; dug my fingertips into my legs. He was laughing, throwing me in the air to catch me in solid Bellovian arms. Telling jokes that barely made sense and were all the funnier for it. Watching my training sessions with his chin high. Promising me it would be okay when only he could tell I was scared. Steadying my hand while teaching me to breathe through my trigger pull. The whole time he knew I wasn't actually his daughter. Never in my life was there a hint that he cared one way or another.

And the way he had looked at my mother... I had counted on that light like I counted on the sun to break through the clouds. Now I couldn't remember how she had looked back at him. Now he was gone and she was here and my memories of home felt empty.

I had sent the commanders to our house. My mother had left him. He saved us and we only brought him death. Where were our gods of peace and love and strength now?

I was going to explode. I was going to silently shatter.

Crumble to nothing. Blow away in the wind. It was too much. I wanted Nico and he was so far away. I felt the Trish trees brush my mind, the memory of escaping to them in my dreams. It was tempting to drift away, but I was mad at the gods and there was a chance they were what called to me.

The doors of the balcony opened and panic clawed at my throat. I couldn't see my mother now. But it wasn't her footsteps that approached. These were the heavier, careful steps of Oken. He stopped before me and I looked up from where I gasped for air. He hesitated. Then, he bent and grabbed my wrists, unwrapping my hold on my legs and pulling me to my feet. He drew me close and folded me in his arms, pressing me between him and the wall and blocking out the world.

The Bellovian strength of his hard chest and arms was comforting and familiar. The pressure of his hold loosened something inside me and I finally sucked in a full breath. The tears began to fall.

Oken held me as I broke. My tears soaked through his shirt. He just held me tighter and tucked my head under his chin. The Bellovians may not show their affection easily, but no one could hug like them.

I didn't know how long it took. It felt like forever. It didn't feel like enough time. It felt like a betrayal to my father when the pain eased and I found myself breathing. I stopped shaking and the panic faded, replaced by a hollowness in my chest. Oken's warmth began to fill it, to support me.

I couldn't have that. I moved in Oken's arms and he loosened his grip. I went back to the wall and sat down. Oken took a seat next to me and we stared through the balcony's strange stone balustrade at the city of Helsa.

"My dad is dead." And I was exhausted.

Oken nodded, a sad smile pulling up one corner of his mouth. "I'd like to tell you the hurting stops, but it won't really."

I slid my hand into his large, calloused one and sighed as the hole solidified its place in my chest next to Dani, Garris, and Fisher. I might not have seen him die, but imagining the light gone from his eyes was... I couldn't do it.

"He would have liked you," I said softly.

"I'm a very likable person." I gave a shaky laugh and rested my head on Oken's shoulder. I was so tempted to fall into him. To let him help me carry it all.

He held perfectly still. We sat until my breathing steadied.

I sighed. "I should go check on Natasha."

Oken stood and helped me to my feet. With a pang of regret, I pulled my hand from his grasp once I was standing. If I hurt his feelings by doing so, Oken didn't show it. He simply turned and led the way back into the room of Trish.

Everyone was turned expectantly toward the piano in the corner where my mother was taking a seat. Fisher's parents still sat in a cluster with Natasha, Savha, and Jenna. The rest of the Bellovians sat off to the side, looking uncomfortable. Oken went to join them. I started to follow, but my mother called out in her gentle voice.

"I know you're mad at me, Fin, but come sing for the ones who aren't with us. We stand together in our loss."

My feet moved to the piano on their own accord. It promised a slight release. A way to honor the dead. Something I could do when I felt so damn useless.

This piano was larger than the one we had back home. It was a polished black and not the nicked wood I was used to. I sat beside my mother on the bench without looking in her direction. She began to play and goosebumps rose on my arms. My mother hid her gifts well in Bellovi, even her playing abilities. Her fingers flew over the keys with Trish speed, adding layers to the melody I already knew by heart. I watched them with fascination. When I was beats away from my part, I cleared my throat and looked at my mother. She was already smiling at me encouragingly, eyes still sad. I looked away, took a deep breath, and let the Trish words out.

The lyrics came strong and clear, pushed out from the base of my stomach, gliding with little resistance from my throat.

Tash has come and blessed our hearts
They've left the gift they give
We mourn the loss. We mourn the loss
Of souls that come and go
Though life is fragile, it is perfect still
We know and we rejoice
The trees whisper and bring them home
We know the loss. We know the loss
And it is perfect still
We move in this world as one
Born and loved and gone
Back to the dirt, we will go
Beneath the roots that all will know
We live in love, peace, and strength
Until our time is done
We love the lost. We love the lost
And never will forget.

CHAPTER 10

I opened my eyes once the final piano chords drifted into silence. Hinze stood directly across the room from me. His smile shook as he led a round of applause, the first I had ever received. It did little to ease the ache in my chest. My mother turned to me on the piano bench and I stood, ignoring her. I began walking back to Natasha. Hinze met me halfway and squeezed my hand.

"Beautiful, Finley," he said for my ears alone, his thanks brimming in his hazel eyes. We reached Natasha and he raised his voice, "My father is ready to speak with you now. I can take you to him if you'd like."

Natasha told Fisher's parents to come to her if they needed anything. His father cleared his throat and returned the offer. He and his wife had been in Helsa longer than the other Trish. Later, they would help Natasha get settled.

Hinze leaned in and said his own words of comfort and support, accepting their hugs but unable to meet their eyes. Fisher had followed Hinze to the Front. They'd gone together hoping to make a difference. To find Natasha and save the Trish. Had Fisher fully understood the risk when he left his loving parents behind?

We exited the Trish Hall. I felt a flash of annoyance when my mother fell into step next to Sam. I wanted a clear head and her presence jumbled everything. Yet I knew we needed someone with more political experience to help us with the king. They spoke in rapid, quiet Trish and I did my best to ignore them, focusing on Natasha as she pointed out different aspects of the palace, from statues to paintings to the clothing the nobles wore. Hinze told her histories and myths to accompany the sights and Natasha listened intently.

Hinze led us down the twisting halls and up a sweeping staircase. A couple more turns brought us to a spacious office done in dark wood. A bright, shifting light beamed down from above. A large table took up the center of the room. Like Hinze's in Honna, it was painted to look like the map of Bellovi, Traesha, Floria, Detono, and some small surrounding islands. The Florian King sat at the head of the table, just above Traesha.

He was not what I was expecting. It was apparent Hinze took after his mother. The king was ghostly pale with thinning blond hair. Even his eyes were rimmed with lashes so fair he appeared not to have any at first glance. He was shorter and stockier than his son. His round stomach jutted against the table. I immediately hated the gleam in his eyes as he sized up Natasha.

Chelsa halted her whispering in his ear and sat down on his other side, also eyeing the Trish queen. The table held several Florians, most I didn't recognize, but three possessed enough resemblance to Chelsa, Hinze, or the king that I knew they were Hinze's siblings.

Unlike Hinze, the other princes kept their hair cut short. The elder was blond like the king; the only features he shared with Hinze were a full upper lip and a slightly hooked nose. The younger brother had even less in common, sporting flaming red hair and a face splashed with freckles, yet the hazel eyes were the same. Both wore gold suits with sashes and pins on their breast pockets. The older brother reclined in his seat, a practiced look of smug arrogance arranged on his face. The look hardened into an angry frown when the Bellovians followed us into the room and lined up against the wall as there were only four empty seats. Most of the other Florians at the table, nobles and generals, if I had to guess, wore the same expression.

The younger brother watched eagerly, perched on the edge of his chair. He grinned at Hinze, his teeth impossibly white. When the king rose and Hinze's siblings followed suit, he practically jumped out of his seat. The youngest princess righted his chair, shaking her head at him. I could tell from the glint in her eyes she had better humor than Chelsa. An easier nature. Her coloring and simple attire did little to draw the eye compared to her siblings, but her smile was by far the most welcoming.

"Welcome, Queen Natasha and... friends," the king said with a stiff, shallow bow. Natasha mirrored the movement, her mouth quirking into a tight smile at the king's not-so-subtle slight of the rest of us.

"Thank you for hosting us, King Mavrick. Helsa is as beautiful as my grandfather always said it was."

The king gestured to the chairs left empty at the table. When he and Natasha sat, we followed suit. Hinze walked through the table to sit between Chelsa and the youngest prince. He ruffled his brother's hair as he sat, earning himself a glare with no fire behind it. I wondered how long it had been since Hinze had seen his younger siblings. He and the eldest didn't bother with a greeting, but Hinze reached to squeeze his younger sister's hand.

"Yes, I remember when your grandfather visited," the king said. "He was a kind man. I'm sorry for your loss. These are my children; Prince Mavrick is my heir, then Princess Chelsa, Prince Liam, Princess Fay, and of course Hinze you know." Natasha smiled and nodded at each of them as they were introduced. "We were very concerned to hear about the attack in Honna."

"It was a jarring experience and a horrible loss of life. May I ask how they got past the boundaries set at the Front?"

The king's smile slipped so briefly I could have imagined it. "They were more motivated in their efforts than they have been. I must confess, with our efforts focused on your country in the north, they slipped our notice. Those who made the push were some of their more trained and able soldiers, not the usual rats they send out."

Rennie stiffened in the corner of my eye at her place by the door. I opened my mouth to contradict the king, but my mother elbowed my side.

"It was unexpected," Prince Mavrick cut in, "but we are readying our retaliation as we speak."

"The elites we've sent should be there already. They will see to the matter quickly," a gruff Florian beside Princess Fay said. He had dark skin, darker even than the Trish and tightly curled black hair. His sash was orange and red, images swirling in the shape of flames. The scar on my bicep itched.

I didn't want to imagine what kind of retaliations the Florians were capable of committing.

"And their air crafts and communications with Detono?

What do you make of those?" Natasha asked. I fought a smile. I'd asked her to bring this up but wasn't sure if she'd brush off my worries as Hinze had.

The king's brow furrowed. "Communications with Detono?" He glanced at a man further down the table who looked puzzled and sheepish. He shrugged.

"Yes. The instructions for their technologies are from Detono. I can only assume the same can be said about a good deal of their funds and materials needed for these machines," I said.

The king slid a cool look my way, gaze following the length of my braid where it had fallen over my shoulder. "I suppose you would know." Natasha bristled on my behalf. "It is worrisome, I admit. Detono was not gifted with abilities like us and has created technologies to bridge this gap, but they've never done anything to cause much concern. Their strength is nothing compared to our advantages, flying machines included. We wondered where the Bellovians came up with their weapon ideas and how they were able to mirror those from Detono. Wilson, why has this information slipped our notice?" the king asked the man, who was now sweating.

"I cannot say, but I'll find out."

"Go."

The man hurried from the room. His coloring reminded me of Mesa. She had told me of the coastal town where she grew up. They made their living spying on the Detonians. That man must oversee those spies.

"Are you certain your abilities will compete with these flighters? What if they—"

The youngest prince snorted so loud it cut Natasha off. Hinze shot him a stern look. He was the only one who didn't stare at Natasha. Chelsa leaned back in her chair, clearly offended. Prince Mavrick's eyes narrowed. They were a light brown under his blond hair. He looked like he'd been left outside too long and faded in the sun. When Princess Fay let out a nervous laugh, the first sound she'd made to call attention to herself, the king raised a hand to calm his children and the Florians down the table, his eyes dancing with amusement.

"Of course, I am certain. Floria still holds the upper hand, and the time has come to show it. This rebellion has gone on long enough."

"How are you planning to end it?" I couldn't hold the question back. The king's eyebrows rose in my direction in a practiced look that made me feel six inches shorter. I straightened in my chair and lifted my chin, my expression cooling to neutrality without thought.

"I plan to remind the Bellovians that I am their king. First, I will cut off their supplies. I am sure you have no objection to my ruining their roads to Traesha. Then, I will send my elite forces to do what is necessary to ensure their surrender."

"That sounds a bit simple," I said. I could feel my mother's tension rolling off her. Was she worried because I was speaking to a powerful king, or did she care about the Bellovians? "Are you willing to take out Bellovian children guarding supply lines? Kill any of them stationed along the Front? Starve the entire country? If you end this war like that, they will always remember it. The rebellion won't stop; it'll only be fueled."

"And *who* are you?" Prince Mavrick asked, the question reducing my every word to a girl speaking out of turn.

Hinze opened his mouth to respond, but Natasha answered first. "This is Finley Cassiwess, my *resa magsai*, leader of Trish defenses, and my most trusted advisor."

"And you side with the Bellovians who just murdered a young Trish man?" The oldest prince's eyes took in the black of my hair with disdain. I was grateful Savha had stayed behind with the Dossens then.

"I don't side with those Bellovians, no. I side with the Bellovians who are just trying to get a decent meal and you're about to make that a whole lot harder for *them* and *not* the ones leading attacks. I side with the Bellovians who have been working on the inside to end this war for years. I side with anyone who wants peace and I think—"

Prince Liam let out a laugh. "Hinze, she's your twin!"

Again, reduced. My face burned and I longed to wipe the smug look off Liam's face. Hinze looked furious. He made to respond when his father lifted a hand for quiet. The Florians instantly stilled. The king turned to me with a cold look.

"You are welcome to your idealist opinions, but this is a war. No matter the position you have found yourself in, you are too young to understand. If we let this petty rebellion drag on while we search for a peaceful solution, more innocent people will die than if I stomp it out as we should have decades ago."

"I have seen more of this war than you have sitting here in the palace. And by innocent people, I think you just mean Florians. Plenty of those on the Front that you plan to stomp had no choice—" I trailed off as the table began to shake.

Anger flashed in the king's eyes. The Florians down the table sucked in a breath as one. I remembered then I was talking to a man with powerful abilities. The king got control of himself and the table stilled. He looked at Natasha in amazement over my audacity.

My heart swelled when she unapologetically lifted her chin.

"We're Trish, King Mavrick. Above all, we value strength, peace, and love. If you don't think the three can exist hand in hand, then this is where our differences begin. We know what it means to have a country crushed under a brutal oppressor. We know the pain of losing what we value and those we love. I won't support the same actions happening to another country, not even the one that attacked my own. The Trish will not stand behind you if you use your gods-gifted abilities to kill thousands of hungry, poor, and uneducated people."

The table trembled briefly again as the king struggled to keep his face neutral. "You cannot possibly think this war will end without bloodshed. They either kill thousands of us or we kill thousands of them."

"Have you ever made any kind of attempt to negotiate peace?" Natasha's question left the king blinking. She pressed on. "Have you ever offered help to those so-called Squalor rats you have cut down so quickly at the Front?"

"Yes!" The king snapped. Even Hinze's face hardened at Natasha's question. "We used to, yes. And now my wife is dead."

A brief silence. Natasha swallowed, but again, she didn't back down. Her tone softened, though. "I know you have ways to contact the rebellion, but have you ever offered true aid to those in the city? The commanders have the Detonians backing them; how can the rebellion succeed without support?"

"The Bellovians have been unreasonable in every interaction we've had with them," Prince Mavrick said.

Natasha glanced pointedly at the wall where Levi, Audrey, Oken, Jenna, and Rennie stood quietly. "Yes, clearly, there has never been a Bellovian who could calm their bloodlust enough to hope for peace and join a rational discussion," she said. "You've known about the rebellion in Vichi for years but only used them for information. I haven't seen any evidence you tried to help them in return."

Levi was nodding, jaw set and eyes flashing. I wondered if the king had heard who Levi was and his ability to calm such Florian outbursts like the ones that had shaken the table. The king had more to fear from the Bellovians than he imagined, but I wasn't going to expose Levi now to make the king see reason.

Prince Mavrick's face reddened. Hinze smirked down at the table, even when it trembled again. The king put a hand on his eldest son's arm and it stilled. I recalled they shared the same ability. Apparently, the same temper too.

The king cleared his throat. He pasted on a smile, shifting the tension in the room as he redirected the conversation. "The Trish and Florians have always been peaceful. I believe the cultures of our two countries complement each other beautifully. We appreciate your input, Queen Natasha. I will reconsider my plans and hope you will continue participating in the discussion. I would like to move the conversation onto the topic of Traesha if you would indulge me." I hated this practiced diffusion. The king was moving on to the real reason he wanted to meet with Natasha if the light in his eyes was any indication.

"Please, go on," Natasha said, although her wariness of the king mirrored my own.

"I want nothing more than for our countries to remain close allies. Times have changed, however, and the distant allegiance we formally shared may not hold in this new world we find ourselves in. I am willing to support you in regaining control of Traesha. I will even supply you with soldiers to help you hold it. This is in good faith of your helping and standing behind Floria in the future. I believe the best way to solidify a promise of this magnitude is also our most traditional solution. I propose a marriage agreement. While my first son has already been promised, I offer Hinze's hand to your majesty along with Floria's aid."

CHAPTER II

T looked to Hinze. There was no way he hadn't known about this. But the way his face drained of color said otherwise. He appeared to be as shocked as the rest of us. Only Prince Mavrick and Princess Chelsa looked unfazed by their father's proposal. Chelsa watched Natasha and Hinze closely, a slight frown on her face. She lifted a hand to touch Hinze's arm. When it simply passed through him, her frown became more pronounced.

Natasha struggled to control her emotions; her hands clenched so tight under the table I could feel the pain of her nails digging into her palms.

Sam was the first to find his voice. "Your Majesty, the Trish have our own esteemed traditions involving the marriage of the queen. She must—"

"There is always time for change and new traditions. Do you think a Florian prince has ever married outside our head families? We speak of new alliances; let us make one. The Bellovians and Detonians are more of a threat now that they have joined forces. Our countries will be stronger together, just as theirs are."

"We will need time to discuss this, of course," my mother said, an easy, calming smile on her lips. She drew the attention away from Natasha, who was breathing audibly through clenched teeth.

Natasha stood suddenly, her chair scraping, and we followed suit. She gave the king a stiff nod. "Yes. Thank you for your hospitality in the meantime." She turned on her heel.

My fingers curled into fists at the king's smirk. He tipped his head in a nod and watched Natasha sweep out of the room. She moved a little too quickly, her Trish speed betraying her desperation to escape the king's gaze. I glanced at Hinze once more before I followed her. He was staring down at his hands folded on the table, completely still and brows furrowed. I realized he was angry. I'd never seen the emotion on his face.

Sam and my mother were close on Natasha's heels, trying to talk to her while she stormed down the hall. They moved swiftly and the Bellovians behind us were practically running to stay with us. How fitting to find myself in between the two groups.

I was struggling to keep up. The force of Natasha's emotions was dizzying, her anger making it hard to think straight. It hit differently than my own would have, befuddling my mind and looking for release. I resisted the urge to slam my fist into a wall. To grab my head to stop it from spinning away. To go back and show the king Traesha's power. All while my stomach turned painfully with the force of Natasha's dread and anxiety.

Natasha was too distracted to hear a word my mother or Sam told her. I couldn't focus on them, the roar of Natasha's fury drowning everything. How loud must it be in her head? We came to the doors of the grand hall where the Trish spent their time, but my mother led us past it to a set of stairs off to the side. At the top was a hall lined with bedrooms where the Trish living in the palace must stay. My mother turned us again to another short set of stairs. This hallway entrance had two wide doors that opened to the chambers inside. A pair of Florian guards stood posted on either side. There was a set of grand doors in the back of the circular area and a seating area in the middle. The rest of the walls sported doors open to simple bedrooms. The room was perfectly designed to hold Trish royalty and their *magsai.*

Natasha took in the chamber and stopped my mother and Sam's words with a hand in the air. "I will heed your council in the morning. For tonight, I need to think for myself." She spoke with careful control. She continued past the seating area and through the grand doors, shutting herself away in the royal chambers. I stepped forward.

"We will be guarding the queen ourselves," I told the guards in Common Tongue, my Bellovian accent harsher than usual.

The guard on the right raised an eyebrow. "I'm sorry, miss, but we have direct orders from the king."

"The king does not decide what happens in the queen's private quarters," I said, the words coming out a sharp hiss. I didn't realize I had stepped forward until the guards shifted into defensive positions. Natasha's anger and my own were a strong force combined. Try as I might, I couldn't relax my features to my usual neutral expression.

The other guard raised her hand.

Levi cleared his throat noisily, narrowing his eyes at her. I realized she was trying to use her ability on me. The guards exchanged a startled look.

"Please tell the king thank you, but no thank you for

us," I said with as much sweetness as I could muster, stepping aside and grasping my hands together to stop their shaking. And to keep from reaching for the guards.

They left with little fuss after that. I slammed the doors behind them. It was the first time in my life I had slammed a door. It felt amazing. I took a deep breath and tried to think through Natasha's rage. Rather than calming now that she was alone, she was working up even more of a storm. It consumed my mind. I held my head together at my temples, leaning against the doors for balance.

I'm not an object up for sale. The king had no right to control my life like that! I am a queen! *I'm trapped here. Surrounded by them...*

I shook my head to clear it, yanking myself forcefully away from Natasha's end of the bond.

"Mom, Sam, you take the rooms nearest these doors. Audrey and Levi, I want you closest to the queen's room. The rest of you can fill in where you like."

"Finley, the *magsai's* place is next to their queen," my mother said.

My eyes narrowed at her before I could stop them. The force of my glare made her step back. I saw her shock and confusion. She'd known me my entire life and I'd never looked at her like this, not even when I first saw her here at the palace.

I forced myself to take a deep breath. "Everyone in this room is here to protect the queen. Levi can do that quite well against the Florians and I don't think anyone could get past Audrey if they tried. You and Sam can hear the threat first, warn us, *and* get to the queen faster than any of them by skipping. I also want to keep a watch. Mom, you'll go first since you didn't have to travel today and are most rested."

"We should do it in pairs. I will share the first watch," Sam said.

"Sure. Fine. You two do seem to have a lot to talk about. By the way, just out of curiosity, are *you* my father?"

Sam sputtered. My mother let out an indignant gasp. Oken fake coughed, the force of it sounding almost painful as he fought a laugh. The familiar sound had me fighting back a smile. Oken's laughter was like a breath of fresh air, dissipating Natasha's storm of anger. Suddenly, I was fully back in my own mind.

"No! Finley!" my mother practically shouted.

I shrugged. "Well, how was I supposed to know? I was just asking." I turned to the Bellovians. "We'll do hour-long shifts; you guys decide what order to go in and whether or not you want a partner to hold you accountable. I'll go last. Just knock a couple of times."

That said, I turned and followed Natasha into the main bedroom, begging Finma to give me words to calm my queen.

She sat on the edge of the enormous bed and was yanking out her braids. I saw from across the room that her hands shook badly while she worked through the strands.

"Natasha?"

"You're angry too," she said, whirling to face me, half-braided hair fanning out wildly around her face. "Are you angry for my sake? Or is it jealousy again? Are you upset you can't marry him yourself?"

I froze mid-step. Natasha's anger was a deep spiral—growing tighter the more she considered the injustices layered upon her over the years. How little choice she'd ever been given. How few people she could take it out on.

"I see how the prince looks at you," she continued. "And it's not like you don't enjoy the attention."

At the spiral base, I felt a haunted fury like the trees surrounding the cleared Bellovian road in Traesha. It was the frustration I had sensed in my dreams.

Did she feel the same anger the land did?

Was this the anger of the gods?

I swallowed, forcing myself to detach from Natasha's fury again so I didn't let loose the biting response that rose on my lips.

"I never considered myself the marrying type." I climbed onto the bed, scooting behind her and reaching for the brush on the nightstand. "But even if that were the case, I thought you knew where my interests lay. Hinze is my friend. I'm not jealous. I'm hurting for both of you."

My feelings for Oken weren't something I was willing to admit out loud in any other situation, but it worked in making Natasha's shoulders relax just a bit. I began brushing the clumped knots she'd left in her hair.

"I *can't* marry him," she whispered, her hands coming to rest in her lap. "I don't…"

I worked silently until she released a deep breath. The rage ebbed from the room. When I finished, she rolled back to lie beside me. I reached over and took one of her hands. It was freezing.

"We'll figure something else out," I promised.

"Like what? If we want Traesha, we need an army. If we want to hold Traesha, we need to keep that army. Those aren't so easy to come by. My grandfather didn't even know where to start. This marriage is the only offer we've had since the invasion. As much as I hate it, I've been waiting for an opportunity like this my whole life. And the Trish, who we are, we're peaceful. Praise Finma, I can't ask them not to be. I can't ask them to kill for me. What if this is the only way to get our home back?"

"But you *can* ask, Natasha. At least see if they're willing to fight for you. Give them a choice. We are peaceful, yes. We *strive* for peace. But I would never have survived Bellovi if we weren't powerful too. If we weren't capable of fighting when necessary. I could feel in that room how much the people still love our country. Not only that, once the people get to know you, they'll love you too. Maybe, for right now, we need to focus on our love and strength. Finma will forgive once there is peace again, but we both know we'll have to fight to get it."

Natasha caught her bottom lip between her teeth, staring at the ceiling. Finally, she rolled her head to look at me. "Don't be hurt by this, but do you really think you can represent them to me? The *resa magsai* is supposed to speak for the people, but you don't even know them. You've spent your whole life surrounded by their enemy."

I moved to lie down too, suddenly unable to meet her eyes. Natasha stilled, surprised by the doubt that flooded me. I had done an excellent job keeping it hidden. Maybe the bond wasn't so entirely transparent.

Who knew doubt could hurt so bad? When I spoke, my voice wavered. "You need an army. You need someone to lead an army. Maybe I can't claim to be Trish after my childhood, but I know armies and war and fighting."

"Maybe the gods sent you there for a reason."

"What happened in Traesha, why my mother left, was too senseless for the gods to have had any hand in it." Was so senseless I often struggled to believe in their presence or control at all.

Natasha fell silent, but she reached for my hand. I was failing. I came in here to reassure her, and now hopeless-ness hung thick in the room. I would almost prefer the anger.

"I've always known it'll take violence to save them, but now that it's all happening..." She turned her head to look at me, tears welling in her eyes. "They won't ever leave us alone. No matter if we win. No matter how. We can't return to how things were."

I couldn't disagree with her, so I just gave her hand another squeeze.

"I think I should consider the marriage, Fin. Hinze seems kind. Maybe this is the best option for our people."

"Why do you think the king wants this so badly, though, Nat? From my understanding of Floria and Traesha, marriage here is very different than what it is there. Here, it's a power move. The king wants you as his pawn. He wants your future children as pawns. He thinks he is making Hinze the king of Traesha and wants Hinze to have an equal rule of the country, if not more. He won't go through on his end of the bargain unless this is the case. Through his son, the king wants control of both Traesha and Floria. His goal is expansion, not an alliance."

"How can you be sure?"

"I guess I can't. I just thought it was in his eyes."

Natasha looked at me for a long moment. "You read people well." She gave me a small smile. "I didn't mean to make it sound like you couldn't help me. You've already done so much." She shut her eyes, but a tear slipped out, sliding down her temple and into her hair. "I don't want to give up my freedom."

The memory of cold, consuming fear flickered. The way she had felt in the prison cell.

"That's what I'm here for."

Natasha nodded and the anger finally eased and gave way to exhaustion. She shifted closer, resting her head against my shoulder.

"I'm sorry I couldn't help you with your mom earlier today," she said.

"You're not supposed to be worrying about me. That's my job," I tried to joke, but it fell flat as I thought about my father.

"I'm glad Oken followed you."

"You are?" Wasn't I failing her every time Oken made my heart race and consumed my thoughts? She needed my focus.

"Yes. He makes you feel better about things. Like whatever is weighing you down gets lighter. I feel it over the bond whenever he's around. Did it help? He looked unsure of things when you came back."

"Oken unsure of himself? Unheard of." Even as I laughed, I remembered his hesitation before hugging me. How I dropped his hand too soon. "He did help. I just don't think it's a good idea to get closer or explore whatever it is between us. It's distracting."

Always focus.

Natasha shrugged and got up. She walked over to the bathroom area but asked over her shoulder, "And why is that such a bad thing? I'd take a distraction right about now."

She wiggled her eyebrows and I smiled, relieved she was acting like herself again.

"I hear Hinze's available!" I called through the door. It warmed my heart to hear her high, tinkling laugh on the other side.

~

THE NEXT MORNING, a gentle knock on the door woke me for my watch. Oken stood on the other side. He grinned at the sight of me and I ignored any feelings that might have stirred. With one last glance toward Natasha, I shut the doors and turned to see him sitting on the couch next to the gun he'd casually left on the cushion. I raised my eyebrows.

"Mind some company? I don't think I'll be going back to sleep soon anyway," he said, making himself comfortable.

I shrugged and sat on the couch with a cushion between us. Natasha's words from last night kept replaying in my head, making my cheeks warm.

"So, who do you think your real dad is?" Oken asked.

I sighed, letting myself fall back into the cushions and looking up at the ceiling. "I have no idea. I guess he's probably dead, or she would have told me by now."

"Do you think they were married?" Marriage was on everyone's mind, it seemed.

"I don't think so. She was young to be married. Young to have a kid at all. In Traesha, they have methods to keep from getting pregnant. It's such a small country they had population concerns before the invasion. She was shocked by how many kids there were in Vichi." Maybe it was my fated bond with Natasha that had led to my existence against the odds.

Oken huffed a laugh. "Yeah, my family of four kids was the smallest in my apartment complex."

I looked down at my hands clasped tight. I knew Oken had siblings, mostly older, if my memory was correct. Yet that I wasn't sure, that I didn't even know their names, just reminded me how little we knew each other. I was fairly certain Oken had lived with his aunt and Mayze after his dad died. I thought about asking him about it all and what his siblings were like. I opened my mouth to do it, but I could only think of his hardened gaze at the Front. How hard the choice was for him to follow Natasha and me. I felt so raw and fragile after the last few weeks that I lost my nerve. I didn't want to hear more about the people I put at risk. At least not right now. Maybe it was selfish, but I searched for something else to say. Nothing felt adequate in the silence.

"You're not what I expected, Finley Larson," Oken said.

My lips scrunched as I fought a smile. "So you've said. And now that the secret is out, it's Finley Cassiwess." I let a decent amount of false sass drip. I didn't particularly want to give up using my father's last name, but the history behind Cassiwess was something to be proud of and I liked teasing Oken.

He smiled. "Finley Cassiwess it is." Even with his Bellovian accent, my name came out like a caress. The hair on my arms rose. "It fits you, but it's strange thinking of you as anything other than a rich and spoiled Larson."

I stifled my laughter, not wanting to wake the Trish in the surrounding rooms. "I was rich, but hopefully not that spoiled."

"Too good to train with us, though."

"Well, my training was more centered around how to keep you all from being able to tell I was so much better than you. Little tricks to keep your Bellovian egos happy."

Oken laughed openly. I enjoyed the sound so much I didn't bother worrying about waking anyone up. "What did you have to do?" he asked.

I explained little things, like how I had to pull harder than necessary when people helped me up so they didn't notice my bones were lighter and how I had to slow my movements even when I walked. I mentioned how hard it was when I was little and couldn't speak Trish in public. Some of the lingering fear crept into my voice.

Oken sighed. "I didn't realize how cruel we all were

until we went to the base. How people treated you. And now I know just how it felt. Everyone hates us here."

"You weren't cruel. You just didn't notice."

"Oh, I noticed."

I melted under his gaze.

When he didn't say more, I scrambled to fill the silence. "You get used to the glares. Just keep reminding yourself their looks don't matter because they don't know you. My dad always said when the looks start to hurt, the worst thing you can do is flinch. Now, I don't care about the glares, just my reaction to them."

"Even if he wasn't your real dad, he was a good dad." Oken wasn't even looking at me when he said the words, so he didn't notice the tears I couldn't stop from welling up in my eyes. When he saw them, he crossed to my end of the couch. I sat up as he neared and settled in close, thighs touching and hands unsure if he should reach for me. "Ah, damn. I'm sorry, princess."

"No, it's okay. I just miss him and you're right. He was a really good dad." I wiped my cheeks and blinked at the ceiling until the tears stopped. Oken cautiously put a hand above my knee, squeezing gently. I took a deep, shuddering breath. When I glanced back at Oken, he looked so worried I couldn't help but give a breathless laugh.

"You want another hug?" he asked.

So badly. "No, it'll make me cry harder. I'm fine, I promise." I needed to think about something else. "Do you know where they sent the rest of the team?"

"I don't know about Yike, just Mayze. They thought she looked young enough that they sent her to Traesha."

"Yike was still with Silken when I saw him in Vichi."

Oken nodded and I worried my lip. It felt like we were

forgetting someone. My stomach dropped when I realized I was thinking of Dani.

"I hope it won't come to fighting Mayze," I said. "Or those kids."

"Mayze wouldn't fight me and I would never fight her. We're family and she cares a lot about the people in Vichi. Once she sees we have their best interests in mind, she'll side with us."

"That's good." I sat back, my body aligned with Oken's warmth.

"We do have Vichi's best interests in mind, right?" Oken glanced over his shoulder at the shut door between Natasha and us.

I couldn't fight the urge anymore. I reached for Oken's hand on my thigh, slipping my fingers between his. "I do. And I believe in Natasha. She'll help Vichi however she can. This war and the commanders are the problem, not the Bellovians."

"But... war is Bellovi."

"Because they don't have a choice. I want nothing more than to give them a choice. If I can stop what happened to Dani, to my dad, to your dad, to *so many* people, I will. They're my..." *Priority*. I looked again at Natasha's door, the truth hitting me in my gut. Natasha was supposed to be my priority. "I just want to help. I don't understand how things got so bad between the countries when we could *all* benefit from ending this war."

Oken shrugged. "People want safety. They want control. They think both of those things are tied up in power. They don't trust people enough to sacrifice anything for strangers."

"Do you think it's possible to change their minds? Do you think we'll ever have peace?"

He thought about the question, looking at our hands. "A year ago, I believed everything they said about the Trish. If I had been sent to the Conquering Ceremony before you spoke Trish to me, I probably wouldn't have seen that the people there look even more miserable than the people in the Squalor. Even Rennie looked uncomfortable seeing the chains; I thought she would have seen it all, given her childhood there. Before you, I wouldn't have realized the commanders are to blame for all that misery, both in Vichi and Shalta. I didn't understand what happened to Dani and that it could have been prevented. In such a short time, you've changed me so much. I don't think I'm some special case. I think you could change so many more people if they listened to you. People also learn from examples. I believe you'll be an example for all of them. Like you are for me."

The room was so still. I could hear Oken's beating heart and feel the anxious sweat on his skin. He meant so much to me. I never imagined how much I could mean to him. I stared at Oken's eyes, so open and honest. My gaze dropped to his mouth, capable of such perfect words. His lips looked soft. He started to smile, noting where my attention was. Even as I was caught staring, I couldn't take my eyes off him. I wanted to taste his smile. He sucked in a breath and—

Someone knocked on the doors to the chambers. I jumped back. When had I leaned so close?

I heard Oken laugh as I went to answer. I grinned when I looked over my shoulder and saw he was equally shaken.

This. This is precisely the kind of distraction I didn't need.

CHAPTER 12

I shook off the moment with Oken and opened the door. Two young Trish girls smiled nervously from the other side. They exchanged an excited look at the sight of me. The younger girl bounced on her toes, trying to look around me and into the royal chambers discretely. Her eyes widened fearfully when she saw Oken.

"*Resa,*" the older one began, nodding her head in a respectful greeting. "Our mother was a maid in the castle before the invasion. She taught us well. If it pleases her majesty, we would like to offer our services and help her ready for the day."

The younger one recovered from seeing Oken and pasted on a smile. I looked to Oken. At his shrug, I turned and led the girls to Natasha and my room.

When I woke her, she hesitantly agreed to let them help her get ready. I settled back on the bed and talked with her through the open bathroom door while the sisters picked out her dress and laced her into it. They painted her face in subtle colors and did her hair. Natasha kept catching my eye in the mirror, raising her eyebrows and giggling like she couldn't believe what was happening. The girls kept up a constant chatter. They told Natasha about their mother and her stories about the late queen. Natasha soaked up every word, thriving in every minute of their Trish chatter.

They braided her hair into a tight knot in such a complex pattern that I could barely follow. When she left the bathroom, Natasha was in a simple green dress that brought out the green in the center of her eyes. She spun for me and I clapped. With a quick curtsy and a smile, Natasha swept out of the room with her chin high. I heard Oken whistle in appreciation and Natasha's laughter.

Over the bond, I felt how relieved she was to dress and look like a queen.

"Just a moment," I said to the sisters before they followed her out. They were enraptured by Natasha. I had a feeling they would follow our queen anywhere. I heard Natasha asking Savha, who had joined Oken outside the room, how she felt and Savha's toneless response.

I forced my attention back to the girls. "How old are you two?" I asked, patting the space next to me on the bed. They shared a look and slowly came to sit next to me. They were nervous around me. Their eyes kept going to my braid. I fought the urge to fidget with the black hair.

"I'm fourteen," Alessa said first.

"Twelve," Masen said.

"Are you two sure this is what you want to be doing? Getting Natasha dressed?" I tried not to sound patronizing, but I could never picture myself content to do Natasha's hair and sew all day.

"Our mother loved working in the castle," Masen started. "You were raised in Bellovi, so I guess maybe you don't understand what a high honor this is." She matched my poorly concealed condescension in her tone. I fought a smile.

"But being a *magsai,* maybe you get that having a place next to the royal family feels magical," Alessa put in quickly, shooting her younger sister a warning look. "Mother always said dressing the queen was like creating a piece of artwork for everyone to admire all day long. She loved Queen Shay and said she was always kind, fair, and giving. I think Queen Natasha will be the same way."

"Before we escaped Traesha, we had to work in the fields. Our father worked harder so we could all meet our quotas. Even when our mother had to stay home with us, he gathered or plowed enough for both of them. He had Trish speed but had to pretend he didn't because they killed people who had it."

"Every night," Alessa picked the story up. She and Masen spoke in one voice, switching back and forth. "Our mother would bathe us and teach us braids and stitches. This was the best part of our days. Even when our hands were hurting from the fields, she would teach us."

"How did you escape?" I asked, already worried they would have a similar answer to Savha's. Fleeing through the woods with the Bellovians shooting at their backs. Their mother or father dropping dead at their side.

"The *Tasha,*" Masen answered like it should be obvious.

"The *Tasha*?"

The sisters shared another look. Alessa scooted closer and Masen mimicked the movement. "Our mother got us passage. The *Tasha* is Traesha's last ship. The Bellovians burned the others. The captain of the *Tasha* was more cautious. She could tell something was wrong; their fate speaker on board said something had happened. She listened to him and knew to hide. When they returned to Floria, the Dossens told them what had happened in Traesha."

I bit my tongue to stop myself from asking what a fate speaker was. The sisters were still talking and this news was too important to interrupt.

"Every year after that, they risked coming to shore in the dead of night on Mags' day, when the dark lasts longest and is at its blackest. The forest let them enter and people knew to meet them in the trees where the Bellovians wouldn't go, especially at night."

"It's hard to secure a spot on the *Tasha*, but our mother found us a place last year. She promised she and our father were coming this year. The *Tasha* took us north, around the mountains, and then back south to Ross Port. Half the crew brought us and the eighteen other Trish inland to Helsa. The king welcomed us, but the crew warned us to behave well around him."

"We can all tell he doesn't like letting so many of us live here. A lot of Trish try to find a job and a place to live in the city as soon as possible. We work in the palace, so we have a room here."

"When we said our father had Trish speed, the king took more of a liking to us." The girls shared an eye roll and my skin crawled.

"And then the crew just left again?"

"Yes, Captain Alson said she's trying to get help for Traesha from other countries when they aren't transporting us into Floria. 'The world is big and full of hope,'" Alessa quoted.

My pulse quickened. "There might be help out there?"

"Maybe, but not enough ships and the captain said many of the islands and lands they found don't know much about warfare or start seeming more interested in conquering Traesha for themselves, so they don't tell them where our land is. We bonded with most islands initially because we were all peaceful people. It's either that or they're too violent or they don't have the resources or they have a relationship with Detono."

"So, most of the Trish here came from the *Tasha*?"

The girls nodded.

"Thank you for telling me." I stood to find Natasha, heart racing.

I hurried to the shared area in the center of our rooms. Trays of breakfast food had been brought up and everyone stood around eating. The mood hung heavy. Everyone still focused on the meeting with the king the day before. My mother was missing from the group, but Lilah, Brea, Mesa, and Londe had joined us. Lilah stood at the end of the food table, talking animatedly to Oken and touching his arm often. For once, her hair was free of its high ponytail and fell like a gold curtain around her face. She flicked it over her shoulder, exposing the bare skin of her collarbone and shoulder. I made myself look away.

I felt pressure on my thoughts. It was familiar now. Easy to let Londe slip in.

How's the stomach? he asked, mouth full of ham as he approached. He offered me a roll of bread with some kind of fruit spread on it. I found it a bit sweet for this early. I must have been sharing too much of my mind because Londe exchanged it for a savory breakfast sandwich.

Thanks. It's healing, but I'm fine. Barely notice it. How's Hinze?

Fay told me he and the king went at it all night. Hinze was already angry the king let Traesha go so easily. The king thinks he should be grateful for the offer to help Traesha like this. Londe shrugged a little helplessly. I winced.

Brea touched my and Londe's arms to speak out loud. My eyes refocused.

"Can we still do training like we talked about?" she asked.

"Of course. When?"

"There are padded rooms in the basement we use to practice our abilities. We could go there now? Or soon?"

"Sounds good to me." I set aside my half-eaten breakfast roll and realized then all the Florians had come dressed ready to train. They looked at me expectantly. "Just let me get dressed."

In Natasha and my room, I swiftly changed into a sleeveless shirt and a lighter pair of leggings that ended above my knee. The thought of training again steadied me. My body missed regular exercise.

Natasha joined me, Masen and Alessa trailing her. They all wore deflated expressions. As the sisters began unlacing the pretty green dress and pulled out a similar outfit to mine for Natasha, I realized why.

"I should at least learn the basics," Natasha said. She didn't love the idea. Any level of violence made her cringe, but she was determined.

I almost laughed, thinking about the angry storm yesterday. Natasha may be capable of rage, but she wanted to banish it through politics, winning negotiations, and biting words. It was only me who wanted to punch the nearest wall. We readied quickly and I told Brea to lead the way. Oken came up next to Natasha and me as we walked through the halls.

"We on for a rematch, princess?"

"You must be a fan of losing," I said.

He laughed, but the sound died quickly. I looked his way in surprise and caught him staring at the handprint scar on my bicep. I hadn't yet worn short sleeves in our time together. I became conscious of how ugly and ruined my skin looked. My stomach panged with the memory of Garris's apology for the scar. I still didn't mind it. It was nice to have a reminder of the kind healer.

I *did* mind the scar's shape. It was the mark of a violent person. A Florian man.

Oken dragged his eyes away, his mouth set in a tight line. He kept close to me after that, watchful of the Florian strangers we passed.

Rennie and Jenna talked behind us, more animated than I'd seen them since leaving Bellovi. Training was a welcome and familiar distraction. Their excitement was contagious. I forced my mind from Oken, not letting it bother me even when Lilah fell back to ask him to show her some Bellovian moves, winking when she did. Natasha linked arms with me.

We passed Liam and Fay on our way to the practice rooms. I had a feeling the king would quickly be informed of what we were doing. I hoped it made him nervous.

We entered the basement and passed an indoor shooting range and another arena with heavy objects, pools of water, and obstacle courses that one needed abilities to complete. I could barely stop my mouth from dropping open as we walked and walked and walked past the vast underground facilities. These rooms offered more than the entire Bellovian training base. An army could and did train here, right in the palace.

We stopped at the room furthest down the hall. It was a

third the size of the elite training arena and the floors and walls were lined with light blue mats. It smelled familiar, like the gym my father sometimes brought me to after hours when it was too cold to train outside. It brought forward memories of discovering myself and learning how to move through the world safely. I missed my father desperately.

Once inside, I called for quiet and paired everyone up, feeling smug when it made the most sense to pair Brea with Lilah, moving the latter away from Oken's side. Savha and Natasha went together, Levi and Rennie, Jenna with Londe, and Audrey with Mesa. I looked twice when Mesa's cheeks flushed. I'd never seen such a soft expression on her face.

I refocused, fighting a smile as I tucked the look between them to the back of my mind. It gave me hope, though. Bellovians and Florians really could get along. More than get along.

I cleared my throat and called out, "Oken and I will demonstrate a few basic moves first and then walk around to assist."

Oken grinned, his reaction to my scar forgotten. He shifted into his fighting stance as I did, the movement as familiar as breathing. We went through the basics with ease and precision. In little time all the pairs were practicing punches and blocking. Oken and I walked around correcting forms and giving advice. At one point, I watched Mesa land quite the hit on Audrey. Audrey laughed in surprise. I remembered Levi telling me she wasn't easily impressed. Mesa's lightning-fast strikes were what it took, apparently.

The room grew hot and stuffy after an hour and Brea raised her hands to cool it. I saw then my mother and Sam had joined us. Sam took Savha and Natasha aside to show them moves I assumed came from *magsai* training. Natasha kept her face guarded. She still hadn't forgiven Sam, but she followed his instructions.

I approached my mother. Her eyes lit when I went to her on my own accord. "Show me what you know," I said.

After a pause, she nodded and took her stance, balancing on the balls of her feet and lifting her hands, palms up, fingers curved gently to the ceiling. I mimicked her. It felt strange to adopt a stance other than the Bellovian one drilled into me by my father. It was a stance for easy movement, not the solid base needed for the Bellovian style of fighting.

My mother moved with a blinding speed I doubt I could have met a month ago. Now, with my abilities nearly fully formed and Natasha nearby, I tracked her movements with ease and blocked her advances. I was young and in practice, but my mother fought with years of experience and comfort with her Trish speed. She went through several attacks, demonstrating and letting me try on her until I mastered the strange *magsai* movements. Most of it consisted of jabbing hits to nerves and moves that unbalanced the opponent, using gravity and our building momentum.

In time we shifted from a lesson to a sparring session and fell silent. We exchanged moves and tested each other's abilities. My mother began to tire before me. I gave in to the smirk playing at the corner of my mouth. Her breathing grew heavier. We circled and sidestepped, ducked and lunged, twisted and flipped. Graceful as the wind through the trees. My mind was made to fight like this. I let go of the Bellovian instincts to calculate and look for specific weaknesses. This was like breathing, like dancing, like pitching my voice and knowing I would find the next note to sing.

I relished each hit my mother landed, a reminder of her power and how much she held back from me. If she had been training me all these years, I would be unstoppable. As unstoppable as she seemed to be.

My belief that she could have saved my father solidified the longer we spared until my anger burst through the surface. I abruptly stopped our dance and hit her with a tight fist to the gut, a Bellovian punch. I ignored the guilt rising in my stomach when she bent over and wheezed. I immediately hated the violence, the line I crossed. Still, rage was a tight coil.

"You say you couldn't have saved him?" I demanded. My voice shook.

It was then I noticed the entire room had stopped to watch us. We had even been joined by several Trish who must have followed Sam and my mother here. Their eyes were huge with shock.

My mother straightened and faced me with a wince. "You can punish me as much as you want, Finley. I am your mother and I will love you for it anyways. I am so proud of who you've become and I rejoice in your strength and the force of your loyalty, even if I must suffer for it."

I clenched my jaw against the renewed anger at her careful, rehearsed-sounding words.

But then the steam left my system. The loss of my father cut deep. I was taking it out on her. Even if she did deserve a portion of the blame, she had not pulled the trigger. She never would have. As I looked at her, I could see the grief in her eyes. The weight she had lost. The sleepless nights in the bags under her eyes. The pale tinge to her skin. The nails she had bitten to the quick.

I closed my eyes and took a deep breath. I wasn't ready to forgive her, but the punishment wouldn't bring him back. It would only have hurt him. My mother saw the fight leave me and stepped forward, wrapping me in the hug I had missed so much since I left our home in Vichi. That morning felt like a lifetime long ago.

I allowed my mother to hold me; my hands limp at my sides. I felt small. Ashamed. She whispered how proud she was over and over. The training around us resumed, Sam pulling the Trish to join Savha. I pushed away from my mother, panicking when I noticed Natasha was no longer with them. I spotted her and Oken together. He was teaching her the fastest and easiest way to break out of holds. I heard her laugh at something he said and smiled. I felt lighter from the hug, the release of anger, and the sight of those two happy in each other's company.

I walked away from my mother and she let me go, too much understanding in her eyes. Rennie was confused about a move Jenna was explaining to her and Brea. I went over to them and let Jenna demonstrate the hold on me, showing them how one was supposed to counter it. When I looked back at my mother, she had joined Sam, but she took the time to smile at me.

I almost returned it.

Sometime later, the children brought sandwiches from the kitchen, led by a smiling Alessa and Masen. We sat in exhausted groups, the children forming a cluster around my mother while she told the stories about Traesha I had grown up hearing. Oken, Rennie, and Jenna joined the kids, curiosity in their eyes. Although they inspired some looks of fear at first, they were soon forgotten and they all listened, sandwiches in hand.

Audrey, Mesa, and Levi spoke nearby, Levi using his hands to illustrate whatever point he was trying to make. Sam sat with the other adult Trish. When I listened in for a moment, I heard him telling them about raising Natasha and our journey here. They stared across the room at her with reverence, following her progress as she walked to my side. I could already feel her muscles growing sore from the exercise she was unaccustomed to. She groaned as she sat down.

"I don't know why you love this so much. I swear I haven't felt you happier than when you were flipping around throwing kicks at Levi a minute ago."

"Well, he can get on my nerves," I said, grinning. "Here, you should probably stretch out a bit." I walked her through the ones I could feel she needed most while I told her what I had learned about the *Tasha* from Masen and Alessa.

"Captain Alson?" Natasha asked.

"That's what they said her name was."

Natasha thought for a second. "I think my grandfather told me about the *Tasha*. He loved talking about our ships and the islands off the coast. He said once that my uncle sailed with a Captain Alson. Do you think he could be alive too?" The thought of having some family left lit Natasha's eyes.

"It's possible. You could ask Alessa or Masen."

"I don't know his name, but maybe they will know something."

I frowned a bit, trying to think through my mother's rare mentioning of Trish royalty. From what I remembered, the queens often only had one child, a daughter. I'd never heard of male royalty besides the men they married who became kings. "I didn't know your mother had siblings."

"She was the only one born from the marriage between my grandparents, but my grandmother had a bit of scandal. Royal marriages are very sacred in Traesha; they symbolized a bond between the queen and her people. Just like the *magsai* do. When she had my uncle by another man, they trained him to become a *magsai*, not knowing what else to do with him. But he had his own scandal within the *magsai* and they sent him away. When I asked my grandfather about my uncle, he said his head was in the clouds and the trees whispered in his ears. That was it. Sam never answered my questions either."

"I had no idea it was like that for the royal family," I said.

It was difficult to imagine the Trish shunning someone to the extent that their niece wouldn't know their name. I thought they were more giving with their love as they honored Tash, but maybe that didn't include the royal family and their *magsai*. A chilling thought struck me. What if there had been other sons born to Traesha's queens? What had happened to them?

"My grandfather hated to talk about it. He only told me that much because I overheard him say something to Sam and wouldn't stop pestering him with questions."

"I wonder if my mom would tell us. If he trained to be a *magsai,* she probably knew him."

Natasha could feel my reluctance to talk to her. "Maybe later. We have enough to worry about without adding my banished uncle to the list. But we should at least try and find out if there's a way to contact Captain Alson and see if they can help us."

"When is Mags Day? They could be bringing more Trish soon."

"Not for another three months, in the middle of winter."

"Hopefully, by then we'll be in Traesha."

"Gods will it, I sure hope so. At this point, I would marry Hinze just to be there."

We tried to keep straight faces for all of ten seconds before bursting into laughter. The king's proposal grew more ridiculous with each passing hour.

And it felt much better to laugh at him than fear him.

CHAPTER 13

atasha had just finished bathing when my mother and Sam knocked on the door to our room.

"We need to discuss the king's proposal," Sam said. The shared chamber was empty. I experienced a flare of panic, realizing I didn't know where the Bellovians were. After a moment, I recalled Lilah and Brea inviting them for a tour of the palace.

I didn't expect them to accept.

We settled down around a table already set with tea. I let my mother pour me a cup with a word of thanks.

She nodded and began, "To start, I would like a better understanding of this prince. As a second-born son, it was clever of him to orchestrate this. Sam? You know him best. Do you think we need to fear him?"

Sam cleared his throat. "I only met the prince when I was traveling with his sister. We traveled to Traesha, but we have only shared a few discussions that were not organizing and plotting our escape. He seems like a respectable young man and quite sympathetic with Traesha. I do not believe this marriage was his idea, but Finley would have a better sense of him."

My mother raised her eyebrows at me, and I explained the circumstances under which I met Hinze. "He's always been kind to me," I concluded, "and I believe he truly does want to see Traesha flourish. Fisher was his best friend and Hinze has made it clear since I met him that helping Traesha is his first goal in this war. That might be based partially on him believing our independence would help Floria, but I could tell he had no idea about his father's proposal until we did."

"Always kind until he was having you tortured," my mother huffed. Her hackles were up. I swore internally. I shouldn't have gone into such detail.

"That was Brea," I muttered, knowing it was a poor defense.

"On his orders. It's not ri—"

"Either way, Hinze isn't the current problem," Natasha cut in. "The king is using both of us. What do you know about *him*? From before the invasion compared to now especially. I want to know just what kind of a friend he has been to my family."

"We should have invited the Dossens then," Sam said. "We'll have to meet with them once they've had time to grieve. They've been in contact with King Mavrick longer than any of us and have lived in this palace for twenty years."

"But the Trish and Florians are allies on the same terms Traesha has always allied with anyone," my mother said. "We were more interested in learning other cultures than gaining friends for wartime. Our ambassadors didn't bother to talk about armies or the war Floria was involved in, no matter how concerning it was. I don't think any of us grasped the scope of the war any more than we could imagine how it might one day impact us. The Bellovian invasion was completely unexpected."

There was a brief pause in the conversation. To live with no threat of war, to be surprised when it made itself known... I couldn't imagine.

"Speaking of other Trish allies," Natasha said, "we heard there is still a Trish ship out there. The *Tasha*. They smuggle the Trish from Traesha to here and they've been in contact with our island friends."

Sam and my mother were stunned into silence. I filled the quiet with what Alessa and Masen told me about Captain Alson and her crew. I couldn't read the look in my mother's eyes. It was something beyond hope and shock. For some reason, her expression made my stomach clench.

We were interrupted by a knock on the door. Londe entered and told us the king had invited us to the great dining hall for dinner to celebrate Natasha's safe arrival. He grimaced in apology when he admitted the dinner would be taking place in an hour. We knew it would be in bad form to decline, but I could feel Natasha's temptation to do so. She thanked Londe and told him to assure the king we would attend. His eyes unfocused as he did just that. Why hadn't he told me through his ability instead of coming all the way up here? When Londe's attention returned to us, his gaze kept returning to my mother. Londe spent most of his time in the palace with Hinze. Was he using this as an excuse to check on my mother for Nico? Had they talked recently? How was Hinze doing with his father's proposal and his grief?

The king hadn't left us time for such questions.

"Will you send up Alessa and Masen?" Natasha asked Sam and my mother when they rose to get ready. Sam skipped away. I went to our bathing chambers and quickly rinsed off the grime from training while Natasha waited for her new handmaids.

I went into the excessive walk-in closet after Natasha had gone into the bathroom with Alessa and Masen. I had no idea what one wore to a large dinner gathering in a Florian palace. I ran my hand over the dresses they had stocked for Natasha within a few hours of her arrival. Most of the gowns shimmered with light, bright colors. Some were textured lace and hand-stitched patterns. I missed my warm knitted sweater and simple leggings I could wear daily in Vichi without a second thought.

Thinking of the dark colors popular in Vichi, I was drawn toward the very back of the closet. Tucked hastily away was a dress made of a soft, navy-blue fabric. When I pulled it out, I saw it was a two-piece ensemble. I tried it on. The top was an off-the-shoulder shirt that flowed loosely to just below my ribs and the bottom a straight-cut pair of pants. On Natasha, they were probably meant to be worn with heels, making them long enough for me to wear in the flats I found. Only the barest strip of my stomach was visible, and the pants hugged my curves in a way that made me stare at myself over my shoulder. All those years of training had given me a toned and powerful body. This outfit showed it off to the fullest. I almost lost my nerve and took it off. Instead, I squared my shoulders.

Decided on my outfit, that left my hair. It was still damp from my bath and hung down my back in uneven waves. I mentally ran through the braids I knew how to put it in but couldn't decide which one I wanted to wear. I was tired of braids. A thought came to me suddenly while I was staring at my reflection in the mirror. I wasn't the same girl I was in Bellovi. The sun had given my skin a darker hue than the clouds and snow in Vichi could ever have achieved. I glowed in the new coloring. It fit me. My scarred cheek stood out pink and stark, but I didn't mind it. Nor the slice of pink showing below my ribs. And the silver peeking out of my head at my roots reminded me of what I was embracing. I wasn't Bellovian. I didn't have to wear a braid to blend in with them ever again.

I straightened my shoulders and looked myself over once more. I rarely gave my reflection more than a cursory glance, but now I looked at what the world saw. My face gave away none of my thoughts. Even standing alone in the closet, I couldn't help but hide what I was thinking. It was eerie, noticing the mask I wore constantly. I looked empty. I carried none of the life and animation Natasha wore. Nor the easy smile Oken had a hard time wiping away. I didn't even have Audrey's closed-off attitude that hid her thoughts while letting people know they would have to work to gain her attention.

I was just blank.

I thought about my father's words, *don't let them see when they hurt you.* I had taken them to heart. Maybe even too far. I turned from the mirror before I could start wondering what this said about me and went to the bathroom, where the sisters were curling Natasha's hair.

"Can I borrow Alessa?" I asked. Natasha raised a delicate pale eyebrow but nodded. Our bathroom had a vanity, and I sat down on the plush white stool and began looking through the drawers as Alessa came to stand behind me.

"Do you know who Mesa is?" I asked her. I found a comb and put it on the counter before bending again to search another drawer.

"Yes." Alessa's eyes widened when I straightened again, scissors now in hand.

"Can you cut my hair to look like hers? Maybe just a little shorter?" I pictured Mesa's shoulder-length hair, how it fanned out so spectacularly when she spun in a kick during training.

I was done with my Bellovian braid.

~

WHEN NATASHA and I entered the Trish Hall, my hair was dried and cut straight across, brushing my shoulder when I titled my head one way or another. Natasha's was swept up high in braids and curls, a simple silver tiara resting above her forehead. She wore a lavender gown with thick black stitching. We felt it together in our bond when the hall filled with Trish and our Bellovian friends turned to stare at us. A hum of power quickened my pulse.

My mother's eyes, the same crystal shade as mine, lit up when she took in my outfit.

"That's a Trish style," she said. I told myself I didn't care about her approval. My insides warmed anyway.

Fisher's father came up to join us. Misha Dossen's features were haggard, but his clothing was pressed and tucked neatly. Savha stood at his side in a simple black dress. She looked exhausted. I remembered the fire that once burned behind her eyes, extinguished since Fisher's death. I hoped she hadn't heard Oken and me laughing this morning while she suffered another sleepless night.

"My queen," Misha swept into a quick bow. "My wife sends her regrets. She was not feeling up for the evening, but I felt someone who knew the workings of the palace should be escorting you. You'll be expected to sit at the high table, a place we have been invited to dine quite a few times, including tonight. It would be my honor to sit with you through dinner. I can help you with names and any Florian manners expected of you."

Natasha glanced at me, worried to realize I couldn't join her at the high table. I gave her what I hoped was an encouraging smile. She gracefully nodded, smile so convincing I would have thought it real if I couldn't feel her nerves as she took the arm Misha offered. The two led the small procession of Bellovians and Trish who had received an invite to the dinner tonight. Several of the Trish joining us lived in the city proper. They now owned businesses or knew nobles to gain these invitations. They watched Natasha and me extra close, not having seen our arrival but well aware of the rumors already spreading. For them, I was too much like the Bellovians I brought with me. I should never have fought with my mother so publicly. Trish edged out of my path with wide eyes. How would I get them to trust me? It was a challenge unlike anything I had encountered before.

My mother began to fall back, clearly intending to walk beside me, but Rennie hurried forward and punched my arm affectionately. I was too relieved to have my friend at my side to care how the Trish reacted to my interactions with the Bellovians.

"How much do you want to bet this will be the best meal of my life?" Rennie's smile was wide.

I laughed.

"You mean it can get better than what we had in Honna?" Levi asked. They fell into conversation about their favorite Florian dishes thus far. I listened to them talk, but my favorite meals were still the Trish ones my mother risked making growing up. They rarely consisted of meat and relied more on the bread and soups she made over the stove. Florian meals had too much salt followed by too many sweets.

Rennie said something especially ludicrous about how the food here made her feel an inappropriate way, and our unrestrained laughter filled the hallway. The Florians ahead of us turned back to stare.

I saw Lilah and Brea making their way into the dining hall with their families ahead of us. Lilah grabbed Brea's arm and pointed at Oken, his tall figure easy to spot over the crowd. Her red dress hugged every significant curve of her body. Brea's dress was purple and cut in a low V. They looked incredible and easily parted the crowd as they walked toward us.

Before I knew what I was doing, I turned to Oken, reaching for his arm. "Sit next to me," I said, my voice only a bit breathless.

"*Maybe.*" Oken drew the word out, and I felt the blood drain from my face. I dropped my hand. He quickly caught it back up, laughter dancing in his eyes. "I'm kidding, Fin. I'd love to." He looked me up and down, but with the smile still on his face, I didn't feel the clenching in my stomach like I did when other men looked at me like that. "Who wouldn't?"

My shoulders relaxed and I returned his smile. It was hard to stare too close at his face. It was too bright and intent and I couldn't help but notice the look he wore was one he saved for only me. I glanced away and saw my mother watching us. I could practically hear her reminding me to *always focus.* She was not who I wanted to look at when Oken held my hand. A bit further up the line, Natasha shot me a ridiculous smile over her shoulder, the tip of her tongue poking out between her teeth as she nodded at me dramatically. I rolled my eyes at her, and she returned her attention to the room full of Florians. Misha led her to the ornately decorated table on a raised dais in the front of the dining hall. They both stood tall and walked with grace only the Trish possessed. The dining hall hushed to watch them. A well-known father in mourning and Traesha's lost queen. Natasha's white hair was a beacon, drawing eyes from around the room. The two of them had clearly been the subject of many conversations that were now hushed.

King Mavrick and his children were already seated. Hinze spoke with Chelsa. I could tell from the tension in his shoulders it was an argument, but they were smiling to keep up appearances. He looked almost as exhausted as Savha. Natasha felt my sympathy for Hinze and when she looked from me to him, I saw her gaze soften the slightest bit. Misha directed her to sit in the empty seat next to Hinze and sat on her other side. She was so nervous that the bond rolled my stomach. Fisher's father began to point out people seated at the nearest tables, probably explaining their stations in the Florian court. Hinze and Chelsa leaned in to contribute. I was surprised by Chelsa's willingness to help.

There was a table of silver-haired Trish to the right. Sam and my mother led us there and we took up the empty seats. I found myself between Savha and Oken. To my annoyance, Brea and Lilah had doubled back to sit on his other side. Lilah made a big show of waving and calling greetings to her Florian friends and family who walked by, often touching Oken's arm and explaining how she knew each person. I got the feeling the shock value of her friendship with a Bellovian was one of the biggest draws for her. She smiled every time her Florian friends did a doubletake. With two empty seats left at the end of the table, Mesa and Londe joined us. Audrey's lips quirked when Mesa settled in next to her, and I fought my own grin.

Lilah said something to Oken, and I felt a flush of happiness at the hollow laugh he gave her before turning to me. "What are you thinking about?"

"I'm trying to figure out who everyone is," I said, gesturing to the different tables. There were ten set up, but only eight territories in Floria. One was for us, the Trish, but I didn't know about the last one.

Savha heard. She tore her eyes from the Florians around us and leaned in close, pressing into my shoulder. The contact filled me with warmth. She spoke in Common Tongue for Oken's sake. "The table next to us has the rest of the king's family, the Hectori's. With Mavrick crowned king, his brother heads the territory. This includes Helsa's affairs and the surrounding land. The king's younger sister and their kids make up the rest of that noble house. Almost everyone at that table is a mover like Prince Mav and the king." Savha noticed Oken's confused expression. Her eyebrows drew together, realizing just how little Bellovians learned about the Florians. I didn't bother telling her that before we were captured by Hinze's during that mission weeks ago, Oken thought Florian gifts were only a rumor started by the Florians to scare the Bellovians into surrendering.

"They can move objects without touching them," Savha explained. She nodded at the table. I turned to see a man lift a hand, the water pitcher at the other end of the table rising and floating his way. He caught its handle and filled his glass, never pausing his conversation with the woman next to him.

"The next table over holds the king's general's family. General Tyron is the one next to the king at the high table.

The Anthez's are the strongest igniters in the country. Their land is to the northeast of the Hectori estate. Prince Mav is engaged to the general's daughter, Tiana. Next over are the Harrowers, known for their ability to control water. They own most of the coast and we call them drowners. They're a serious, quiet family. Fisher always called them downers." Savha's smile shook.

She pressed on, "Then Londe and Lilah's family, the Collins. They have the lands to the south. We call them the messengers. Most of them can communicate telepathically. Some can do more than communicate. Behind us is the Bennick family. They're growers and own the land that borders Traesha. They have a special affinity for animals for the most part, although a good portion of that family can call plants to grow and bloom. The Amiras next to them are the healers. They control most of the land south to the Bennick's along the Front."

Savha took a steadying breath before speaking of the absent again. "Garris's aunt and uncle are the head of that family. Brea's family, the Ross family, is next. They own the smallest territory and work with the growers a good deal, controlling the temperature to help our crops. The second to last table holds the late queen's family. They don't travel south often, and relations have been strained since her passing. They own the land to the north, including the uncharted forests and mountains. The king and queen were married to help relations, but more and more of them are traveling up into the trees. Only the queen's sister comes down regularly. They say she and Prince Liam are the last of the shifters."

There were only nine people seated stiffly at the late queen's table. Liam sat before them at the high table and they looked his way often.

Savha took a large gulp of wine. This was the most she'd spoken since Fisher died. "The last table holds mainly the elites of miscellaneous families and abilities or people who have traveled here. A few people from Mesa's village who are successful spies too. There's a light bender over there. He could make this room dark and then light it again if he wanted. There's Travi, who we think must have been related to the royal family because his ability is basically the opposite of Hinze's, where he can make himself hard as stone."

"Can he really?" Oken interrupted, tone far too innocent. I shook my head at him, unable to hold back my laugh.

Savha snorted and continued, lowering her voice. Oken leaned in closer to hear, his warmth seeping through his shirt where our arms pressed together. "A lot of the Florian abilities are changing. They say the Bellovian Front isn't worth their time, but I think they're just preoccupied with the fact that their gifts are so unstable. They're searching for answers. For instance, for the Collins, they used to focus on communication, but some can now control minds like Lilah. Londe's older sister is considered the top elite at their table. She can make your body do what she whispers in your mind."

At the head of their table sat a bored-looking girl sipping from a glass of wine. She was one of the few who seemed present at that table. Eyes focused on the room around her. She looked up and smirked at me. I felt the hair rise on my arms even with Oken's warmth.

"Or Brea's father can control more than hot and cold. He can alter the weather. Then Hinze and Travi's powers are completely unheard of. I think what worries the

Florians even more are the people like Chelsa, born to the most powerful families, yet they don't have—"

The king stood at that moment and we rose to our feet. My mind was whirling with all the information, fitting gifts with sections of Floria's map in my mind and puzzling over that last thing Savha said. It rose the hairs on my neck. Unheard of gifts. Some are stronger than ever before. I glanced at Natasha. She was looking at Chelsa, copying the princess and lifting her glass. Was the same imbalance affecting us and our power? Our bond was so strong, Natasha's healing gift so rare for the Trish...

The king held up his glass of blood-red wine. My eyes shifted to Chelsa. She didn't even have an ability. What did this imbalance mean?

"To the return of the Trish queen!" King Mavrick boomed. The Trish happily drank to that. "To our continued alliance and the end to this war!" More cheers and drinking. Natasha forced her smile. She appeared confident and stunning standing in front of the room. "We have much to celebrate, so let the feast begin!"

I looked around at the elite Florians the king wished to unleash on Bellovi to end the war. Some possibly as strong as Natasha and me. Londe's sister was still smirking.

I couldn't help but examine their faces as one would an enemy.

CHAPTER 14

The food was as spectacular as one would imagine from the wealthiest kitchen in the land. Our table fell silent and tucked into the seeming hundreds of dishes brought in from the kitchens. The only thing that could spoil the delicious meal was the sight of Hinze and Natasha sitting uncomfortably beside each other while King Maverick smirked at them in satisfaction. Misha Dossen and Chelsa kept leaning in, talking to them to ease the tension, but the proposal loomed too heavy.

My stomach was full to bursting when I finally sat back from my plate. The desserts were presented, but I didn't have much taste for the rich sweetness of the cakes and puddings.

"Fisher loved these," Savha mumbled next to me, holding a chocolate fudge bar covered with crushed nuts. I didn't even think she meant to say the words out loud from the way she pressed her lips together. I gave her a sad smile. I was so relieved she was talking again. It eased the sting of hearing Fisher's name.

"My dad would have killed for one of those," I told her,

pointing to the apple crumble in front of Sam. "He always insisted we didn't follow his mom's recipe close enough when we made them, and we'd have to make a second batch. They tasted the same; he just liked cooking with us when he had the time and would eat both batches within a few hours."

Oken couldn't have understood what we were saying in Trish, but he reached over and rested his hand on my knee under the table to comfort me. The unexpected gesture eased the tightness in my throat.

"How many more of us will die before this is over?" Savha whispered. She broke her chocolate bar in half with a quick snap and showered her plate with crushed nuts.

I met her eyes but didn't have an answer. I'd asked myself the same question too many times. She looked at Oken's arm, reaching for me under the tablecloth. She smiled a bit, only one corner of her chapped lips turning up. "Enjoy every moment you get."

I squeezed her hand on the tabletop. "I'm scared to," I admitted.

Lilah claimed Oken's attention as if she sensed my hesitation. I did my best to ignore her while she scooped her favorite pudding onto his plate and insisted he try it. Savha watched her with an eyebrow raised before looking back at me.

"Oh, please. You're not afraid of anything." The tiniest bit of her old fire lit in her eyes. She turned her hand over on the table and gripped my fingers back. "Thank you for singing the other night. I don't think we'll have a moment to do a true life ceremony for Fisher, but that was perfect."

"I wish I could do more."

"Me too." We fell silent, our eyes going to the bouquet of flowers in the middle of the table. Savha sniffed. Pressure burned the back of my throat. My too-few memories of Fisher flooded my mind. It was a relief when the king called for our attention once again. His oversized chair scraped loudly on the dais floor as he stood.

"My son, Prince Mavrick, has a splendid idea. This Seventhday night, we will hold a ball in celebration of Queen Natasha's return and our alliance." The king's cheeks were rosy and his words slurred just a bit. His glass of wine was nearly empty when he toasted from it. A cheer went up around the room, and after a few more words from the king, everyone rose to leave the feast. Natasha hurried over to me once she got a chance to break away.

"He's insisting Hinze and I have the first dance," she hissed. We glanced back at the king, who laughed loudly and slapped Prince Mav on the back. Prince Mav's answering smile didn't seem quite to reach his eyes. A young woman with dark skin and flaming red braids held his arm. From how she looked at him, I knew it must be the fiancé Savha mentioned.

My stomach dropped. With or without Natasha's agreement, the king would present her and Hinze as a couple and the means to ending the war.

The king cut a sly glance our way. My hands clenched into fists at the smile on his face. I looked away and caught sight of Hinze slipping away through the wall.

"I'm going to talk to Hinze," I said. I didn't know how it could help, but I wanted to get his take on the situation. I hastily told Oken goodnight and slipped between the many bodies leaving the room to get to the door first. Hinze was turning a corner down the hall, but with a skip, I caught up to him quickly.

"Can we talk?" I asked.

He didn't respond for a moment, his eyes searching my

face. His expression was uncomfortably similar to the one he had worn in Traesha's dungeons. Right before he nearly kissed my bloodied face. My stomach twisted and I regretted chasing him down. I forced the flicker of anxiety back and squared my shoulders. I had no reason to fear my friend. Hinze caught himself and blinked, pasting on a smile. "Sure. Let's go up to my chambers."

We followed the main hallway off the dining room, Hinze pausing to show me where the ball would be. The walls of the room were a muted red and the floor was covered with small black and white tiles that were difficult to look at too closely. I was finally beginning to get my bearings in the vast palace when we came to a foyer with stairs going up and down. The downward stairs went to the training rooms. Hinze led me to a staircase going up instead. At the top hung a large portrait of a woman who could only have been the late queen. I saw a great deal of Hinze in her soft smile and thick auburn hair. Princess Fay was almost a perfect copy of her.

Hinze led me to the right. While we walked, I could feel the distance growing between Natasha and me. This was the furthest we'd willingly been apart since I rescued her. The tug on the bond was uncomfortable. I could tell she was fine, but being away pressed me with anxiety. I told myself she was either sitting in the Trish Hall or getting pampered by Alessa and Masen. When I felt a flare of amusement for her, I imagined her sitting with our friends and Oken making her laugh.

We came to an olive-green set of doors. Hinze took my hand and walked us through it.

"Sorry," he said when I pulled back in surprise. I should probably be used to him doing that by now. "I locked the door once when I was younger, having a tantrum as we princes do, and threw out the keys. As punishment, my father never replaced them, so I would have to clean up after myself. I have found I don't mind being the only one with access."

Feeling slightly trapped, my laugh sounded forced. Nevertheless, I did enjoy the insight into Hinze's younger days. I let it warm me as I turned to him. "How are you?"

Hinze shrugged. "I miss Fisher. And my father has been unbearably smug about the marriage proposal. He has been trying to pair me off since I came of age. I always refuse, but I suppose it was only a matter of time. I have asked him for years to send real help to Traesha. I should have known this would be how he would finally offer it to me."

Hinze sat down hard on the couch, his brows low and eyes almost entirely brown. How long had it been since his mood was light enough for them to look mostly green? I sat across from him. He pulled ruthlessly on the small braid he wore. I let him stew for a time, not knowing what to say. He surfaced from his thoughts with a sigh.

"How are you liking the palace?" he asked.

I laughed at the sudden change in topic, and Hinze smiled faintly at the sound.

"It's big." His smile grew with my words. "I never dreamed there would be so many Trish people here."

"They keep finding their way. I think my father is growing tired of housing so many. A good deal of them have found work outside the palace, but my father thinks he is owed for his generosity. He likely believes his proposal will compensate for some of that." It would seem we couldn't avoid the topic.

"What exactly does he think he'll gain from the marriage?"

"He wants Traesha to become part of Floria. The land

there is fertile, and the people seem so strong to him...." Hinze searched for the right words. I hated that I was on edge enough to get the sense he was hiding something from me. "The elites my father keeps close are like a collection to him. He has his guards all over the country looking for especially powerful gifts, and you saw the shows in the city that people put on trying to catch his eye. He's gotten worse since my mother was killed in front of us. I think he fears that sense of helplessness. He wants to control Traesha, then Bellovi, then whoever else stands in his way with the armies he pulls from all three countries."

"But even if you and Natasha marry, she'll rule Traesha, not him."

"Yes, but is she just going to kick out the Florians my father sends to defend Traesha from the Bellovians? Is she going to make it so no Florians stand on her council? Work in her castle? Enter marriages with her people? Many Trish have adapted so well here; my father thinks this is the next step to fully blending our countries. And with the vast majority of people being Florian, and a Florian prince on the throne in Traesha too, who will look like the ruling figure of both our countries?"

"That's exactly what I worried about." It was my turn to sigh. A blended country didn't bother me, but the king's hands in it did.

"You look beautiful tonight." Hinze's words came out in a rush. "I like the haircut."

I blushed and resisted the urge to pull down on my top to hide the strip of skin on my stomach exposed. "Thank you."

Hinze's face was bright red, his stare so intent I stood and went to the window. His view was of the wall surrounding the palace and the tops of the city buildings beyond. The setting sun cast it all in a haunted light.

"I just... I have to say this before I lose my chance," Hinze said. I heard his steps approaching and closed my eyes. I was so stupid to come here. Stupid to think he needed my help in any way but this. Something was breaking in my chest. The idea of an easy friendship. The sense of safety I'd felt with Hinze. "I'm not interested in Natasha, Finley. I'm interested in *you*."

I fought back a cringe as Hinze came to my side and gently took my arm, right on the handprint scar, and turned me to face him. I couldn't stop thinking about the locked door. I opened my eyes and swallowed.

"You're so beautiful," he said again, his voice barely above a whisper. "And fierce and brave and strong. You make me forget about everything else."

Everything else? Did he mean my Bellovian upbringing? The way I left him behind? Or his own problems like his grief? His duties as prince? Natasha? Gods knew I couldn't forget about her.

"Hinze..." I started, but he leaned in, his lips beginning to pucker. His hand ran up my arm. I jumped back more quickly than I intended to and was left staring at his hurt expression from across the room where I had skipped.

"Hinze, we can't. It's too messy and complicated. You could be engaged to my queen in a matter of days!"

Hinze let out a breath, his hurt shifting to exasperation. "Not if I refuse. Not if Natasha refuses, as I expect she wants to. I know you both think you somehow stand a chance in this war without Floria's help."

"*Somehow?*"

"I just mean, with all the *magsai* and skippers dead...."

He threw his hands up. "Come on, Finley. You can't possibly find an army to take on Bellovi *and* Floria."

"Taking on every country in war is not the only option here, Hinze." My tone was patronizing. Anger flashed in his eyes.

"Not the only option? You are delusional if you think there is any other way to live in peace when your land is so valuable. My father was right about one thing. You don't understand this war at all!" It was his turn to sound condescending.

I leveled him with a look, all the awkward feelings from dodging his kiss fading. I stalked toward him, pointing at his chest.

"Are you forgetting who grew up in Bellovi? Are you forgetting who spent her childhood training to win a war she didn't believe in? Hiding her hair and heritage from everyone around her so she didn't get herself and her family killed? Or maybe I should remind you about the rebels I saw living in hiding in Vichi, starving through the cold days because they'd rather that than war with *your* people. Maybe I should tell you that when my secret did come out, they attacked my family even though you promised to help. Tried to help. But it didn't work. They killed my father. Do I need to remind you of that?"

I let myself glare at him. It felt so good to let the emotion show. "You don't get to tell me I don't understand how complicated this war is, Hinze. You don't get to tell me I don't know how the Bellovians think and am an idiot for believing they don't all need to die for this war to end. You don't get to tell me it's black and white, us against them, kill or be killed. You don't get to tell me you understand this all so much better than me." I jabbed his chest with my finger on the last word, narrowing my eyes further when he let it pass through him.

"I'm sorry!" He lifted his hands in surrender. "Finley, I—"

"After talking to you in Honna, I thought you understood, at least on some level. I thought you saw a different way to end this all. You could make such a difference in this war, Hinze."

"By marrying Natasha," he replied in a flat voice. He knew that wasn't what I meant at all. I pinched the bridge of my nose and took a deep breath, running out of words.

"I think it's time I went to bed," I said. His face fell, but I ignored the pity rising in my chest and clung tight to my anger. He didn't think Traesha stood a chance without his father's help. He thought without this marriage, Natasha was powerless.

He thought without a marriage to Natasha, *he* was powerless. How could someone so untouchable not see the potential there?

Hinze clearly wanted to say so much more. His eyes were pleading, but I crossed my arms and stood by the door, waiting for him to let me out. "Finley..."

"I can't talk about this right now. I have to focus on Natasha."

After another moment of hesitation, Hinze nodded and helped me through the door, hand lingering as he stayed on the inside. I fumed the entire way to our chambers, trusting the bond to guide me through the twisting palace halls and stairs. Jenna sat alone in front of the fire in the center area, a pad of paper resting on her knees and a pencil in hand. She nodded at me and returned her attention to her drawing.

"So, that didn't go as planned," Natasha said as I entered our bedroom, gleam in her eyes.

"Nope!" I threw my hands up and went to change in the closet. From all my emotions, she could probably guess precisely what had happened between Hinze and me. Natasha muffled her laugh against a pillow while I pulled off the Trish outfit. Only that sound could bring a smile to my face at that moment.

THE NIGHT of the ball approached quickly. Every morning we went down to the padded room in the basement to train. A large group of Trish now joined us, even some who lived and worked in the city. At times they cringed from moves intended to inflict the most pain, but they surprised me with their determination to learn. Shocked me when they turned to me more and more often for direction. I could tell Natasha hated the sight of their fists, but it filled me with hope. We never asked them to train, yet they came willingly. I didn't know if it was Natasha's presence, thoughts of revenge, or hopes of reclaiming our home, but they came and put in the work. I was confident it wouldn't take much to convince them to fight for Traesha. To go to war for their queen.

The fact that they were slowly growing less wary of me filled me with relief. I was supposed to be their connection to Natasha. Their representative. I couldn't do that if they saw me as an angry Bellovian and were too afraid to approach me. I made sure to take time with the Trish who grew comfortable with me. I asked them about life in the city and palace, learned their names, and tried to be open with them about my childhood and finding Natasha. There were some topics I didn't elaborate on. I had to share too much of myself with Natasha to give it all to them, but I made an effort to let down my mask.

Sam took a particular interest in training the children of fallen *magsai*. Though much accelerated, he followed the lessons they would have taken in Traesha. He asked Natasha and me to attend occasionally. I had nearly as much to learn about the *magsai* ways as the little ones. Most of them still shied from my black hair, but they adored our queen and tolerated my presence to be near her. Only one boy who seemed to be around our age sat near me during lessons. His name slipped my mind after our first meeting, but he was quick with a dry joke at Sam's expense, so I warmed to him instantly.

Sam watched him and the other older children closely for signs of Trish speed. Apparently, there were early markers they used to recruit *magsai* guards. My mother laughed when I asked her if I had shown any.

"Always focus, remember? Why do you think you had to work so hard just to blend in?" she had asked. It was jolting to hear those words spoken by her again.

My mother worked with the other Trish. Even without the ability to skip, they were faster than the Bellovians and Florians who joined us but had to learn how to convert that speed to force. The Trish let their speed lead to grace instinctually. Their bodies answered instructions so quickly there was still time left to temper movements, to adjust postures, to add a sway to hips and an extra flair to gestures. It was difficult for them to give up these frivolous motions and instead go right for the punch without flourish, only speed and strength. I felt like a lumbering workhorse when they gathered, talking in Trish with high voices and deliberate expressions. Even my mother gentled in their presence. My skin itched when I was around them and my thoughts always went to the other side of the hall where the Bellovians sparred loudly. I still had so much to work on to be one of the Trish.

I often caught Savha looking longingly at the potential *magsai* training while she followed my mother's instructions. She showed no markers for skipping, and I resented the requirement for Trish speed among the *magsai* as I watched her face. Just because someone lacked blinding speed didn't mean they couldn't be a loyal defender of the queen. I needed to ask Natasha about it. We would have to change so much when she became ruler. Why couldn't we change this?

Aside from the children, we had a group of about fifty Trish training every day. A small percentage, but maybe they'd spread the word and encourage others to join. My mother guessed there were about four hundred of us in Helsa. It was her lowest estimate, but the number made me cold.

Even if they all came to train, it wasn't nearly enough to build an army.

Hinze's silence toward me made our access limited, but we eventually gained permission to use the shooting range through Oken asking Lilah to ask Liam who asked Chelsa who reluctantly cleared it with the king. We spent hours teaching the Florians and a few Trish to shoot with the limited number of guns provided. The shooting range shared a wall with the elite gym, a room reinforced enough for them to practice their wide range of abilities but not so sturdy we couldn't hear the crashes from Prince Mav or the heat that came through the vents when the igniters were working. They fought each other hard and always had an Amira nearby to heal them.

Natasha had a few opportunities to work on her own

healing abilities. She was better at it when I was close, just like I was stronger in her presence. She liked to heal my bruises and scrapes at the end of each day to practice and once put Brea's sprained ankle to rights before a palace healer could get to her. Working on these abilities felt much more natural to her than combat training.

As the days passed, the Bellovians grew familiar with the palace and were accepted among its more open-minded occupants. One day while we were in the shooting range, Prince Liam came in and pestered Audrey to go into the elite's gym with him. I knew Prince Mav was in there and shot her a warning look. She agreed anyway, likely to get Liam off her back. I heard one crash next door and she came back looking smug, covered in dust as she always seemed to be after using her abilities.

"Turns out I don't need to practice," she said before rejoining Mesa at the knife-throwing station, shaking out her two braids. They were getting closer every day. Tensions in Mesa's quarters had been high since the king learned they'd missed a Bellovian alliance with Detono, so Mesa spent most of her time with us. She found more in common with my Bellovian friends than the Florian court. Audrey seemed content to build a friendship just with her, not bothering to warm up to any of the other Florians or Trish people.

Levi and Rennie similarly stuck close together. Florians avoided him at all costs, and Rennie loved to see how fearful they grew when he was near. I caught the two of them sharing more than one whispered conversation and knew their thoughts were on the rebellion back home. Every time I saw them conspiring, I felt a twist of guilt and wished we were doing more. All Natasha and I had obtained were vague promises for help, an unsavory marriage proposition, and a ball. Levi had only come here hoping to aid the rebellion, yet the king refused to speak with him or any of us about the situation in Bellovi. He had become very adept at turning the conversation to marital matters.

We saw less and less of Jenna during training. I wondered where she went off to until one day, she walked into our shared room covered in paint splatters. She possessed such a happy glow that I debated telling her to just stick to her art and forget about the war entirely.

Oken got along with everyone, like always. Lilah's persistent attention earned him invites to Florian gatherings and sometimes he even attended, going alone without a care about his safety among the nobles and elites. Now when we walked the halls, Florians our age nodded and waved to Oken as we passed. He always returned the greeting, calling them by name and gifting them with his smile.

He had even become a favorite among the Trish children. He constantly threw himself around the padded room as they pretended to fight, making the kids look like they had Audrey's superhuman strength. No one made those kids laugh like Oken could. He joined the circle gathered around my mother when she told Trish stories and ended up surrounded with kids giggling and hanging off him, making my mother wait for them to quiet down. His less-than-apologetic shrug softened her features every time.

She often called me over to sing for them. I obliged as it was the only way to get the kids to look at me with something other than fear. Oken's eyes never left my face, even with kids climbing his shoulders trying to get his attention.

I did my very best to ignore all these things. *Always focus.*

I failed miserably.

In the background of all this, during the stillness of the night, the trees' incoherent whispers grew louder. I didn't tell anyone about their persistent presence and knew it was only a matter of time before I'd be able to understand their angry words.

THE MORNING before the day of the ball, Prince Liam made an appearance at training. He stuck with Brea and Lilah, the three of them making an unusual amount of noise as he cracked jokes. They laughed almost as often as the Bellovians.

He approached me as we were winding down for the day.

"I don't think we've officially met," he said, thrusting out a hand. His skin was soft and sweaty.

When I didn't respond, he gave me a cocky grin unlike anything I had seen on Hinze's face. "This is pretty fun," he said, gesturing to the groups stretching.

I resisted the urge to roll my eyes and nodded. Clearly, the young prince had no experience with situations where this kind of training was the difference between life and death. *Pretty fun* wasn't what I was aiming for.

"And this is your Trish army you'll be using to reclaim your homeland when the queen refuses my father?" he asked, sliding me another look.

I wanted to smack the smile off his face. "Who knows." My tone must have said more than I intended because the smile faltered on his lips.

"We all want to see the Bellovians out of Traesha, *resa.*"

"For different reasons, *prince.*"

"You really trust them?" He jerked his chin toward Levi and Audrey. Levi was crippling her strength with his abilities, making it a fair fight. When he landed another blow, Audrey swore loud enough that a Trish mother covered her son's ears and glared in her direction. I smothered a grin.

"More than I trust you," I said.

I left him, going to Rennie and Jenna's area. The two of them quickly joined together to attempt to take me down—Rennie quite hilariously as she ran at me with her arms spread wide, letting out war whoops. That girl had energy to burn now that she was getting regular meals. I didn't bother to look back at the prince as I let her hike me up on her shoulders and throw me in Jenna's direction, forgetting as she did that I was lighter than her usual partners and tossing me quite hard. Jenna and I both went down in a fit of laughter and tangle of limbs. Oken was laughing so hard that he grabbed the wall to keep himself upright. Not that I looked to him first.

There was only one person in the palace I hadn't seen often. I asked Savha about Hinze that night when we met for extra help with her training. In the evenings, we ran outside on the vast palace grounds or sparred next to the pond when she asked for extra practice.

"I haven't seen him very much either," she admitted. "It's... hard. We both remind each other too much of Fisher."

I nodded, pain flaring in my chest. Savha looked better, but she didn't sleep enough, and I knew half her motivation to gain Trish speed was born from the need to distract herself. She was improving steadily and getting faster every day. I learned she was turning seventeen in a month and was quick to assure her if she had Trish speed, it may still take some time to kick in. I hadn't been able to skip until I was seventeen.

We went back up to our quarters when we finished.

After bathing, I found Savha and Natasha giggling on the bed, dresses thrown all around them. I raised my eyebrows and fought the urge to comment on how good it was to see Savha's smile. I made room for myself, letting an obnoxiously orange gown fall to the floor. Natasha crinkled her nose at it.

"I thought you weren't coming tomorrow," I said to Savha.

The now-familiar hollow look crept into her eyes, and I regretted my words instantly.

"Natasha asked me to come with her and run interference between her and Hinze. Also, you never told me you talked to him, and he all but confessed his love for you."

I had been very careful not to. That drama seemed insignificant compared to her hurts. I tried to glare at Natasha, never imagining the queen was such a gossip. Her exaggeratedly innocent expression as she suddenly grew busy looking at the dresses made it difficult to stay annoyed.

"Emotions were just running high." I pointed at Natasha. "Thinking he might be stuck with this one his whole life probably made him desperate for someone else's attention."

A pillow flew at my head from Natasha's direction. The laughter started all over again, and I was relieved to see Savha's eyes light with amusement.

"Gods, imagine if my first dance is with the man who ends up being my husband," Natasha said, shaking her head.

"You said your grandfather taught you to dance," I said.

"Okay, my first dance that *isn't* with my grandfather." Natasha rolled her eyes. She pulled a pink dress onto her lap and began flattening it, petting the soft fabric.

"Imagine being engaged at seventeen!" I laughed.

Natasha's hands stilled. "We're eighteen."

I blinked at her, and Natasha continued, her voice growing gentle. "We were born six months before the invasion, Finley."

It took me a second to realize my mouth had dropped open. I stood quickly, thinking about finding my mother right then and there to demand the truth. But it had to be true. I hadn't even stopped to think about it. I knew Natasha was born before the attack, and I had to have been born at the same time to be *resa*. I had just never put it together. I sat down with a huff, trying to push down the anger that still burned toward my mother when I thought of her lies.

"Damn. I guess you *really* don't have to worry about your Trish speed not having developed yet, Savha."

CHAPTER 15

" Is that one for me?" I asked Alessa and Masen.

They lifted their bleary eyes from the green ball gown they'd been sewing for Natasha all night, faces etched in identical horror. I didn't feel too bad for them; they had been the ones to decide none of the Florian dresses were adequate even when Natasha protested. I fought a smile.

"N-no. We didn't think—"

"This is for the queen—"

"But we could alter one of the other—"

I took pity on them and interrupted their stammering with a laugh. "I'm joking. I have an outfit."

Their shoulders slumped with relief. I had already decided to wear the Trish two-piece from the feast again.

"Be nice, Fin," Natasha said, coming out of our room, fighting a smile of her own at the sisters' expense. While she might have insisted a brand-new dress wasn't neces- sary, I could feel how much she loved it as we walked past the sisters to go to training. They shared a smile when they saw the way her eyes lingered on the fabric between them.

In the basement, Natasha was distracted and unmotivated. After getting neatly beaten by Rennie a fifth time, she walked across the room to Londe and Brea.

"Please work on my dancing with me," she begged Londe.

I didn't know why she bothered; her steps were perfect, thanks to her grandfather's lessons. Londe moved with surprising ease and offered only a couple of suggestions. Even so, she stuck close to the Florians the entire training session to practice her steps and ask how balls progressed. Misha Dossen was at her side and offering his own words of advice.

"Oh, I love that dance, Londe!" Lilah called off to my right. She stood by Oken's side and turned to him. "Do you know it? I could teach you at the ball."

"Doesn't look too difficult," Oken replied.

I turned away to hide my smile.

After barely touching her lunch, Natasha insisted we hurry upstairs to get ready. We found a rack of lavish clothing waiting for us in the common room of our chambers. On it hung suits tailored to fit Oken and Levi's tall Bellovian frames and long dresses for Rennie, Jenna, and Audrey. The last dress on the rack had my name on it. I fingered the cool material. It shimmered a silver so rich it looked blue in the folds that caught shadow.

"I picked that one out for you," my mother said from behind me. "The color suits you."

I couldn't remember wearing any clothing that color in Bellovi, but I took the dress. It was heavier than I expected, the weight reassuring.

"Natasha told me I'm older than seventeen," I said, looking up from the dress to confront my mother.

She sighed. "There were lies I had to tell you to keep you safe and happy for as long as possible, Finley. You were always smaller than the Bellovian children. It helped in those early years to say you were younger. I won't pretend I did everything perfectly, but I did my best. I hope one day you can forgive me." She smiled gently. "And get better at math."

I resisted the urge to smile back at her. I was so tired of holding my anger. It was much easier to pretend our relationship was how it had always been. But each time I tried, I thought of my father's face. The bloodstain on the floor of our home. My mother reached up and pushed back some of my hair.

"It looks good short," she said. "And I'm glad you stopped wearing the hat." Her eyes went to the silver creeping out through the black.

"Thanks. And thanks for the dress." I turned and went to change, leaving my mother with her hand still in the air.

Masen insisted I let her paint my face. She pulled out products I had never seen before. Seeing the bright colors of the pallets, I begged her not to go too crazy. In the end, I had shimmering shades of silver to match my dress on my eyelids, smoking out to a dark gray. She surrounded my eyes with a thin line of black. My cheeks had a dusting of pink and another shimmer right on my cheekbones that caught the light when I turned my head. She pulled up the top half of my hair, braiding it into a little knot before putting a gentle curl in the rest. Natasha clapped when she saw me, her face painted with just enough color, her hair pulled up on top of her head, and the small tiara in place.

She was stunning.

We were ready last and joined the rest of our friends on

the lower level in the Trish grand hall. The wine was flowing, and Oken came over with two glasses. When Natasha refused, saying she wanted to keep a clear head, Oken handed me mine and clinked my glass with the one in his other hand.

"Save me a dance tonight?" he asked.

I raised an eyebrow. "Can you even dance?"

"I'm a quick learner." He winked.

"We'll see about that." I grinned when Oken drank to that. I took a drink to hide it, watching him over the rim and suddenly feeling much happier that the king had decided to throw this ball.

We drank and mingled. Our Florian friends joined, and Trish filled the hall as they arrived from the city. It was the most Trish I had seen at once. Most wore pastels and summery fashions, and they were a sight I could get used to. Their silver hair and natural grace gave the room a serene, otherworldly quality. For a moment, I let myself imagine Traesha as it was before the invasion: a country of people all doing what they could to make their world more beautiful. They were peaceful and smiling and loved any excuse to dance.

It was hard for me to believe a place like that had existed.

Oken stayed near my side even when Lilah and Brea showed up in gorgeous, intricate dresses that left me wondering if they would even be able to dance. Lilah shot him a bright smile and Oken waved before turning back to me. I said the first thing that popped into my brain, desperate to hold his attention.

"It turns out I'm not actually seventeen. My mom lied about that too."

Natasha smirked and moved away to mingle with more

of the Trish joining us. Rennie came up to my side. She wore the navy dress my mother had found for her. It brought out the dark blue in her eyes so much that they looked indigo.

"How old are you then?" Rennie asked, a smile playing on her lips. I caught Oken's worried expression and realized why she was fighting laughter.

I widened my eyes and went with it. "I'll be fifteen next week!"

Oken snorted through the drink of wine he had just taken, red coming out of his nose. He sputtered and reached for a napkin. Rennie and I burst into laughter watching him dry his face, his eyes watering profusely. "You're joking," he realized. His features relaxed and he joined in the laughter.

"Yes. I'm eighteen. Could I pass for a fourteen-year-old?" I looked down at the silk of my dress hugging my curves. Rennie smirked.

"Definitely not," Oken said, his voice deep and smooth as honey. I blushed and looked away. I was glad to see Rennie enjoying our flirting and felt ridiculous for the jealous flares I used to experience watching the two of them.

"What's so funny over here?" Levi asked, stopping at Rennie's side.

"This one's going to be the death of me." Oken pointed at me accusingly.

"We all accepted that the moment we followed her over the Front," Rennie said with a shrug.

A weight dropped in my stomach, stealing my breath. Rennie felt the change in the air when I stilled. Oken stepped closer to me, shooting her a look.

"I mean that only in the best way, princess," she said hastily.

"Princess?" Lilah and one of her friends I had yet to

meet had come up behind Oken. The friend was staring at me with wide eyes. "Are you royalty in Bellovi?" the girl asked.

I didn't know if it was the wine, the excitement of the night, or the sudden release of the tension from Rennie's words, but we all lost it looking at her clueless expression. When Levi could pull in enough air, he explained there wasn't any royalty in Bellovi, only stuck-up rich girls, and we broke into laughter again. Lilah's friend looked even more confused, and Lilah's cheeks turned pink. Both girls sparkled with diamonds and gold, their wealth evident even from the healthy glow of their skin. They turned to get more wine when it became apparent how out of place they were. I felt slightly bad excluding them and was glad Oken moved away to ease the tension, pouring out the drinks for them and glancing back at me over his shoulder.

His smile was gentle and soft, utterly different than the grin he usually had plastered on his face. My breath caught.

Eventually, Natasha returned to our group and took my hand. "Will you walk in with me?"

It was time. Everyone prepared to leave, checking outfits one last time, chugging the contents of their drinks. I caught Oken fixing his curls out of the corner of my eye. The Trish lined themselves up in pairs to follow behind their queen.

"I'd love to," I said, taking Natasha's gloved hand. The white silk was soft to the touch. Her fingers seemed so small, encased in the expensive fabric.

"Don't forget our dance!" Oken called behind us.

Hoots of laughter from the Bellovains. I blushed. Natasha laughed. The bond was lighter than it had been all day.

"Maybe you and Oken should lead the dancing while I hide from Hinze," she muttered under her breath.

"Maybe someone should cut them off already," I replied, glancing back at the empty wine glasses scattered where I had been standing with the Bellovians.

I caught Lilah's eye and saw her glance between Oken and me. She didn't look mad, but I couldn't read her expression. It made my shoulders edge upward. As harsh as Lilah could be, I did value our friendship. Not to mention how much she had done for the Bellovians by extending invitations and introducing them to the younger members of the Florian court. Because of her, I rarely worried about my friends walking the palace halls.

When we reached the front of the procession, Natasha donned a smile and straightened her back, every ounce of her a queen.

The ballroom was already bustling when we arrived. We waited for the man standing at the door to announce us. His voice boomed through the hall, and I realized what the housekeeper in Honna's abilities could be at full volume.

The king and his children had not arrived yet, so I sipped another glass of wine while we waited. Natasha gave in and grabbed one for herself. I couldn't blame her. At this point, her stomach was a painful knot of dread. I told myself I was only experiencing Natasha's emotions each time my stomach fluttered thinking about the dance Oken wanted me to save for him. More titled Florians trickled in, most of them members of the elite. In the far corner, a small orchestra played. A Trish girl named Sadie played along on the piano next to them. I thought about Nico with a pang and pulled my gaze away.

The Florians were dressed in swirling skirts and bright colors. The Bellovians with us nearly fit in with the clothing my mother had found them. Only when the Florians looked close enough to notice their paler skin, tall and muscular builds, dark eyes, and black hair did they eye my friends suspiciously. Natasha got pulled into conversation with an older Trish man and stepped away. I stayed close to my Bellovian friends, protective instincts torn between her and them as I stood on high alert.

"If looks could kill," Rennie muttered out the side of her mouth.

Oken was doing fine. His new Florian friends found him and pulled him away to meet families or other young nobles. He was one of the tallest people in the crowd, making it easy to watch his progress around the room. Everywhere he went, eyes followed him.

Jenna and Levi stood with Rennie and me. With Levi near, our group received most of the glares. Mesa had Audrey with her. They were already across the room, talking to a family of people who shared Mesa's small frame and muted brown coloring. Mesa reached and casually adjusted one of Audrey's braids.

"They all look so..." Jenna began, watching a group of Florians laugh as they walked by.

"Healthy?" Rennie tried.

"Blinding?" Levi snorted and nodded at a couple standing a few feet away. They wore matching outfits in a startling orange striped with white.

"Unbothered?" I tried.

"I was going to say beautiful, but I think you guys were more accurate. I can't believe they just live like this. Were the events in Vichi ever this lavish?" Jenna asked me.

"No, not at all. We would have a good meal, but just war talk to go with it. The Conquering Ceremony in Traesha was the closest I've seen to this. No one danced, though."

"Sounds about right," Levi said. His eyes dimmed in the light of the Florian chandeliers and yet again, I wondered if he regretted leaving his rebellion to follow Natasha and me here. What a waste of time this must be to him.

A pair of Florians walked by, bumping into Jenna while communicating with the messengers' distant eyes. Levi shot a look at them and they started, eyes focusing abruptly. They stared at each other in confusion before hurrying on, looking back over their shoulders at us fearfully. Levi laughed a bit and grabbed Rennie and Jenna's arms. "Let's find some more wine," he said.

"You coming, Finley?" Rennie asked. I spotted Londe and Brea at the drink table and shook my head. They would be fine. I couldn't get too drunk or stray too far from Natasha when she was this tense. At the moment, she was distracted and playing with a Trish child who had come up to her. His silver hair bounced in a sphere of tight curls around his head and his front tooth was missing. His father stood nearby, looking beyond proud to see his son had captured the queen's attention.

"She's just like her mother," my mother said, stopping at my side. "So good with the people. A kind heart."

"She's nervous."

My mother nodded. "She cares. We can start worrying about the fate of Traesha when she doesn't."

"Do you think she should marry Hinze?"

"I don't know." I could see my mother's thoughts turning. She never spoke without careful consideration and would never decide her stance on an issue of this magnitude after so little time. "I want to get to know both of them better and see if they could make one another happy. An unhappy couple ruling a country is toxic. Yet not all relationships between strangers of different lands are doomed. Teo taught me that." Her smile shook.

"I hadn't thought about that. I tried to talk to Hinze about it." It was so easy to remember a time when I told my mother everything. I missed her insight.

"How did that go?"

"He tried to kiss me," I said, my cheeks growing warm just remembering.

My mother gave me a sympathetic smile and patted my cheek. "Well, at least we know he has good taste."

The same older Trish man who had pulled Natasha away earlier approached us now.

"Is this one yours, Elise?" he asked. His eyes were a light gray that nearly matched his silver hair. They twinkled when he smiled at me. "She has your hair."

My mother laughed, touching her dyed strands. "Yes, this is my Finley. Fin, this is Asa Gamsa. He was a *magsai* advisor to Natasha's grandmother and her mother. He retired from the position a few years before the invasion."

"It's a pleasure," I said. And it was. I loved being surrounded by Trish, but meeting and building a community of *magsai* was something special. "Are you going to step in and help advise Natasha?"

"Oh no, my days in politics have been over for years and years. I'm too out of touch at this point. I focus on the arts these days. That's my granddaughter over there." He waved a hand in the direction of Sadie at the piano. "When the castle was taken, all I knew was that I had to get my family to safety. The Bellovians attacked the throne room so quickly..." he trailed off as though he wasn't sure why he began speaking in the first place.

"Asa also taught me to play the piano," my mother told me, covering for his sudden quiet.

Asa smiled brightly. "You were one of my best pupils. Oh, look, here comes Miss Molvish and my grandson."

Savha came up with the boy who always stood near me in Sam's lessons with a dry joke on hand. He shared his grandfather's light gray eyes and kept a shadow of dark gray hair growing on his face. His facial hair was the first I had seen on a Trish man. It was dark and less shiny than the silver hair on our heads and sparser than the beards I had seen in Bellovi and Floria. Most Trish had very little body hair to speak of, including me. The scruff suited him well.

"Wesley," he said, catching me grasping for his name.

I smiled and stuck out a hand. He accepted the Bellovian gesture after a slight hesitation and shook it. "Finley."

"Oh, we all know your name," he said with a laugh.

"How do you like the ball so far?" Savha asked.

I shrugged and opened my mouth to answer when the man at the door banged his staff loudly on the wooden floor. The room swept into a respectful hush.

"May I present, Princess Fay." Hinze's little sister entered wearing a rose-gold ballgown; her hair swept up high in a style similar to Natasha's and a broad smile on her face. She dipped her head at the room, the lights catching on the slim band of diamonds on top of her head. She stood aside and took Liam's offered arm after he was announced. His grin and wave were far too enthusiastic to be considered dignified. Hinze came next and stood aside to offer his arm to Chelsa as she was called forth.

"Prince Maverick the Second and his betrothed, Lady Tiana Anchez."

Mav's fiancé smiled, chin tipped up and hand secure in Mav's elbow. They made a formidable pair. I could nearly feel the heat and tremble of their power combined. Tiana had dark brown eyes that swept the room with a lofty look that ensured no one forgot who the next queen of Floria would be. Mav looked dashing and neatly bored at her side.

The king was announced last and swept past his coupled children to lead them to the throne and cushioned chairs at the front of the room. Natasha's eyes followed Hinze and Chelsa intently, emotion swirling on her end of the bond. Once the king stood before his throne, he brought up his arms and shouted at the audience. "And now for the celebration! My son, Prince Hinze, has the honor of leading us in the first dance with Queen Natasha of Traesha! Their dance symbolizes the beauty of our countries and the peace of our union!"

The room erupted into cheers and Hinze walked over to bow to Natasha. She nodded back and I had to admire her once again for never conceding to bow to any other person. She held out a hand, and Hinze took it. The dance floor cleared as they walked to its center. When the music struck, Hinze gently pulled Natasha closer, his free hand coming to rest on her waist. I felt the adrenaline in her blood as if it was my own. The whole room watched with bated breath as they stepped gracefully into the dance.

I had to admit they made a beautiful pair.

The music was the only sound; everyone stood enraptured watching them. I noticed Hinze's lips moving. The tension between Natasha's shoulders slowly eased, the knot in her gut loosening. I should have thought to assure Natasha that Hinze would be kind. That he would try to make this easier on her. She let out a surprised laugh she quickly silenced with a blush and Hinze grinned. As the song ended, Natasha was still smiling. Hinze looked more relaxed than I had seen him in days. He bowed to her again when the final cords drifted off and she gave him another nod. He took her hand and led her back to my side, giving me a small smile that I was more than happy to return. Natasha's relief and the wine made my head light.

When the next song began, Mav and his fiancé led it, quickly joined by Liam and Fay. Soon the dance floor was spinning with bodies. Fisher's father came over to ask Savha to dance, making her eyes sparkle with unshed tears when she took his hand. I could only imagine how much she wished it was Fisher leading her onto the floor. Natasha was swept away by Asa and Wesley surprised me by offering his arm. Eager to avoid an uncomfortable moment alone with Hinze and spotting Lilah pulling Oken to the floor, I accepted.

"Let's see if you dance as well as you fight. We have to make sure growing up in Bellovi didn't drain all the Trish out of you," Wesley said.

I prickled at his words. "My mother taught my brother and me." I thought about the nights with her at the piano, Nico spinning me around the room with so much grace and perfect rhythm that it had always left me breathless. "He's an incredible dancer. Better than anyone I see here."

Wesley stopped us at a spot on the floor he felt was suitable. "You have a Trish brother in Vichi?" he asked, his steel-gray brows lifting.

"No, I have a Bellovian brother in Vichi. Are we going to dance or not?"

I heard a snort to my left and looked to see Londe passing, an almost sad smile chasing the sound. Something began to dawn on me then, but Wesley nodded and pulled me close for the first steps, spinning me away before I could fully interpret Londe's expression. I followed with ease, even when I could tell we were tapping into our Trish speed and moving much faster than the people around us. He danced like the whole room was watching and I realized, belatedly, they were. My heart was pounding when the song ended, and even Wesley looked flushed despite his dark complexion. He opened his mouth to speak, but I cut in before he could.

"Thank you for the dance." I walked off the floor and away from all the eyes watching us. I had never felt more Trish than I had while dancing with Wesley but having all those Florians share in the moment took away the pleasure. I went to the drink table and picked up another glass of wine. Scanning the crowd, I saw Natasha had ended up near the king. She soothed my concern over the bond. She was deep in conversation with Chelsa, the king barely paying attention.

I was hyperaware of his presence when Hinze came to stand at my elbow. "That was something," he said, nodding to the dance floor I had just vacated.

"Thanks."

He played with his braid. I wondered if he realized how often he reached for it. "Listen. I am sorry. I didn't mean to react the way I did. This has all just been... so much. Watching you and Wesley reminded me of watching Savha and Fisher. They used to dance like that all the time." Something softened in my chest. Hinze cleared his throat. "I really do want to help Traesha. I love your culture and how gentle you all are with each other. I just don't know how to go about it."

He stared at me too intently. What was he searching for

in my face? A solution to his and Natasha's predicament? Returned interest? Forgiveness? I broke eye contact and saw Oken over his shoulder. He stood across the room, but now he was with Mesa and Audrey rather than Lilah and her friends. He discreetly put a hand on his chest, tapping twice with a questioning look in his eyes—the Bellovian hand signal used to ask if someone needed assistance.

I deliberately grabbed my left wrist and drummed my fingers on the skin. With a grin, Oken began making his way through the crowd toward me.

"I don't know either, Hinze," I said, looking back into his polished-looking green-brown eyes. "I know your father put the two of you in a hard spot, but maybe you should ask Natasha what she wants from you and Floria bef—"

"Finley!" Rennie came up and grabbed my arm. "You must come help us. We're just embarrassing ourselves out here." She waved a hand in Levi, Jenna, and Oken's direction. Hinze gave me a stiff smile and walked away. I experienced a swoop of guilt as Rennie led me to Oken.

The Florians were giving my circle of friends space, avoiding them as though one of them might grow suddenly violent if bumped.

"Beautifully executed rescue, Jaspers," Oken said in a near-perfect imitation of Silken's brisk tone. It made the hair on my neck rise. Rennie gave Oken a sloppy salute. I glanced to the piano when Wesley's sister slid into an upbeat Trish melody. I smiled at my friends and it only grew broader when I felt Natasha's approach.

"Do you know the steps?" I asked when she stopped at my side. She glanced around as if making sure no one important was nearby to witness what was about to happen but smiled when she nodded. I took her hands and we faced each other.

"Watch closely," I told the Bellovians, my voice taking on the quality it gained when I led training sessions. "We do the steps twice through, each person taking a turn to lead and then we switch partners. The taller dancer leads the first round."

Laugher rose where the Trish gathered. They followed the steps and changed partners at top speed a short distance away. Natasha and I began. We crossed ankles, spun under each other's arms, leaned and jumped and spun together as the dance called for, with me leading first and Natasha following. After two rounds, we spun apart. We grabbed the two nearest people, Natasha with Jenna, while I caught Rennie's hands. Rennie was clumsy but laughed while she struggled with the steps in the long dress she wasn't used to. We barely muddled through our time together before I spun away to Levi, and Natasha joined hands with Mesa, who already knew the basics of the dance. Levi did an adequate job, having watched two rounds by this point. When we separated, he and Jenna linked up, Mesa and Audrey joined hands with uncharacteristically sweet smiles, and Natasha took a turn teaching Rennie. My hands were free for Oken's. I laughed so hard I nearly missed a step when he surprised me by smoothly following the steps, smiling smugly from ear to ear with his curls bouncing in time. I didn't want to spin away after leading my round but was pleased to find Savha had joined us and went through the steps with her. The song ended with loud whooping from our corner of the room and applause from the Trish . Sadie beamed from her piano bench.

The orchestra took a break, and Sadie began playing one of my favorite songs, the love story of the Florian igniter and the Trish queen who didn't give him a chance.

"I think it's time for our dance," Oken said, coming up behind me. He placed a hand on the small of my back. My heart stuttered.

"No, that was it just now. I only promised one," I teased and turned to look at him, leaning into his touch. His fingers curled into my waist, his golden-brown eyes crinkling at the edges with his smile.

I forgot how to breathe.

Shaking his head and tutting, he guided me onto the dance floor. I glanced back to see Wesley had made another appearance, this time leading Natasha to the floor with an expression of near awe. They were striking together, all light silver and willowy.

Oken watched the other dancers until we found a spot, then pulled me as close as they stood and followed their slow steps.

"I'm impressed. I didn't think you had much experience dancing," I said.

Oken shrugged. "I think training so long helped. It's like learning a new move, just set to music."

We swayed for a time together and I closed my eyes. Oken's scent was like the air back home when it snowed. Crisp and clean. I lost myself in the song, humming along and enjoying Oken's proximity.

"This is the song you hummed in the forest."

I opened my eyes to see him watching me intently. "Yes." Our first mission felt like years ago.

"I should have known you wouldn't have learned anything like this in Bellovi. Are there words?"

"Yes."

"Sing them for me." Oken spun me once and pulled me back even closer than before. I obliged, singing just loudly enough for him to hear. His amber eyes danced under the light of the chandeliers.

The song ended, and Oken swept into a bow, looking up at me from under his lashes.

My heart stopped at his next words.

"Let's get out of here, princess."

CHAPTER 16

I told Oken to meet me in the hall and quickly crossed to where Natasha stood with Mesa's family, Chelsa, and Sam. Chelsa was answering Natasha's latest question with a wary expression, glancing over her shoulder. Natasha shook her head and opened her mouth to respond, only to pause when she became aware of my proximity and the butterflies in my stomach. She turned to me with a knowing smile.

I spoke in a low voice. "Oken and I might go get some fresh air. Will you be okay here without me?"

Natasha's grin only grew more mischievous. "I'll be just fine."

I eyed Chelsa. She looked harmless now, but she tried to have me imprisoned in Honna not too long ago. I spoke too quietly for her to hear. "Have the king or Hinze tried to talk to you or done anything?"

"Not yet. The king seems content to sit with Prince Mav and his fiancé. Hinze disappeared a little bit ago. I'm trying to figure out the princess's thoughts, but she's not very forthcoming."

I nodded. Chelsa wouldn't try anything with Sam so close. "Just be careful. You sure you're fine alone?"

"I'm fine, Fin. This hasn't been nearly as bad as I thought it would be." Pride had become a pleasant glow on her features. She was handling the finery, dancing, and politics like the queen she was born to be. All self-doubt was gone for the moment.

"If you need anything, let me know." I began to back away.

"And how will she let you know?" Sam asked.

I hadn't expected him to overhear us. My first reaction was a childish fear he would tell my mother I was sneaking around with a boy. I pushed the worry away, reminding myself I wasn't happy with her anyway.

"Through the bond, of course," Natasha said. "Have fun!"

She pushed me toward the ballroom doors and winked. She returned to her conversation with the princess and Florian spies without missing a beat.

Oken stood down the hall. He'd taken off the dark blue jacket that had come with the suit and stood holding it in a white long-sleeve shirt and black pants. I let myself experience a silly rush. A shock as if the girl I had been in Vichi was coming back to life. *Oken Sars* was waiting for me. He smiled at the sight of me. He knew who I was. He liked who I was. He was here for *me*.

I was happily ridiculous. In my excitement, I accidentally skipped to his side.

"You sure you want to miss out on the party?" I asked when I stopped next to him, pushing my hair back when it flew forward.

"I'm sure." His smile grew.

I didn't know why I kept pressing. "Won't you be missed? I'm sure Lilah's looking for you already."

"What's this? Finley Lar— wait, what's your last name again?"

I laughed, and the sound bounced around the hall around us. Oken pushed off the wall and began walking next to me. "Cassiwess."

"Finley Cassiwess, *resa magsai* to the queen, former Bellovian commander, and leader of future Trish armies, is jealous?" He wiggled his eyebrows at me, and I pushed him away. I laughed again when he exaggerated the force of the blow, stumbling into the wall next to him. He bounced back to my side with a grin, and I reached for his hand. The motion felt as familiar as breathing.

He squeezed my fingers. "But no. Lilah's not looking for me. We talked."

I raised my eyebrows. "Talked?"

"Yeah. And everything is fine. She likes me, mostly the idea of me, but I've always been clear and she understands. She's a flirt. I can admit I am also a flirt. It's just a fun distraction from all the terrible stuff around us. We're friends and she's not pining for me. She very stiffly claimed to be happy for us, but I think that was for show."

I sighed with relief and stepped closer to Oken's side, pulling his hand over my head so his arm rested across my shoulders. I kept hold of his hand, keeping myself securely against him.

He was so good. A pang of guilt in my chest told me I should have communicated better with Hinze like Oken did with Lilah. It had been easier to pretend Hinze wasn't interested in me and now I had hurt him. I swallowed the bitter lesson. I should apologize. The next time Oken and I danced, I didn't want to cause someone else pain.

Yet I still couldn't entirely forget Hinze's lack of faith and how much it stung.

We went up the stairs and to the main level of Trish quarters. Oken kept up a commentary about the ball, making me laugh and asking me questions about how I learned to dance. I heard his nerves in his constant chatter, and it warmed me to my core. I tightened my grip on his fingers. Soon we would cut off each other's circulation.

We went through the main Trish Hall and out to the balcony where he had comforted me after seeing my mother here for the first time. I let go of Oken's hand and stepped out from under his arm. I walked up to the balustrade. Placing my hands on the cold stone, I stared out at the twinkling city. Half the windows held lights lit with electricity, the other with candle flames. Some were lit with the ability of the Florian inside, the windows glowing a soft blue.

Oken settled next to me, leaning to rest his elbows on the railing and bringing our eyes closer to the same level. He caught a strand of my curled hair the wind had blown out of place. He twirled it around his finger, briefly brushing the sensitive skin on the curve of my neck.

"I like it short. It suits you much better than the braid."

My breath came out shaky. I turned to face him, ignoring how it felt when his hand lingered in my hair just a beat before he lowered it to the railing again.

"What are we doing, Oken?"

He battled internally for a moment, likely fighting the urge to say something stupid like *standing on a balcony*. "I like you a lot. Why do we have to be doing anything with that right now besides enjoying ourselves?"

"Because it's distracting. I have to put Natasha and my people first. There's a war out there. People are dying and starving and counting on Traesha to make a difference. And Traesha is counting on me to fight. I just— I have to focus." *Always focus.* The words pulled heavy in my chest.

Oken thought for a time, his eyes roving over the city lights. I couldn't read his expression. I wished he would touch me again. "I put my people first, too, Finley. And that includes you. I may not know you well, but I know you feel the same way. You may be a shut book, but I've learned something pretty important in our time here."

"What's that?"

He turned to look at me again. "Natasha has an incredibly expressive face." Oken gave me a cheeky grin, and I blushed. "She gives you this look every time you look at me. It's the same look Rennie gives Levi when they see Audrey with Mesa. My point is I know you enjoy being with me. I know you feel something when I'm near, something strong enough for Natasha to feel over your bond. I wasn't sure for a long time, but I am now. I think I knew when you said goodbye to me when Dani died, but I still couldn't read your face. I just remembered how you touched my cheek and how much I wanted to run after you and ask what you had said."

I didn't know how to respond to that. Oken rubbed a hand through his hair, gathering his thoughts before he pressed on. "We all followed you here, so we're your people too. The Trish are your priority, fine. Understandable. Completely. But I don't want anything to do with the commanders. I want to help you and the Trish because what the Bellovians have done to your country is wrong. What my dad helped do was murder and slavery and I want to do my part to put it right... If that doesn't make me your people, I don't know where I fit in all this. I don't know why I'm here if you don't want me by your side, helping you fight. But either way, I have your back, Finley. And I do think you have mine. That trust isn't a bad thing. Letting people in, it's not a bad thing. It makes us stronger. It *focuses* our efforts. And this is war. I've seen enough of it to know we won't get through the hard parts without some good. And this is good."

He paused, lifting one of my hands and speaking into my knuckles, lips gently brushing my skin. "I promise I won't ever get in your way, but this thing between us is as easy to give in to as breathing. How much can it hurt?"

He said exactly what I had thought in the hall. It was so easy. Too easy to be around him. "What if I'm with you and something happens to Natasha because I'm not with her?"

"Then we stay close to Natasha just like we have been."

"What if... what if something happens to you?"

Savha's hollow eyes. My mother's broken smile. I already felt so shattered.

"Then you'd regret not spending every amazing moment in my company that you could have," Oken said, flashing a smile that was sad and perfect and hopeful. I realized he'd asked himself the same thing and knew his answer. Even if something happened to me, he wanted these moments.

My voice came out in a whisper. "I've already lost so much... You think this could be so simple?"

"If we make it. But we won't know unless we try. I'd rather regret exploring this than regret denying it."

"And what exactly is this?" I needed him to say it. To spell out exactly how he felt.

Oken reached up again, tucking my hair behind my ear and away from my face. He kept his hand there, fingers curled in the hair warm from my neck. For being from a culture unfamiliar with touch, Oken was getting too good at this. He was giving me the look that was only mine. My world had turned so ugly and brutal. The brilliance of his lasting smile hadn't faltered. I needed it like I needed the reminder of sunshine, the sound of Natasha's laugh, and the glances my mother cast my way to ensure I was doing okay.

It terrified me how much I needed it. It steadied me each time. He really did make everything easier.

"It's precisely what you think it is, Finley."

My heart fluttered sporadically.

He bent closer.

I leaned into him.

I was about to have my first kiss.

We froze. The doors to the Trish Hall shut with a decisive snap, and footsteps echoed from inside. Just like that, our moment broke.

I groaned and fought the urge to pull him closer despite the intruders. Oken seemed to read the struggle in my eyes. He huffed a quiet, shaky laugh and took his hand out of my hair before he straightened. At that moment, I knew hatred for the Trish that interrupted us.

I turned back to the balcony doors and peered inside. Of course, it was my mother and Sam. I rolled my eyes. The two of them sat down before the fire burning in the corner. My mother reached toward the flames, seeking their warmth. Their backs were to us, so I opened the doors just a bit more to hear what they were saying. I couldn't resist the chance to eavesdrop. My mother had left me with too many unanswered questions.

"—makes me worry, Elise," Sam was saying.

"But why? Why is this so concerning for you? The link forms between every queen and their *resa*."

"With Shay, I could feel her, yes. I had an idea where she

was and if she was ever frightened or anxious, I had a sense of it and it drew me to her. When she broke her arm when we were kids, I felt it enough to cry from pain, and people were amazed I had such a strong connection. We were still so young, and our abilities had not developed. But even with the strength of our bond, I didn't feel her every emotion." Sam leaned in closer. "Sometimes, I think Finley and Natasha can read each other's minds. Finley can tell if Natasha so much as *pinches* herself. Natasha can summon Finley even if she isn't in trouble just because Finley can feel when Natasha *wants* her nearby. When Natasha is angry, I can see it burning in Finley's eyes. A bond this strong... it's unheard of, Elise."

My insides chilled and I wrapped my arms around my middle. Oken couldn't understand the Trish conversation or probably even hear their low voices, but he stayed close and quiet. He carefully draped his jacket over me. I gave in and leaned into his warmth.

"But why is that so bad?" my mother asked.

"I don't know if it is. I don't know what it means, and *that* is what scares me. We were taught everything about the *magsai* history and have never heard of anything like this. I worry about their influence on each other. I don't know if you've ever seen your daughter truly fight, Elise, but she does not shy from a challenge. If she keeps getting hurt or even gets herself killed, I fear what that would do to our queen. To the triangle and our country as a whole. And what if Natasha gets influenced by this reckless behavior and takes unnecessary risks? What if Natasha's rage fuels Finley? I have tried to be optimistic, but I cannot see their connection being anything but harmful. The queen and her *magsai* need to think and feel independently for Traesha to be balanced. Natasha should be of one mind, the mind for the royal line and alliances, and Finley of one mind for the people."

"But the land is in such danger. Maybe the gods gave them this bond for the strength to reclaim it?"

"Or maybe we've been cursed and that's why the Bellovians overthrew us to begin with."

"Don't say that, Sam!" my mother hissed.

But she didn't disagree with him and the protest didn't sound as heartfelt as I would have expected.

"The Florians are getting stronger despite their diluted bloodlines. The ones with abilities are truly terrifying. The Bellovians and Detonians are creating technologies we never dreamed of in Traesha. Our gifts from the gods barely compare to all of them, and only a handful of us are left with the ability to skip. Our land is just a small spec to the north in this war, and our queen could soon be reduced to the wife of a Florian prince. Even the *resa* bond is going haywire to the point where Finley nearly lost her mind when Natasha was upset by the proposal. I've seen Natasha mad as a child and she's been working her whole life learning to control it, but the look on Finley's face was one I've seen before on Natasha. And you know your daughter does not show her feelings easily. Natasha's rage was that strong."

"And she isn't used to the anger," my mother said. "She's always been even-tempered."

Sam nodded. "They share too much. One person alone cannot be expected to control all their emotions. Now put two peoples' emotions into one and make that person the queen or the leader of an army. How can they rule without being sound?"

I didn't know when I had taken Oken's hand, but I was squeezing it now.

Sam wasn't finished. "And I admire how Finley sympathizes with the Bellovians, I really do. But I grow fearful when I see the same love cross Natasha's face. It is the same as seeing Natasha's rage in Finley's eyes. It isn't the queen's emotion. Natasha cannot give in to Finley's desire to protect the ones who destroyed us. She cannot do that and keep her people happy and in her favor."

My mother sighed. "Finley adored Teo, the man I married in Bellovi. And her brother and now Oken and her team. She's so loyal to those she lets in. If Natasha is experiencing that loyalty, I agree she can't make decisions about their people without being influenced. Finley needs to focus on the queen."

Always focus. Yet I couldn't let go of Oken's hand. I was failing in this war, failing in my duties. And they had barely even begun.

"And there will be fighting. We would be foolish to think Traesha can get out of this war peacefully."

"They're still girls, Sam. They have their ideals, which may lead to a few mistakes, but wanting a peaceful solution is not bad."

"Until they refuse to fight."

"You already said it yourself; Finley doesn't back down from a fight," my mother said.

"And Natasha is stubborn. She will strive for a peaceful solution and fight for it in her own way. Which solution is better? Will Finley's desire for violence be amplified when our queen experiences it and makes the kill orders? Or will Natasha's desire for peace infect Finley and make her so hesitant we lose?"

My mother reached up and pinched the bridge of her nose. "I see what you mean, Sam. But what can we do about it?"

"We need to make them listen to us. We need to advise them until they are thinking like Trish. You must repair your relationship with Finley, and I must fix my relationship with Natasha."

"I don't know how... he told me to run... I was wrong to listen. Finley has every right—"

"Stop, Elise. We're alive right now because we abandoned the people we love. If we don't move forward—" Sam's voice caught. He cleared his throat and pressed on. "All that matters is finishing this war. After. After, we can grieve and decide what the war made us. We just have to get them through this."

My mother's following words raised the hair on my arms. "What about Sylas's prophecy?"

A heavy beat of silence. "What prophecy, Elise?"

I knew my mother well enough to hear her indecision in her pause. "You didn't hear? He told Shay. She didn't want to hear it, said it wouldn't come to pass for years. They fought so long about it. He was so worried."

"About what? What did the trees tell him? Why would Shay not tell me?" Sam had never sounded so young.

"The trees told him—I think it was about Natasha and Finley, but I don't want to put more pressure on them. Shay could be right."

Sam stood abruptly, body agitated even when his voice came out eerily calm. "What did the trees say?"

My mother took a deep breath before reciting,

"*When royal blood runs thick,*

Death will break brittle bonds.

When royal blood falls,

Traesha will invade the eastern lands.

When royalty burns bright—"

The doors to the Trish Hall opened, and laughter spilled

in, cutting off my mother and the eerie prophecy. The new voices apologized for interrupting and moved off to find a different room. I held my breath, waiting to hear the rest. Instead, my mother and Sam rose by unspoken agreement to find somewhere more private. I watched their retreating backs. The tension in their shoulders was mirrored in my own.

I moved away from the doors and sat back against the wall. Doubt came, a crushing flood. The one thing I hadn't truly questioned was the bond itself. I thought the strength of it was a sign of our power and that it would help our cause. Yet, according to Sam, it wasn't the source of strength. It was an omen. It too was corrupted and layered. My easy friendship and duties with Natasha had been comforting. I was trying to make the bond my priority. What did this mean?

Oken pulled me closer, resting his cheek on my head and waiting patiently for me to explain. Did I love the Bellovians too much? Was my loyalty and desire for peace going to doom Natasha?

Death will break brittle bonds.

Oken squeezed my hand when I only continued to grow tenser. It didn't feel like a mistake with him sitting by my side. I wanted to put Traesha first, but why should I regret this? I *couldn't* regret every push I made to help the innocent in Bellovi. It was the right thing to do.

Death will break brittle bonds.

I shook off the prophecy and replayed Sam's words over in my head. I was so much more powerful with Natasha nearby. I should probably have died from my stomach wound. I hadn't heard of a royal with her healing ability since the first family ended with Stessan Finley. They said the ability was lost when she and her daughter drowned at sea, and the Hollis family's next daughter was born with white hair and a *resa*, beginning the Hollis reign.

But could our heightened abilities really be wrong? So far, they had only helped us. But maybe our bond was a flame burning too bright.

I stood, and Oken followed, wordlessly taking his jacket when I handed it to him. He draped it over his arm, unbothered by the night air. It was nothing compared to the freezing temperatures in Bellovi. His hand was warm in mine. I looked at our linked fingers. *I should let go.*

"Princess," Oken spoke softly, and I looked up. "Only as long as it makes things easier," he reminded me. He lifted our hands and kissed the back of mine. I felt just a little bit better.

"I should talk to Natasha," I said. "Sam was saying things about our bond... he's worried." I didn't even know what to think about the prophecy. *Death will break brittle bonds.* I pushed the refrain from my thoughts. There was no use thinking about it when I hadn't heard all of it.

"Where is she?"

She had just gone into our room. Was it truly bad I knew that? "She's upstairs."

"Let's go. I told everyone I'd keep the first watch. I should probably be up there if she is."

I left Oken in the common area of our quarters and found Natasha already in a nightgown, her white hair falling freely. She patted the space next to her in bed. Her posture was rigid. She didn't want to hear what I had to say. She dreaded learning why I was suddenly so full of doubt.

"Start talking," she said.

I did. All of Sam's worries and my mother's agreement

came spilling out. The only part I couldn't voice was the prophecy.

"Our bond is that strong?" she whispered when I finished.

Brittle. "I guess so."

"And he thinks the power is too much." Fear twisted our stomachs. I tried to distance myself from the mingling sensation, to distinguish which fear was mine and which was hers, but they were too intertwined.

"Yes. He believes it could make us unstable."

How can they rule if they're not sound?

Goosebumps rose on Natasha's arms, and I took her hand. I wanted to know what she thought about Sam's views on her sympathizing with the Bellovians because of me but was afraid to ask. What if she only felt like I did because of the bond? What if she only told me exactly what I was thinking? Were they my thoughts or hers?

Would she care about the Bellovians at all if I wasn't here? Would it matter to her if the country starved? Would she have encouraged the king to go through with his initial plans for stamping out the rebellion?

"I need to sleep on this," Natasha finally said, pulling her hand from my grasp.

I nodded and left the bed to get ready for sleep. When I returned, she was on her side facing away, pretending to sleep. I knew through the bond that she wasn't. I was hyperaware of everything it told me. How much did it tell her? The sheets were cold when I slid between them.

Natasha's breathing didn't even out for a long time. Once it did, I fell asleep only to be thrown into the forest.

I stood in the dancing shadows of the trees. They waited for me to speak first, their whispers hushing when they found my frustration matched theirs. It seemed to excite them, but still, they waited.

What was the end of the prophecy? *I demanded.*

The trees shook. The triangle, singer. The triangle.

What about it?

It will break. It will break. It will break. It will BREAK. *The trees grew louder. Rustling intensely. A cacophony of hissing shouts. Overlapping and filling my ears, my head, my body.* IT WILL BREAK. IT WILL BREAK.

I shot upright in bed. Sweating and shaking, I threw back the covers and went to the shared living area. Oken was finishing his watch, but he made space for me on the couch. "I'll just wait to wake up Levi," he promised without needing me to explain.

I curled up next to him and breathed easier. I forced the trees from my mind and ignored the way their words were still echoing in my head. I didn't sleep and we didn't speak. When another hour passed, I was steady when I stood.

"You can go to bed now," I told him.

Oken studied my face. He touched my hair. I caught his hand and kissed his knuckles like he kissed mine earlier.

"Sleep well, princess."

"You too."

I paused at Natasha and my door, and he paused at his. He smiled at me, something so wistful and sweet on his face. I slipped inside before I let myself smile back. I eyed Natasha and the cold bed. Oken's warmth lingered. For the first time, I was relieved I had someone to make this all easier. Something told me no matter what happened, I wouldn't live long enough to regret Oken Sars. Not if I lived a thousand years.

CHAPTER 17

The following day Natasha received a breakfast invitation from Princess Chelsa and Princess Fay in the former's chambers. Natasha accepted quickly and retreated to the bathroom to get ready. Alessa and Masen were wide-eyed as they followed. No doubt, they felt the strange chill that had fallen over our bedroom. Natasha barely spoke to me and the cold shoulder was too familiar. Just like the Trish who still cringed from my black hair. Her brow had been furrowed in concentration most of the morning. I only felt the barest flutter of nerves from her end of the bond as she anticipated breakfast with the princesses.

When the time came, I walked Natasha to the royal quarters. She paused at the top of the stairs. Everything between us through the bond was so jumbled or muted that I had no idea what she was about to say.

"Look. I know you aren't a huge fan of Chelsa, and the invitation was just for me, so I think it would be best if I go on alone. You'd rather be training or something anyway, right?"

Strange how yesterday morning I would have smiled and been relieved by her words; today, they felt like a slap in the face. Natasha barely waited for my nod before she turned for the door a servant held open.

I stood there feeling lost long enough to become worried Hinze might catch me standing so close to his room. I turned and hurried to the bottom of the steps. I was so distracted I didn't see Londe until it was too late. We collided, and his eyes shifted to focus as he reached to catch me, barely managing to keep me from falling.

"You alright, Finley?"

"I'm..." I didn't know. I felt unbalanced even as he steadied me; it was all I could do to clear my expression. I tilted my head back, looking for a break from the dark palace walls and the heat of the corridor. No one from Brea's family had been by lately to cool it.

Londe's smile filled with understanding. He adjusted his grip on my arm, tucking my hand into his elbow to lead me. "Come with me. This place gets to be a lot. I know what you need."

His attention slipped away to communicate with someone else, but he continued guiding me through the halls. I paused when we reached the main doors of the palace. "Londe... I can't leave Natasha."

"Finley, judging by the look on your face, I think some space could do you good. It's okay to be two separate people still. I let Sam know you're leaving. He's going to stay close in case she needs him."

I bit my bottom lip. With the doors open, I could see the sky beyond. Rich blue with a shining sun and enough clouds to keep a gently cool breeze rolling over the palace lawn. I trained with Savha outside often but hadn't left the palace walls since we first entered them.

"You've barely seen the city, Finley."

I'd never had Londe's attention focused on me for so long. I found myself wanting to keep it. His quiet was easy; his mind occupied enough that I never felt the need to fill the silence. His expression was concerned. Did his ability clue him into my inner turmoil? Without really understanding how it happened, I found myself outside the palace doors, down the long gravel drive, and leaving the high gates.

Londe's entire demeanor changed away from the royal home. I'd noticed on a few occasions how he and his family drew attention wherever they went. Their pale coloring and distant eyes put them apart. It was clear the divide grew from a certain level of fearful respect.

"So, are you and Hinze doing any better?" he asked.

My stomach tumbled. "I think so, but it's painfully uncomfortable still."

"I'm sure you two will be back to normal in no time."

"I hope so. Things are hard enough as it is."

Londe's mouth twisted in a poor attempt at a smile. "Yeah."

He seemed to shake himself out of darker thoughts and began his tour of Helsa. Surrounding the palace were the grand homes of the elites. Londe pointed out his family mansion with a bored flick of his hand. I stumbled at the sight of it. Harsh and towering and cut with strangely uncanny precision, it was stunning. The yard and open windows belied the lack of voices within, and I nearly shivered thinking of all the distant gazes that must walk those halls. Almost entirely composed of some gray, shimmering stone, it was surrounded by only red rose bushes. The silence, green, red, and gray swirled together and looked like a painting propped up off the street.

Londe drew us past it without another comment. We also passed Garris's family home, both of us hushing after Londe said his name.

"How have you been? With that?" I asked.

"It hasn't been easy. Then take in saying goodbye to Ni —" Londe cleared his throat. "And Fisher. It hasn't been easy."

I frowned at my shoes, wondering at Londe cutting himself off. I thought of Nico's distant looks as his fingers flew over piano keys. How both of them softened when speaking about their "contact" on the other side of the Front. My steps slowed to a halt.

"You two...*You're* the reason Nico stopped dating!"

Londe pressed his lips together, but his body slumped from relief with the words in the air between us. He cut me a glance. "Is it completely ridiculous? I've only seen him once." Londe scoffed at himself and scratched the back of his head.

I couldn't help my laugh, suddenly feeling lighter. I jumped forward and wrapped Londe in a hug. He was grinning widely when I stepped back and grabbed his hand.

In the back of my mind, a pang of hurt sparked at yet another secret kept from me, but I focused on being happy for my brother.

"Tell me more. Tell me everything! When did it turn into more? Was he completely awkward when you started communicating? Were you worried he'd be hideous? I know I ask constantly, but have you heard from him recently?"

Londe laughed. He ticked off his fingers as he answered each of my questions. "It was a gradual thing. He was incredibly and endearingly awkward. No, I wasn't worried, but he was worried I'd think so. And he most definitely isn't hideous. And I have, but I can't tell you the news yet." He looked back toward his family home. "We should go deeper in the city where fewer people bother to listen."

He obliged me with stories of his and Nico's blooming love. Embarrassing tales from Nico first learning to communicate mentally, when Nico would let his thoughts wander and give Londe more information than he wanted. Eventually, Londe learned to treasure the insights. He told me of Nico telling him about me, how when Nico played the piano, it made it easier for him to focus and send messages so that now every time Londe heard music, Nico came to mind. How Nico's voice in his head became just as beautiful as the Trish melodies. How Nico influenced his love for Trish culture as much as Savha and Fisher did.

He told me of their excitement to meet in Traesha. Nico's horror when he learned I'd become involved and his desperation to help our parents. Londe's voice caught and he admitted Nico had kept Londe there with him when he returned to the house and found our father's bloodstain in much the same way I had. He'd been there comforting Nico the entire time Nico packed our family's belongings.

"I should have told you. I should have told you everything then, but I wasn't strong enough to comfort both of you. It was taking everything from me to hear him in so much pain."

My throat was tight. "Thank you. For being with him. Always do just that." I squeezed Londe's hand.

By now, we were clear of the mansions circling the palace gates. Shops and houses and some apartment buildings lined the streets, though not nearly as condensed and upward as the Vichi living situation. Londe pointed out a bigger building and explained it had been bought by a Trish family and converted into a theater. They had brought plays and music when they fled Traesha, preserving a considerable part of the culture and sharing it with the Florians with great success. The sight of the building stirred pride and hope. The doors were locked, so we couldn't go in and see it, but that didn't stop me from imagining myself inside and on stage singing.

I listened to stories about Nico and realized how my world had condensed to the tension within the palace for too long. It was amazing to remember why I fought and see the outside world again. Londe was right; I needed this. It felt unnatural to let my shoulders relax. Not even the bond pulling at me could drag me down as we passed children playing and the incredible street performers.

Londe led us to a cafe with outdoor seating along the street and ordered tea and pastries I'd never heard of. Luckily, they were savory, not the sugared fruit that was so common in the palace. I ate three and felt like I had forgotten to breathe by the time I finished. Londe and I continued talking in our minds, making me lose track of how much I was consuming and getting rid of the need to pause between bites.

With the pastries done and our tea kettle nearly empty, Londe cast a glance up and down the street.

It was still early in the day. Those shopping were unhurried and sun-kissed, wearing bright colors far less jarring than the court fashion. It was nice seeing them laughing, chatting, and strolling. I wanted to envy their ease. Wanted to resent their way of life while Bellovi and Traesha struggled. Wanted to hate King Mavrick and everything he provided for his people. But I couldn't. This was what I desired for the people I cared for. What I felt looking at the Florians enjoying the warm day was longing. The type of longing that solidified my goals.

I inhaled deeply. I could feel Natasha, but she was far

enough away and occupied with the princesses. I'd barely felt her tugging me toward her or her emotions infecting my own, just discomfort over the distance that I realized was inherent in the bond. This wistful sensation I had watching the Florians was all my own. Natasha's view of the Florian lifestyle was jaded with resentment and envy. What would she do to these people to better our own?

I hated thinking about her so negatively and tried to be fair. She expected them to fight for what was right. She didn't hate them. She hated that they were happy and content to ignore Traesha's state.

Londe spoke out loud, maybe aware that I had a dull headache growing from concentrating on keeping my thoughts about Natasha out of our conversations. "Nico's last message was quite concerning."

I stiffened. "How so?"

He fidgeted with his napkin, staring at the table and talking in a low voice. He was aware of my sharp hearing. His words were barely audible even to me. "One of the rebels was looking through a high commander's office in Vichi. He found messages coming from Floria. The first was a location in Honna hours before the attack there. The next were updates on the palace. Who is here, the elite's abilities, how you are training the Trish, and Natasha's healing."

The hair on my neck rose. I had to set down my tea before my unsteady hands spilled. "Who?"

"Nico's doing what he can to find out with no luck. Either way, we have a spy, and they've been with us at least since Honna."

Frustration and betrayal rose, a burn in my throat. It took so much for me to lean on those around me. I was working so hard to trust. For this to be the result...

I cleared my throat and sat up straight. "What should I do?"

"Right now, I don't know what there is to do. Whatever the spy has reported, the damage is done. Watch your people close and be careful where you speak. Keep any new plans or developments only between those you trust. I've been doing my best to listen, but it is dangerous to do so without being let in willingly." The hair on my arm rose when I realized he meant listening to people's thoughts, not their conversations.

"But I trust them all. They followed me here; they risked their families...."

"I never said it was a Bellovian, Finley. It's more likely the spy is Bellovian, but with Detono backing the commanders, we have no idea what kind of power they hold or promises they can make."

I pinched the bridge of my nose. I wanted to trust the Bellovians, but why would a Florian spy for the commanders?

I would have to tell Natasha. Cold spread through me. Her feelings toward the Bellovians had already grown warier since I'd told her what Sam said. The rift between the Trish and Bellovians would only grow. Our team would fracture and our strength diminish.

"And we have no idea who it could be?"

Londe shook his head. "Nico said the boy saw more files but was interrupted while looking through them. He could try and go back—"

I shook my head. "Hue doesn't need to take the risk. He's too young to be caught up in all this anyway."

"That's what Nico said." Londe was a master at smiling with sadness.

I leaned back in my chair, watching the unbothered

Florians go about their business. This time, I couldn't stop the envy stirring in my chest for their simple lives.

"*Resa!*" I was walking down to the training rooms in the basement when I heard my name called.

"What?" I snapped the word when I saw it was Liam. I was irritable from two nights of little sleep. Between Natasha's cold shoulder and watching every friend I had for signs of deceit, my nerves were stripped raw.

"Whoa!" Liam threw up his hands. I didn't care for the amusement dancing in his eyes. "Would you be less snippy with me if I looked like this?"

He grew tall and thin like the average Bellovian man. His eyes darkened to a deeper brown, and his hair went from red to black. I rolled my eyes at him, which only made him smirk. "Or maybe it's just this look in particular that gets you going...."

He turned into Oken before my eyes. A muted, less appealing Oken, the features all the same but worn without Oken's light. I balled my hands into fists. Turning, I kept walking, and Liam let out a laugh that was nothing like Oken's. He shifted back into his former self, panting slightly from using his abilities and hurrying to keep up with me.

"What do you want?" I asked.

"What do you want, *Your Highness?* You need to work on your manners if you'll be staying in our palace much longer. Especially since I'm being nice enough to come to tell you your queen was summoned to see my father about an hour ago, and they haven't left his office since. Elise and Sam are in there, too. I heard Mav mention another attack on the Front before he went in."

I froze. Liam stumbled to a halt next to me and grinned at having caught me off guard. I had known something was off with Natasha but hadn't realized it was a different emotion than the turmoil we'd been in the last two days. She was still confused, but to leave me out of a meeting with the king, to bring my mother and Sam instead...

It was suddenly apparent how little Natasha needed me and how easily I could be left outside of the room once she decided I was doing more harm than good. *Death will break brittle bonds.*

I needed to know what was happening. I left Liam behind and skipped to the office where the king first made his marriage proposal. For the first time in two days, I really listened to the bond. I didn't like what I heard. I knocked loudly, not caring about my lack of manners. Hinze opened the door, his expression pinched.

"*Resa,* kind of you to join us," the king said from his seat at the head of the table. I could have cut the tension in the room with Oken's knife in my boot. My mother gave me a tight smile when I pulled out the seat next to her. Natasha didn't look up. "Why don't you catch our guest up on the latest development, Hinze?"

Hinze cleared his throat. The effort was in vain. When he spoke, his voice remained strained. "The Bellovians have pushed through the Front in the south. It would seem they're using further range weapons and growing even more aggressive by the day. They were stopped and fell back again as they did in Honna. We believe they are testing the lines. More troubling than this, however, are reports from our spies in Detono. Two have been reported missing after following our lead to look for correspondence with Bellovian commanders. One found a message about a planned attack, apparently bigger and more organized than those at the Front. They think it will take place in a few weeks, but we still do not know where they plan to send forces."

The king turned to me, giving me the full force of his cold, colorless glare. "And now here we are fighting a war on two sides that was spurred by the queen's sudden appearance in Floria. A queen who has yet to give me an answer regarding my more than fair proposal. A queen who has brought the enemy directly into my palace, including a man who could turn most of my guards defenseless at any moment."

The king did little to hide his anger, letting the table tremble enough that even Chelsa stopped resting her elbows on it. Natasha looked from Hinze to the king, her gaze level. I felt her helpless fear, and I struggled to think of anything to say that would stop her from agreeing to marry Hinze right then and there.

"How about we give Queen Natasha a chance to prove she would even be a valuable ally?" Prince Mav said, pulling the attention in the room away from the king and Natasha. His voice was smooth, unaffected by his father's fury.

"Continue..." the king growled the word.

"We've all heard the commanders' threats to burn Traesha down if the Bellovians think they are about to lose it." I hadn't heard these threats but kept my face neutral despite this new fear rushing through me. It stung that there was no surprise from Natasha. "Should that happen, it would take years for us to benefit from an alliance. Years for their crops to return to what they had once been. Years of us supporting them in the meantime. What we can use now, at this moment, are soldiers. More elites are preparing to leave the palace for the Front as we speak, but why should we be the only ones using our abilities to end this war? We've seen the Trish training and how strong they are. What are they preparing for if not to help us defend our countries? And if that's the case, why not start now? We don't even need many. We're just sending enough of a force to push back at the Front while we prepare our full army. One Trish soldier who can skip is equal to at least twenty regular soldiers."

Natasha stared at Mav like her worst nightmare was coming to life. I truly hated this room.

A slow smile crawled onto the king's face. "I haven't seen you make any moves to reclaim your country, and without a solid yes regarding this marriage between you and my son, Mav is right. I am getting very little out of this whole situation, and I've been supporting your people for years without any compensation." King Mavrick nodded, resolute. "I am sending five teams with my top elites to patrol the Front and the coast between Detono and us. These teams will include Mav and Hinze, my sons, and their friends. I think asking you to supply three people to each team is more than fair. It's time for Traesha to join this fight. As their queen, you'll be the one to ask this of them."

I stared from Natasha to the king to Hinze. As weird as things were, I didn't want to be in Floria without my friend nearby. Especially as everything kept turning for the worse. The king's chair scraped against the floor as he stood. "The transports will be ready to leave this time tomorrow along with the brave Florians who have already volunteered to fight for their country without hesitation. If you'll excuse us, we must ensure they are ready for their journey."

"I'll do it," Natasha whispered before the king could sweep out the door. He didn't try to hide his smile when he turned back around. Natasha didn't see it, staring straight ahead at the opposite wall. I shivered at the force of her feelings. It took everything to keep my face neutral.

"Yes, it was decided already." The king laughed, but the wicked glint in his eyes told me he knew what Natasha meant.

"No, I'll marry Hinze."

Hinze's face dropped, defeated as he nodded. My stomach rolled and I didn't know if it was Natasha who was ready to be sick all over the table or me. The image of both of us doing so nearly raised a hysterical laugh.

What was happening?

"I'm thrilled to hear it. However, I do still need rein-forcements. This alliance will work best when we are helping each other mutually, starting now and ending with my son and your children. We can discuss wedding details when the war is more settled. Welcome to the family, Queen Natasha."

CHAPTER 18

Natasha's emotions coiled. A whirlwind of despair, regret, and dread. My mother had a hand on Natasha's arm as we walked. Her voice sounded muffled to my ears when she said Natasha's name, but Natasha couldn't hear her at all. A memory hit her with such force I watched it in my mind's eye with her and stumbled.

Natasha's grandfather stood tall, walking as though gliding through the trees with Natasha's tiny hand in his. She barely reached his waist at this time in her life. She clung to every word out of his mouth, swinging their hands happily. He stopped suddenly and plucked a flower from the branches above his head.

"This is your Traesha. You can't reach it yet, but someday you will. When our land is yours again, you must protect it and cherish it as though it were as fragile and beautiful as this flower."

"How? How do I reach it, Grandpapa?"

He shook his head. "You must grow first. And you must protect it even before it is yours, or you will have already lost it. Begin watering the earth now, my love. Work on your own heart first. You must bring peace, Natasha. That is why we have a royal family. That is why you were born."

I wrenched myself from Natasha's mind. She stared ahead in horror. I wanted to comfort her, but there was too much between us right now. She likely wouldn't welcome my attempts.

Across the bond, Natasha's anger began to simmer, hungry and ancient. Exactly like the forest in my dreams. I thought about peace and the triangle breaking. *It will break,* whispered in my ear. I smelled lavender and wished I could just be alone in my head. Without the trees pulling me. Without Natasha's intense emotions. No kings or wars or magic.

"What would you like us to do, Your Grace?" Sam asked.

"What can be done? We must speak to the people." Natasha's voice shook.

I fought to center myself back in my own mind.

The bond between us urged me close to her side as if she was in physical danger. Without even realizing it, I stepped closer. Natasha shifted away. I swallowed the lancing pain.

I forced the hurt back. Ignored the whispers. This wasn't about me. It wasn't about how unfair our fight was or how helpless I felt. This was about the Trish in the hall we approached, the ones Natasha would have to ask to risk their lives for a country many hadn't seen in nearly twenty years. Some had never seen it at all.

We entered the hall. Everyone lounged in the afternoon breeze drifting in through the open balcony doors. The Bellovians were in a corner and playing a makeshift board game with a few of the Trish our age. Levi deliberately pushed his troops forward with a smirk, making Oken cry out in protest. Wesley and Rennie laughed.

A hush fell over the room. Heads turned in our direction, expressions wary seeing the look on their queen's face.

"I..." Natasha trailed off. A mother shushed her silver-haired child by the piano. Natasha cleared her throat and forced strength into it. "I have a troubling announcement. King Mavrick wishes for our people to contribute to the war efforts, threatening our alliance if I should refuse. I must ask now for fifteen volunteers," her voice cracked, "who would be willing to travel with the Florian elites to push back the Bellovians at the Front."

The child began to cry, fearful of the terror on their mother's face.

Sam positioned himself in front of Natasha and took a knee. "I will go, Your Grace."

Natasha's eyes slid shut. After a brief hesitation, she conceded a single nod. Sam's face was pale as he stood, jaw clenched. He looked at my mother and she lifted her chin with determination. He'd planned for the two of them to stay close with us, to counsel us as Trish and save us from the instability of our bond. It fell on her now.

Unless I removed myself. Natasha didn't want me around anyway. What was I good for? Fighting and war. I had been born for the violence. It had always felt that way.

I went to move forward and join Sam. It only made sense. I was trained, I was the leader of the Trish armies, and I was half the problem keeping Natasha from a stable rule. But Natasha's eyes snapped open. The look she sent me stopped me in my tracks. Everything in me screamed to take the place of anyone in this room, but with clenched fists, I followed her silent order and stilled myself. She cowed me quickly—a strict, awful command in a single look and burst of feeling through the bond. I clenched my jaw tight enough to hurt.

Savha stood. Natasha began to tremble. Two brothers, Reese and Nass, who were in their thirties, stepped forward. Cassa patted her partner's hand and joined them. An eighteen-year-old girl with *magsai* parents named Salena stepped forward, chin jutted forward. Wesley pulled himself from his sister and grandfather's hands and went to Savha's side. Two more Trish stepped forward. I hated that I didn't know their names.

There were so few of us here already. We waited in tense silence for the next volunteer. What would happen if there weren't enough? Would Natasha be forced to pick? Would we have to go door to door in the city? Asking for volunteers from those who didn't even want to train with me? Maybe they'd be more willing, having lived more closely with the Florians they might want to fight the king's battles—

"I'll go."

Everything stilled at the sound of that voice. I couldn't look to where the Bellovians sat, even when I heard Oken walking toward the cluster of volunteers. I knew his voice and his footsteps and his scent that carried toward me on the breeze through the open balcony doors. I couldn't think.

Natasha hesitated, probably experiencing the emotions on my side of the bond.

Oken noticed her pause. "We're your people too now, Natasha. I should be allowed to fight. We know how the Bellovians think and what they'll do more than anyone else here. The king would be an idiot to turn me away."

"Or me," Audrey said.

The air was so thin. I was dimly aware of my mother's hand on my arm, supporting me gently.

Mesa stared at Audrey and indecision warred on her

features. Then, nodding, she took the other girl's hand. "If he'll count me for one of yours, I'll go for you, Natasha," she said.

Jenna glanced at Fisher's parents. "Me too," she whispered.

"We'll go too," Rennie said. Levi nodded at her side.

"Thank you all." Natasha did nothing to hide the tears welling in her eyes. "I'll speak with the king."

She turned and I followed. Sam and my mother stayed behind, motioning for the volunteers to come forward to speak with them.

"Nat, you should let me go," I said once we were alone in the hall. "They never even wanted to fight."

All I could picture was Salena's pale face.

"No, Finley. I need you at my side."

"But distance could help our bond," I tried, thinking to use the fear Sam already placed in her.

"If you want to be with Oken so badly, go tell him not to volunteer. You're staying with me." I cringed from the force of Natasha's sharp tone. Her words stung, but Natasha was so caught up in her thoughts she didn't stop to acknowledge their effect.

I didn't realize how quickly we'd been walking until we reached the Florian training room seconds later. Trish speed was now so effortless for both of us.

I reached for Natasha's arm, unsure what I wanted to say but needing to get it out before we went before the king. She cut me a glare that stilled my hand and dropped my stomach. Her rage in the bond shifted to consume me. This time, it was anger at myself. My hand fell to my side. Unable to sort through the emotions of the bond, the anger and disappointment flushed at the forefront of my mind, bringing me so low I let my eyes fall to the floor. I meekly followed Natasha to stand before the king, feeling worthless. Deserving of her anger. Why couldn't I do one thing to help?

Useless. I was useless here.

Come back, singer. Come back. The triangle. The queen. We must protect. We must protect.

I was only half in the training room. Half my awareness was with the trees, rushing with the angry breeze. Prince Mav stood shirtless in the center of the room, a massive black cube of some strange metal floating in the air above him. Beads of sweat gathered on his forehead. The king stood to the side, talking with Lilah's father and Mav's fiancé, Tiana. She watched Mav like a prized possession. She tensed when Natasha stalked toward them. I didn't trust the fire behind her eyes or her clenched fists. Protective instincts yanked me away from the Trish trees. Their rustling leaves hissed to silence.

"Back so soon? I'm surprised it took so little time for you to pick your soldiers," the king said. I wanted to physically wipe the smug look off his face.

"They volunteered," Natasha said.

"Oh? And who were the brave souls?"

Were. I envied Tiana's ability to burn this place to the ground. With a dead voice, Natasha listed off the volunteers. Lilah's father stopped her when she mentioned Oken. "Isn't he the Bellovian boy? He's friends with my daughter."

Natasha reluctantly nodded.

"I asked for Trish volunteers," the king snarled.

"You asked for our people," I hissed back, anger still too close to the surface. Natasha's shot me a warning look.

"The Bellovian boy was telling me some of what he has seen and learned in Bellovi," Lilah's father broke in. "He could be useful, my king. And Lilah told me there was a girl with Bellovian strength. Did she volunteer?"

Natasha's head jerked a quick nod. The king considered her before his eyes slid to me.

"You won't be joining them?" he asked, disappointment evident.

I schooled my features. I wouldn't give him the satisfaction of seeing I was also disappointed or how I reeled from being a disappointment.

"Finley stays with me as my *resa*."

"Pity," the king said. "I accept your contribution, but I have no need for the Squalor girl with barely any Bellovian training or the one who can take away our abilities. I would be an idiot to trust him at the Front with my people. Savha will also stay behind; I've had just about enough of Hinze's moping around and wouldn't want him losing another one of his little friends. I realize this brings you to less than the desired number of volunteers, but given your willingness, I will let it pass this once." The king turned to me. "Keep up the training, *resa*. We may be needing more troops in the days to come."

I opened my mouth to retort, but Natasha pulled me away. She led me from the training room. The loud crash of Mav's block flying into the opposite wall followed us out the door. The king laughed, loud and unencumbered.

At the top of the stairs, Natasha continued back to the Trish Hall. My feet were too heavy to follow. The air still too thin. The din of soft Trish voices too oppressing. For the first time, I genuinely wanted distance from Natasha and our people. I wanted this brittle bond to go silent. I needed it. I turned and skipped out of the palace, finding my way to Savha and my running path. Already dressed for training, I began running around the extensive palace grounds, sometimes in bursts of Trish speed, sometimes a slow jog. I felt too much of Natasha and too much of myself and too much of Traesha. The bonds tugged chaotically. I couldn't get my head straight.

Always focus. I pushed the words away with a bitter laugh.

If I slowed down, the reality of it all would catch up. I ran and ran. Dani. Garris. My father. Fisher. Nico, in the midst of it all, at risk. The failing, unhelpful rebellion. The spy among us. Hinze hurt and leaving. Oken leaving. Failing the Trish. Natasha's engagement to Hinze. Hinze's engagement to Natasha. The growing strength of our bond. Natasha's coldness because of it. The prophecy. The trees and their ancient anger. My uselessness.

Oken leaving.

My brain skipped from problem to problem, leaving me dizzy.

I ran until I couldn't think and the satisfying burn in my legs was all I felt. I ran until the sun began to set behind the palace and my lungs ached for air. I ran until I looked up and saw Oken on the balcony outside the Trish great room, leaning with his elbows on the balustrade with his long legs crossed behind him. He glanced down, caught me staring, and a smile graced his features. He lifted a hand, beckoning me. Without a thought, I skipped through the palace and to his side.

"Don't go," I said, breathless.

He didn't even jump; he'd gotten so used to my speed. He turned to me, and I thought about the last time we stood here side by side during the ball. The last time I felt happy.

"I know you don't mean that," he said, smile turning sad.

He was right. I would rather a capable Bellovian go to war any day over the untrained, gentle Trish in the other room. I tried to swallow, but my throat was too tight. But why did it have to be him? What more did fate want from me?

"What about getting to Mayze?" I asked him.

"I'll come back soon. If not, you'll get there. I know you'll help her."

I will help her, but Oken should be there. He shouldn't have to go. I didn't want him to leave me.

Oken stepped closer. "Let me see, Fin."

I blinked in confusion.

He sighed as if he shouldn't have to explain. I stepped back, unable to face disappointing him too. I dropped my eyes and inhaled sharply. His hand reached out and steadied me. His voice was so earnest when he spoke. "Let me see what you're thinking. I can't stand how you hide it all the time."

Was I still hiding all the raging emotions I felt? I hadn't even realized, and now that I did, I wasn't sure I wanted him to see. I didn't want him to see my hurt, my fear, my longing, my helplessness. I didn't want to burden him or anyone with all that. I didn't know if I trusted it.

The bond had let Natasha in and she left me ragged.

I trusted Oken with my life. I wanted him here, guarding my back in every battle. But this was different. This trust that wasn't physical. I didn't know if I was capable. Hadn't everyone I trusted refused to return the favor? Hadn't they all let me down? The spy in our midst. Natasha with her stony silence. Even my parents and Nico kept so many secrets from me. Nothing hurt like what they had done. Secrets and lies and their constant belief I would be strong enough on my own.

Was I? Did I have to be? Did I want to be?

No. That's why Natasha hurt so much. She was my queen. Was it fair to lean on her like a best friend?

I couldn't lean on her, but I didn't want to stand alone anymore. I wanted one person who would put what I wanted and needed first. I craved it so badly that my chest hurt.

Oken drew closer still. The night air shifted through his curls, and I smelled the clean scent of him, like a clear stream in the cold Bellovian woods. The air just before the clouds released their snowflakes.

I drew in a lungful of it. I savored it.

"Please, princess. Tell me there's something here." The way he said princess made my whole body warm. I stared into his eyes; the sunset reflected like burning gold in their depths. They showed every emotion he felt. Vulnerable and trusting. A want that mirrored my own. It took my breath away. It was precisely how I always fantasized he would look at me during those frozen winter months growing up in Vichi.

So hopeful.

It took some effort, but I forced my face to relax. There were muscles around my eyes I didn't even realize I kept tense. I drew in a shaking breath. "I want more from you than I can give you, Oken."

"For now, Finley. Our world won't always be violence and war. If anyone can end it, you can. I want to be with you every step of the way, and then one day, there will be real time for us."

He always had the perfect words ready. I let loose the smile building from the flutters in my stomach. The smile I wanted to let out every time I saw Oken. And I let myself feel hope, too. I lost myself to it.

Oken's returning smile was brilliant. Stepping so close our bodies aligned, I pulled his face to my own. Our kiss started soft and sweet, just like I dreamed a first kiss should be. But as it grew deeper, I wanted to explore every part of his mouth, of him. Because underneath my joy, this was still a goodbye. I wanted every taste I could get before he left me and I had to stand alone again. I wanted and wanted and wanted.

I backed away just long enough to pull myself to sit on the balustrade, bringing our faces level and bodies ever closer. He pressed into me, his arm around my back the only thing keeping me from falling onto the lawn far below. I relished the excuse to cling to his hard, warm body. At times the force of our kiss made me lean back, but I only felt more of a thrill as I trusted Oken not to drop me. I trusted everything to him, and it felt so damn sweet.

Our kiss was fire and war and friendship. It was silent promises kept and made.

It melted my insides and planted me firmly in my mind. The bond was a distant hum I ignored with ease. We took turns laughing breathlessly. We took turns moaning against each other's lips. We coaxed the fire with lips and hands, the burn that had us pressing closer still. It was so good.

It was only Oken and me. His kisses convinced me I was everything. I could have lived in that moment forever. His body against mine, my legs wrapped securely around him. His arms holding me tight in a way that would never let me fall. When he pressed forward with one last, hard kiss, I clung to his shoulders to keep him close. I made a noise of protest.

"I'll come back," he promised, breathless. The night sky twinkled above us, and I wondered how long we'd been out here. It wasn't long enough. "You're the most incredible person I know. I want everything you can throw at me. I want more of this forever. I'll always come running back to you."

"You better," I tried to make my voice threatening but failed miserably. I kissed him again and his lips curled into a smile. When we broke apart, he scrunched his nose and rubbed its tip against mine.

"Whatever you want. Natasha might be my queen, but you'll always be my princess." There was no smoldering quality to his voice this time, only an overly thick layer of sweetness.

I pretended to gag and watched him laugh with a sense of wonder. How was this brightness mine? That ache to hold him close and keep him safe almost robbed me of breath. I joined in his laughter instead, pressing our foreheads together.

The sound of our happiness was lost to the open night.

CHAPTER 19

The next morning, Natasha asked Alessa and Masen to help her into the simplest dress in the closet. It was dark gray, and although it hugged her curves and flowed beautifully to the floor, it reflected our somber mood perfectly. Natasha couldn't look me in the eyes. I had been planted firmly in my own head since my kiss with Oken and let the sensation of him linger, blocking out most of her frustration and disappointment so I could deal with my own emotions today.

I dressed in my usual leggings and a dark red shirt. My focus slipped despite my resolve, and a flicker from Natasha crossed the bond. In that moment, it was grief I felt. She was grieving as if the soldiers leaving today had already died at war. It made my skin crawl with irritation. I thought of every time the train had pulled out of City Center loaded with seventeen-year-olds. The parents who forced cheers as their children were whisked away. I had known this feeling my entire life.

Her lack of faith renewed my focus. Hopelessness was

the ultimate defeat in war. I didn't want her emotions in my mind.

We went downstairs to the Trish Hall for the goodbyes. Oken stayed close to my side the entire time, making it even easier to block out Natasha. My mother joined us and we moved among the volunteers. She offered words of encouragement. Oken and I offered words of advice.

"If you see an orange packet of dehydrated food, that's the so-called meatloaf. Do *not* eat it," Oken told Wesley with a shudder, making him and everyone listening laugh. The room brightened briefly, Oken's power clearing the air enough for everyone to breathe.

I leaned into his side. How would I breathe when he left?

Too soon, everyone had gathered. With a thrill of rebellion, I remained among the Bellovians in the back of the procession as Natasha took her place to lead us to the palace doors. Sam was at her side, offering his arm. A twinge of pain from her end of the bond made it through as she tucked her hand in his arm. It stung that he was leaving her again. And she hadn't even fully forgiven him.

I looked to my mother. I hadn't fully forgiven her either. My esteem for Sam rose just the slightest bit that he would let my mother be the one to stay behind, helping us heal our rift instead of him and Natasha.

I thought of my father with a wave of grief. I missed him so much. It hit often and with no prompting.

Oken leaned in close. I heard him inhale the smell of my hair. I didn't want him to go. All that would be left was the pain between my mother and me, Natasha's coldness, worries about a spy, Levi and Rennie noting how useless we were to the rebellion, and the king's politics.

I wanted to deny needing my mother's help. How

would I have handled my mother leaving instead of Sam? The pain of the thought robbed me of breath. It was then I knew I wasn't angry anymore. Oken was leaving, Natasha didn't want to speak to me, and I had one person in this palace who would love me unconditionally, no matter what mistakes she or I made. If I couldn't have both of my parents, it didn't mean I had to starve myself of the one I had left. I knew and had known this whole time my father would have hated this more than anything.

We reached the doors of the palace, slowing to funnel through. There were transports outside, waiting to carry my friends off to war. They could have taken my mother from me just as easily as Sam. I kept my grip on Oken's hand and turned to my mother, wrapping my free arm around her. I hid from the world briefly, my face in her neck, drawing in her familiar scent.

"Don't leave me," I whispered in Trish.

"I'm here, Finley."

I couldn't meet her eyes as I stepped back and nodded, slipping back into my place beside Oken.

He sighed in relief. "That makes me feel better about leaving."

My mother laughed. "Can I hug you goodbye, Oken?"

"Um, okay." Oken stiffened with surprise, but after a beat, he hugged her back. I felt a wash of pleasure realizing how far the two of us had come. The Bellovian in him still wasn't used to touch, but he was comfortable with me. There was no hesitation from him with me anymore. No uncertainty. He reached for my hand first when we continued out the palace doors.

Too soon, we were on the palace steps. A line of transport vehicles, mostly full of elites, idled. Noting how the empty seats were spread across the transports, I realized our people would be separated and hated the thought. My hand tightened around Oken's. He took in the line of Florian transports. The Trish had somehow ended up behind the Bellovians, hiding behind their bulk and fearless approach. With me at his side, Oken went first to Natasha where she stood ready to send her people off.

"Until I see you next," Natasha said, the expression far harsher in Common Tongue.

Oken nodded and shook her hand.

He turned to me, one hand slipping under my jaw and tilting my chin up. In front of everyone, he kissed me. His kiss said goodbye and I'll be careful and I want to come back. I put equal feeling behind my response. Goodbye, you better, I need you back. When he pulled away, the world dimmed.

"Stay strong," I whispered.

"I will," he sealed his promise with another fleeting kiss.

He climbed into the back of the transport vehicle where he was directed. I stayed at Natasha's side, a step further away than I would have stood a week ago. We said goodbye to Sam next, and I was relieved to see the older *magsai* get into the same transport as Oken. Although Sam had not entirely warmed to me, I knew I could trust them to watch out for each other.

Lilah and Brea were also in the same transport as Oken. The promises in Oken's kisses meant I was glad to see them together, to know he had friends by his side, even if they weren't the Bellovians we knew. I saw the terror in Lilah and Brea's faces just before the doors slammed. They weren't ready to see battle again. My heart broke and I felt again that it should be me going. Even if they returned safely, this battle would take a heavy toll.

Natasha bid each person who volunteered for her good-bye. She made sure to give them her blessing and wish them well. I appreciated that she said goodbye to the Bellovians and Mesa with equal enthusiasm as she did the Trish.

"Until I see you next," she whispered mid-hug over and over before kissing each cheek of the volunteer.

I told them all to stay strong, the Bellovian goodbye even more fitting when I spoke it in Trish to those who understood. Levi, Savha, Rennie, and my mother stood still behind us. Hinze stayed where his father had placed him at Natasha's other side until it was time to follow his brother into their transports. He accepted the hurried, shy kisses Natasha brushed on his cheeks. Blushing, he found his seat. Prince Mav finished saying his goodbyes, and my heart sank as he went to sit in the front of Oken's transport.

"Just a moment," Londe called to the driver when it was his turn to get in the same transport as Hinze. I hadn't known he was going too. Another blow. I hadn't even had the chance to introduce him properly to my mother. She would have loved to talk to him about Nico. Londe's eyes had been distant all morning, deep in conversations we couldn't hear. He climbed the steps and stopped in front of me.

"Can I have a quick word?" he asked.

I nodded and followed him to the side of the drive.

I expected us to walk until we were out of hearing range, remembering his wariness to speak within the palace walls before. Instead, Londe went as far as it took for us to be out of sight before he tugged in my mind.

I'll be able to contact Nico more often when we're close to Bellovi again. Anything you want me to tell him?

I considered his offer, feeling guilty that my mother wasn't being given this same opportunity. *I have a lot to tell him. But just tell him I love him, I miss him, and I'm still going to try and do whatever I can for the rebellion from here. I just have to figure out how.*

Finley, you're already doing so much. The fact that you're still thinking about them is more than everyone else.

Will you ask him to look into the flighters if he can? And whatever the commanders have planned? But to stay away from Silken. Even just thinking the man's name made me shudder. I fought the urge to tell Nico to keep out of it all entirely.

He's smart and already doing all those things. Will you be okay here?

I think so.

You and Natasha need to work things out, Londe's tone turned slightly chastising. *The rebellion, the Trish, none of us can risk having you divided.* "You two need each other," Londe finished out loud, kindness softening his gaze.

I swallowed and nodded. He wasn't Nico, but he loved Nico. His hug was a close second at that moment.

"Make sure he's being smart," I said. Londe nodded. I could practically feel his excitement to be close again. At least one person was approaching the Front with something other than dread. "And take care of Hinze."

It had hurt when Hinze barely paused to wish me goodbye. That there was so much friction between us. The lack of hope in his eyes as he let Natasha kiss his cheeks chilled me to my core.

Londe smiled sadly. "I'll try to stay in contact. You're a bit more difficult, though. Your mind is too closed off. Try to listen for me."

I nodded and inwardly cringed at being closed off. I didn't want to know what that meant about me. We parted ways. I rejoined Natasha. My mother took my hand. Londe went straight to his transport and climbed into the passenger seat.

I couldn't help but feel we were losing a war we had barely even joined as Natasha watched the transport vehicles drive out of the palace gates with her fiancé and people inside. I no longer had the strength or motivation to fight her emotions. I let the heartbreak consume me, for once sure it was a mirror of my own and not an overshadowing.

~

THE DAY PASSED IN A QUIET, stunned haze. It was done. Trish people were at war, sent on Natasha's order, and our number of allies within the palace walls was drastically reduced. Natasha disappeared into our room, and the back of my eyes stung with the force of her tears. She'd held them back until she was alone.

The remaining Trish went to our hall with stooped shoulders. I lingered at the doorway, but I hadn't known the Trish who left very well. I didn't know how to offer comfort. In fact, while the wary looks at my black hair had nearly stopped, today I once again received pointed looks. They knew I was trained and had faced war. It made no sense why I was still here when everyone could feel the wall standing between Natasha and me. I wanted to know these people. I wanted to be the bridge between them and Natasha. I wanted to be their voice and for them to come to me. Instead, it felt like another brittle bond I would break after centuries of tradition.

I turned from the room, never having felt less worthy of my title.

I caught sight of Levi and Rennie walking the gardens through a window. Their black hair shone in the bright sun.

They probably wished to speak outside of Trish hearing. Their shoulders were tense with the Bellovians' departure. They talked to Audrey for a long time this morning about messages she should try to get to the rebellion, but they were worried for her. For all our Bellovian friends likely facing war on two sides once again.

I was adrift. I didn't feel comfortable among any of my people. I felt guilt no matter who I looked to. I missed Oken already, if only because I could count on him to always appear happy to see me. He welcomed me without hesitation. He smiled, and I had to smile back. Even now, I could feel the ghost of his lips on mine. My hand strayed upward constantly to touch them, pressing into the tenderness left by the force of his affection. I hoped he felt me lingering similarly. The slight bruises assured me I hadn't imagined it all.

I went to the basement training rooms. They were empty now. Not even the constant crash of Prince Mav's training rattled the halls. I shuddered to think what kind of chaos he would unleash at the Front. I wandered to the shooting range but stopped early at the knife-throwing table. I pulled Oken's knife from my boot, Mesa's knife from my waist. I stuck them perfectly into the center of the target over and over. I didn't know how much time had passed before Savha joined me. She stood and watched my technique for a time and then began to practice at the table over. She was a terrible throw, but it was nice to hear more than one set of knives thudding against the target. I knew I wasn't alone in my helpless anger. Savha's presence grounded me. Fisher's death stood between us, but she didn't look at me any differently than she had before the call for volunteers. She understood why Natasha kept me close and how I felt about it all.

"Princess Chelsa went in to talk to Natasha," Savha said.

This surprised me. "I guess she needs someone to talk to," I said. I threw my next knife a little harder than the one before. It sank up to the hilt into the target.

"Your mom was in there for a while, but Natasha didn't want to see her. What do you think Chelsa and her are talking about?"

"I don't know. Natasha doesn't want me to know." Savha heard my helpless frustration. We fell quiet again. *Thunk, thunk, thunk.*

At dinnertime, Fisher's parents came looking for Savha, drawing her out of the training room to escape the palace tension and go into the city for dinner. The silence between us had offered a pained comfort. The silence when she left was just hollow. Realizing I hadn't eaten all day, I went to the kitchen to find food. I wove through the many bodies working to feed the palace and talked to Mari. Alessa always went to her when she needed to get food. Mari was an igniter who worked the oven and baked most of the breads and cakes. She had a warm smile and a soft spot for Trish people. She gave me a large roll and a bowl of soup. I made her stop there even when she asked me repeatedly if it would be enough. This would have been a feast for me in Vichi.

I missed those simpler times.

The sun set while I sat by the lake and ate. It was peaceful and warm. I felt something loosen in my body and suddenly remembered how adept I used to be at being alone. I was fine. I was always fine. I could survive this just like I had everything else. I settled back in the grass. It was better than snow. The Trish stares were better than the Bellovian open glares I grew up facing. I could and would handle this. I was strong. Time would pass and get easier. This hurt, but it would pass. There was a war, and I was comfortable and protected in a grand palace. I had no right to feel so sorry for myself.

Feeling more centered and optimistic, I readied to face Natasha. Like it or not, we were stuck in this together. Londe was right; we needed to fix this rift. We needed to figure out our place here and how to find our power. Uselessness wasn't an option anymore.

Natasha wasn't sleeping when I entered our room, but I figured she would pretend to be like she had the last few nights. At least Chelsa was gone. Now that I was here, my courage stumbled. Briefly, I considered moving into Rennie's room and taking Jenna's empty bed to give Natasha some space.

To my surprise, Natasha sat up when the door clicked shut behind me. It was the first time we'd made direct, unguarded eye contact in days. It was so strange not to know where I stood with her. I didn't even try sorting through all the conflicting emotions I felt between us. With her red, puffy eyes and pale face, I could read her features better than I could decipher the bond. Finally, something shifted in her expression and the link between us. Guilt flew to the forefront and her eyes filled with a fresh round of tears. I skipped to her side at the exact moment she crumpled against me, knowing I would be there.

"I'm so sorry, Finley. I know I've been just awful. Everything has just been so much, and I feel so terrible."

It was remarkably easy to cling to each other. I couldn't stop my own tears. Our emotions mixed, mirroring and mingling so we worried together. I let it happen, refusing to fear the bond along with everything else.

"I don't know what to do. I don't know what to do." She repeated the words over and over until they lost meaning.

When she paused to breathe, I cut in, "We'll figure it out. It's not like we can mess things up more than they already are."

She sat back on her heels with a small laugh and wiped her cheeks. She reached and wiped my cheeks too. With her fingers already wet, she left my cheeks even damper than before, but I didn't protest. She closed her eyes, likely experiencing my crashing waves of relief as we sat together and the wall between us came down.

"I am so sorry, Fin. I thought distance might help us with whatever Sam is so worried about, but trying to block you out made me feel worse every day. I couldn't even think straight. It's already better now that you're here. I'm sorry I took everything out on you. And I'm sorry Oken had to leave."

"It's okay, Nat." I looked down at my hands, remembering the feel of Oken, his soft curls around my fingers and skin warm under my touch. I pushed the memories away when Natasha's face grew sadder, feeling how I longed for him. "I'll miss them all, but we'll have to make even harder choices as we go forward. And it's not like any of this was your idea. I blame the king and Oken for volunteering." I rolled my eyes in mock annoyance. Natasha's lips quirked in an attempted smile.

"But I should have the ideas. I should have power. I'm useless here! And now I have to marry Hinze—" She swallowed hard. "I can't get married, Finley. It didn't even help us." She moaned and dropped her head in her hands.

"It can't be too late to take it back. No one can force you into marriage."

"If I back out, we lose the alliance. The king told me we

can wait until the war is settled, and he wants Mav to marry first, but after that—" She shuddered. "I just wish...." But she didn't finish the thought, and I didn't want to push her.

"That's more than enough time to figure out how to get out of it," I tried to keep my voice light and joking. Natasha gave me a shaky smile.

"I'm scared."

"I'm scared too. But I think all this just means we *need* each other." I paused. She wouldn't like the direction my thoughts had been taking lately. Bracing myself, I pushed forward, knowing that as the leader of her defenses, it was my job to speak up. "I think it's time we called all the Trish together. Everyone in the city. We give them a choice like we have been, but those who are serious about saving Traesha need to be training. Every day. And training harder than we have been. Training to go to war and fight as a group." As a small army.

"You want to make them all train?" I heard her real question: *you want to jeopardize what makes us Trish?*

"Mags gave us our speed for a reason. It's time to use our strength. We need to stand on our own. The king needs to know we don't rely on him anymore. That none of this is for him. We must be strong enough that he can't force our hand again."

"I agree, but I don't like the thought of using violence to get there. There's so few of us here." Natasha stared at the ceiling. "I just wish *I* could do more. Even if I'm queen, how can one person make a difference? How do I free my people without the king's armies? How do I lead my people with so few of them here? I'm not even able to train them to fight. I can barely even put someone in a headlock."

"There's a reason there are two of us. We'll make a

difference," I leaned in closer, "or we'll all die." I shrugged as if each option was equally likely to happen.

Natasha rolled her eyes but couldn't stop her laugh. The mood lightened. Somehow saying something so pessimistic gave us the sense of hope we'd been missing.

As we settled down in bed, our bond hummed, relaxed and content. Natasha kept looking at me and tugging on our connection as though to reassure herself I was close. The pillow I used smelled faintly like Princess Chelsa. The image it produced of her lying here and talking with Natasha like this was inconsistent with the uptight Chelsa I knew.

The chaos sparking through the bond the last few days finally settled. Natasha and I talked late into the night, covering everything, including Natasha's hesitantly blooming friendship with the Florian princesses and what she had learned about Florian beliefs through them, such as the theory that the gods we worshipped were simply extremely gifted Florians. We sat in discomfort with that thought and quickly moved on to her situation with Hinze, my first kiss with Oken, my diminished anger toward my mother, Londe's news about the spy, and how much we hated the king of Floria.

The only thing I left out was the beginning of the prophecy my mother had recited. I didn't want to make it real between us. I told myself it was because I didn't know the whole thing and didn't want to worry Natasha unnecessarily, but I knew I was avoiding the topic. It felt good to complain and even laugh about everything else that was happening.

Not as good as it would have felt to actually be doing something, but we went to sleep feeling better about the world hanging over us.

CHAPTER 20

In the morning, I woke well-rested for the first time in days. I realized just how much the bond had been fogging my thoughts. Fighting it wasn't helping anyone. I was finally strong enough to sort through the tangled mess of issues building in my head. The need for a Trish army and the spy took precedence on my list. I left the palace walls while Natasha was having breakfast with the princesses again. I skipped to the Trish theater Londe had pointed out. The side door was unlocked, and the area within was dimly lit. I walked through a dark hall accented in gold, which undoubtedly shimmered when the chandeliers were lit overhead. I entered the auditorium. Past performances seemed to hang in the expectant air. I took in the vast space, head tipping back and heart pounding.

They had designed it with the Trish castle in mind. Paintings of the forest, mountains, and sea covered the walls. There was more gold detailing and arches over the stage like trees. It was breathtaking. It was the art and beauty of Traesha. It made me homesick for a place I had only visited briefly.

"Hello?" I called in Trish. There was a clattering like someone knocked over an instrument, then a woman came out from the side curtain of the stage. Her silver hair was swept up in a loose bun.

She froze when she recognized me. Fear flickered in her eyes. She gave me a stiff and shallow bow, unsure how to greet me. "*Resa magsai*, welcome." She pitched her voice loud enough to draw out another person from backstage. "I'm Issa, and this is my partner, Fin."

I smiled a bit at the coincidence of our similar names. Hoping to appear friendly to ease their furrowed brows, I walked slowly up the aisle toward them. "I'm Finley. This place is beautiful." They didn't respond, and I cleared my throat. I wasn't good at this. I found myself gentling my tone and movements, trying to emulate my mother. I wanted to seem more approachable, less Bellovian. It made my skin itch to try. "I have a request to make of you both. Feel free to say no." I said the words, but the fear in their eyes clearly stated they wouldn't feel very free to deny me anything. I held back a sigh.

"What can we do for you, *resa*?" Fin asked. They stepped close to Issa's side, a hand on her back.

"The queen and I would like to gather the Trish. To speak with all of us in the city about what is to come."

"What is to come?" Issa repeated, more worry darkening her expression. She and Fin shared a look, no doubt thinking about the Trish who had just left the city to go to war.

"Yes. We need to address everyone, so we move forward together and in agreement. I was hoping we could meet here. Do you have a show tonight?" I'd already checked and knew they didn't, but I felt the need to give them a reason to say no to me in their fear.

They exchanged another look. Finally, Fin shook their head. "We are at your service. It would be our honor to open our doors for Queen Natasha."

Not for me.

I forced a smile. "Thank you. We plan to meet at nightfall. If you can, spread the word. We'll send people out of the palace to let everyone know too."

They nodded so stiffly that I hurried out. I couldn't help but take one last glance around the beautiful space. In another life, the first time I stood on that stage would have been to sing, not to discuss war. People would have wanted to hear from me. They wouldn't be so afraid I had to invoke Natasha's name to get them to agree to let me up there.

I lifted my chin. That other life was why I was here, why I was fighting. I wanted that better life for all our people in the future, just like I told Jenna when I convinced her to join us. If it made the Trish hate me now, that was fine. It should be the least of my worries.

It wasn't, but it should be.

AFTER LUNCH, I sought out Levi and Rennie, the last Bellovians in the palace. I found them in Rennie and Jenna's room. Jenna's bed was made up perfectly how she left it. I sat down on it heavily and Levi moved from the window to join me. He looked tired. His hands fidgeted in Jenna's blanket, weaving his fingers through the holes of the knitted yarn. I leaned against the footboard and Levi lounged in the pillows. I watched him carefully. For whatever reason, I trusted him almost as much as Oken. His blunt, simple way of speaking made deception hard to imagine. Then again, so did Rennie's. She shifted to get more comfortable on her bed, laying on her stomach and propping up her chin to watch us. Her covers and pillows were strewn about and her clothes spilled out of the closet and onto the floor. Jenna's closet still held the Florian clothing she was lent, all hung up or neatly folded on the shelf.

I steeled my nerves and began. "Do you guys have any idea how the Bellovians knew Natasha was in Honna?"

Rennie arched an eyebrow. Levi considered the question before frowning and shrugging. "I figured they were either making a random push along the Front or saw Hinze and thought he'd be going to the Honna house. Although, I suppose most Bellovians wouldn't necessarily recognize the prince, so I've leaned toward the first theory."

I desperately wanted to believe him. Rennie, always so perceptive, read something in my face and question that Levi missed. "Are you trying to accuse us of something? I know you and Natasha were fighting, but you don't need to make enemies of everyone," she said, frowning. "I think it's clear how badly we need to stick together."

"I trust you more than anyone in this palace beside Natasha. But Nico was able to contact Londe. He said the Bellovians have been getting regular updates on Natasha's movements. Hue found them in his father's office."

Levi leaned forward, alarmed. Was his surprise genuine? He had spent years spying and sneaking around Vichi. Maybe he was honest to a fault in most conversations, but I had to remind myself that he knew how to lie. How to work with people to get what he wanted.

"Since when?"

"Honna. Then the attack happened. It had to be an attempt to recapture Natasha, right?"

"Sure. But that means it could be one of the Florians," Rennie pointed out.

"They hate us, Rennie. Why would they spy for Bellovi?" Levi asked.

"Well, they might want to rule Traesha more than they hate us. What if they're trying to use the Bellovians to wipe Natasha out?"

Levi sat back again. I had to admit she had a point.

"Neither of you know anything? You haven't seen anyone sneaking off to send secret messages?"

"Just Levi," Rennie said with a laugh.

I looked at him sharply, stomach dropping. He held up his hands.

"To the rebellion! Hue made me this transmitter thing," Levi pulled a blocky black object as big as his hand from the backpack he carried with him everywhere. The handheld device had one button on the side and speaker holes on the other. "He created it before I left. It's not very advanced, but it's the only thing that sends messages this far. Well, aside from Londe. It trades recorded voice messages. It's only two-way, though; I can't talk to anyone but him and he swore not to show his transmitter to anyone else. And you met Hue; you know he'll keep his word."

"Can you ask him more about who the spy is? Last Londe heard from Nico, they still didn't know much."

"I can try. But I'm sure it was just a briefing Hue found. If he knew more, he would have told Nico. Maybe he could look again and try something to figure it out." Levi worried his lip and fiddled with the transmitter. I didn't like the idea very much either. Hue was so young to risk. "This thing only sends one message at a time," Levi said. "I'll have to wait until he responds to my last to ask him or it'll overload the system. He usually responds around this time, so it shouldn't be too long."

I took the transmitter and looked at it closely. It had

been so long since I last held Bellovian tech. I remembered how advanced our night vision glasses had been. The flighters. How much did they have access to through Detono? Were they holding back?

"What was your last message?" I asked, handing the technology back.

Levi's face fell. He turned the transmitter around and around in his hands. "Our main headquarters was discovered."

My heart stopped. Commander Gale was a family friend and owned the home used as the rebellion headquarters. What had happened to her?

"Those who didn't get away were sent to the Front," Levi continued. "Nearly a third of us. The commanders killed two of the committee members in the square as an example. I told Hue they could expect the elites to be at the Front and that they should find somewhere else to hide, maybe even risk going deeper into the Squalor. But at this point, it's looking quite helpless. They'll either be captured and killed by commanders, go to the Front to be killed by the elites, or starve."

I swore. The news only ever got worse.

"Do you really think one of us is spying?" Rennie asked.

I sighed and let myself slide down on the bed, accidentally thunking my head on the footboard. Pinching the bridge of my nose, I stared at the ceiling.

"I don't know what to think," I said. "Honestly? No, I don't think you guys did it. I don't think Oken, Jenna, or Audrey did either. I don't think the Florians did it. I don't think Savha did it. I don't know who to suspect or how they would even be sending information. I don't even know if it matters that the commanders know Natasha is in Helsa. It's not like they wouldn't have guessed she'd come here."

"Is this why you're having a Trish meeting today?" Rennie asked.

"Partially. You two should come, of course."

Rennie gave me a crooked smile. "You aren't doing a good job of treating us like potential spies."

I laughed. "No, I guess not. But you know the old saying, keep your friends close and enemies closer."

"I don't think that means inviting potential spies to secret meetings," Levi said.

I shrugged. "Either way, I want to keep my friends around as much as I can. I'm glad the king didn't make all of you leave."

"Me too. I have never been happier to be a lowly Squalor rat. There's no way the food is this good at the Front, even on the Florian side," Rennie said.

We let out empty laughs. The rebellion starved while we joked about food.

"How can we help them? From here?" I asked. I needed desperately to do something. Anything.

"They need somewhere to go, but it's not like we could get them here. The king already complains about the Trish refugees. I can't imagine him taking in Bellovian ones. Even with so many captured, over three hundred rebels are still hiding in the city and living in the Squalor."

"Maybe Natasha would let them into Traesha if we can get the country back." Maybe that was just my influence through the bond.

"Why don't we just help you get the country back?" Rennie asked. She posed the question like it was an obvious option, but I sat up suddenly. The possibility stole my breath. It had never crossed my mind.

"We could attack on two sides...." I said slowly. Years in the Bellovian school system took hold. I immediately calculated the advantages and mapped out attack routes. We'd still be a tiny army, but with Trish and trained Bellovians, it would be a force. A country protected by children wouldn't know how to counter all the strategies this opened up. They would hesitate when faced with their own people.

"How would they even get there?" Levi said, bursting the hopeful bubble building in my chest. "The snow is about to set in heavy, and it's not like we have a way to transport them."

"They could steal from lots like we did. Hue could easily get himself a cycle from his dad. Probably more than one," Rennie said.

"Nico still has my dad's old one, I bet." The thought of seeing my brother again in Traesha left me grinning. "We can at least let them know that Traesha would welcome them if we ever got the country back. The forest is huge. The rebellion could hide out in the trees until we get there. And it's warm there, so camping isn't an issue until we get a signal to them to move in for the attack. Whoever can get out of Vichi should."

"I wasn't a huge fan of your forest. Those trees seemed almost alive. And angry," Rennie said, shivering. I nodded. She had no idea.

"I can tell them to try to get to Traesha. I don't think I'll have room for this message and to ask about the spy, though," Levi said.

"You'll help me watch over Natasha? Protect her even with a spy here?" I asked.

Levi rolled his eyes. "What do you think we've been doing this whole time?"

"Okay, give me a second," I said. "I need to check with her before we invite a bunch of Bellovians into Traesha."

"Don't want the invasion round two." Rennie sounded

so much like my father just then that I couldn't hold back my laughter.

I tugged on the bond, and Natasha joined us just seconds later. The wispy hairs that had left her braid were windblown from skipping. I quickly explained the situation, sucking in and holding a breath when I finished. I prayed Natasha would continue to sympathize with the rebellion even after what I told her about Sam's fears. That it wasn't just me. That she really cared.

Natasha looked to Levi. "Will they support me as their queen? I find it hard to believe the rebels fighting to leave Bellovian control would submit to someone else, especially someone royal. I've heard how you all use our titles."

Levi had the grace to blush. "They're fighting Bellovi because it's cruel and offers them the choice between starving or going to war. If you present them with a third option, I think they would find you to be the best choice by far. They would fight for you."

"The best choice...." Natasha sat back, her pale eyebrows furrowed. My heart sank. Even after everything, I thought she would like this idea more. Natasha sighed, shooting me a look. "If they get into Traesha before us, they'll have done it all for nothing. The Bellovian children hold Traesha strong and no one is fighting them because they are so young. I won't condone killing a bunch of children to get my country back."

"The rebels will know to hide in the forest," I said. "No one patrols the trees between Bellovi and Traesha. The trees won't let them. The rebellion can camp out there until we can join together to attack. We'll use the element of surprise in our favor, taking the children captive rather than fighting to kill."

Natasha nodded slowly. "I must think of our people too.

I can't just invite a bunch of Bellovians. You understand why."

"Then I guess this all boils down to you deciding who your people are," Rennie said. She pushed herself into a sitting position, her deep blue eyes more serious than ever as she held Natasha's gaze. "You've already agreed to let Bellovians fight in place of Trish for you. When I asked Savha about what Traesha is like now, she told me there are quite a few half-Bellovian children in your country, mostly a result of violence and Bellovian soldiers taking advantage, but still loved by their Trish parents. Do these kids need to suffer for the crimes of their Bellovian parents? Some of them are my age and are treated the same as the Trish around them: enslaved, beaten, and hungry. And if you choose to shelter half-Bellovian innocents, why not full? Are you only going to help those with Trish blood, or do you stand for more than that? It's time to start thinking beyond terms like Trish and Bellovian. Not even your *resa* fits neatly into either one of those categories."

I tried to hide the hope I felt from Natasha. I wanted this decision to be her own. I didn't want her to change her mind or regret her decision later because she felt I had influenced her.

Natasha rose from the end of Rennie's bed and went to the window, looking out over Helsa. Did she see the diversity on the streets? Did she see how well the people from Traesha and the eight very different estates mingled and lived side by side?

"I don't want to be here anymore," she muttered, sounding exhausted. Natasha turned to me. "I trust you, Finley. No matter Sam's warnings. And we *need* an army. If you think this is good for Traesha, I think it is too. And if it isn't, I know you'll do what it takes to set things right. I want the support of the Trish, though. You can send your message if you can convince them at the meeting tonight. Tell the rebels to head east to the ocean when they reach the forest and stay in the trees as they go up the coast. About fifteen miles south of the city, there is an abandoned dock where we used to build our ships. There will be shelter and other supplies. My grandfather always wanted to hide out there, but Sam thought it was too risky to enter the trees and alert the land and therefore Bellovians of my presence."

"I don't think I can fit all that on the transmitter," Levi said, frowning down at the small device.

Natasha gave him a long look. "You want to go tell them yourself."

How did she see so plainly what I had missed on my friend's face? Rennie's eyes widened when she looked at Levi. Excitement stirred in the air.

"You could leave the transmitter with us," I said slowly as the plan came to me. "Then, when you get to Hue and his device, we can tell you when it's time to leave the docks and join our attack."

Levi nodded, a smile edging up the corners of his mouth.

"Can you get back into Bellovi? Cross the Front? I'm sure it'll be worse than ever," Natasha said. I was touched by the concern in her eyes.

"I think so... it'll be a lot easier to blend in with the Bellovians without you and Fin. And I don't have to worry much about the elites, given my ability. If rumors are true, there hardly even is a set Front anymore. It'll be chaos. I should be able to slip through. And maybe find some of our rebels along the way. Spread the word to them to get to Traesha."

"I'll go too!" Rennie said. The thought of adventure or maybe just being able to do something lit her face.

The sense of loss I had experienced yesterday watching the Florian transport vehicles take my friends to war deepened. It seemed everyone had a place and was doing their part, while Natasha and I had to stay here juggling court politics and training in secret.

I suppose this is what I deserve for leaving so many friends behind to find Natasha when this all started. My team at the Florian base and the Florians in the Trish dungeons. Now, they felt free to leave me and I had no right to complain.

"Good," Natasha said. She nodded a few times, her resolve growing firm. "Good. You two will speak at the meeting tonight. If the Trish agree, you should leave right after. The sooner you get to the rebellion, the better."

"You think they'll agree?" Rennie asked.

"I do. I have faith in the two of you. Convince them and then go. We must help whoever we can in this war. We will only succeed by working toward our common goal together."

Natasha squared her shoulders and left the room. We let out a collective exhale of relief. Levi grinned at me and a smile of my own tugged up my lips.

I must have had a good deal of faith in Rennie and Levi too because I felt as though the plan was already in motion.

❧

I DIDN'T KNOW who Natasha talked to for us, but a sleek transport with tinted windows arrived with the sunset to take us into the city. The driver pulled around the back of the theater. Issa and Fin were at the doors, ready to greet us. They bowed when they saw Natasha.

"Judging by the number of full seats and people standing in the back, almost everyone has arrived," Fin said. Their eyes lingered on Levi and Rennie. Widened when they saw my mother and the Dossens haul large, clanking canvas bags out of the transport.

"I'm happy to hear it," Natasha said.

The couple led us inside. There were several chairs set up on the stage. Those who lived outside the palace were easy to spot by the fearful looks they cast in Levi and Rennie's direction. They avoided my eyes when I sat next to Natasha, the silver at my roots not yet noticeable enough to reassure them. My mother went to stand by the doors to the street, welcoming those who came in, greeting some old friends, and prepared to turn away anyone who wasn't Trish. We didn't want any of the king's people catching us unawares.

Once everyone was settled, Natasha rose from her seat. She stood at the front of the curved stage. Her white hair swallowed the dim bronze lighting. The room fell silent immediately. Reverently. She straightened as the hush washed over her. This was what she was meant for.

"Welcome," Natasha began in Trish. Her voice carried efficiently with the building's acoustics. The hair on my arms rose and I wanted to sing a note just to see how the sound traveled through the space. "May the gods bless us with peace, love, and strength. As we move forward, these qualities are all I desire for the land of Traesha. I believe they will help us immensely in the days to come, but I have learned recently that these three words take on many meanings when working in tandem. In honor of this, I will include our Bellovian guests in the conversation." Natasha cleared her throat and switched to Common Tongue.

Many Trish shared uncomfortable looks, the faces of those from the city tightening. I silently willed them to listen, to be more open. A few relaxed, almost as if they felt my urging.

"Too many people want to take control of our gods gifted land. They have murdered us, enslaved us, and chased us away. They have created a rift between us and our gods. We are stronger now that we are together, but one piece is still missing from the blessed triangle. We can no longer deny it is our duty to do whatever it takes to save our land and our people. I don't know many of you personally. I never got the chance even to know my mother. But my grandfather loved the Traesha of his memories. He told me stories and stories about my grandmother and my mother, the last two queens. A similarity between the two of them was their fascination with other lands. I believe that if we had discovered Bellovi by sailing south rather than to the west, my foremothers would have done what they could to help the poor and starving there. Only people in as desperate a situation as the Bellovians could turn so cruel. I will give the Bellovians present an opportunity to speak about the rebellion and the hope they represent for both our countries."

Natasha gestured for Levi and Rennie to come forward before returning to her seat. When Rennie made no move to talk, turning uncharacteristically bashful, Levi stepped to center stage.

He surveyed the seated Trish, and I remembered Levi as I had met him in Vichi, walking among the rebels, giving directions, and helping his people. While annoying when I was in a rush, his slow, deep voice captured attention effortlessly. I had forgotten he was a leader until he stared unflinchingly at the group of Trish sitting wary and unhappy before him.

"Some of you probably know, or maybe most of you know by now, that I have abilities like the Florians. When Finley explained how Floria once included Bellovi among its people, it made sense. The Bellovians are known for their gift of incredible physical strength, but I think there are more like me who can take *away* strength. I believe that is why Bellovi was able to separate in the first place and why this war has dragged on for so long." Levi began strong, capturing attention and overcoming the tension in the room. My insides chilled at his words, though he was only confirming suspicions I already had.

"The commanders know the Bellovian people have little love for them. When I watched fifteen- and sixteen-year-olds taken from their families to fight in Traesha, I saw what love the people still held was dying. The people of Bellovi have been taught that winning this war is the only way to save their home. The only way to get the resources they desperately need to feed their families. The commanders painted the Traesha invasion as a struggle. They said your people were barbarians we overcame. They said your lands and crops were something we had earned. Some people believed them. Most people were just thankful to have something to put on the table finally. No one living in the Squalor that makes up two-fifths of the city even knew we had taken over a land called Traesha."

Even my mother had stepped away from the door to listen to Levi speak. Natasha reached over and took one of my hands. I'd been clutching them together in my lap. My fingers were stiff when Natasha pried them apart.

"My parents were members of the rebellion. It's all I've

ever known and all I've ever wanted is to find some way to help the Bellovian people, especially those in the Squalor. I can tell the Florians here don't know what it means to be truly hungry. None of them know what it is to lose their family and home. They haven't felt true fear. But standing in this room, I am among kindred spirits. *Both* of our countries have been lost to the commanders. We know suffering and we know it because of *their* actions." Levi paused to take a deep breath and glanced at Rennie. Even when he continued quietly, our sharp senses ensured we heard his following words.

"When I was eleven, I watched my sister die. My father's abilities were the same as mine, but she was truly special. She didn't take; she amplified. The day my sister died, a boy came to our house on the border between the Squalor and the city. He told us our mother was in trouble and the rebellion had sent for our father. When my father ran out the door, the boy turned to smirk at my sister and me. At that age, I didn't know what a look like that meant, but I remember my sister reaching for me. The fear in her eyes. When our father didn't return that night, she told me it was time to hide. She was only thirteen. I remember her determination as she bundled me into as many layers as I could wear before we left the house in the dead of winter. The snow was falling thick, and Hattie kept looking back at the tracks our boots left. We found an alley where the snow hadn't drifted and she pulled me close, promising we could wait there until morning. Then we could look for our parents. It only took them an hour to find us. When she heard the voices approaching, Hattie pushed me into the back of the alley and told me to run. I did but stopped when I realized she wasn't following.

"I watched the three Bellovian soldiers round the

corner, one of them in a commander's uniform. Hattie raised her arms and I felt her draw my gift, process it, heighten it in a way I'm not capable of to this day. Their knees weakened, but Hattie wasn't fast enough to stop the woman in the back from shooting her. Hattie probably could have survived the wound; it was high in her chest, practically her shoulder. But as she lay bleeding in the snow, she used all her strength to use my power to drain the life from the soldiers so I could get away. I could barely even feel it. It was the first time I realized the full extent of her gift. As far as I know, it was the first time she really used it. My sister was strong and smart and loving and she died making sure I lived. I believe in the people of Bellovi because, for me, Hattie was the epitome of all they can be. She could have done so much damage, but she wanted peace. She wanted to help. I've learned since that my father was imprisoned that night and my mother was killed. The commanders held my father in a cell where they trained his abilities and forced him into compliance. I know this because my friend Audrey was in the cell next door. He helped her escape and they meant to return to the rebellion, but only she survived."

Levi paused and let out a shaky breath. I was stunned. He'd given no indication he knew those cells while we were freeing Natasha.

Rennie stepped up next to him. She found courage in the desire to give Levi a moment to collect himself. "My parents were both killed in the war. They were very young. My father volunteered when I was just a baby and when I was old enough, my mother left me at my aunt's to join him. They thought they were fighting for a better world where I would have enough to eat. My aunt was cruel and gave almost all the food to her six children, even food bought with the money my parents sent for my care. When I was eight, a winter fever hit her home, and three of her children died. She resented me for living when they didn't. Life got so bad for me there that I ran away, going deeper into the Squalor. I begged for rations and slept in hidden corners. I learned how to pick locks, to steal, to convince people to give me what they could while I smiled my thanks and took more without their noticing. I learned how to defend myself, first with a knife, then with a gun." She looked at Levi significantly. "Levi sold it to me and told me about the rebellion. Without that cause, I hate to think what my life would have become. The rebellion saved me. It strives to save as many others as possible, but I worry about what they have become since I was captured and sent to war. The Bellovian commanders are getting closer and closer to discovering them. We all know what will become of them when that happens."

She fell silent, and Natasha stood. She gave first Rennie a hug, then Levi. The Trish didn't even blink at the contact, and hope unfurled in my chest. I smiled at my friends as they passed me on their way back to their seats. Natasha watched them sit, and I could feel resolve strengthen within her. She turned to the Trish.

"Rennie and Levi speak the truth. If you all agree, I have given the two of them permission to invite members of the rebellion to Traesha. Those who can make it will flee to our country for safety. When the time comes, they will help us retake our land. The rebellion and I have a similar goal for the world. Since our country was taken from us, we have all known it will never return to the land of little diversity our people had known. We can't turn a blind eye to the suffering of others, or we are just as bad as those who have turned a blind eye to ours. Therefore, I will invite the rebels to live among us. Do I have your support?"

There was a tense pause. My mother began to clap in the back of the room. Asa and Sadie joined her. Through the rows of seats, Trish nodded and clapped. My eyes stung with tears I wouldn't let fall. I had never felt more connected with them.

"My *resa* has some ideas on how we will reclaim our home."

Natasha lifted a hand in my direction. When she gave me an encouraging smile, I slowly rose and faced the room. I looked to my mother standing by the doors. The pride shining in her eyes made me stand taller. I lifted my chin and swallowed my nerves.

"It's time for the Trish to fight back," I said. They shifted in their seats. I let my words linger as I waited for them to settle. "We have enemies on all sides striving to diminish our resources, culture, and people for their own gain. If our enemies succeed, it won't matter that Finma asked us to establish peace. It won't matter that we believe in our gods at all. Our ways won't exist. We need to return to Traesha; unfortunately, I can't see how we can do that without a fight. Without using Mags's strength. It's time we all trained more seriously and focused on the offensive. Separate from the Florians and exploring everything our unique gifts allow us to do. I will lead multiple training sessions each day, at the palace and here in the city if any of you know a place."

Fin was nodding and I relaxed a bit, knowing we'd be able to use the large stage and back rooms. "During these sessions, my mother and I will train you in the *magsai* fighting style, which focuses on disabling opponents without ending their lives. In this way, we will strive to uphold Finma's values and do our part to end the useless waste of lives. We will do what we can to maintain peace, but we must prepare for times when that is not enough."

I paused and nodded to my mother. She skipped to the bags we'd left beside the stage and opened them to reveal piles of shining swords, all slim and razor-sharp. Many gasped at the sight of the *magsai* traditional weapons. The shining silver of their blades were etched with roses, trees, animals, lyrics, and other tributes to the land of Traesha. The Dossens came forward to help her hand out the weapons they had brought from Traesha twenty years ago and showed me just this morning.

They armed many of the adult Trish. The sense of empowerment weapons allowed washed over them. My mother handed me the last blade. One side was decorated with the leaves of a vine and the other had the words from my favorite song. *He could have burned the world.*

It was the sword that had been above my parent's bed in Vichi all these years. It had scarred the pads of my fingers and inspired my dreams. I had thought it lost. Figured it was decorating the back or belt of some commander. Had my mother taken the time to get it when she could have been saving my father? I swallowed the bitter anger again, the grief of childhood memories. I accepted the *magsai* blade.

It fit perfectly in my hand.

"We brought these swords when we first came to Floria as an offering to the king when we saw how much they valued fighting. We found them in the back corner of the weapons room a few weeks ago," Fisher's mother said. I was relieved to see her looking better. She'd hidden in their rooms for days. This was only the second time I'd seen her since we delivered the news of Fisher's death. She stood tall with a *magsai* sword in her hand.

"You expect us to fight with these?" a woman asked from the back. She held the blade away from herself like it might attack at any second.

"I expect you to fight," I said. "We're as fast as guns. Our powers are just as intimidating as the Florians. Our blades make us stronger." My words drew dubious looks, most of the room knowing full well they didn't have Trish speed. I pushed forward, my gut telling me it didn't matter. "As I said, with my mother's help, I will train you in the traditional martial arts of the *magsai*, but our blows must be placed quickly, accurately, and the disablement must last the entirety of a battle. If we are being rushed by an army with guns, we must be able to match them and over-power them. In some instances, I think arming ourselves will be the only way to do that. Gods willing, we won't have to use the blades, but I'll never forgive myself if the situation arises when the difference between victory and loss is matching our opponents for violence. If the difference between your survival and death is the ability to use a sword."

"If we're killing our enemies, haven't we already lost?" an older man called.

"We may have as individuals. We will always live with that guilt." The dead eyes of the first man I killed flooded my vision. I still woke from nightmares featuring them and all the others I had ended. "And while we may ruin ourselves, we're saving our culture so the next generation can uphold the values we cannot. I'm willing to pay the price so they stand a chance. So they have the opportunity and life we were robbed of."

Natasha stepped forward again. "There can be no

exceptions to this training. All will come when they are able and learn how they can best participate in their own way. We *will* retake Traesha. We *will* give the refugees from Bellovi a home. We *will* remake a land the gods would be proud of. Speak of this meeting and our training with no one outside this room."

The Trish stood and many cheered. Others looked at the swords in their hands uncertainly. But no one openly dissented. Natasha took my hand and gave me a smile full of doubt. The sentiment echoed in my own heart. I prayed to Finma that the Trish wouldn't have to use the weapons in their hands. I prayed to Mags they would be willing to when the time came. Lastly, I thanked Tash for every person in this room as they stood for our queen.

CHAPTER 21

Levi and Rennie packed what they could carry while I lingered in their rooms. Natasha stayed nearby, offering silent comfort through the bond.

"Will you give this to Nico?" I held out a letter on the thick castle parchment Natasha had secured for me. The words within were too brief and inadequate, but writing them down had lessened the pain of missing my brother. I thanked him for telling me to find Natasha. I told him about her and finding our mother and how confused I was about everything. I told him how excited I was for us to be in Traesha again soon. In a postscript, I indulged myself and told him just a touch about my first kiss.

Folded inside my letter was one from our mother. Nerves flooded as I handed the papers to Levi, who tucked them into his backpack. If something should happen to my friends, would the commanders find those words? Find a way to translate the Trish and decipher who they were for? Would they learn too much about who I cared about? Who Natasha and I were?

Rennie and Levi were too relaxed for me to worry for long. Their confidence and the ease with which they slipped through the world would bring them home safely. Too much depended on their success for them to fail.

It was the dead of night when we left through the back door of the empty kitchen. We hesitated at the palace gates, my arms twitching to pull them into tight hugs, but their wary eyes stopped me. They may be rebels, but they were still Bellovians, and I had to be careful about forcing my physical affection on them.

"Until I see you next," Natasha said solemnly, just as she did for the other volunteers. She pressed quick kisses onto their cheeks, making them stiffen but also smile.

"Stay strong." The words came out raspy through my tight throat.

"You too," they replied in unison. We shared a shaky laugh, and they turned into the night, climbing the palace gate and walking straight down the center of the road beyond. The homes of the elites rose on either side of them, but Levi had no cause to worry.

I watched them go, clutching the black transmitter in my hand and praying that returning to Vichi wouldn't be the death of them. Natasha touched my shoulder before leaving the silence of the night for our bed and giving me a moment to spiral and worry without it mingling with her concerns.

I imagined Levi and Rennie's journey as if I could use my will to lead them to success. They would walk through Helsa until they found a transport. Levi would get it started as he did the transport truck in Vichi. They would ride as far as they could, possibly stopping in the next town to switch the transport out. I pictured them getting right up to the

Front, crossing without the elites being able to target them, and then blending in with the Bellovians on the other side. Then, they may steal another transport, or if our luck continued to hold, maybe the train would be making a trip back to Vichi. They would return to the Squalor, to the square with the one-armed statue. They would spread word. See Nico and pass along my letter. He would help them prepare and then it was straight north to Traesha, through Trent and the mountains until they reached the forest I loved so much.

And the cold road the other Bellovians had cleared through the trees. The anger and darkness and shift in the whispers around the sight of the invasion. The anger that haunted my dreams. I shivered. Would that happen to my friends? Would the magic of the trees understand their intent? Could I convince the trees to welcome them the next time I dreamed of the forest in Traesha?

I froze, a memory hitting me. It was said the trees knew our future. Was it possible they had already given me the answer?

Before I could get too embarrassed by the strangeness of what I was about to say, I quickly scaled the gate and ran after Levi and Rennie. As I approached, they were debating heatedly about what type of transport they should steal.

"Wait," I said, grabbing Rennie's arm. They both jumped at my sudden appearance. "When you get to the trees of Traesha's forest... tell them *nisashan*."

"Tell the *trees*?" Rennie asked.

"*Nisashan*?" Levi checked, his tongue struggling with the word. I nodded slowly, feeling ridiculous. Could this be who the trees wanted me to give the word to when I left Traesha? The message hadn't made sense, but if the forest could really tell the future...

"Just promise you won't forget it."

"*Nisashan*," Rennie tried. It sounded just a bit better coming from her, though her face was nearly horrified by my request. I let go of her arm.

"Right. I'm sure you remember how different the trees there are. They're alive. They know things." I was blushing hard now. I hadn't told anyone how they spoke to me or my dreams. "They gave me that message. Don't forget. *Nisashan*."

They smiled, only looking at me a little bit like I was utterly insane. Straightening their packs, they promised to remember and continued while I watched, standing alone on the dark street between the elite's mansions.

I felt eyes on my back, but when I spun around, only the gates and the sleeping palace stood before me. I shook my head and returned to the kitchen. Everyone who had followed me from Bellovi was gone. For a brief, dark moment, I was concerned over having lost all the allies loyal to *me*, not necessarily Natasha.

But I shook away the thought. The Trish were my people. They deserved my focused attention. They deserved a queen and the *resa magsai* to represent them. To protect them. It was time I embraced the duty. Time I ignored their wary looks and made them listen to me and trust me. To fight for our queen.

THE TRAINING SESSIONS began early the following day as planned. The earliest occurred in the Trish Hall before the palace residents went about their days. Then, I would go into Helsa for more sessions. Back and forth, I would lead lessons for the just over four hundred adult Trish in the city, working around their schedules. The biggest group was the seventy who would meet me at the theater after dinner. Fortunately, I had my mother, my desire to avoid the Florian royal family, and the ability to skip to make it all possible. I hoped.

I pushed Levi, Rennie, and everyone else who had left from my mind and centered my focus on the Trish waiting for my guidance. I would give them my full attention whether they wanted it or not. Rennie was right in that we should be willing to blur the lines of race moving forward, yet I still couldn't shake the clear image of an entirely Trish army skipping with me into battle. It was a fantasy I used to indulge in while staring at the sword I now carried at my hip. Closer than ever. Still so far. Even the fifty-three Trish who were able to gather for the first lesson watched me with distrust. Few wore outfits conducive to exercise. They would learn, though. They had to.

In my mind, we all possessed Trish speed, making us a force like nothing else in this world. A force that was careful, blinding fast, and precise. There would be no senseless casualties like Dani and Fisher. Fewer deaths period if they mastered the debilitating fighting style of the *magsai*. I knew it was impossible, but I went into the training session as if I possessed the ability to will their speed into reality, and some instinct in my gut told me this was the right approach.

The room was cast in blue shadows as the sun rose on the other side of the palace during our first session. Cool morning air drifted in through the open balcony doors. I forced my eyes to the Trish, away from the balustrade outside and the heated memory it contained. The Trish fidgeted and exchanged glances while I stood before them. I already had a good idea where I was starting with most of them after our basement training sessions, but the room with all the couches and tables pushed against the walls barely held us with the new additions from the city. I separated us into two groups, sending half to my mother's side of the room and keeping half on my own. My mother grinned at me and I was bolstered by her confidence. We turned at the same time to instruct the Trish before us. Natasha sat at the piano bench, not touching the keys or joining in the fighting. She just sat and doubted, brow furrowed as she watched.

"Let's begin." The words were enough to shift their expressions into nervous concentration. As the hour passed, there were brief smiles with every mastered move. By the end of the first session, Trish I'd never spoken to approached me with questions. One woman from the city even touched the top of my hair and said she liked how the silver looked with the black. They were small gestures toward acceptance, but they made me stand taller.

Finally, there was something building in my interactions with the Trish. Not the bond I had with Natasha, but a connection. A feeling I knew was mutual as they studied me and began stepping closer, warming to me with every passing moment together. I realized then how fully I'd been distancing myself. How my sense of worth after a Bellovian upbringing made me feel like I couldn't be close. I loved my Bellovian friends, but I had missed something special by avoiding the Trish surrounding me. Something integral to my role as *resa*. We could all feel it blooming and how it deepened with every hour I spent with them.

My mother and I worked the Trish hard and ourselves harder. Natasha invited Trish to fill the rooms the Bellovians had vacated in our chambers. They now kept a watch as I slept soundly through each night, asking the trees questions and wishing desperately I was close enough to decipher their incoherent whispers.

I fell into bed exhausted with each sunset. I could feel Natasha's worry for me, but I couldn't stop. Couldn't slow. Not when I was finally doing something useful.

Ten Trish developed the ability to skip in the two weeks that passed. A shocking number. Each time another person jumped from one spot to another for the first time, my mother glanced at Natasha in wonder. Each time I wondered why I felt no surprise. Those Trish now came skipping to train every morning even if they lived in the city. They arrived breathless and unseen. They chattered at me excitedly and insisted on practicing with me at top speed. They flocked to me in a way that was entirely unfamiliar but not unwelcome. They gave hugs and touches that I had craved. They were slowly filling a hole I hadn't acknowledged within myself.

Regularly working at full speed was incredible. I had never in my life felt so consistently centered.

Under *magsai* training, we were changing, becoming more confident and empowered. Touching our roots to Traesha in a physical way that many of us had been denied. The Trish no longer talked about Florians and the king as saviors who gave them a home and purpose. They were beginning to look at Natasha and me that way as we showed them their own strength. Natasha's feelings were mixed over this change. I was entirely thrilled.

My mother trained us with the swords, standing in front of the room and demonstrating how to grip the hilts and basic maneuvers. For the first time in years, I was as inexperienced with a weapon as everyone else in the room. One day a woman who worked for a carpenter in town arrived with a sack full of makeshift wooden swords. We took turns sparing with each other using them.

Natasha never touched a weapon. I could feel her internal battle every day we sparred and practiced maneuvers. It was one thing for her to watch us work on hand-to-hand, another to see us armed. While we trained, she circled the room, healing bruises and pulling out splinters. Her presence silenced any complaints about the violence we were indulging in, but her spirit suffered alongside all those who felt what we did was wrong.

Eventually, Fisher's parents, perhaps sensing her distress, began pulling her aside and tutoring her on foreign policies. They read over treaties and studied previous Florian marriage agreements. Asa took his turn coaching her in ruling, offering her a perspective her grandfather hadn't known. It helped distract her, but the more she was immersed in Trish history and culture, the harder she frowned at the sound of our wooden swords cracking together.

Yet, as her doubt grew, I became certain we were doing the right thing. How much of that was proof my Bellovian childhood had corrupted me, and how much was my belief we could change this war? I began to accept the answer to questions like those hardly mattered.

We didn't know what to make of the fact that my abilities noticeably surpassed everyone else's and continued to improve each day. Soon my mother had little else to show me with the swords and no one stood a chance against me. As they watched me improve, the Trish began to address me as *resa* with a reverence they had previously reserved only for Natasha. It left me unsettled.

Three weeks of training passed. I stared at myself in the mirror of Natasha and my bathroom, my blood ringing from the work I put in during my last session. I tried to force the feeling away, but sometimes it scared me to feel the strength of my body, the speed I could now unlock without a thought. I no longer feared the Florians who stared at me. In fact, at some point, something in my face had stopped their stares altogether. I practically blinked in and out of existence with my speed. I accomplished so much so quickly during the day that only an especially difficult training session could still my mind. There was so much to do and no one could keep up.

Another four Trish could skip. Two of them didn't have a history of skipping in their families. Savha trained with more optimism than ever. Her goal drove her hard. She attended as many sessions as she could, the ashes left from Fisher's death stirring in her determined gaze.

We were well on our way to becoming a force to be reckoned with, even among the Florian elites.

I knew what I was doing was right but couldn't fully relish my growing strength with Sam's words echoing in my head with more and more urgency. Whenever they crossed my mind, I had my own worries to add to his list. He didn't know I saw Natasha's dreams or that I slipped into her memories with her when she was upset. He didn't know how the trees shouted in my mind. He didn't know sometimes I skipped so much that I had to draw on my father's lessons to remember how to slow down again.

What if it was our unstable bond making me so fast and strong? What if there was no limit? What if we reached the limit and burned out before we saved Traesha? What if I did turn into a monster and forget everything the Trish held dear while I told myself the whole time I only did it for Traesha's protection? What if Natasha turned with me as our minds interlocked? What if I, if we, became everything the Trish were fighting against? What if the prophecy was worse than I feared and I was fulfilling it without realizing?

I held up my hands and stared at myself, remembering how my heavy wooden sword had cracked through Chaz's like lightning striking a branch, leaving him standing there with just the splintered hilt. The room had gone silent and they had all stared. Savha had smiled at me like I was the answer to all her prayers, the fire back full force in her gaze.

"By Mags," Asa had breathed. My mother tried to hide her expression, but I had seen the thin line of her lips, the tension in her shoulders.

I watched the tremor in my hands in the mirror. Would I ever get used to this strange sense of disconnection from my body? I was feeling it more and more lately as my strength grew. Like my mind couldn't even fathom what was happening. Couldn't keep up with the change. I wanted more. I wanted to be strong enough to stand a chance, but what was the price? Would Traesha suffer it?

Natasha neared, and the shaking stopped.

"Can I?" she called from outside the door. I didn't answer, but she opened the door when she felt my assent.

Half the time, we didn't even need words anymore. What would Sam say to that?

Natasha placed her hands under my own. I noticed the splinters embedded in my skin for the first time. With her long, shaped nails, she plucked them out and, with hardly any effort, healed the small holes.

We wondered at our strength together. We feared it together. Natasha took a deep breath and speared me with a look.

"We use it to save Traesha. That's all that matters."

I nodded, and she left the bathroom. I straightened my

back and picked up my sword from where I had left it on the vanity.

He could have burned the world.

My eyes were fever bright in my expressionless face when I checked my reflection one last time.

I missed Oken.

I missed laughing.

CHAPTER 22

Five weeks into the intensive training I led with the Trish, Natasha and I made plans to explore the city with Savha and Sadie between sessions. We were stopped at the doors of the palace on our way out. "Would you like us to gather you a guard, Queen Natasha?"

Sadie laughed and pointed at me. The guards looked confused, but Natasha waved, grabbed my arm, and kept walking. Since her engagement to Hinze was finalized, the Florians treated Natasha like any other member of the royal family. Elites and nobles even spoke to me more respectfully with the Bellovians gone and my association with them a distant memory.

We wove through shops, watching people make art or show off their powers. Messengers spread news of positive developments along the Front, praising the king and the strength of his elites. The fact that they never shared any bad news made my skin crawl with memories of Vichi. We were never told the entire story back home, either. The city was in a mood of celebration, bright clothing and smiles around every corner.

Natasha, Savha, and I were terribly out of place. Natasha and I were too distracted and sullen to celebrate anything. While the training had initially inspired us and made us feel useful, weeks had passed in monotony. The king refused to meet with Natasha or give us direct updates about our people fighting for him at the Front. There had been an argument between Natasha and Chelsa one breakfast over it. Natasha had been downcast ever since. Savha's dim expression and occasionally caught breath led me to believe she was thinking about the number of times Fisher brought her to these stores. They loved shopping together. My heart tugged, remembering how he smiled at her as she bartered for the best prices in Honna.

The three of us made quick work of spoiling the mood for Sadie, who grew less and less enthusiastic as she showed Natasha and me around. My thoughts were on the next lesson in an hour and I was trying to place myself on the tangled city streets so I could get to the theater on my own.

"Let's just go to one last store. It's right around the corner here," Sadie said, almost pleading.

Sadie was sweet and eager. I could tell she was trying hard to get Natasha to enjoy herself. The king had made such a snide remark at dinner the night before that Chelsa had hushed him even though she and Natasha weren't speaking. I couldn't even remember what it was he said. It just fell into the growing number of slights he had directed toward the Trish as reports came back from the Front. Apparently, the Florians felt they were carrying the pushback, that our people had shown too much weakness.

I couldn't care less what they thought. They would see soon enough.

We followed Sadie willingly, exchanging looks and

trying to rally a good mood for her sake. Natasha tried to spend time with all her subjects, dining in their homes or asking them to take walks in the garden. This was Sadie's first invitation and she'd wanted to go into the city.

The tinkling bell on the door announced our presence. I gasped. Savha reached for my hand, smiling knowingly. The swirling gold on the walls, the cleanliness, the pastels covering the racks. It was a piece of Traesha tucked into the busy city.

My heart squeezed to see Natasha confused by our reactions. She didn't even know her country enough to recognize how easily she should be able to breathe here.

A man stepped through the curtains leading to the back room. I knew Shan from training. He startled so roughly that he dropped the bundle of handkerchiefs in his arms.

"My queen," Shan jerked into a bow. A child ran out between his legs, giggling at the sight of the fallen silks.

"Papa, you dropped the little blankets," he said in a darling combination of Common Tongue and Trish. It startled a laugh out of me. When I was little, I used to do the same at home. Of course, my mother's reaction when I would slip from one language to the other was more severe than this man's. Shan only smiled fondly and ruffled his son's brown curls. The pale green of the child's eyes matched Shan's, but the rest of him appeared entirely Florian.

We exchanged smiles as the boy began picking up the handkerchiefs, his expression serious as he worked.

"This is a lovely shop, Shan," Natasha said. She was beginning to understand its significance.

"Thank you. I do what I can to remember home. It manifested in this." He spread his arms to the store, and a

Florian woman came out of the back. Shan moved to tuck her under his arm, but she stepped away with wide eyes.

"This is the queen?"

He nodded with pride, but her expression tightened when she caught sight of my hair.

"I heard she brought those Bellovians. You aren't welcome in here," she bit out.

"Oh, no!" Shan nearly shouted. "That's the queen's *resa*, dear. She's Trish."

But I had said goodbye to all my Bellovian friends. To Oken and Jenna and Rennie and Audrey and Levi. They left to fight for my queen and her king in a war this woman had never truly experienced. To fight for someone who hated us on sight. My brother was in danger every day. My father already dead. Battles loomed in my future. I was wrung out and unsure of even my own body. I was tired from lessons and of being glared at when all I wanted was to help.

I was running out of patience.

"I'll wait outside," I said tightly. Shan's face paled.

I turned on my heel and left, sending Natasha assurances through the bond that I didn't want to be followed and urging her to stay to look around. The bell tinkled again as the door shut behind me; the sound was far too cheerful for my temper. The sunlight was blinding. Frustration and defeat warred. The memory of my father's smile stung my eyes. That woman had no idea. No idea.

It was all just so unfair. Hatred like that was so damn unfair. I wished I had another word for the feeling in my gut that didn't make me feel like a child stomping my foot. But it just wasn't fair. None of this was.

Commotion a few blocks over caught my attention. I skipped to investigate. I only made it so far before I had to slow and pick my way through the hoard of cheering people lining the wide street leading to the palace gates.

My heart lurched at the sight of the royal transport coming down the road. Elites were returning from the Front.

I pushed my way back through the crowd, shouted complaints following me. Natasha was already there. Sadie and Savha insisted we go ahead since they couldn't skip. Natasha and I ran as fast as she could to the palace entrance, skirting the crowd and barely slipping through the gates before the transport. We arrived at the palace doors windblown and clutched each other's hands. My stomach sank slightly to see only one transport was returning and not the line of them that had left well over a month ago.

The transport parked and unloaded. The Trish brothers Reese and Nass exited last and stood apart from the Florians being welcomed home. Natasha and I were next to them in an instant.

"You're back so soon!" Natasha said. As far as I knew, she'd barely met the brothers before they left, but now she threw her arms around them. Relief poured through the bond.

There was a hardened look on the men's faces when they stepped back and nodded at her. What had they seen in the last few weeks? If the devastation in their eyes was even a hint of life at the Front... I swallowed hard.

"We were sent to Honna and told to hold off the section of the Front there. The igniters..." Reese trailed off.

"We regained ground quickly," Nass finished with a whisper. "They evacuated the town because of the smoke."

I looked to where Mav's fiancé hugged her father, the king's general, and suppressed a shudder. Nothing in the older man's smile suggested he had committed the atrocities that had put the broken looks on the Trish brother's faces. Completely unbothered, he let out a booming laugh in response to something Tiana said.

"So much of the forest burned," Reese said, shaking his head. Natasha and I shared a look, remembering the tall, haunted trees along the Front. I thought of the Bellovian soldier from the Squalor, hiding and unaccounted for in the trees. Who would even know if they had burned?

"The Bellovians retreated quickly, although many were caught in the flames. They've been quiet along that portion of the Front since. The king called most of us back."

I felt guilty for the hope that fluttered in my stomach at the thought of Oken returning soon. This was in no way something to celebrate. Natasha hugged the brothers again and spoke quietly in Trish so only we could hear.

"I'm glad you're back."

"We've been training every day," I put in. Natasha shot me a look, no doubt thinking the brothers deserved time away from violence. "I would love to see you at one of the sessions tomorrow. Go and rest for now."

We didn't have a choice. The violence was at our heels, no matter what had happened to them.

The brothers nodded, too tired and worn to react further. They disappeared to clean off.

We turned and stood shoulder to shoulder as the elites happily reunited with their friends and family at the palace. "Do you think the king wanted to send Trish to the Front just to scare us with stories like that when they returned?" I asked Natasha in a low voice.

"At this point, everything he does seems like a threat."

Chelsa walked by, trying to catch Natasha's eye. Natasha hardened herself enough that I only felt annoyance. Chelsa sighed and walked on. A small part of me was glad their relationship was shaken. I had learned the difficulties of friendship with Florian royalty the hard way. Natasha needed a clear head when dealing with them.

Three days later, another transport returned, bringing back Salena and Cassa. Since she left, Cassa's wife, Ferras, had developed Trish speed. Ferras laughed in delight as she flew down the stairs and into Cassa's arms at breathtaking speed. Salena watched them with a small smile. Her eyes were dimmed and ageless. When her boyfriend, a Florian guard, stepped forward to greet her, Salena just shook her head at him and turned away. His red and orange sash marked him as an ignitor, though not strong enough to battle among the elites.

I was scared to ask what Salena and Cassa had seen at the Front to cause this change in Salena.

Turned out it was much the same: death and more death with Trish standing witness.

The latest news stated the Florian show of force had caused quite the retreat. The king was insufferable. He strutted around his palace, letting no one forget his victories.

"I don't know why I waited this long! Here is your peace, Queen Natasha." He lifted his wine glass before the dining hall. Natasha had no choice but to raise her own.

I refused. Only Savha's hand on my arm kept me from breaking my wine glass. Even my mother was openly glaring. She'd been training harder than ever, grief powering her strikes.

The Trish who returned joined our training and told stories that added a layer of urgency to our sessions. Each day, lessons ended later than the day. The Trish were asking more questions and focusing their attention on mastering complex combinations at faster and faster speeds. When Wesley returned, he, Sadie, Salena, the brothers, Cassa, Ferras, Savha, and I stayed in the Trish Hall even later than the rest, often missing breakfast while we worked hard enough to break a sweat.

The improvements I saw were extraordinary, but I went to sleep every night worried it wouldn't be enough. I often thought of Mav's words: *One Trish soldier who can skip is equal to at least twenty regular soldiers.* Given our small numbers, we desperately needed an advantage like that. No matter what the king proclaimed, I knew this war was far from over. And the few of us able to skip were not enough.

A few days later, the fourth transport returned. I looked anxiously for Oken's floppy, black curls among the occupants, but Hinze and Londe were the only familiar faces. I went to them, raising my eyebrows at Londe in question.

The commanders know Natasha is here but have not received any new information in some time. Nico is worried they're planning something. It's been quiet around him for days now. And he sends his love and misses you greatly.

I blinked away a sudden rush of tears. Even Londe's voice in my mind sounded tired. And sad. His shoulder stooped. I wanted to ask about Rennie and Levi, if Nico had seen them yet, but Londe's terrifying sister and head of the messengers went up to him and wrapped him in a tight hug, eyes unfocused.

Hinze pulled at his braid, and I was glad Natasha had chosen today to go into the city again, this time with my mother, Masen, and Alessa to shop for fabric.

"Is everyone else coming home soon?" I asked him.

Hinze glanced to the other end of the foyer where his father stood before he replied in quiet Trish, his voice strained. I winced at the hurt in his eyes and how easily he'd guessed I was asking about Oken.

"Everyone that has returned was sent to the Bellovi border...except Jenna. She was with me but went missing while we were destroying a supply route." Hinze's eyes cut to an igniter standing nearby, and my stomach rolled.

Memories of the chaos of fighting both Bellovians and Florians in Honna assailed me.

"No..." I breathed the word.

Londe stepped closer, away from his sister. "We didn't find her body, so we think they captured her."

Hinze nodded, but he looked as sickened by what happened as I felt. "We looked everywhere. I even went through the nearest base, but she was just gone."

"And she... she wouldn't let me contact her," Londe said carefully. I caught the significance of the statement in his voice. I felt my face pale, fear replaced by betrayal. If she wasn't dead, if she was purposefully blocking out Londe, the mystery of the spy was as good as solved. I pushed the thought away. I wouldn't believe it until I knew for certain and I would worry about her safety until then too.

"And the other transports?" I asked to distract myself from coming to any conclusions.

"Mav told me before we separated he was taking the rest of the elites to Detono to see how deep their alliance with Bellovians went. My father told him to bring the other Bellovians with him. I do not know why and I haven't heard anything about their mission since."

"Thank you." The words felt funny coming out of my mouth. I was anything but grateful to learn this. I was cold with dread. Hinze walked away, things too strange between us to make small talk. I could see from the look in his eyes that I didn't want the rest of his updates from the Front.

Hinze went to stand next to his father. He put a hand on the king's arm and spread his gift as though he was worried for his father's safety. The king barely acknowledged his son, talking loudly with the Florian generals about the commanders' cowardice and the end of the war in sight.

"What will they do now without their trees to hide behind?" he asked loudly. Everyone around him laughed except for Hinze.

My hatred for the Florian king increased each time he opened his mouth.

I escaped the crowd and the king's jeering voice. The one place guaranteed to be empty of Florians right now was the shooting range downstairs. As I went, I sent Natasha what I hoped she would take as a warning of Hinze's arrival. Although, from my emotions over the last ten minutes, she had probably guessed as much. Her response was anxiety and I winced as my stomach rolled painfully with hers.

Chelsa and I both started when I entered the shooting range and found her there. She was the last person I expected to see. She dropped the gun she'd been using on the table with a clatter that made my heart jump. I knew I was faster than a bullet but didn't necessarily want to keep testing this skill.

"I was just practicing." She sounded defensive.

"It's okay. I can leave if you want the room." A glance showed the target in front of her was perfectly intact, while empty cases littered the ground at her feet. I hesitated in my retreat.

"Do you know how to shoot?" I asked.

Chelsa snorted. She glared at my shoulder, seeming unable to look in my eyes. "Of course, I know."

I tucked away the new knowledge that Chelsa was a terrible liar.

"Show me." I crossed my arms. Just from how she went to pick up the gun, I could confirm she was lying. I went to her.

"It's easier without you staring at me," Chelsa tried to force annoyance into her tone, but it fell flat in the face of her embarrassment. Without a word, I began shifting her grip, stance, and angle of the gun. I carefully moved her fingers so she wouldn't injure herself.

"Try now," I said. She was too timid in her trigger pull but managed to hit the very edge of the target.

Chelsa was quieter than I'd ever known her to be over the next half hour while I worked with her. In that time, we didn't mention her fight with Natasha, the Front, or the engagement, but as *resa* and princess, these things hung in the air between us.

When she was consistently hitting the same general area, Chelsa lowered the gun. "I just wanted to feel useful," she said. My stomach twisted. I trained for the same reason. She set the weapon gently down on the table, now empty of bullets. "Natasha won't talk to me. Mav and Hinze went to the Front, and Fay's been an anxious wreck the whole time, barely leaving her rooms. Liam's up to something but won't tell me. I've never seen him practice his ability so much. And now, my father listens to Tiana more than he ever did to me. With the general returned, every plan involves the igniters, and the other families are growing annoyed. Especially the drowners. They're content with the victories, but angry none of the glory is going to them."

Chelsa huffed a frustrated breath. I frowned. I'd been so focused on training; I hadn't paid any attention to the politics and Florian drama in the palace. I still didn't even know the details of why she and Natasha were fighting.

The princess continued before I could form a response. "I am the cleverest. Without abilities, that's how I make myself valuable. My father has always been resistant to listening to his advisors, but he would listen to our mother and then to me with her gone. Now he's, I mean, I know I have my prejudices, but I don't want to indulge what he plans. I want the Bellovians defeated, but I don't think burning down their forest with them inside is what it will take. I think you were right from the start. We all know that isn't where the commanders are."

This wasn't the girl who wouldn't listen to Hinze defend me. The girl who threw me in a wine cellar and locked the door. Was this the girl Natasha knew? Maybe even influenced?

Chelsa continued, "And now, if they're truly allied with Detono, who have always been a big enough threat to station spies over there... He won't listen to me. He thinks he won. With Traesha secured through Hinze's marriage and Bellovi defeated, he thinks he should turn his focus to Detono. Who knows where he'll go after that?"

Chelsa had been staring at her gun, but now she looked up at me. "I... I'm sorry for how I treated you. And I'm sorry that the marriage with Hinze and Natasha was my idea." Her voice cracked. The rift between them made much more sense, but the tears that brimmed in Chelsa's eyes were unexpected. "I see now how unhappy I made them. You have to understand that I have enjoyed getting to know Natasha, and I love my brother. I've just never had to worry about him getting hurt, and now Natasha is going to be family, and I can see that means you will be too. Just take care of yourselves. Be careful and protect her. I look at my father and I barely recognize him. I don't want to think what that will mean for you all."

"Chelsa, I think the people you should be apologizing to are Natasha and Hinze."

Chelsa frowned, but it cleared when she took a deep breath. "Thanks for the lesson." Chelsa put a tentative hand on my arm.

I struggled internally. I should accept her words. There were too many rifts and not enough allies in the Florian palace. But anger surged, learning Chelsa was the one to put Natasha and Hinze in their current position.

Chelsa left the room. I let out a frustrated huff, pinching the bridge of my nose. I was angry at this situation, but for once, it was my own anger. A heat I knew how to sift through and not Natasha's consuming rage. In the center of it all stood the king, General Anthez, Prince Mavrick, Tiana, Silken, and the rest of the commanders.

And then there was us. Nico, Natasha, Oken, the rebellion, Chelsa, me, Hinze—so many people were being reduced to helplessness by the whims of proud rulers. So many soldiers reduced to ashes by people who have never imagined how it felt to be powerless. I hated it. I hated it so much my insides burned.

I was tired of holding back. I stared at the target Chelsa had left covered in holes from my teaching, the silence of the room deafening after so many gunshots.

A distant rustling sounded at the edge of my consciousness. The scent of lavender overpowered the smell of discharged bullets. The trees were calling me. *It's coming. It's coming. We must protect. We must protect.*

They wanted me home. They wanted to give me strength.

I wasn't helpless. I was trying to play by *their* rules.

They were fitting me into a box when I knew from the whispers and my bonds that I was something no one had seen before. It was time for change.

I reloaded the gun. I fired over and over in the center of the target, flooded with memories of my father's voice in my ear as he taught me. All his encouragements as he secretly protected his Trish family. As he went behind the commanders to help the starving in Bellovi more than anyone else.

I wiped my tears and lifted my chin. He hadn't played their games either. I *was* my father's daughter.

CHAPTER 23

That night Hinze returned to his place at Natasha's side in front of the dining hall. My stomach twisted watching them shift their meals around their plates, neither of them eating. They both wore their emotions so similarly, they might have been cute together if the situation were different. Chelsa watched them as closely as I did, biting her lip and, I hoped, thinking about what I had said. The king cleared his throat and stood with his glass raised. The sloshing wine was blood red and had already stained his teeth.

"Here's to the Florian victory of the Front! For too long, I have been lenient. No more! The Bellovians have retreated to their cold city where they belong! Let's drink to the future of Floria! To Prince Mav and Lady Tiana and the power they represent!" Cheers and drinking. I mumbled a quiet and sarcastic whoop. "To Prince Hinze and Queen Natasha and the alliance they form!" I couldn't make myself drink that time. "To many victories to come!"

Natasha's smile was little more than a grimace. When she drank to the king's words, she downed her entire glass of wine. The Florians cheered long and loud, but after what Chelsa told me, I caught the underlying tensions. Londe's sister, the powerful head of the messengers, glared at Tiana with a hatred so burning it rivaled the other woman's power as an ignitor. The head of the drowners was turned in their seat, whispering to a grower. Members of the miscellaneous elites watched the other tables with unimpressed expressions. Most of them had been discovered throughout the country and didn't have a court family to claim. They were loose and powerful cannons at the king's disposal only because he ruled the country they were born in. If the court was as imbalanced as Chelsa feared, would that be enough to keep them all loyal?

Would this weakness of the king's be a good or bad thing for Natasha and me?

As soon as it was appropriate for us to leave, we retreated to our room. Natasha took off her dress in a flurry, gasping for air once freed and sitting on the edge of the bed in her slip. I gave her a moment, going to the bathroom to get ready for bed. When I came back, she still hadn't moved.

"Will you help me with these braids?" she asked.

"I'd be happy to." I retrieved the brush and crawled to sit behind her on the bed. I could have quickly combed out the braids with my fingers, but I took my time like I would have before my Trish speed set in. Her hair was as soft and white as a cloud on a summer day.

"I spoke with Chelsa," she said. "She apologized for our fight but said she told the king it would be a good idea for Hinze and me to get married." Natasha gasped with the hurt of saying the words out loud. Betrayal a sharp pain in her chest. It made me wince. "Will you sing?" Natasha asked, her voice catching.

When I looked up at our reflection in the bathroom mirror, I saw tears on her cheeks. I undid the last braid and began to brush her hair with slow, gentle strokes.

I sang quietly, conscious that my mother was on watch in our shared sitting room and could hear every word. The Trish melody was her favorite lullaby to sing to Nico when he suffered nightmares as a child.

Hush, sweet child,
The moonlight is our dear friend.
The air is warm, the ocean mild
The trees sigh; day comes to end.
Hush blessed child,
Tash sings from above
And though Mags may be wild
They too, bow to love.
Hush precious child,
The night is what Finma loves best
She gave us the moon with a smile
And sat back to watch us rest.

Natasha wiped her cheeks and crawled under the covers without another word. I climbed off the bed and set the brush on the nightstand. Outside, the moon was full and bright. I stood at the window and stared up at it. I cleared my head and let the feeling of Finma's protection wash over me. The moon wouldn't move me so if the god of peace had given up on me, right? Would I feel comfort from this sight if she didn't exist? I swear I could hear waves gently crashing against the beach in Traesha. A whisper that may have been the trees, calm for once as they reached for me.

Traesha beckoned me more than ever. I was so tempted to gather Natasha and just leave. Let the king grind his court to the ground and never let Hinze and Natasha enter a marriage they didn't want.

Could Natasha hear Traesha calling us? Did she know to listen for our home?

But there was Vichi too. Maybe Levi and Rennie had successfully gathered and run with the rebels, but what of those too scared to join? Those too afraid to resist the commanders? Those too weak to travel? What about those who wanted to fight? I couldn't deny there were still too many who seemed to genuinely enjoy war. Even the committee leading the rebels had fully intended to continue the bloody fight for power. Bellovians had been taught their entire lives to long for battle. Were they capable of change? If I could figure out a way to negotiate peace, would it last? Would it even matter?

I could tell sleep wouldn't come for me anytime soon and went out into the sitting room. My mother sat at one end of the couch, wrapped in a blanket. I went to her and settled on the cushions, resting my head in my mother's lap as I had all my life. Her fingers were more familiar than my own when she ran them gently over my arm, raising goose-bumps in the way that I loved. She paused when her fingers met with the scar on my bicep, but only for a second.

"I'm scared, Mom," I whispered. "What if I can't save her? Or them? Or Traesha? What if Nico gets caught?"

"You have always been the strongest person I know," my mother said. The wood cracked under the heat of the flames in the fireplace. "If anyone can save us, it's you. If we are beyond saving, it is this world's fault, not yours. Sleep, my dear, blessed, precious child." She leaned forward and pressed a kiss to my temple.

It took some time, but I let my mother's lavender scent wash over me and tricked my mind into pretending it was a simpler time. That my father was in an exhausted slumber on the other couch and my mother and I were unwilling to leave him alone. I pretended Nico was plucking away at the piano; brow furrowed as he practiced a difficult section over and over. I was home in Vichi, just a child content to hide with her family. Us against the world. Full of dreams and hope. Incapable yet of making true mistakes.

At some point during this fantasy, I slipped into sleep.

AFTER TRAINING THE NEXT MORNING, I sat with Natasha while Alessa and Masen readied her for the day. It was sweltering and we had all the windows open, praying for a breeze. Even the light material of my leggings felt too warm for a day like today and I wore a cropped, sleeveless shirt in the hope of cooling off. Natasha dressed in a simple yellow sundress that made her complexion glow. The sisters braided her hair upward and let the majority fall freely in a ponytail. I didn't miss carrying the heat and weight of my long hair. Alessa was brushing a light layer of makeup on Natasha when Masen went to answer a knock at the door.

"Message for you, Your Grace," Masen said when she returned. The small letter in her hand held only a few sentences written in Trish.

"Hinze and Chelsa want to meet after lunch for a walk around the garden." Natasha looked up, eyebrows high. "Do you think she meant her apology? That she will try and help us get out of the marriage?"

"It's possible," I said. Having Chelsa on their side might be a good thing either way. It was the least she could do after causing this situation in the first place.

I didn't know how to feel about the flutter of excitement from Natasha's end of the bond. She flipped the letter and wrote that she would join them on the back. Natasha checked over her appearance a little longer than usual before we went down to lunch.

We sat through at least an hour of the king planning a week of festivities. He was spreading the word, bringing all the elite families to the palace, and inviting Florians with powerful abilities to participate in a series of competitions. All to celebrate his victory over Bellovi. Hinze gave his father stiff, tired smiles, and Natasha nodded without hearing him. I longed to ask the king which triumphs he was claiming. Bellovians had been pushed back from a position they had held for almost a hundred years, but they weren't defeated. There was no change in Traesha or Vichi. No one had heard from Prince Mav or the rest who were sent to Detono. Not even a true surrender had been offered. No peace agreements negotiated.

Dread was a near-constant twist in my stomach. The Trish seemed to be the only people in Floria preparing for the continuation of this war. No matter the king's prideful thinking, this wasn't over. The commanders would retaliate, I was sure. The people in Bellovi, like Silken, would fight to their last breath no matter the opposition. I remembered the look in his eyes, the cunning when he spoke of the gifted army. The army he wanted me to lead. Then the acceptance when I rejected his offer. It was nothing compared to the anger he felt toward the king of Floria, yet I knew Silken wouldn't let it go. He would make good on his threat. He would treat me like an enemy. If that memory was enough to raise the hair on my arms, the king had no idea what was coming for *him*.

At one point, I didn't think I could bear it anymore. I opened my mouth to speak, but Savha placed her hand on my leg under the table and shook her head at me. *Not yet,* her eyes seemed to say. I wanted to ask her *when* but knew she didn't have an answer. The king wouldn't listen to a warning from me. I'd already tried, mentioning the gifted we'd seen in Command Hall and the possibilities flighters presented. He didn't listen. The king would learn his due. My anger wouldn't bring that time any sooner and my words would not impact him until that day came. Likely not even then.

I could only hope his people didn't suffer too harshly for his blindness.

I excused myself from the table after barely eating. I could feel Natasha's eagerness to leave the room too, but I paused when I realized her emotions weren't a mirror of my own. She wanted to go but not to escape the king's boasting. I looked back as I left the dining hall and saw her talking with Hinze and Chelsa, a slight blush on her cheeks. Hinze was refilling her glass and gave her a small smile. Chelsa said something to make them laugh, and Natasha's stomach fluttered.

With everything else happening, I hadn't noticed her attraction. It hit me that Oken had always been around when Hinze was before, inducing butterflies in my stomach that must have overshadowed the ones Natasha experienced. I tried to read the bond more clearly now. It took concentration, but I'd never focused on a specific feeling like this before. I saw now that Natasha was glad I was leaving so she wouldn't feel my eyes. She was *enjoying* herself. Why did she want to keep it secret? Did she worry I'd get between her and Hinze?

The worry she constantly felt for the people around her was absent. The threat of war momentarily lifted. Hinze was safe. He wouldn't be hurt and with his gift, he could protect her and the people around her better than I could.

I'd missed all of this completely. I knew Natasha was genuinely angry the king was forcing the marriage and saw now how this confused her feelings immensely. She didn't want to be excited to go on this garden walk, yet she was.

I pulled out of the bond, unsure how to feel about this new knowledge. I thought about her laughter when I returned so angry from Hinze's room. Had it been tinged with relief? Was I happy for my friends?

Guilt swept through me as I realized what an invasion that search through the bond had been. Did Natasha read my feelings for Oken as clearly? My cheeks flushed at the thought. I had just read Natasha's most private emotions like a book after she'd taken such care to keep them hidden. Once again, I resented the strength of our bond. I should have fought the temptation to look, but why could I even do so?

I turned for the basement. I craved the oblivion that training provided. There would be a few Trish downstairs, but it wasn't a scheduled session. Liam and Fay were already down there in the gym for the elites. The king's children were feeling the stress of the war more than I thought. I hadn't even noticed the two of them missing during lunch. I watched Liam shift in front of the mirror, turning into one of the guards I had seen walking around and then one of the women who worked in the kitchens. How often was it Liam I saw around the palace and not them?

He let the illusion slip with a grunt of effort after only holding it for about a minute, and my worries settled. Still breathing heavily, he turned and asked Fay something. Our eyes met, and I hastily turned away.

I continued to the shooting range and took up a long gun to practice, but my mind was still full of questions even as I tried to focus on shooting. There was no mistaking Hinze or Mav's strength, but Chelsa was still without an ability and I wasn't overly impressed with Liam's. Fay was just showing hers, another mover like the king, yet it was coming to her slowly. How powerful would she grow? I'd seen her looks of worry when she glanced at her older sister.

What was happening to the Florians to make their abilities so unpredictable?

I stopped. What if the same imbalance made Natasha and me so strong? The question felt like blasphemy. Our bond and power came from the gods and their will. Yet my faith had always felt more like a habit. I pushed it aside with ease to contemplate the problem. Something gave us abilities and something was meddling with them. My power felt natural, like sunlight on skin. Maybe the natural world, and perhaps even the gods, was more affected than we knew. Could it be the war? Could it be the gods dying? The land hurting and taking it out on us? Was the balance upset in some other way? The only other recent change was Detono's presence in our land, the technologies they sold to both Bellovi and Floria. The same weapons that helped Bellovi take over Traesha. But Bellovi had already been losing its incredible strength and that was why they sought the guns. Wasn't it? Or did they simply need range, then they began to weaken when—

I reloaded a third time when my thoughts were interrupted by a humming noise in the distance. A familiar buzz that washed over me and left me frozen.

In a daze, I set down the empty gun and turned on my heel, flying up the stairs with panic rushing hard behind me. Reaching the foyer, it was apparent none of the Florians heard the droning. Not even the Trish I passed heard. I was too intimately attuned to the sound and it was coming steadily closer. I didn't want to believe what my ears were telling me. I reached the level Hinze's room was on and went to the balcony at the end of the hall. It gave me a view of the city in the direction of the Front. I barely stopped in time and still hit the railing hard enough to knock the wind out of me. I gasped, clutched the stone balustrade, and squinted over Helsa as the hum consumed me.

What I saw had me stumbling back. Flying toward Helsa was a cloud of black. A swarm of massive flighters. Unlike the two I had seen before, the bodies were long and wide. Hanging from the bellies were the guns Oken had speculated would be deadly. The sun glinted off the windshields. The largest began to lower at the city outskirts and landed. The rest carried on, sweeping over Helsa's furthest reaches.

I stared at the flighters, stuck in horror and the gently, sickeningly satisfied unfurling of my dread.

I'd been right.

Shouts began to rise from the city beneath me. The citizens looked for the source of the noise that now reached their ears. I was rooted in place. What could I even do? A transport door wouldn't take out a force like that.

The first flighter reached the city. Two flaps on the bottom opened and a large object shaped like an oversized bullet fell out. I clutched at the rail again.

"No!" My shouted warning did nothing to help the innocent people in the street.

The bomb dropped. When it landed, the world stopped for the explosion. It knocked out an entire building. Fire began to spread, fueled by whatever was in that bomb and the dry, dry heat of the day.

Screams breathed life into the chaos.

The other flighters began to open the flaps on their undersides. The enormous guns swiveled. Bullets and bombs.

Death had come for Helsa and its boastful king.

CHAPTER 24

I knew I should help them. My feet were rooted in place, my insides frozen. *Go help them. Go help them.* The mantra was a numbed echo in my head. I couldn't move. I might be sick. I might try to kill all the commanders. I might die from loss of hope. How? How could I do anything to stop this? Nothing I did to prevent this attack had done *anything*.

I had known war my entire life, heard of the lives lost at the Front and the destruction of the throne room in Trae-sha. Yet I had never imagined this level of devastation. So quick and violent. An entire building of homes and people collapsed.

I watched helplessly as each bomb, so innocent and tiny from this distance, slipped from the flighters. I watched their arcs as they fell. I felt the explosion they brought in my ears, drowning out everything except the screams that followed.

I was so small. I held just a silly little sword at my hip.

Each scream stabbed at my core. *Go help them.* Satisfaction had left me long ago. I should have done more. Tried harder to make the king take me seriously rather than getting swept up in Natasha's fury and biting back my words.

I should have prepared Helsa, not just my Trish.

I shouldn't even have deserted in the first place. My family would be safe, and I could have learned of this plan from the inside among the commanders and put a stop to it.

Each death piled on my shoulders.

I was the only one who knew what the Bellovians were capable of. The only one here who had anticipated what the flighters would mean for this war. It was here and happening and I could have prepared every citizen now screaming in terror.

The world tilted painfully. Emotions all my own were a coiled pain in my gut, in need of release. *Go help them.*

How?

I swallowed the acidic taste rising in my throat. I smelled something horrible. I didn't want to think what it was, but I knew. I knew with certainty. Impossible from this distance, but not. My nose had picked out the scent of burning flesh.

More buildings went up in flames. Jets of water rose from the wreckage as drowners took action and worked desperately to put out what fires they could. The Bellovian flighters drew closer and I could see now that the black writing on their sides and wings was unfamiliar. Detonian. The balustrade under my fingers began to crumble.

I tore my eyes away from the horrors of the city to stare at the marks my strength had left in the stone.

It was the reminder I needed. I was capable. I could help. Somehow.

Breathing quickly, I turned from the burning city and

ran. I skipped so fast I didn't even have the time to take in the faces of the shouting people I passed as I dodged them neatly. Too neatly. When did I learn this control? My vision tunneled and created a path my body followed on its own accord. I ran through the halls and slipped around corners as though time had paused to let me through.

Power fed by emotion thrummed in my blood. I didn't have time to think about the deafening build; I could only call on it as I ran.

I sent up a prayer to Mags and wrapped my hand around my sword hilt. The world was burning, and I needed every ounce of strength they had to offer.

I followed our bond, pausing at each Trish to tell them to arm themselves. To be ready. When I saw those who could skip, I sent them into the city with a sour taste in my mouth. They needed to gather our people.

"Spread word to gather at the theater for now. The rest of us will meet you there."

Each Trish nodded without hesitation, and I could feel as they drew strength from my resolve. They would be my army today. I felt it like a bond, tugging them to readiness like Natasha was pulling me to her. There weren't enough of us. Some still didn't want to pick up a sword. They were untrained and unable to skip. But this was my army. The only way I could help. There was no time for any of us to question it.

Natasha made her way back into the palace. She was full of horror and confusion but not worried about her safety. She must be holding on to Hinze. He could keep her safe. It wasn't until I felt the familiar lightness come over me that I realized he might be able to keep the whole palace safe. My hearing marked when the flighter flew directly overhead. I braced for impact but felt nothing except a flush of warmth when the bomb hit the ground under the palace. Its flames passed by harmlessly and then were swallowed in a blink.

I ran to the main foyer and passed Savha and my mother, swords already in hand.

"What's happening?" Savha called over the roar of another aircraft passing too low over the palace lawn.

"Bellovians!" How else to describe the chaos?

"Where's the queen?" my mother asked.

I turned and took them to Natasha, running painfully slow to accommodate Savha. Hinze was pushing against the wall as if he was the only thing keeping the palace from collapsing. Natasha was white-faced and shaking but unharmed and clutching Chelsa's hand. I heard lightning-quick feet on the stairs and soon, we were joined by all the Trish left in the palace who could skip.

The doors to the king's meeting room burst open. His face was red with anger, his hands trembling in a way I could feel in the walls. Eyes unfocused, the head of the messengers followed. Soon Fay, General Anthez, Tiana, Brea's father, and the other elites came running to his side.

"Thank you, Hinze. You can let go now." Hinze slid to the ground with a groan at his father's words. He lost consciousness, and the lightness disappeared. Natasha knelt to revive him with her healing hands. My first thought was for her and I dropped to her side, grabbing her arm as though I could keep her safe in the same way that Hinze was able to.

The king marched to the door, red cape billowing out behind him and his top elites close on his heels. Before stepping out into the sunlight, he paused and removed his crown, setting it carefully on the side table. With Hinze now awake, Natasha and I followed. The Trish were close on our heels. Their presence steadied me as we went outside and stood at the top of the stairs. The king and his top elites walked a short distance down the drive, spreading out and flexing their arms. More elites came from their homes just outside the gates, calm as they looked to the king for direction. I almost shouted for them to get on with it already, the sound of screaming far too loud.

The air crackled with energy. Static lifted my hair.

The king moved first, lunging forward and thrusting up his arms. Three of the flighters in front of us shot upwards and back, their metal crunching inward as they crashed into the flighters behind them. Six flighters lost control with one show of power.

Fay mimicked some of her father's movements. She was far less dramatic yet equally effective. Far stronger than I had thought. With a frown and flick of her wrist, she turned the steering mechanism of one of the flighters. Her target swerved and took out two other flying machines. I saw her neck veins bulge, her auburn hair snapping in the wind as she tried to slow the flighters' descent and direct them out of the city. Her arms shook in the air. Once the flighters cleared the buildings, she released her hold on them and let them drop into the sparse, dry lands surrounding Helsa. Fay turned her attention to a bomb that had just been dropped. With another flick of her wrist, she sent it shooting back into the sky, where it hit the flighter that had dropped it and exploded. The king stepped forward again and stopped the shower of debris, directing it to the same place Fay had sent the other flighters along with the others he had crushed in that time. In this manner, the two of them began clearing enough flighters that I pulled in my first real breath since I heard the hum of their approach. Maybe the Florians were right not to worry. Natasha squeezed my hand as relief bounced back and forth in the bond.

A flighter got through the king and princess. It flew overhead and I tipped my head back to watch its progress. A blast of heat blew my hair back. Tiana and her father sent up two columns of flame. The fire washed over the aircraft as it opened to drop another bomb, and the flighter blasted apart. We ducked and I shielded Natasha with my body as the flames licked downward. Hinze reached for me, almost casually sharing his ability, and that action alone told me how little he trusted Tiana and the general. Before the fire could touch us, the two igniters brought their hands together with a clap and the flames appeared to swallow themselves. Fay turned at Hinze's shout and directed the rest of the debris to land away from us.

Two flighters were close on its heels, and Londe's sister watched them near, her eyes unfocusing when her targets grew close enough. Her lips moved rapidly as though she was speaking to herself. The flighters veered to the right. They were so close that I could see the copilots shouting angrily at the people steering, but the pilots didn't seem to hear. The two flighters flew away from the city and then, with a sudden jerk, crashed into each other, going down in a smoking spiral.

The crackling energy in the air intensified, and my ears popped as the pressure around me changed. Brea's father lifted his arms and the wind picked up, making his jacket and the king's cape billow and snap. I saw General Anthez glare in his direction as the flames encasing his hands sputtered out. Brea's father clenched his fingers into fists and lightning flashed out of the previously clear sky with a sudden burst of thunder. Six flighters were hit, lightning flickering and sporadically jumping from one to the next as they fell from the sky. Pushing his arms forward, Brea's father redirected his gusts of wind out and the flighters were swept away. My mouth dropped open in shock at his power.

All around, the top elites rid the city of the attacking swarm without moving from their spots. Those further from the palace weren't as strong or effective, but they were doing their part to take the aircraft down and deal with the aftermath of the bombs. The shadow the flighters had cast over the city dissipated. Some weren't gifted enough to clear the falling flighters and their crashing and the subsequent explosion were as harmful as the bombs that would have been released. Most focused on halting the bombs' progress, likely learning from those who dropped flighters.

In this manner, the gifted saved rest of Helsa from the bombs. By then, a commotion was rising in the streets.

"What now?" King Mavrick barked, squinting toward the road on the other side of the palace gate.

My stomach sank as I realized the shouting was entirely unrelated to the wreckage the flighters had caused. The elites shifted, turning their attention downward. I stepped forward, surprised to find Hinze was still holding my arm when my movement pulled me out of his grip. The Trish behind me were silent, and I thought about those waiting in the city for my command. I had a feeling I knew what was happening. I'd seen it before, but not on this large a scale.

I picked up the sound of gunfire and cycles revving and whooping. I remembered the larger flighters that had landed on the city outskirts.

The bombs were just the beginning—possibly only a distraction.

"I'm going to get a better look," I said. Natasha nodded

and took my hand. We turned and came face to face with Hinze and Chelsa. They stared at the palace gate, stricken even though they could not see the city beyond. Hinze's hand was still outstretched like he wanted to reach for me again as destruction reigned over his city.

Natasha pushed us between them and called over her shoulder to the Trish, "Wait here!"

The prince and princess looked ready to protest our leaving, but we skipped away before they could say anything. We sprinted back up to the balcony where I first watched the flighters approach.

We arrived just in time to see the palace gates blown inward with an explosion that knocked the king and his elites back almost to the palace steps. The Trish scrambled to help them, awkward with their swords in hand.

Natasha stilled. The enormity of the attack became clear from our vantage point. There was so much fighting beyond the palace gates. Much like in Honna, Bellovians tore through the streets on their cycles, shooting their guns and attacking innocents. Their black hair, cut short or a long braid whipping in the wind made them easy to identify. There had to be hundreds and hundreds and still more of the enormous flighters approached, bringing more fresh soldiers and their cycles. It looked as if the entire population of Vichi was here, though I knew that wasn't true. The Bellovians in the city streets whooped and whooped, victory closer than ever. They took advantage of the chaos left in the wake of the bombs.

Yet some stopped at upturned carts to scoop up food, all violence gone as they ate. Even in the destruction, the sight broke my heart.

All wore glasses like the ones I wore during those few days I was a commander in the Bellovian army. I had a peculiar sensation watching them. They could have been me if I had never been taken by the Florians. If I was still trying to figure out a way to take them down from the inside without harming my family. If my father was still alive. If I hadn't discovered I was a *magsai*.

But I was. I was *resa*. Their blood did not run in my veins. I looked down at my handprints in the stone on the railing. I was stronger than they would ever be.

A strange calm flooded me. *The bonds. Singer, singer. The bonds.* I nodded to the whispers. I was born entirely for this. I looked at Natasha. "We are stronger than any Trish has ever been because we need to be."

Natasha held my gaze steady. "Save this city so we can leave it."

We let go of our fear of the bond. Stopped tiptoeing around its potential. I dove into it mentally. I smelled the Trish forest and ocean breeze as our combined strength rushed through our clasped hands, finally freed from the restraint we hadn't fully realized we had placed on it.

I was washed with all the anger Natasha had worked so hard to suppress. How the injustices our people suffered fueled her even while she strived to honor Finma. She let the anger focus her, focus us, directing it at the Bellovians killing innocents in the streets of Helsa. The world became sharper, the edges ruthless. I embraced it.

Through Natasha, I felt myself. My physical confidence and how I spread it to others. I saw how the Trish looked to me when I entered a room. I saw how their strength was unleashed in my presence. I realized then it wasn't Natasha helping the Trish around us find their true speed; it was me. I saw the bond I shared with our people that she would never have. The envy she felt, but the acceptance.

I let go of Natasha's hand. We shared one last look

before I skipped back to the Trish gathered on the steps below, yanking on this newly discovered bond. I felt those gathered on the steps as they looked to me. I felt those at the theater. As one, we tightened our grips on our swords.

Natasha was a pinprick of energy I was tied to in a way that allowed me to gauge her exact distance. The Trish people were warm buzzing lights that drew me. I could feel them similarly attuned to my presence. The bond to them wasn't as strong as the *resa* bond. I couldn't tell their emotions or thoughts, but I could send out my own. It was more like the way the trees of Traesha beckoned me, but I was the trees. It was a strange and foreign power. Too ancient to have at my disposal, yet there it was. It didn't feel as natural as slipping into the forest in my dreams or calming Natasha. *Brittle bonds.* I shook my head and focused. It didn't matter. People were dying, and this was a risk we had to take. This was war.

The gates were still falling into smokey ruins. The Bellovians emerged through the hole they'd created, dust covering their black uniforms. I thought of Audrey. Florians on the streets behind them fought back with their abilities, mostly nobles with great power. I was so glad at that moment that my Bellovian friends were all gone. They wouldn't have survived here, just as they almost hadn't in Honna. I caught sight of a face in a uniform and thought it might have been a boy from my class, someone Oken grew up training with.

I shut down the memories. My throat burned.

The Bellovians swarmed the main streets like ants, but they were being fought off with jets of water, simmering heat, flames, and clutching their heads. The tension in the air shifted. I knew exactly what was coming and stepped forward, the Trish on my heels. The king lifted a hand to stop me from his place on the ground, surrounded by guards. "Just go back. You'll be in the way of my elites."

I scoffed. How could he retain this ego when he was reduced so low? Bleeding on the ground, he still thought himself more powerful. I was brimming with the power of Traesha and he thought himself capable of controlling us. His hand fell at the look on my face.

A Bellovian in red pulled forward on his cycle, stopping right in the middle of the waging madness. Two more followed. Their eyes were empty, faces grim. They made no movements to show their power unleashed, but the Florian who had been throwing bricks at the Bellovians with her ability suddenly stumbled. The stream of water dousing a nearby fire sputtered out. The Bellovians, now unopposed, lifted their guns without thought, shooting everyone in sight.

Screams escalated. The king's eyes widened as his guards staggered and his nobles fell—the red uniformed Bellovians making their way closer.

I raised my sword and let my power flow. Unhindered. Standing before my people, I called upon Mags.

"*Stisha colm!*" I cried in our beautiful language.

I ran and felt the Trish draw on my power, Mags flooding them too. Savha was at my side, her Trish speed finally released and her face set in a determined expression. We flew at the Bellovians on their cycles, vengeance screaming in our blood. An army of skipping Trish, coming from the palace and city, every single one able to tap into the speed of the *magsai*.

It was fate.

It was exactly as I imagined.

We ran through the palace gates with a cry that turned

the heads of those we passed just before the sound was caught in the wind.

I moved faster than I ever had, the Trish fanning out behind me to protect the powerless Florians. We relieved the Bellovians of their guns and slashed the tires of their cycles. We left them unconscious or bleeding. Once we'd cleared the palace gates, I skipped deeper into the city, the Trish spreading out to defend the streets behind me, clearing them in seconds. Commanders, gifted Bellovians, those from the Squalor, on cycles or on foot— none of them stood against my army.

It hurt knowing the red uniformed Bellovians had less choice in their situation than even the others who went through the sham process of "volunteering," and yet they were the ones we had to focus on. I knocked them unconscious, but with my power fully unleashed, I worried I had caused more damage than intended. I couldn't dwell, though. None of us could. This was war and war didn't leave time for hesitation even when one possessed Trish speed.

I reached the edge of the city so fast that the sudden open space took me aback. The last of the Bellovians were just arriving on their cycles. The larger flighters were about to touch down with more, but they weren't a problem yet. I ran down the line of those approaching with my sword held low. I slashed their front tires. Soldier after soldier flipped over their handlebars. The crunch of their bodies hitting the ground and building walls at top speed would live with me forever.

The stream of Bellovians leaving the bulky flighters on cycles ended, and I returned to the city. In the streets, the Florian elites recovered from their shock and rejoined the attack. I was aware of the Trish drawing strength from my seemingly endless reserve. I felt it when Wesley made a killing blow, his entire body recoiling. He turned and heaved up the contents of his stomach before he dodged another attack and pressed on. He was the first Trish to knowingly end a life, but more soon followed.

Natasha was in agony. We all were, but those of us on the streets couldn't stop to dwell on what this meant for our people.

"Bring them in!" I barely yelled the words, but every Trish in the city felt and understood what I wanted. They began to round up the disarmed attackers, killing only when their hands were forced. As I ran, I took Bellovians out with blows to their jaw and back of their heads, knocking them out to be bound by the Florians scrabbling behind the wake of the Trish. There were so many, but Prince Mav had been wrong. A Trish soldier was worth far more than twenty of theirs.

A transport truck turned at the other end of the street. I saw the dark hair of the Bellovian behind the wheel, the twist of hate in their face. I sucked in a breath and skipped to meet it, turning and ducking my head with my shoulder jutted. A crunch, a whoosh of impact, and it flew over me, the shape of my body now dented in the front bumper. It flipped and landed with a crunch on its hood. Its occupants were silent. The driver's glossy stare visible through the cracked windshield. I shut off my brain, felt Natasha, shook out my arm, and carried on.

The Trish worked the attackers first onto the main roads, then toward the palace. I ran by Sadie as she took on a red uniformed soldier with Bellovian strength, catching a punch the woman threw in her palm and putting her sword through the Bellovian's stomach. I froze, skidding on the debris in the street. We stared at Sadie's hand, limp and broken from the impact. I remembered her sitting at the piano bench as if she were part of the instrument, just like Nico.

The price of war was already too many lives. It shouldn't be this too. Shouldn't be art and beauty and passions. The consequences were grave enough already.

Before we could mourn the loss of Sadie's talent, I felt Natasha's presence again. We could barely see her through the buildings, but her white hair stood out like a beacon where she remained on the palace balcony. Sadie gasped and flexed her fingers, her hand in perfect condition once again. She smiled at me in thanks though I had done nothing, and skipped away to her next victim. I gave them strength, but Natasha was their protection.

My blood rushed with our shared power in the bond. The whole city hummed with it—the scent of lavender mixing with blood and ash.

I was skipping from Bellovian to Bellovian when my ear pricked at the sound of sobbing. I skidded to a stop in time to see a woman pointing at a burning building.

"He was right here! My baby!" she screamed.

I didn't think. I darted inside, running too fast for the flames to touch my skin. I burst through a doorway at the top of the stairs, following the sound of cries, pleas for Mama. Fire bellowed out at me, but I skipped through it and into the room. Before I even breathed in the smoke, I handed the woman her toddler, the boy crying and coughing. Alive. A group of elites I recognized from the king's events began to douse the fire, fearfully looking over their shoulders for Bellovians as they worked. So far, the latest wave hadn't approached the city. I hoped they were hesitating. That they would retreat at the threat of my army.

I continued, helping those I could and taking out any

Bellovian in my way. Even without the call for retreat, some were running back to the flighters that had brought them here. I let them go, so my Trish did too. The king wouldn't be happy about it, but there were too many Bellovians to capture and kill them all.

I was skipping past an alley when I heard a voice that stopped me cold. I closed my eyes just long enough to suck in a breath and ensure my hands didn't shake. I turned and crept on silent feet into the shadows between the buildings.

"Where is our next wave?"

"Their commander won't send them in. She says it's too dangerous."

Silken's voice was death itself. "Tell her to get her teams here *now*. And contact Detono. Tell them to send more flighters! I know they have them. I told you before; we get one shot at this!"

"But we have too many soldiers on the ground!" the woman beside him protested. "If we drop more bombs, it'll—"

"And what good are they doing? We were supposed to have the palace by now! I thought you said we'd taken down the gates already!" The enraged panic in Silken's voice almost made me smile. I tightened my grip on my sword, raising its point as I stalked closer. None of them had seen me yet.

"They're holding the gates and pushing back. We can't get past them."

"The elites can't fight," Silken insisted. "We had them disabled!"

"It isn't the elites," I said directly behind Silken.

He whirled, his eyes widening behind his glasses. When he recognized me, his expression shifted—darkening and twisting in a fierce snarl. I saw it then, everything he was capable of. He was far beyond the patience he once possessed to act kind like my father to persuade me to his side. As he had promised, I was his enemy. I saw all the hate and violence he was capable of in his depthless eyes. The desire for power, revenge, and victory. Ending me was the fastest way to reach his objective and the most satisfying. His fist clenched.

"Larson!" he barked. He moved forward to hit me, but his hand crunched into bricks behind me when I easily dodged the blow. His other hand raised with his gun at the ready. "You fucking traitor." He spat at the ground at my feet.

I stepped forward, right into the glob. My boots were already covered in ash and blood. He held the gun, but he was the one to take a step back. I knew then I had won. It wasn't the sweet feeling I anticipated. Something cold was unfurling in my chest. Silken's eyes were on my blade. I was the biggest threat here. I was the monster.

"She's Trish!" the woman shouted. They were her last words. My sword moved faster than my thoughts. A quick swipe, a spurt of blood. I barely had time to understand what I had done before she fell. I waited for regret, but it didn't come. There wasn't room for it yet.

The other commanders raised their guns, and I grabbed Silken, spinning him quickly, so he shielded my front. I moved too fast for them to draw back, to stop the flex of their fingers. They shot, and I darted out from behind Silken, killing them all before they could pull their triggers a second time. Blood slipped in spurts from slits in their throats and stomachs. It was splashed on the tan brick of the alley walls. On my face. My sword. My hands. Everywhere.

Silken slid down the wall, his hands pressed against the two bullet wounds his comrades had left in his gut.

"Your father would be disgraced." His words gurgled as though he had water in the back of his throat. I smelled that it was yet more blood. "You don't even know what he was capable of. What he did for our people. You're ruining everything he worked for."

"My father was killed," I said, my voice too calm. "After you reported my actions. But this wasn't only for him." I stepped closer and pressed the tip of my sword to his throat. "How many did you send to the Front? How many did you watch faint from a life of starvation when you pushed them to run for miles and made the call to end their lives? Was your fight worth it? Were your victories worth it? What do you think of the Trish now? Do you feel our power?"

Silken smiled, blood pooling under his lips and darkening his teeth and gums. He answered all my questions in two words. "Not enough."

I pressed my sword into his throat, my entire body leaning into the slow motion. The blood he was choking on released. It poured thick down the front of his shirt while I held his eyes, watching them dim. The hatred in his gaze never once wavered, remaining even in death. All he cared about was this war and his enemies.

That was all he would ever know.

The fear that came each time I thought of him finally broke. A frigid wash. I sucked in a breath.

"Finley!" I heard my mother's gasp but felt nothing when I looked up to see the tears pooled in her eyes. I had no idea how long she had been standing at the mouth of the alley. Her sword hung at her waist, the blade still clean. I turned away and watched my arm move to wipe the blood off my blade on Silken's pant leg. Every moment he had haunted me replayed in my mind. But he was only one commander. Not even the highest rank.

I bent and took his glasses off, turning from his dead stare. I ignored my mother and put them on to hear the voices coming through.

"Commander Silken report! How are the ground forces? Should we send another round of flighters or the cycles? The Detonians want this finished."

"It is finished," I said.

I stepped over the bodies and around my mother, leaving her staring at what I had done. She didn't move to stop me as I passed. "Sound the retreat."

For whatever reason, they listened. I stepped into the sunlit street. There was a high-pitched ringing in the ear of the glasses, along with shouts as the commanders protested. The Bellovians froze.

Never in all our years of this unending war had this sound carried across a battlefield.

I noted the relief on their faces.

CHAPTER 25

The eyes of the fallen followed me. I didn't have the will to consider what it meant to be so familiar with the weight of their stares. I couldn't brush it off, but I could move beneath it. The top right of the glasses showed Silken his position from the Bellovian base. I ran toward it, desperate to confront the leaders of this attack before they left. They argued over the speaker, claiming the retreat signal hadn't come from base. The soldiers retreated anyway. My legs ate up the distance. The miles disappeared so quickly that the glasses glitched and I threw them off. The sound of their shattering against the brick wall was fleeting and satisfying.

I went to the slim flighter grounded in the center of the bulky ones used to transport the soldiers and their cycles. The large flighter that never released its occupants was already lifting into the air. A dusty, dry wind surrounded the fleet. Soon it would be chaos as the retreat took place and the soldiers I outran returned. The heat of the sun made the camp waver. The open flighters looked like they'd been settled in the sand and empty for ages. Looped straps hung in tight rows from the ceiling; all the soldiers within had used to steady themselves during the flight. How long had they stood there for the journey?

The flighter was enormous, and nearly everyone it had carried here was within Helsa. How many wouldn't be able to return? How many straps would hang limp and useless for the trip home?

I paused and looked over the intricate technology. The extensive wings and droning motors. The mountains of sand that the arrival of the flighters had displaced. I looked down at the sword in my hand and swallowed. As I moved again, I prayed all the flighters here could still get air born. That those scattered in ruins on the city outskirts were damaged beyond repair or replication. As harmful as this technology was in Bellovian hands, I didn't want the Florians having it too. This war would only escalate and nothing would be left.

I glanced back down the dirt road to Helsa. Smoke billowed and I could still hear so many screams. This couldn't keep happening.

The sleek, smaller flighter in the center had a ramp leading up to the door. I paused before entering. They had attached a disk to the top, wires snaking down into the door. I figured it must be important, so I jumped on top of the flighter and ripped it off. From the sudden silence and following objections within, I must have cut off their communication. Only the retreat signal remained, emanating from the speakers on the surrounding flighters. I dropped onto the ramp leading inside as the first commander stepped out to investigate. My sword to his throat, I pushed my way inside.

The small area was full of panels and the sound of

static. Six commanders turned to stare at me. But my eyes went to the girl in the back.

"I had to protect my family," Jenna whispered, her face white as death behind the glasses she wore. Beside her was a map she had drawn of the palace.

"I know. I can't say I'm surprised." It was still a crippling blow to have my suspicions confirmed.

The commander I held at sword point made to take advantage of my distraction, reaching for his gun. I threw a quick elbow and heard his jaw snap out of its socket. He went down, and another commander rushed forward, only to fall at my blade. The rest remained frozen in place, my speed shocking them into stillness. I turned back to Jenna.

"Finley, please!"

My blood roared so loudly that I almost didn't hear her. I didn't want to hear her. I remembered her sketching; the city, the palace, the people we met. Careful details to help the Bellovians identify us. Identify Natasha. Identify Oken. My thoughts went to his family, the fear so familiar and sharp.

"Fisher died for you." I thought of raining flowers, warm hugs, Savha's laugh.

My grip tightened on my sword, the leather warm in my hand. The words on the blade flashed.

I could burn them all.

Jenna's eyes dropped to the weapon and she fell to her knees. "I didn't want to hurt anyone but my family... Commander Silken said if I could find you or wait for you to find us, he would reward them. I stopped reporting after I met Fisher's parents, but I had to go back to Vichi to make sure my family was okay. My sister's been sick for months. The winter fever is running rampant. Please, Finley!"

I blocked out her words and adjusted my grip again. My arm was getting heavy.

What would Fisher want? What would Natasha tell me to do?

What did I know to be right?

I raised my blade and Jenna flinched, her hands clutching her sketchbook to her chest. Fisher's father gave her that sketchbook. Oken had asked countless times to see what she was working on, always making her smile with his compliments as she eagerly showed him.

I swung my sword down and Jenna shrieked. I saw the forest sketched into the dust of the prison floor. I thought of the birds that seemed to take flight even in that tiny, cold cell. I angled my blade and slashed the lines of wire next to her. The transmitter with Detonian writing on it stopped humming. The trailer was silent. Dark save for the hot sunshine coming in through the blinds on the windows. Jenna's gasps were the only sound. Dust swirled in the air.

"It's finished. Take it all and leave."

I left her behind.

My head cleared as I jogged back to Helsa, the adrenaline leaking out of my system and exhaustion beginning to settle in. I heard the hum of flighters as they left one by one. I still couldn't believe they were retreating.

The wash of detachment from battle began to clear. I was coughing on ash and smoke. My clothing was uncomfortably soaked with blood. Blows I had landed and death I had seen and blocked out in the moment came rushing back.

My thoughts darkened. I imagined it was the ashes of those who burned that caught in my throat and I gagged.

There had been people burning in the building I entered to save the child. I forgot I had seen them until now. The black and red blistered corpses.

Leaning against a building, I lost the contents of my stomach. The image of my sword freeing blood and ending lives wouldn't leave my mind. So many glassy eyes now stared from my memory. I couldn't catch my breath and threw up violently until nothing was left inside me. Spitting and wiping my eyes, I blindly continued.

The screams had quieted. There was wailing and grief, but mostly a shocked silence that echoed in my mind.

The war made monsters. After all those years of training, I never expected to be an exception. I had seen so much death and pain, but I always knew I would. I had ended lives, but I always knew I would. I had already broken some part deep within myself weeks ago. It simply continued to shatter the longer I kept up the fight. And I was nowhere near finished. I would be a fine, lifeless powder soon enough. The thought slowed my steps.

I was already so tired.

I needed to return to Natasha, but I heard another person calling for help every few steps. I shifted piles of rubble and bodies to dig them out. More haunting images I couldn't focus on for long, or I worried my mind would snap. I was checking a man's pulse when Fin skipped to a stop at my side. Their nose was bleeding and mixed with the soot smeared over their sharp cheekbone. "We're taking the injured to the healers on the palace lawn. Want help?"

I shook my head, stood, and clenched my trembling hands. This man was beyond help. He wore a bracelet, bright string woven with clumsy large and small loops—a gift from a child.

I helped carry children and unconscious figures to the

sanctuary set up within the palace gates. It was effortless to find the nearest Trish person and summon them through this new bond, bringing them over to help lift larger objects or people. After eleven trips inside the gates and back, I caught a glimpse of Natasha still standing on the balcony, rooted in place. Ash drifted through the air around her, darkening her white hair.

As soon as our eyes locked, the bond flared. Had I been muting it again or her? I moved to go to her, but my steps faltered. I didn't deserve a place at her side. I didn't deserve a place in Traesha.

I saw everything. Her melodic voice drifted through my mind in the way Londe's might have. The way the Trish trees did. The world stilled and our power hummed even louder between us. *I don't know if we are worthy for our positions— of Traesha— but I thank Mags you are my sword.*

Tears burned the back of my throat. In a heartbeat, I was at her side. We looked over the devastating wreckage that was Helsa. Once so alive and carefree. Healthy and beautiful. My shoulders slumped in defeat. What we had accomplished today was not a victory. It was only a sign of my failure. I should have pressed the king. I should have heeded the warnings. I should have made them listen. I should have focused on the big picture. My mouth tasted like burnt flesh, and now that I was still, I thought I might crumble. I braced myself on the balustrade, recoiling when my hands fit neatly into the imprints they'd left earlier. I was so strong, but I wasn't strong enough to save them. My eyes slid shut. I thought of my mother, so strong but not strong enough to save my father.

I forced my eyes open. Forced myself to face the war. Because *this* was war. The battle was only a moment. War lasted so much longer. I wished for weaker vision and dulled hearing as I took in the horror wrought.

"We are *strong*," Natasha's voice was low, full of wonder. I followed the direction of her gaze to our people bringing in the injured. Appearing and laying down another person before disappearing in another blink. Even Alessa and Masen flitted from place to place, bringing blankets, bandages, and water. Every Trish skipped with ease, using the ability to help. Pride filled the smallest fraction of the emptiness in my chest.

Near the palace stairs, a healer was working on the king. A metal bar from the palace gate was lodged in his thigh. His eyes rolled when the Amira elder yanked it out and tried to stop the blood. Every healer was sweating, and their bloodied hands shook with fatigue. A few had already collapsed in exhaustion. A man who looked like Garris gripped the hand of a crying girl. Sweat drenched the back of his shirt. He tried to heal her stomach wound, but he was swaying with the effort and nothing was happening. I glanced at Natasha, wondering why she hadn't gone down to help. She surveyed the lawn below with her eyebrows drawn, worrying her bottom lip.

"You saw how I helped Sadie?"

I nodded.

The healers couldn't keep this up. Now that the battle was finished, none of the other elites were of much help besides those putting out fires and Hinze. I saw him walking into the collapsed buildings to free those trapped inside. Even flames passed through him harmlessly. He looked surreal, like a ghost drifting through the wreckage of battle. The only person in the city not covered in blood or ash, his face was unreadable as he carried people out of buildings or rumble. What else was he witnessing inside the wreckage? How much innocence was lost every time he walked through those walls alone? I swallowed again, willing myself not to be sick. More dry heaving wouldn't help anyone. The Trish promptly took the injured from Hinze and brought them into the gates of the palace, another person too many for the healers to help.

I could hear so many more crying throughout the street. My gut twisted painfully. "Natasha..." I was begging. Why was she just standing here?

"We're stronger than all of them," she whispered. Was she in shock? I grabbed her hand and nearly dropped it, yelping. The power crackled between us, pressurized like the air when Brea's father called on lightning.

The exhaustion from battle vanished. I had never been so awake.

Natasha stared at our hands, then lifted her chin to take in Helsa again. We stared at the war, and I followed Natasha's lead, allowing the energy between us to build. Natasha nodded like something suddenly made sense to her. The crackling, buzzing power under our skin canceled out any other sounds. Trish below paused to look up at us. They felt it. *Brittle bonds.* I held my breath. I watched Natasha close her eyes, her lips moving in silent prayer. She raised her arms and mine moved with her. We stood over the city with our hands in the air, ash swirling around us.

The force that was life built between us. I felt Natasha drawing from me and knew she needed more. I reached for the trees. They were always on the edge of my consciousness these days. I directed their whispers to the well of energy Natasha drew from.

Our power flared. It was Traesha. Ancient trees and the souls buried beneath their roots. It was stories about three gods. A triangle. So much energy I didn't think my skin could contain it. It bounced between Natasha and me through our bond, growing stronger and stronger until the air shimmered between our fingers. When I looked at Natasha, she glowed. The sun of the hot day dimmed in comparison to my queen. To us.

When it reached the point where I thought we would burn alive, Natasha cast the bright force outwards with a high tinkling laugh that rang in my ears and raised the hair on my arms. The light erupted like a strong wind, touching everyone in the gates, blowing through hair and clothing out and out to the furthest reaches of Helsa. I heard the crying halt as Natasha and I were engulfed in the blinding light and I could no longer see the war.

CHAPTER 26

*W*e dreamed.

We had white hair our grandfather worked on for hours as he taught himself to braid.

We watched our mother in the mirror's reflection. She patiently dyed our hair black, frowning and pulling the color through strand by strand with quick, graceful fingers. Our eyes met in the mirror, matching icy blue. She was so sad and worried.

We gasped when Sam set us on top of a horse for the first time and returned his smile when he told us every queen should know how to ride. Our tiny shoulders straightened with pride and possibilities.

We drove a cycle through the streets of Vichi, the air too cold and hour too early for anyone else to be out as our father laughed his booming laugh behind us. We had done that. We made him laugh.

We learned to dance, first with our grandfather, standing on his shoes while he moved in the dusty cabin he and Sam had found. Then with Nico, our mother playing the piano and our father smiling while he watched.

We were standing at the edge of the forest in Traesha, begging our grandfather and Sam to let us go in, just for a moment. It pulled to us so forcefully we almost couldn't hear them tell us no. The risk was too great.

We watched Oken walk into the dingy classroom and stare out the window, head resting on oil-stained knuckles morning after morning as we learned battle formations and gun mechanics. He was so beautiful.

We sat while our grandfather talked us through the Trish history and culture, his eyes green like the underside of a leaf and far away.

We said goodbye to Nico at the train station, whispering words in a forbidden language, dread filling our hearts.

We lived through our grandfather's death and reached out desperately through the bond.

We saw the castle in Traesha with Bellovians dressed in black going inside one after another to celebrate a victory that destroyed our people.

Our vision blurred with rage.

∾

I SAW THE LIGHT DIM. I saw Natasha and I collapse. But I wasn't in my own mind. Like the trees were able to carry me away in my dreams, I saw through different consciousnesses. I knew where I was as I shifted through the pairs of Trish eyes looking up at Natasha and me. I was Savha, heart in her throat as she watched us fall. I was Masen, staring at all the injured who were no longer groaning in pain. She turned to look at the balcony with wonder.

We were lying still, but my bonds were not. The trees were whispering, singing in my ears. The ocean crashed and the wind stirred the dying crops. Heads lifted in the fields, silver hair shining under the sun despite layers of filth. I felt the power of the Trish here and in Traesha. I watched through my mother's eyes as my body shifted. Her relief was forceful enough to make her cry.

I OPENED my own eyes and pushed onto my elbows. I gently prodded Natasha, sending her what strength I could through our bond. A wave of dizziness hit me, but her eyes opened. I felt sick. That wasn't natural. My body felt strange and distant, like I had left it uninhabited for too long.

"What happened?" Natasha whispered, struggling to get up.

I didn't answer. *Brittle bonds.* This unstable power. Was it only me? Did she not hear the trees? Feel the people? See what we'd done through their eyes? I didn't understand, but for now, I smothered the fear. It didn't matter as long as I used it to save Traesha.

Natasha was still staring at me, waiting for some kind of answer. I wouldn't tell her. I couldn't. Not when she glanced down at the palace lawn and pride flooded her features. I knew she thought this was all her power.

It didn't matter where it came from; it was hers. I would give it to her.

It left me feeling so depleted. On edge, like something else was under my skin with me. The trees were still in my head, whispering, always whispering words I couldn't make out.

I didn't want it, but I would use it for my queen.

Our eyes held. Helsa continued burning below us. I

reached for Natasha's hand and, with some difficulty, pulled myself to my feet and helped Natasha stand.

I was drained. Emptied of light and self. The bonds were all that kept me standing.

"We know we're strong enough," Natasha said, voice firm though her body shook. She braced herself on the balustrade, eyeing the indents I had left. "The gods have given us everything we need. Their message is clear."

I nodded, though, in all my bonds, I hadn't felt any gods. "It's time to go home."

CHAPTER 27

"You healed them all," my mother whispered behind us. She had skipped and now stood in the balcony doorway, eyes shining.

Her words didn't make sense, swirling disjointed in my mind as I searched for their meaning. I remembered looking through Masen's eyes but hadn't understood the significance of what she saw. I noticed the king was now standing, craning his neck to see where we stood on the balcony. His leg fully healed. His expression slack with shock.

I looked at Natasha. She was smiling; her cheeks flushed red and eyes bright. The air between us smelled so strongly of lavender it was nearly unpleasant. Her whole being buzzed with remnants of the energy we had created. She looked beautiful. Windswept and ethereal. Confidence radiated outward.

For the first time, she felt she deserved the crown waiting for her in Traesha. She raised her chin, copying the stance I had taken a thousand times.

My mother moved in the doorway, dropping to one knee for our queen. I did the same, a smile that wasn't real stretching my lips. Natasha buzzed with happiness, but I was still empty. I knew I was relieved Natasha had stopped their pain. I knew what she did was amazing. But my hands were still covered in blood, drying and cracking when I curled my fingers into trembling fists.

With my head bowed, I could see the Trish below us fall to their knees, many crying out to Natasha in Trish. *"Stisha colm!"*

The king's face darkened when the Florians, now healed and unburnt, did the same; heads dipped in gratitude. The dead remained lifeless, but everyone else could move on their own, no matter how injured they had been seconds before. Some looked bewildered, having been yanked from unconsciousness or the brink of death with no idea how they'd ended up within the palace gates.

Tears welled in my eyes as I felt Natasha's pride. I let her elation overpower my emptiness. She filled the bond, and I let myself vanish within it. I felt her thanking the gods with her whole heart. I felt how keenly she wished her grandfather could see this. Her victory. Natasha reached and helped me to my feet. We smiled, mine still painfully forced, and waved down at the people below us. More and more streamed in through the hole in the palace gates, clapping and chanting for the queen of Traesha. I even heard my name a few times among the shouting, mostly rising from the silver-haired Trish directly below. The Florian elites kept people from coming too close to the king or palace steps, but that didn't diminish anyone's enthusiasm as they cheered. I was amazed they could rejoice so wholeheartedly after what had just happened. As they stepped around the bodies there hadn't been time to cover.

My stomach rolled again. I swallowed hard. Once. Twice.

The Bellovians may have waited this long to fully use their ties with Detono and their abilities, but I knew attacks would soon take place now that they had shown their hand. Those captured stood silent where they had been gathered to the side, guarded by elites. The anger in their eyes was chilling, and there were few commanders among them. Horrors like today would no doubt continue. I looked down at the Florians' smiling faces and hoped they were ready for what was to come.

Natasha and I wouldn't stay to protect them.

I noticed Natasha watching a particular place in the crowd and followed her eyes to where Hinze was now walking through the bodies gathered below. Chelsa ran forward to hug him. She was as filthy from helping the healers moments ago. Hinze didn't release his ability in time to accept her hug. She ran through him and turned back with her eyebrows knotted. He seemed to struggle, trying to accept her hug, and finally shook his head and kept going. He stopped inside the king's circle of protection but stood a few steps away, holding himself awkwardly. Natasha felt a crash of sympathy even while she basked in Helsa's adoration.

With a final wave, Natasha turned to my mother and me. After seeing the failed hug, she wasn't as enthusiastic as she'd been seconds ago. "I want to go home. The gods have shown us it's time." Natasha gestured to the healthy crowd, and my mother's eyes widened. "Can you ensure the Trish are packed and ready to leave tomorrow? Only what they can carry."

My mother nodded, and Natasha moved to leave the balcony. My mother gently grabbed her arm when she passed.

"Queen Shay would be so proud. Your mother knew you

were destined for great things. We all knew. But this... what you've done today was unimaginable, Your Grace."

Natasha blinked and thanked her before skipping to our room. I knew exactly when she had shut the door behind her. When she collapsed into sobs of relief. She had been so desperate to feel worthy. I marveled at how we could feel so utterly opposite in this moment. Where she felt her place now deserved and settled, I felt like I needed to vomit again.

I barely held my own tears at bay. We *finally* had power. We could do something. Natasha could be something besides a ruler in title over a conquered people. This dread in my stomach wouldn't help Traesha. I had to keep pushing. Move forward until this was finished. Then I could fall. Then I could drown in the darkness of these memories of battle edging in. I focused on Natasha's relief and refused to acknowledge the pain cracking my heart.

My mother and I watched the crowd on the lawn disperse. It was disconcerting to see so many people mourning and celebrating simultaneously. Half of Helsa was still raging fires. The drowners and igniters were exhausted trying to keep the flames at bay. Homes, businesses, and bodies burned while the Florians and Trish rejoiced over Natasha's actions. I had to turn away.

My mother reached for me, and I flinched away before I could think. Her hand dropped and her eyes filled.

For a moment, she struggled to find her voice, and I feared what she would say. "I'm proud of you, Finley. And I thank the gods every day that I'm still here to tell you that myself." She reached again, setting a hand on my arm the same way she had Natasha's. I let her, even though my skin was crawling. I wished for Hinze's gift.

"But you saw what I did," I said, shaking my head at the

memory. The gushing blood down Silken's front. "I'm not like the Trish. I'm more like *them*. Like Silken. I can't—" My breath hitched. I couldn't be like Natasha. I couldn't be gentle like my mother always told me the Trish were. It would only get worse.

"You didn't have to do that, Finley. You didn't have to be judge and executioner, but you did carry out justice. I believe that truly. Not every *magsai* is or was perfect. Just as not every Bellovian is bloodthirsty or Florian privileged and unchecked in their power. We had our laws and passed sentences even when Traesha was at its most peaceful. You aren't the first *resa* to swing her blade to right wrongs or protect those around us. We just don't talk about these things. We never did. It was the queen and her *magsai's* duty to protect the peace in Traesha, and while we were forbidden to speak on how we did it, I don't think we were ever unjust. And neither are you."

I couldn't say my mother's words made me feel any better about my actions, but I was glad she was still here. When she reached for a hug, I went into her arms. Our embrace was short, but it was one of trust and forgiveness. Soon, I was walking to our room, knowing Natasha was through the worst of her tears and wanted me near once more.

I REACHED the stairs to the Trish landing and spotted Hinze climbing them ahead of me. I must have made a noise of surprise because he paused and turned to me.

"Finley." His voice was flat and hollow. He'd never addressed me like that. It was enough to make me hesitate to join him on the stairs. "That was amazing, what Natasha did."

"Thanks. Are you going up to see her?" She would welcome the visit. Complications be damned, she would want to say goodbye.

"No. Maybe. I—I don't know where I'm going." He pulled on his braid and then shoved his hands into the pockets of his pants. "I think I was going to Fisher's room." He looked so pale and diminished, I felt like I could see right through him.

I recognized the trauma haunting his gaze—the confused emptiness. Without Natasha's emotions fueling me, I would look the same as he did. I found myself desperate for his commiseration. For someone to suffer with me so I didn't place it at Natasha's feet. So it didn't infect her through the bond.

"I can't believe you saved the whole palace like that," I tried. I needed him to keep talking. I needed something from him that assured me he was still here. Still with me.

"I should have done more," he said. He couldn't even meet my eyes.

"Hinze?"

"I just—" His hands balled into fists in his pockets and he turned away, staring out the nearest window. His eyes trailed a piece of ash as it floated inside. "I can't believe they did that." The venom he spat behind the word "they" rose the hair on the back of my neck. Hinze scoffed at himself, lip curling in a sneer so out of place on his kind face.

I regretted it then. I regretted every moment I pushed him away and avoided him. I regretted that I didn't just talk to him when I had the chance to interact with his sweet demeanor instead of this.

"I know," he continued, "it sounds stupid and naïve. But there were so many bodies in those buildings. We're nowhere near the Front and they just took what power they had and, and they killed so many innocent people. They took away our ability to defend ourselves and slaughtered everyone they could."

"The commanders—"

Hinze cut me off. "I understand it now. Why my father wanted to send in the elites earlier. How he could burn the forest with them inside. Why he wanted to take Traesha and starve the Bellovians out. Why Traesha and Floria *need* to be allies. I thought it was cruel for him to use his strength like that. I should have been admiring how much restraint he had. *They* didn't even hesitate. They just..." He pressed the toe of his boot into the piece of ash, smearing it.

My blood-flecked hands were shaking again. "We can't just turn around and do the same to them, Hinze. It will never end that way. The people in Vichi, in the Squalor, are just as innocent as the Florians you mourn now." I swept an arm out toward the burning city, my words horribly inadequate to my ears. What the Bellovians did today was unfathomable, but the thought of turning around and doing it back? It swayed my unsettled stomach with renewed force.

Not to mention, could the Florians even retaliate now that the Bellovians had shown their abilities? How many more red uniforms waited to be unleashed? How far did their power extend?

Hinze's eyes darkened to a murky brown, their usual metallic shine dulled. His mouth set in a firm line.

How long had it been since I'd seen him smile?

"We can't hold back, Finley. Not anymore. Not after today. Not after Fisher. After Garris. We can't pretend the Bellovians are capable of peace. We can't believe the Detonians aren't part of the fight. My father is calling for his army. We will march on Bellovi, and they will not be able to do this to us ever again. This war has gone on far too long. We have been far too lenient."

The hair rose on my arms. I opened my mouth to respond, to argue for the rebellion and people like Rennie, Oken, and Nico, who struggled in Bellovi enough as it is, but Hinze was finished listening to me defend them. He walked down the stairs and stepped around me.

"Hinze!" I started after him and grabbed for his arm, but my hand passed right through. I was suddenly certain he wasn't there at all. What had happened to the prince who gently explained the history of our lands? Who advocated for my people with such passion that I learned to hope? Who let laughter shift the color of his eyes as flowers rained around us? The boy who used the last of his strength to enter my cell and make sure I was okay? Who grabbed my face when it was covered with blood and looked at me with hope?

Why couldn't I protect anything? It all unraveled.

Tears burned in my throat; one fell down my cheek. My voice was choked. A panic rose in my chest that I couldn't fight down. The force of it left me breathless. "Hinze?"

He didn't turn. His laugh was humorless. "So, this is what it takes for you to show anything toward me. The threat to your precious Bellovians."

I stared at his back, something cracking deep within. And here I thought it had all shattered already.

It seemed impossible that his voice was capable of falling even flatter. "My father will want to meet with you and Natasha. He wants the wedding to take place as soon as possible. The Trish will enter a mutually beneficial alliance or—"

"Or what, Hinze? He'll march on us, too?

Hinze shrugged. He didn't look back. He passed through the nearest wall. Gone.

I choked back a sob, shuddering. I couldn't start crying now. I was disgusted with myself when the sudden longing for Oken rocked me. If I let the tears fall, I may never stop. I focused on Natasha again. On the trees calling us home. The more I focused on their whispers, the less I was capable of feeling. It helped dispel the image of Hinze walking away on top of every other horror I'd seen today. Even after our fight, I'd always known I could rely on him. I always trusted his kindness.

The war made monsters of us all.

After a deep, painful breath, I turned to climb the stairs. Natasha was standing at the doorway at the top, her eyes wide and dry.

"How could he still think he has such power over us?" she asked. She actually laughed.

She was talking about the king, unconcerned by the rest of Hinze's words. I was so distant, half in Traesha. My voice and the bond betrayed none of my feelings. I knew my face was a blank mask. "I don't know. The Trish just saved the city."

"And now we're leaving it," she said firmly. "Did you let them know to pack?"

"My mother said she would spread the word."

"Good." Natasha nodded. "I don't think I can stay here a second longer. People are starting to cry again. They're mourning on the palace lawn where the bodies are. I wish I had been faster."

I stepped forward to comfort her, relieved her giddiness had ebbed. I heard two sets of footsteps on the stairs, light and graceful.

"So, it's true?" Alessa asked. Her hands and the front of her dress were covered in blood like mine.

"We're really leaving?" Masen clarified. The ash in her hair matched its shade of silver almost perfectly. When Natasha nodded, their smiles were all I needed to know we were doing the right thing by our people. Within minutes, Natasha and I each had a packed bag. Masen and Alessa ran to get themselves ready.

It took ages to scrub the blood from my body. Even longer to start feeling slightly clean. Natasha and I climbed into bed. She reached for my hand immediately.

"Do you think that was the gods?" she whispered.

The blinding light, the warmth, and absence of sound. The power we cast out. The bonds growing so strong.

"What else could it have been?" Yet even as I asked, I felt the gods had become an overused explanation. Right now, I didn't feel I needed a reason for all that happened. If any being had a hand in what occurred today, they were cruel and thoughtless.

"Us? Our strength? But I think it was the gods. I think they gave us our abilities so we can do what needs to be done for Traesha. I think they've been preparing us our whole lives for what we must do."

I squeezed her hand. "Maybe you're right. And if you're wrong, I'll follow you anyway." My voice sounded hollow.

Natasha let out a small laugh, not noticing. Her body relaxed as the day's events caught up with her. I forced myself to still and tried to follow her into the escape of sleep. It eluded me stubbornly. I couldn't stop thinking. Remembering. I could feel the warmth of the Trish consciousnesses over the new bond, unfamiliar and over-whelming with Natasha's emotions quieted. I focused on my eagerness to return to Traesha tomorrow to keep my mind busy.

Every time I closed my eyes, I saw the stares of the dead. I saw Hinze's broken expression. Remorse pressed me into the mattress and made it so I couldn't even bear holding Natasha's hand. The same regrets kept repeating. I should have told anyone who would listen about the flighters. I should have told every Florian the Bellovians had a plan and would attack. I shouldn't have let the king take Oken and Audrey and Mesa. I shouldn't have pushed Hinze away just when he needed his friends close.

I was *resa* and at the moment, that meant nothing but power gone to waste on a girl who couldn't find her voice. Who was afraid to face her strength.

I finally, silently, let myself cry. Hinze's words replayed in my head. *So, this is what it takes for you to show anything towards me.* I turned my face into the pillow so I wouldn't wake Natasha and let all the broken pieces scrape and poke and cut until I could hardly breathe through the pain.

Natasha slept on. Traesha in her dreams and a smile playing on her resting lips. It was then I knew for sure she couldn't feel my side of the bond like I felt hers. *I* was the problem. I felt too much and I had the unstable power. I was the reason the bond was so brittle.

I was alone even in this.

CHAPTER 28

I eventually cried myself out, but sleep never came. Relief swept over me with the first touch of dawn. The palace was still hushed as I gently shook Natasha awake. I forced out a small laugh, trying to match her merriment when she opened her eyes immediately with a brilliant smile. She was so excited not even my turmoil through the bond could touch her vibrant happiness. Did she feel it at all?

We dressed quickly, Alessa and Masen coming in yawning to pin Natasha's hair back in braids. I looked where my ashy, blood-soaked old boots sat by the closet. They were a gift from my father, but I couldn't make myself put them on again. With yet another dark wave of mourning, I laced my feet into the new boots the sisters had found for me weeks ago. These were a dark blue color made of strange leather. Natasha surprised a huff of a laugh out of me when I turned to see she wore the same outfit; only her top was green to my blue. She looked beyond proud of herself over my reaction.

"Today isn't the day for dresses," she said primly.

My smile still didn't feel quite natural. "You're right about that."

I hoped the rest of the Trish understood what today entailed. What had my mother told them and would they listen? Would they be willing to leave a place after nearly twenty years with just what they could carry? Not to mention the journey ahead. I was already reaching in deep, gathering strength for it. Strength the Trish would no doubt need to draw on before the day was done. It wasn't as easy to find as yesterday, I was tired and heartsick, but it was still there. The powerful bond between them, me, Natasha, and the land. All working together to give me strength. A well I had just begun to tap.

When we were ready, my mother was the only one in the common room waiting for us. She beamed at Natasha and me when we joined her.

"I believe everyone here is packed up and waiting in the Trish Hall. The rest are at the theater."

"They've had plenty to eat?" Natasha checked.

My mother nodded.

"Clothes they can run in?" I asked.

My mother laughed and turned for the stairs.

"Enough water to—"

"Yes, yes, and yes! Now come along,"

Natasha looked at me, eyes full of reluctant hope. "Is this really happening?"

"What's stopping us?" As I said the words, I thought about Hinze's message to Natasha last night and the king's plans for our people.

Natasha straightened her back. "Nothing." She swept out of the room.

As my mother promised, the Trish waited in our great room. Many looked as exhausted as I felt. Most had eyes rimmed with red. While no Trish had died, they had lost friends and loved ones in the destruction. Many were still smiling and talking animatedly. An awed hush descended on the room when we arrived, many not having seen Natasha and me since we'd shown our power the day before.

We were approached immediately. It was the Trish store owner named Shan with Fin at his side. I read their faces and swallowed, knowing what was about to happen and praying Natasha understood.

"Please, Your Grace," Shan said, falling to his knees. Fin winced. "I have a Florian wife and child. I can't just leave them here."

Fin didn't bow. They stood tall as they spoke next. "And Floria needs our art more than ever. Issa is helping the city Trish get ready, but we'd also like to stay behind."

Natasha regarded them both briefly, her excitement only taking a minor stumble. "Follow at your own pace," she allowed reluctantly. I winced internally. She didn't understand.

"But I have a store here," Shan replied, his hands coming together. His wife had kicked me out, and his child spoke an adorable mix of Trish and Common Tongue. He had a made life. Fin swallowed. Neither of them meant to stay behind for now. This was their home.

Natasha's eyes turned cold as she finally read it on their faces. A wave of disbelief came from her end of the bond. She had not accounted for this possibility. She hadn't considered many had made happy homes away from Traesha and wouldn't come running back at the first opportunity.

"Stay if you must," Natasha said in a stilted voice. "You and anyone who chooses to be left behind will live under King Mavrick's rule then. Consider yourselves his people, not mine."

Fin's mouth swung open. I knew they wanted to preserve Trish culture here to help the Florians. That their location didn't change who they were, their identity as Trish. Natasha couldn't take that away.

Shan dropped his head, accepting more quickly than Fin. His silver hair fell to cover his eyes. Natasha stepped around him dismissively and regarded the rest of her people waiting before her.

"I won't force anyone to follow me, but we are leaving now to save our people and our home. If you choose to stay away from this particular fight, you can call yourself Florian and live out the rest of your days here. Likely join the king's army when he calls it. You will live under his rule. Otherwise, I hope you have said your goodbyes. You will see them again when the war is over. When Traesha is free and our people are at peace. There is even a place for them in Traesha, but not in this fight. We will be skipping home and those who can't keep up will have to make their own way." Natasha's tone made it clear she didn't think she should have needed to say any of this. She thought the loved ones they would be concerned about were those enslaved in Traesha. She turned to Fin and told them to tell those waiting in the city the same thing.

Fin frowned and nodded. They skipped away. I felt the loss.

A rumble of voices broke out, asking Natasha how she expected us to run all the way back and still fight to free our country after. When they would see the Florians they were leaving behind. How the children would come; if she expected them to be carried the whole way. Natasha was cool and confident, saying the gods would protect us and give us strength like they had the day before. I never realized how much the Trish in Floria had lost their faith until they continued to pester her with questions. *Brittle bonds.* The tension, the volume of their protests, and the kindling of Natasha's anger all became too much. On top of everything, I had someone else to worry about.

I slipped out while she and my mother tried to reassure the crowd.

I walked to the balcony and settled my hands on the stone of the balustrade. This one was smooth. The memories it contained so much more pleasant than the one marred by my handprints. Helsa was drastically different than it had been when I last stood here, kissing Oken and floating on top of the world. Only a handful of streets had avoided damage from the bombing or flames. Helsa had been remade in black and gray ash. No one walking on the streets smiled anymore. Whatever victory felt after the Bellovians retreated and Natasha healed the city had faded, leaving everyone dazed and displaced.

The stone was still chilled from the night but slowly warmed under my palms. I closed my eyes and let myself slip into the memory of Oken, holding it close until my cheeks flushed. The thought of him eased the weight on my chest long enough to pull in a breath.

I couldn't wait to get out of Helsa, but my heart broke when I imagined Oken returning only to find we had abandoned the palace. I recalled the dark hate in Hinze's eyes last night and didn't think Oken or any of my Bellovian friends would receive a happy welcome. Hopefully, the friends Oken had been able to make would protect him. I silently begged Lilah, Brea, and Mesa to keep my Bellovians safe, even from Hinze.

I pulled the letter I had folded this morning from my pocket. Kneeling, I fitted it carefully into an indent formed at the top of the curved stone column. It was a reach. Oken likely wouldn't find it, but I couldn't go without leaving something to let him know where we were. That I hadn't abandoned him completely.

Returning to the Trish Hall, I saw the faces in the small crowd had shifted from incredulous to fearful. Natasha stood firm, but the doubt was affecting her. I sighed. This was another task that fell to me. I pulled on the new bond I shared with our people, the same bond that had allowed me to unlock Trish speed in each of them. They turned as one to look at me.

I lifted my chin and cleared my expression. "We will run to Traesha. I've run further to help our queen when I was weaker than you are now. We all share the same strength and Traesha will gift us with more. When we get home, we will stop the Bellovian children from burning our lands and remove the chains they have kept our people in. The land is still strong. We are still strong. We can do this, I promise. I swear it."

I stood with my chin high and let them feel my confidence. I gave them a glimpse of the energy stores I discovered yesterday. The expressions on the Trish's faces changed to mirror my own as their backs straightened. They began shifting like they couldn't stand still after a taste of power. Wesley, Sadie, and Savha grinned at me where they stood by the piano. I walked through the crowd to join Natasha.

"We're ready when you are, Your Grace," I said, sending up a habitual prayer of thanks to Mags.

Natasha smiled at me, but the look in her eyes was different. She couldn't feel my connection with the Trish, and a twinge of jealousy now marred her eagerness. It stung that her people trusted me to lead them over her. I didn't have time to assure her they only looked to me because it was a fight that awaited them. I taught them to wield the swords strapped to their waists and backs. I gave them the gift of the *magsai*. When we returned home, when this war was over and we no longer relied on our strength, they would look to her.

I highly doubted any of them would be able to stand the sight of me when the dust settled.

Shan slipped to the front of the crowd of Trish, heading toward the door. He worried his lip, eyes darting from Natasha to the doorway. I thought about his child and hoped he'd stay. No kid deserved to lose a parent. As the Trish shouldered their bags, he sighed and left the room. I hid my relief from the bond as well as I could.

Natasha and I led the Trish from the great room. My mother, Wesley, and Savha followed on our heels. I loved that Wesley and Savha elected to stay nearby. In my head, I was already making plans to invite them to the ranks of the *magsai*. Once I learned how that worked. All that information would be available once we returned to the castle unless the Bellovians destroyed the Trish books. I found this easier to think about than continuing to dwell on yesterday's events. I began sifting through the other Trish, wondering who else I would pick to invite among our ranks of official *magsai*. Would it even matter if we were all fighting? Would the title mean anything if everyone who could go to war did? I had to believe one day we wouldn't need everyone to fight. When that day came, only a select few would still want to carry swords. These were the Trish I needed to identify now.

We moved silently through the halls. Trish grace and speed meant we reached the stairs to the main foyer undiscovered. The palace slept on, and I felt a twinge of worry for them. Would they survive without us? How many were we dooming by giving up on their king? I found myself wringing my hands and forced them still.

A tense alliance with the Florians could negatively impact Traesha for years. Generations. Was this the right call for our people?

Thank the gods Natasha was too excited to feel my doubt, but my mother must have seen something on my carefully arranged face. She squeezed my shoulder and nodded. Just that was enough to calm me momentarily.

We descended the stairs and halted. King Mavrick was waiting for us. I squared my shoulders in the face of his anger, stepping closer to Natasha's side. Shan's wife and child stood beside the king. His children and highest-ranking elites flanked him.

Out of all the Florians, Londe was the only one I would have wanted to see and bid goodbye. I wished he was here and awake so I could tell him I would meet Nico in Traesha if the rebels had made it. But Hinze was the only friend of mine among them. His face a hardened mask. He hadn't slept either.

Shan stood at the bottom of the stairs in front of us, staring at his wife in horror. She remained at the king's side, expression grim and her grip firm on their child's arm, even when the boy made to run to his father.

Natasha placed a hand on the storeowner's arm and stepped around him. Shan's face darkened and he slipped into the ranks of the Trish. "How could you tell?" he asked softly.

The woman's eyes rounded, seeing the decision made on her husband's face. The child began to cry, pulling at his mother's grip and calling for his father in a jumbled mix of Common Tongue and Trish. My chest went painfully tight. The mother shook the child's arm and shushed him, casting an anxious glance at the king, but the king didn't bother to look her way. She had served her purpose when she informed him of the Trish's departure. He took no further notice of the crumbling family.

The child pulled and pulled until he slipped from his mother's grasp. She stumbled after him, but he was quick on his feet—swift like the Trish children waiting in their parent's arms behind us. I felt a spark of connection with him like I had the rest of the Trish. I thought again about what Rennie said about the importance of blood. How little it mattered. The boy ran into Shan's arms and his mother began to sob. The king pushed her aside rather roughly.

"What is the meaning of this?" he hissed at Natasha.

"We are leaving to save our country. You have made no move to do so. In fact, at this moment, I fail to see how this alliance is benefitting myself or my people," Natasha said, an echo of the king's previous scorn in her voice.

"Thousands of people died here yesterday. You think I'm worried about Traesha when the war is literally on my doorstep?"

Natasha spoke loud and clear, head high and anger bright in her eyes. "No. But you weren't worried about Traesha twenty years ago when the war was on ours. Or in the years it has remained there firmly. I think you have enough to worry about here and I have enough to worry about in Traesha. Do you know how many thousands of us have been killed since *your* war struck Traesha? How little effort you put forth to save us?" Natasha shook her head, rage shaking her voice. "And how many did we save yesterday, even after your lack of loyalty?"

She stepped closer to the king. "The last numbers we were able to gather told us *over half* of our people have been killed while you did *nothing*, and we still came to your defense yesterday. The battle proved to us our strength. Proved we should never have listened to Florians who insisted we aren't strong enough to save ourselves. We can't afford to waste any more time waiting for you to keep your promises. I've had enough."

Natasha sent the king a withering glare. The shock on his face made it clear he had little experience being spoken to like this. Satisfaction fluttered on Natasha's end of the bond and she made for the door. We followed. I heard Savha release a strange sound behind me and turned to find her rising off the ground—toward the king's raised hand.

"You think we are weak," the king said, a terrifying calm in his voice. "I assure you we are not. You do not want us for your enemy, Queen Natasha." He curled his fingers toward the ceiling and Savha rose a few more inches. Her eyes were wide with fear, she struggled against the king's invisible hold.

I thought of metal crushing inward and flighters crumpling.

Natasha's voice was low with fury. "*Put her down.*"

"I take orders from no one. The Bellovians murdered my wife before my own eyes. They burned my city. They will pay. If you care about your country, you will stand with me. Together we will *end* them."

I moved. In a quick skip, I was right in the king's face. He stumbled back but retained his grip on Savha.

"Queen Natasha said to put her *down*."

The king's lip twisted into a sneer. His eyes were wild in a way I had never seen in a human's expression. He reminded me of the starved dogs in the Squalor. Hungry, snarling, and cornered.

The king flicked his wrist, and Savha went sailing toward the wall. Fay lifted a hand, and Savha slowed, but the princess wasn't as strong as her father, and Savha continued through the air like a limp doll. Hinze lunged and caught Savha's ankle, making her pass through the wall unharmed. I blew out the breath I had been holding.

The king turned to his son, his hand still lifted in a threat. Hinze raised an eyebrow as though daring his father to try something. He was untouchable. He stalked toward the king of Floria, only going solid long enough to move me aside. His gentle touch filled me with relief. My friend was still there.

Even the elites in the room stared at the king in horror.

"Savha is my friend, Father. She has been for years."

"They are all traitors!" the king spat.

"Don't let your fear of weakness blind you," Hinze whispered, intending for only his father to hear, trying to ease the king's humiliation, but the Trish could all hear the words spoken.

"We are not weak," the king hissed back.

"No, but given the Bellovian powers, we are not as strong as the Trish. We need them on our side if we will ever end this war."

The king went to push Hinze out of his way, but his hands passed uselessly through his son, and he stumbled clumsily. Hinze stepped aside so the king could look up at the Trish on the stairs waiting to pass and experience his full embarrassment.

Natasha moved forward again, calling to the king over her shoulder, "We will be in touch regarding a continued peace between our people."

"It will not!" the king shouted. "You have made a new enemy this day!"

Hinze closed his eyes, defeat etched on his tired features. Savha came to stand behind me, her face ashen but eyes ignited with anger. Her fire was back. She spared Hinze only a nod before following Natasha. I met Hinze's eyes, but he turned away before I could shift my expression into something readable. Drawing in a sharp breath, I refused to watch his back as he walked away from me again and went after Natasha.

Shan was speaking rapidly with his wife. Angry and yet still pleading. His son's arms were firmly clasped around his neck. She pointed at the king. Defeat slumped Shan's shoulders and he shook his head.

"Then go!" she shouted.

I hurried away from the private moment. The Florian-Trish child cried softly behind us as his father carried him into the line of Trish. I stopped to look back at our followers. Their expression determined, we all pulled on my strength.

In seconds we were running. Skipping. We passed the theater and our people there joined us. Fin and Issa stood on either side of the door, expressions bleak.

Natasha and I led the way to Traesha, needing no directions. Just as strong as the bond between the two of us, the land of Traesha called us home.

Singer, singer.

I'm coming.

The triangle. The triangle.

WE STOPPED TO REST TWICE, more for the sake of the children among us and those who had to carry them. We slept and ate from our packed bags. The next morning, Cassa approached Shan and offered to hold his son for the last leg of the journey. The small child appeared happy to be transferred into Cassa's gentle arms. I learned she and Shan were cousins and had fled Traesha together after the attack. I didn't know if it was a comfort for Shan yet, but I was glad to learn he had family to support him. I prayed when the dust settled, he'd be able to work things out with the boy's mother. I prayed Natasha would let him.

The sun was bright as it chased away the coolness of the night. We had slept huddled together in the fields of the Bennick's land. I couldn't believe how far we'd traveled. A herd of cattle grazed to our left, unbothered by our presence.

The Trish forest was so close I could taste it in the air.

"We can't just go and slaughter the children," Natasha whispered for my ears alone as she tied the laces of her boots.

I cringed. Is that what she thought my plan was? "We don't need to. You saw their parents' faces when they were taken. You saw how afraid they were on the train. I don't think they'll fight as hard because of it. I'm hoping we can talk sense into them, especially if the rebellion is there to help us. Having familiar faces will help."

"I have a feeling they're instructed to shoot on sight."

I shrugged. I thought of my class at fifteen. It had been the year Oken started working as a mechanic and kept hiding tiny, whirling engines around the classroom. He'd hum at perfect pitch along with the buzzing items, so our teacher had no idea where to look. Even I hadn't been able to hold in my laughter at the silly prank. Fifteen-year-olds were just kids. We'd been savoring the freedom we still had and the respect afforded us by people who knew most of us would volunteer soon. These kids had been robbed of their childhood and the last couple years of classes that truly delved into battle strategy. They would follow orders, but they didn't know what they were doing. They'd been thrown into war too early, too young, and too scared.

Then there were people like Mayze. For Oken's sake, I hoped I found her quickly. For my sake, I hoped she was happy to see me.

"We'll disarm them."

Natasha worried her lip. "Will we be quick enough? Most of those remaining in Traesha couldn't escape because they didn't have Trish speed."

"I think I can change that," I said. Natasha raised an eyebrow. "I mean, I can change that." I put all the confidence I could into that statement. "Again, don't forget we'll have the rebellion at our back. Even the confusion their presence will cause might be enough to overtake them."

"If they made it," Natasha looked in the direction of Traesha with doubt. We hadn't heard from Levi yet. I placed an arm around her shoulders.

"You, my queen, need to have more faith."

Natasha snorted but rested her head on my shoulder for just a moment, drawing on my strength. "Let the rebellion know to be ready," she said, straightening. She nodded at the Trish, "And make sure they are too."

"I will."

Natasha went to Shan and the other parents, telling them it would be best to leave the kids together in the forest when we reach Traesha. She went to Alessa and

Masen last, putting them in charge of the little ones when the time came and ignoring their protests.

I pulled the small black transmitter from my pack and pressed the button. "We will be there in an hour. Move for the city and be ready to fight. Keep casualties to a minimum."

I released the button and the transmitter beeped once. I prayed that meant it sent successfully, though not entirely sure which god would aid technology, and slipped it back into my bag. As we readied to run, I drew on my strength yet again. The Trish energized while I explored whatever it was connecting them to me. I felt like I was just brushing the surface of my power, yet any stooped shoulders straightened, and a giddy burst of laughter sounded to my left. Savha was bouncing on the balls of her feet. Natasha returned to my side with a smile.

"Shall we?" I asked. At her nod, we began running faster than we had yesterday.

The Trish shouted at each other excitedly over the wind as we slipped through the first trees, not yet in Traesha. I heard Wesley and Sadie laughing about something to my right, falling slightly behind as they tried to catch their breath.

We paused when we reached the outer edge of the Trish forest, the power of it overwhelming.

My mother's voice rose above all the others, and we slowed in the trees. We walked, but with the speed and grace of our people, we still traveled quickly over the forest floor. She'd been talking to Asa, but now she spoke for us all. The story brought me back to a childhood of her tucking me into bed each night and whispering about the gods.

"There is a land high in the north," my mother began. Natasha reached for my hand. Her hair fluttered in a breeze

I didn't feel, her eyes shut as she breathed in Traesha for the first time in her memory. The trees sighed above us. Their whispers paused in Natasha's presence. "Where three gods made their home in perfect harmony. The land they blessed was warm. The flowers only the richest colors. The ocean kissed the white sands of the beach. The sun beamed. The trees sang with life."

Above us, a flock of small white birds took flight.

Welcome, singer. Welcome. The trees whispered in my ear. I smiled up at their leaves, but no one else paid them attention while we walked and listened to my mother.

I remembered how it felt to hear this story surrounded by the gray walls of our Vichi home, snow blowing outside. My childhood imagination didn't compare to the beauty of the land I walked in now.

"The gods were lonely and invited the people from distant lands to come live with them. The first complained of the heat and left to go south. The second stomped through the flowers and turned them into crops, only seeking a profit. They were cast out to the east. The third used the forest and open spaces to practice their abilities to throw flames, water, and play tricks with the eyes. They thought themselves so strong that they challenged the gods. Yet when Mags stepped forward, they cowered back into the forest. Few returned.

"The gods gave up finding anyone to share this land with until the day Finma danced with the flowers, sang with the trees, swam in the ocean waves, ate from the fields, and lay under the silver moonlight. When she woke, her belly was swollen. Soon, she pushed out a silver-haired child, as perfect as the moon. She taught the babe to love the land and cherish all peace she could find. Men heard of the silver-haired beauty and traveled to meet her. Soon,

Finma's daughter gave birth to many silver-haired children. Her hair turned white, and she ruled them and her lovers until the day she died. When her soul left this world, Mags, Finma, and Tash decided to follow her beneath the roots where they rule to this day.

"They gifted the first-born daughter of the queen with white hair, a name, and a bond. Through the bond, the new queen knew to rule with justice and love. Through the bond, she was protected. Through the bond, she and her partner protected the land. The first queen and every queen since have been tasked to rule with love, peace, and strength. To carry out the gods' will. The land flourishes when the people do. In this way, the gods bless us and watch over us. In this way, we protect each other and our land. In this way, we know peace and strength and love." We traced a triangle in the air together.

When it was just my mother and me, this was the point where she would end the story by asking me if I knew what name the gods had given the first queen. I would swell with importance and tell her the name had been Finley. My mother smiled at me now, her thoughts no doubt traveling in the same direction.

I squeezed Natasha's hand, and we picked up the speed to a jog. The trees came alive as we passed. The wind in our hair smelled like home. The leaves danced wildly. Birds sang and circled above. A pack of wolves began to howl and another answered their call far away. Insects lit and swirled around us, making Natasha's eyes widen with wonder. The grass was soft under our boots. I saw deer running. The land celebrated. Natasha glowed with a wash of power.

If I concentrated hard enough, I could feel the Trish waiting on the other side of the tree line. They were so very tired.

I could barely breathe through the energy saturating the air, like a gust of wind that hits so hard you forget how to inhale. It was a hundred times more intense than the last time I walked through these trees. I squinted at their branches, waiting for the familiar anger or foreboding. For now, they were content.

The triangle was complete.

CHAPTER 29

We reached the tree line and paused to take in our land. Standing on a gentle rise, we had a view of the fields surrounding Shalta. The crops were yellowing and brittle. It may have been my imagination, but they seemed to flush with green with Natasha's entrance. I could see the castle sparkling in the distance. Beyond, the ocean stretched impossibly far. We fanned out, standing between the trees silently, waiting for the strength I promised. I removed my pack, tucking away the transmitter. I drew my sword. Natasha nodded at the writing on the blade, letting her tight control over her rage slip as she saw the state of our homeland. A large part of her wanted me to burn them all. This was one thing I could not give her, but I'd give her our country back.

This next moment depended entirely on me. It was my gods given task to fight for this country, to lead our people in only the necessary violence.

My mother's words ringing in my ears; I wanted to make the gods proud. If they were out there. I wanted to believe they were. *Mags be with me.*

I stepped from the shadow. The trees took notice of me then. When I was separate from Natasha, their whispers called out. *Nisashan, singer, singer. Nisashan.* The wind gusted, bending them. The whole forest bowed toward me and cheered with its rustling leaves. I still didn't know what *nisashan* meant. It sounded like acceptance. Like welcome. My eyes slid shut. I was so strong here.

I lifted my arms and shoved my consciousness toward the condensed swirl of power waiting inside me. My breath whooshed out as the force of it surged. For a brief moment, I saw everything. I saw through the trees, through the people. Fear crashed down as I separated from my body, but I couldn't stop. Not yet.

I knew when every enslaved Trish straightened. I felt their consciousnesses perk toward me, ignoring their duties when the energy in the wind touched them. I stirred what I now knew slept within each of us. Abilities awakened and their strength renewed after nearly twenty years. I felt brief stings in my own wrists and ankles when our people snapped off the chains with quick movements they were incapable of seconds ago.

My heart raced. I snapped back into my mind, the trees wild behind me. I hadn't even moved, but I knew I had just won this battle. The wind pushed my hair forward when the Trish behind me took off at top speed, following my silent signal and moving to reclaim our land.

I began to run, quickly outdistancing everyone else despite their head start. I was unstoppable with the triangle lifting my power. Every Bellovian I passed held a gun for only as long as it took me to overtake them. I broke the weapons over my knee and tossed the scraps to the side. Panicked shots rang out when the Trish began to fight back.

Rage leaked from Natasha as she ran the forest perimeter, taking in the rest of the land and approaching the city. It was nothing like what her grandfather had described. The Bellovians had ruined it. I battled her influence before the rage could spread through me, infecting our people and making them cruel.

Brittle bonds. I monitored them carefully. It took so much effort that my head started to pound.

I heard Bellovians whooping close to Shalta, where Natasha was heading. There was no fear in her. It had to be the rebellion. I smiled. Levi, Rennie, and Nico were close. They made it.

Bellovian after Bellovian was forced face down into the dirt. There was childlike crying, or children crying, I suppose. They were so young. I made myself immune to the sound. I knew they weren't being hurt.

A deep voice shouted near the city, yelling into a cornfield—a commander barking orders to fight back. I came up behind him and swung my body upward, wrapping a leg around his neck and bringing him down hard. While he flew toward the ground, I relieved him of his gun and flipped onto my feet. Before he knew what was happening, he was looking up into the barrel of his long gun.

"Call them off." The calm in my voice was eerie. I had so much to control inside me, it was infecting my demeanor even in the heat of battle. I knew my face was as blank as ever.

He touched the button on his glasses. "Burn it do—"

I didn't let him finish his sentence. The shot rang loudly through the fields, echoing in the earpieces of the Bellovians. The cold wash of a kill swept through me. I swallowed and looked over my shoulder, catching sight of a head of white hair. Bellovians began shooting in earnest, but through our speed or the gods' grace, every bullet missed. A few Bellovians tried to start fires, lighting matches that would never have finished the job with the lush crops now full of life. Some ran to the forest edge, seeking shelter, but the trees grew dark, their branches whipping wildly, and the children backed away. Only one made it to the Bellovian road and a tree fell, blocking the path.

It all took less than five minutes. The shortest battle in history. Quick and precise like the Trish. I had just decided the threat was over when I felt an urgent tug on the bond from Natasha. I followed it, skipping to the lawn between Shalta and the trees. She was standing in the middle of the grass. I could feel the desire consuming her at the sight of the castle. The trees still bowed in her direction, now with a new intensity.

The Bellovian rebellion was behind her, some still seated on cycles and others out of breath from the run here. Their guns were raised. My heart skipped when I saw them, Levi at the front.

A girl in a commander's uniform stood ten paces before my queen, her mid gun pointed directly at Natasha's head.

"Tell them to stand down!" In the time it took the girl to shout the command, I was behind her.

"I recommend lowering the gun," I said low in her ear. The girl spun, but I caught the gun's barrel and pointed it high before she could shoot me.

"Finley!" Mayze gasped. Her eyes, a honeyed brown so like her cousin's, grew wide. I yanked the gun from her grasp and she fell to the ground from the force of my pull.

"You…" She took in the rebels, Natasha, the silver in the roots of my hair, and the Trish who came to stand behind me. "You're a *traitor*," she shouted, rising to her knees.

"Deserter. You're betraying all of us! Your family. Oken. Jenna. Rennie—"

"Right here," Rennie said, stepping away from the group of rebels. Mayze's eyes grew impossibly wider. "And oh, look! Her mom's here too!"

But she didn't mention Nico. My heart plunged.

"And if you're wondering why my father didn't make it to this little reunion," I lowered myself to Mayze's level, "it's because the commanders came to my home and killed him."

"Well... you deserted. If they killed your father, it was for planting the seed of thought needed to make you do such a thing. You knew the consequences and so did he."

I stared at Mayze in disbelief. This was the sweet girl who sewed old clothing back together to donate to the people in the Squalor. This was the girl that came to my mind when I thought of Bellovians with gentle natures. This was Oken's cousin. He risked everything for her before he even knew me. Even after. He had been convinced she'd see things the way he did.

I gestured toward the Bellovians standing behind Natasha. "I'm trying to help the Trish *and* the Bellovians. This war is a waste of lives."

Mayze looked at the dirty, tired faces of the rebellion. "My family isn't here," she said stiffly. "You saved, what, a hundred Bellovians? Two hundred? There is an entire city still waiting for the food shipments from Traesha. You've *starved* them all."

"If they stopped spending all their money on this war, they could have enough to feed their people!"

"If we didn't have the weapons we did, the Florians would have killed us all by now!"

I shook my head. Behind me, I could hear the Trish

leading the Bellovians from the fields at the point of their guns. I highly doubted the freed Trish knew how to shoot those guns, but the Bellovian children didn't know that and were compliant.

"You won't convince me I am in the wrong," I said. I noticed how much she had changed. How even kneeling, she stared at me with stubborn confidence and pride. The red commander patch bearing two stripes on her shoulder stood out stark against the black uniform. What had she done in such little time to earn a second stripe? I stepped forward and ripped the patch off. She made a noise of protest that I ignored. I turned to the Trish arriving from the city and fields with their Bellovian prisoners.

"Any Bellovians with this patch marking them as commanders should be taken to the dungeon," I called.

My mother appeared at my side and took Mayze's gun from my hand. Her head was high, her smile wide. "Your father would be proud," she whispered just for me. My throat tightened.

My mother told Mayze to rise and instructed the Trish with commanders to follow her. She led them in the direction of the castle.

Mayze shouted at us over her shoulder. "They'll know soon enough what happened here! They will come with their armies and technology and kill all of you this time! You're making a mistake! All this will lead to is more death and it'll be on your hands, Finley!"

My mother pushed Mayze forward. The Trish shifted uncomfortably, their grips tightening on guns they didn't know how to shoot.

Natasha turned to address the Bellovian rebels. I studied their faces, looking for the remaining committee leaders who had turned me away when I asked them to help me free Natasha. Commander Gale stood proud and met my eyes with a smile, but I only spotted a couple of the leaders, looking as gaunt and uncertain as the rest. Could they feel Natasha's rage? Did they fear I would harbor anger? A part of me did. I couldn't help but associate the committee turning me away with the bloodstain I had found shortly after, proof of my father's death. Could they have helped him? Would they go back to their power-hungry ways once they had settled here? Would their bids for power infect this land next? There were only two, but I didn't know how many of the rebellion stood with them rather than Levi.

Even after Rennie hadn't mentioned him, I searched desperately for Nico.

"The Trish will help you find emptied homes to move into," Natasha told the rebels. The Trish straightened. They may feel my instructions through our connection, but a direct order from the queen was irrefutable. "I place you in charge of the Bellovian children sent here. Teach them about the peace we are searching for and the futility of fighting against us. If you find them unwilling to live here peacefully, they will join their commanders beneath the castle."

The Bellovian children stood quietly. Resignation, fear, and tears on many of their faces. They looked so much younger than fifteen and sixteen. The Trish I had trained in Floria moved to help the rebels. Those who had just been freed stood apart from the rebels, tension heavy between them. Their faces turned incredulous when the Trish from Floria greeted the Bellovians warmly, especially Levi and Rennie. The two of them were all smiles.

Levi slipped away from his conversation with Sadie and approached me. "This is more than I could have hoped for," he said. But something was off in his tone. I stiffened, prepared for the worst. I knew Levi wouldn't dance around any bad news.

"They took Hue," he said. Whatever happiness this success had brought me drained away. We were too late. "When his father asked for more volunteers, they asked why Hue should be exempt. Apparently, he couldn't think of a reason. They probably took him to a weapon-making facility with his talents and not the Front, but it may only be a matter of time."

"We don't even know where the Front is anymore," I said, heart sinking. King Mavrick was ready to move it to Vichi in retribution. "What can we do?"

Levi's face was drawn. "I don't know." He'd saved many of the rebels, but Mayze was right. We hadn't helped the city. The feeling of inadequacy was crushing. Levi and I sighed at the same time.

Rennie walked up and pressed a letter in my hand with a soft smile. "Nico sends his love."

I tucked the letter into the pocket of my leggings, knowing I couldn't read it here. I couldn't cry yet. I wanted to demand them to tell me why he wasn't here, why they hadn't convinced him to join them.

A Trish boy our age stepped forward. His hands were still covered with dirt from the fields, the last two fingers missing on one. Savha stiffened. It was the boy we'd seen during Hinze's mission. The one the trees showed me in my dream. The hair rose on my arms. I knew he was important, but not if it was a good or bad thing.

"They aren't just going to let us go," he said. "What will we do when they come?"

The gathered crowd looked to Natasha and me. The boy stared at Natasha, trying to keep his face clear of the awe and desperate desire for her to provide answers. To provide safety at last.

I could see hope bright on all their faces, especially those who followed us from Floria. They had come to expect the amazing from us. The power in our bond stirred in response to their gazes.

Natasha looked at me and I stepped forward. "You all felt it when the queen and I returned," I spoke Trish, trying to reassure them despite my black hair. Eyebrows lifted as they realized I was *resa*. The boy recognized me and narrowed his gaze. "Trish speed has been granted to each of you because of us. We are so capable and strong. If they come, we defend our gods gifted land. The Bellovians succeeded all those years ago because they surprised us. This time we will be prepared."

The freed Trish shared anxious looks. They didn't like that answer any more than the Trish in Floria first had. But those who had trained with me for weeks now nodded in agreement, their eyes steely. I experienced a strange mix of grief and pride when I saw how their chins rose. They drew their swords and raised them high with cries of "*Stisha Colm!*"

Natasha watched, desire to do more burning in her chest. She longed to keep whatever innocence they had left intact. We finally had our home and she wanted to keep it. But she wanted to rule as her grandfather taught her.

Natasha craved peace. Her rage had settled at the sight of the commanders being led away. All she had wanted was Traesha.

The wind gusted again, the trees swaying toward her. Natasha closed her eyes, and I felt her brushing against her side of the bond. She yanked at it, drawing from me with such force I staggered a step.

Running and the day's events had loosened many fine hairs from her braids. They lifted now with the crackling energy in the air. In a sudden hush, the winds stilled and when our queen addressed us again, her voice was a low murmur, only for Trish ears.

Breathing grew difficult as she kept pulling from my well of power—the power connecting me to the trees. I wanted to trust her, but panic crawled up my throat. She could take whatever she wanted. I was powerless. I forced myself to breathe. It was hers to take. Hers to take.

"We need to know how to fight, but we can also be protected. Our land has suffered alongside us all these years. It calls to me now."

The trees began singing. *We must protect. We must protect. The queen. The queen.* I glanced around, but I was the only one listening to them. I heard my panic echoing as Natasha asked for more.

Natasha turned her back to us, staring up at the forest. The smell of Traesha intensified in the air. Lavender. The warm salt of the sea. An indescribable tang: *magic.*

Natasha lifted her arms slowly as though they were burdened under a great weight. The trees groaned in response. Their whispers grew frantic. The waves crashed against the distant shore too loud. The birds in the far trees took flight with startled squawks. No one noticed when my knees gave out or the effort I used to right myself again.

It took a moment to see what she was doing, but the trees began to grow on the distant forest's edge. Peeking just over the tops of the trees in front of us at first, they continued stretching higher, higher. Worried curiosity got the better of me and I skipped to the base of the growing trees, stumbling multiple times as Natasha took and took. I was the only one who risked approaching them.

I trusted her and the forest not to hurt me.

She asks us to protect. She asks us to protect. The whispers were strained. I nodded weakly. I felt the same command from Natasha in the bond. I thought of the dark forest, so unwelcoming to the Bellovians unless they knew to say *nisashan.* They *had* been protecting, but Natasha asked for more.

Was she asking too much?

I placed my hands on the shifting bark, panting and craning my neck back to watch the trees grow. I felt Natasha's presence all around me. The trunks grew thicker as they reached ever higher and I stepped away in awe as they melded together, their branches twisting and intertwining, hugging trunks and creating a gapless wall of bark. There was anger in their movements. Pain. Desperation motivated the trees and I couldn't tell if it came from Natasha or the land itself or me. Their whispers grew incoherent.

Black edged my vision. Through the bond, I urged Natasha to stop, but she brushed my concern aside. I had no choice but to watch on in horror.

The trees rose higher and higher until I wondered if even a flighter could clear their tips.

Until I doubted it could ever be reversed.

I watched Natasha cut us off from the rest of the world. Everything suddenly so final.

The trees finally stopped shifting and groaning. They settled into their new role as the wall surrounding Traesha. I placed my hands on them once again. Natasha stopped pulling from my strength and I worked to catch my breath. I remembered the crashing waves on our beach, unwelcoming and dangerous.

How would Oken ever get back to me now? He promised.

And Nico. Choosing to stay behind to help the Trish and even Florians because he still believed in our alliance. The trees let in little light, but I could see in their shadows. I slid down the silent trees to sit at their base. I leaned back and felt exhaustion and frustration and too much. I pulled the letter from my pocket and read Nico's beautiful Trish scrawl.

Dear Finny,

I miss you, Mom, and Dad so much. I'm sorry we couldn't talk longer in Traesha and I couldn't explain more. Londe tells me you were able to rescue the queen. I'm so proud of you, Finley. I knew every day when you left to train that you would be the change in this war we all needed. Know I believe in you and I always have. Even before you could run like the Trish, even before you were resa. I have always been proud to call you my sister.

I hope you understand why I have to stay behind. Without Hue, Levi, Gale, or the rest of the rebellion here, we'd have no way of knowing what the commanders are planning. It wasn't an easy decision, but it was the right one. I think the Bellovians may attack Helsa, and I've been trying to warn Londe, but communication can be challenging. I have to try, though. My place is here in Vichi, behind the piano. I'll join you as soon as I can.

All my love,

Nico

P.S. Good work finally making your move with Oken Sars. Atta girl.

The last sentence made me smile through the tears that ran freely as I leaned my head back against the wall of bark.

Natasha decided our place in this war with one sweep

of her arms. The Bellovians and Florians could destroy each other for all she cared now that Traesha was safe.

I still cared too much. Nico and Oken were so far away now. The fighting I finally believed we could make a difference in was on the other side of the wall, the sword at my waist as useless as it had been above my parents' bed. I dropped my hands and pushed off the ground, turning from the wall and making my way back through the forest slowly. The trees were silent. Recovering.

A deer stepped boldly into the path in front of me. It had nothing to fear now.

Natasha was still standing where I had left her, safe and greeting the Trish who bowed and kissed her hands and wept in thanks. Natasha was crying right with them. The Trish from Floria found their family and friends they hadn't seen in decades. My eyes filled again watching them reunite. I spotted Alessa and Masen in the arms of their parents. They pointed to Natasha and her intricate braid with pride and their mother laughed, hugging them tighter. I kept walking. My dark hair was enough for them to let me pass unacknowledged. I went around Natasha, not ready to talk.

"Finley!" I turned to Gale as she shouted my name and shook her hand.

"I'm glad you're here," I said. When the rebellion base was discovered, I had been worried that the commanders would tie it to her.

"Yes, it was a close thing, but Nico heard about them discovering my parents' home was our base and was able to warn me in time. It was hard to lose the intel I was gaining within their ranks, but at least I'm alive. Have you heard any news of Helsa? They were planning an attack."

My smile wobbled at the mention of my brother and the bloody battle. "We were able to save the city before we came here. With our speed, we were able to stop them. The Trish can be quite a force."

Gale and I both looked at the wall and sighed. A force that was now sheltered from the war we could make such a difference in. "Your father would be so pleased to see this." She gestured toward the rebels and Trish speaking. A committee member called for Gale's attention while giving me the cold shoulder. I almost laughed and nodded as Gale left with an apologetic shrug.

Wesley and Levi were chatting nearby, Wesley acting something out animatedly with his hands swinging in front of him as if he held a sword. Rennie came up and pretended to get hit with the invisible blade. The three of them burst into easy laughter. The freed Trish watched in confusion.

A few children with black hair and delicate Trish features pointed at them and tried to get their parents to take them closer. Shan's son played in the dirt with two other children, their heads, blond, silver, and black, bent together to look at a worm. My heart went out to them. I saw hope again in their little triangle.

I continued into the city. I passed a few Trish returning to the celebration on the lawn after dropping off commanders. Savha stopped to smile at me.

"We did it," she said. "I wish Fisher and my father could see."

"They can. I know they can." I drew her into a long hug. Her tears wet my shoulder; sad or happy, I couldn't tell.

There was singing coming from the direction of the trees now. It drifted closer and I knew the celebration would probably move to the ballroom. Savha stepped back and tilted her head in the direction of the sound.

"You coming?" she asked.

"I might join later. I need a minute." She nodded and went toward the beautiful Trish voices. I couldn't find it in me to sing. Only one song seemed relevant right now. *He could have burned the world.*

I walked blindly through Shalta until I found myself before the castle. I tipped my head back to take it in. The white, gold-streaked marble gleamed in the sunlight. Proud as if it understood what had happened here today. I went slowly up the steps, remembering how I had done so last time with Mesa at my side and my hair a completely black braid.

The floor of the hall was dirty after so many had passed through straight from the fields to bring in their commander prisoners. I walked past the base of the spiraling staircase.

The throne room doors had been barred shut, by Bellovians or Trish, I didn't know. I yanked out the heavy bar and slowly pulled open the door on the right. The first thing I noticed was the frigid temperature of the air, then the smell. When I stepped inside, it reminded me of Helsa as we'd left it. The walls were still blackened by the flames of the Bellovian bomb that killed the royals and the *magsai*. There were a few pieces of ruined furniture, but the room had been cleared otherwise. Even so, the smell of death was heavy in the air. No one had cleaned it since the late queen had died besides the rest of Natasha's family and their *magsai*. The memory of the bomb that killed them lingered.

I shivered and stepped back, closing the door gently before I turned to the stairs. It had been a mistake to look. I felt so torn. I wanted to help Vichi, but they had done that to Natasha's people. To my people.

I tried to shake the effect of the throne room as I climbed the spiraling steps circling to the top of the tower point. For the first time in a long time, I was in no rush to go anywhere. I felt lost and aimless. I wanted to be in the forest but couldn't look at that wall. I wanted to be with Natasha but couldn't share in her smiles. I wanted to be with the Bellovians, but they reminded me too much of Nico and Oken and the city starving to the south. I wanted to be with the Trish, but I had forced them to fight and the memories from my kills still threatened to overwhelm me. To break me.

When I touched my cheek, it was wet from tears. Yet the next mirror I passed reflected a face otherwise devoid of emotion. What was wrong with me?

The first level of the stairs led to the library. The walls were still full of books and a promise to answer all my questions. The Bellovians had so little interest in these books they hadn't even felt a need to destroy them. I wondered if any of the covers held the answer to the power Natasha and I possessed. If they could tell me whether I should fear it or embrace it. It was good they remained. I would try to feel happy and relieved later.

I continued upwards to the next floor. This circular wall held paintings, sketches, and tapestries that took my breath away. I hurt over Jenna's betrayal in a fresh wave and looked away.

I explored a bit and found a doorway to a music room filled to the brim with instruments I had never seen before. Another room held sculptures made in a material I couldn't name. One near the back had been left half-finished. When I walked around, I found the other side splattered with a dried brown I realized was blood. I swallowed and continued; the still faces chiseled into stone were now haunting to look upon.

The next level held rooms full of desks. The offices closest to the stairs contained mechanical devices that could only have belonged to the Bellovians. Stacks of letters I'm sure held important correspondence we now couldn't use to help war efforts littered the desk. Shoved into the furthest office from the stairs was a room carelessly filled with papers and books covered in tight Trish writing. I sat and riffled through some of the brittle pages. Many held blueprints of ships, houses, and mills. Others were logs of food production, another a half-drawn map of the islands and lands the Trish had yet to discover. There was still nothing drawn to the south of us. The island of Detono was nowhere to be seen, though Floria was marked in detail.

When I stood to leave the room, the sun was setting outside the window, and my body was stiff. Exhaustion pulled at me, the well of power finally spent with the creation of the wall. My head was still pounding. I went up to the next level and found bedrooms. I peeked into each, and my heart skipped a beat. The Bellovians had made use of these rooms, but they left the artwork on the walls. The paintings told the story of the *magsai*. Every room had hooks to rest a sword above the bed. Some had large beds that took up nearly the whole space. Some had two smaller beds. Even with the black Bellovian clothes strewn across the place, I knew these must have been the *magsai* rooms. Which one had my mother lived in? Which one had been Sam's? Which one would be mine?

The last set of stairs took me to what I knew would be the royal bed chambers at the tip of the tower. I stepped onto the landing hesitantly. The wall was lined with portraits of royals, all with striking white hair, circling up into the point of the tower ceiling above.

This floor possessed a force that welcomed me like the forest, but I could tell it had pushed away the Bellovians just like the darkening trees. The top floor of the castle held no trace of the invaders. The layer of dust at my feet was evidence that no one had stepped here in years until today. There was only one small set that was fresh and led to the room to the left. Perhaps the spirits of the royal family protected this place like the trees protected the land. Perhaps the gods couldn't stand this last bit of their strength destroyed.

I looked at the five doors and wondered which royal family member had lived behind each one. How could only one still live when every inch of this castle had been built as a testament to the strength of Traesha's queen? I moved toward the one furthest to the left, following the footprints, and gently pushed the door open.

Natasha was already inside. She must have passed me while I explored. Our bond hadn't warned me; its strength sapped as much as my own. Natasha looked down into the crib taking up the center of the room, clutching a blanket close to her chest. Her eyes were misty with tears. I walked forward and looked down into the crib with her, a strange sense that I had seen it before overtaking me.

"Are you angry?" she whispered.

"I don't know." My voice was flat. I shook my head and sighed. I walked to the window and looked out at Traesha. There were lights throughout the city, but it sounded like almost everyone was in the ballroom. "I wouldn't say I'm happy, though," I admitted.

"I have to keep Traesha safe. It's why I was given life."

"You did that, Natasha. They would all be proud," I said.

My eyes strayed to the chair to the side of the crib. The imprint of the woman who used to sit in it was still in the cushions. It was a blessing the Bellovians hadn't destroyed Natasha's nursery or evidence of her mother's love.

"We saved them," Natasha said. A tear slipped down her cheek. I walked to her side and wrapped an arm around her. She leaned into me, resting her head on my shoulder. We comforted each other through the muted bond. Our flickering power assured us it was enough that we were together.

If I wasn't entirely convinced, I didn't let Natasha know.

Acknowledgments

This acknowledgements page is a little harder to write, mostly because Daughter of War and Weapon of Rulers were one book for the first draft, so a lot the people I thanked the first round are also who I want to thank here. So thanks to you all once more. Love you!

But a special thanks is owed to Sarah, for breaking the book into two and making them both so much better.

Thank you to everyone who read book one and agreed to read this one and let me know if it "held up." Thanks Delaney, Wyatt, and Kaycee!

Thanks to Ben, who stood in as my proofreader and let me bounce ideas off him during for my final round of edits.

Thank you to everyone who enjoyed Daughter of War enough to keep reading Finley's journey. You're making dreams come true.

About the Author

Kelly Cole graduated from the University of Wyoming where she studied English and Creative Writing. She is working on a self-publishing career, beginning with her debut novel Daughter of War. Kelly is most active on Instagram and enjoys sharing her latest and favorite reads. She lives in Wyoming with her two crested geckos and her dog, Maya. She spends most of her time writing and playing endless hours of fetch (not with the geckos).

www.ingramcontent.com/pod-product-compliance
Lightning Source LLC
Chambersburg PA
CBHW060614300726
48975CB00005B/1565